J.

Bangkok Tattoo

Bangkok Tattoo

John Burdett

LARGE PRINT

This large print edition published in 2005 by
RB Large Print
A division of Recorded Books
A Haights Cross Communications Company
270 Skipjack Road
Prince Frederick, MD 20678

Published by arrangement with Alfred A. Knopf,
a division of Random House, Inc.

Publisher's Cataloging In Publication Data
(Prepared by Donohue Group, Inc.)

Burdett, John.
  Bangkok tattoo / John Burdett.

  p. (large print) ; cm.

  ISBN: 1-4193-5429-9

1. Police—Thailand—Bangkok—Fiction. 2. Intelligence officers—Crimes against—
Fiction. 3. Large type books. 4. Bangkok (Thailand)—Fiction. 5. Prostitutes—
Fiction. 6. Mystery fiction. I. Title.

PR6052.U617 B363 2005b
823/.914

Printed in the United States of America

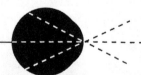

**This Large Print Book carries the
Seal of Approval of N.A.V.H.**

For Sofía

Israelites, Christians and Muslims profess immortality, but the veneration they render this world proves they believe only in it, since they destine all other worlds, in infinite number, to be its reward or punishment. The wheel of certain Hindustani religions seems more reasonable to me.

—Jorge Luis Borges, *The Immortal*

What? Could perhaps, in spite of all "modern ideas" and prejudices of democratic taste, the victory of optimism, the achieved predominance of reason, practical and theoretical utilitarianism, like democracy itself, its contemporary—be a symptom of failing strength, of approaching old age, of physiological exhaustion? . . . what is the meaning of—morality? . . . all things move in a double cycle: everything which we now call culture, education, civilization will at some stage have to appear before the infallible judge, Dionysus.

—Friedrich Nietzsche, *The Birth of Tragedy*

PART 1

THE OLD MAN'S CLUB

CHAPTER 1

Killing customers just isn't good for business."

My mother Nong's tone reflects the disappointment we all feel when a star employee starts to go wrong. Is there nothing to be done? Will we have to let dear Chanya go? The question can only be decided by Police Colonel Vikorn, who owns most of the shares in the Old Man's Club and who is on his way in his Bentley.

"No," I agree. Like my mother's, my eyes cannot stop flicking across the empty bar to the stool where Chanya's flimsy silver dress (just enough silk to cover nipples and butt) drapes and drips. Well, the dripping was slight and is more or less finished (a rusty stain on the floor turning black as it dries), but in more than a decade as a detective in the Royal Thai Police, I have never seen a garment so blood-soaked. Chanya's bra, also hideously splattered, lies halfway up the stairs, and her panties—her only other garment—lie abandoned on the floor outside the upstairs room where, eccentrically even for a Thai whore, she has taken refuge with an opium pipe.

3

"She didn't say anything at all? Like *why*?"

"No, I told you. She dashed in through the door in a bit of a state holding an opium pipe, glared at me, said, 'I've done him in,' ripped off her dress, and disappeared upstairs. Fortunately, there were only a couple of *farang* in the bar at the time, and the girls were fantastic. They merely said, 'Oh, Chanya, she goes like that sometimes,' and gently ushered them out. I had to play the whole thing down, of course, and by the time I got to her room, she was already stoned."

"What did she say again?"

"She was tripping on the opium, totally delirious. When she started talking to the Buddha, I left to call you and the Colonel. At that stage I didn't know if she'd really done him in or was freaking out on *yaa baa* or something."

But she'd snuffed him all right. I walked to the *farang*'s hotel, which is just a couple of streets away from Soi Cowboy, and flashed my police ID to get the key to his room. There he was, a big muscular naked American *farang* in his early thirties, minus a penis and a lot of blood from a huge knife wound that began in his lower gut and finished just short of his rib cage. Chanya, a basically decent and very tidy Thai, had placed his penis on the bedside table. At the other end of the table, a single rose stood in a plastic mug of water.

There was nothing for it but to secure the room for the purposes of forensic investigation, leave a hefty bribe for the hotel receptionist—who is now more or less obliged to say whatever I tell him to say (standard procedure under my Colonel Vikorn in District 8)—and await further orders. Vikorn, of course, was in one of his clubs carousing, probably surrounded by naked young women who adored him, or knew how to look as if they did, and in no mood to be dragged to the scene of a crime until I penetrated his drunken skull enough to explain that the business at hand was not an investigation per se but the infinitely more challenging forensic task so lightly spoken of as a "cover-up." Even then he showed no inclination to shift himself until he realized it was Chanya (the perp, not the victim).

"Where the hell did she get the opium?" my mother wants to know. "There hasn't been opium in Krung Thep since I was a teenager."

I know from her eyes that she is thinking fondly of the Vietnam War, when she was herself a working girl in Bangkok and a lot of the GIs brought small balls of opium from the war zone (one of them being my almost-anonymous father, of whom more later). An opiated man is more or less impotent—which reduces much of the wear and tear on a professional's assets—and not inclined to argue about fee structure. Nong and her colleagues had always shown special interest in any American serviceman who whispered that he had a little opium back in his hotel. Being devout Buddhists, of course, the girls never used the stuff themselves, but they encouraged the john to get stoned out of his tree, whereupon they would extract exactly the agreed fee from his wallet, plus a tip somewhat on the generous side to reflect the risk inherent in associating with drug abusers, plus taxi fare, and return to work. Integrity has always been a master word for Nong, which is why she is so upset about Chanya.

We both know the Colonel is arriving in his limo, because his damned signature tune "The Ride of the Valkyries" is booming from the stereo as his car approaches. I go to the entrance and watch while his driver opens the rear door and more or less pulls him out (a beautiful cashmere Zegna sports jacket, fawn colored and somewhat crumpled, pants by Eddy Monetti on the Via Condotti in Rome, and his usual Wayfarer wraparound sunglasses).

The driver staggers toward me with Vikorn's arm over his shoulder. "It's fucking Saturday fucking night," the driver complains with a glare, as if it's all my fault. (We prefer not to investigate even capital crimes on Saturday nights in District 8.) The Buddhist path can be much like the Christian in that the karma of others often seems to get dumped on your shoulders from out of nowhere.

"I know," I tell him as I make way to let him pass, and Vikorn, sunglasses now thrust fashionably onto his hairline though slightly askew, also glares at me blearily.

There are padded benches in intimate little booths along the back wall of the club, and the driver dumps Vikorn down in one while I get some mineral water from the fridge and hand it to my Colonel, who empties the bottle in a few swigs. It is with relief that I observe the rodent cunning return to those frank, unblinking eyes. I tell him the story again, with a few commercially focused interjections from my mother ("she makes more for us in a month than all the other girls put together"), and I see that he already has a plan to maximize wriggle-room should things get difficult.

Within ten minutes he is close to sober, tells his driver to disappear with the limo (he doesn't want to broadcast that he is here), and is staring at me. "So let's go up and take her statement. Get an ink pad and some A4 paper."

I find the ink pad that we use for our business stamp ("The Old Man's Club—Rods of Iron") and some sheets of paper from the fax machine, which Nong installed for those few of our overseas clients who don't have e-mail (we tried for *hooker.com* and similar domain names, but they had all been taken, including *oldman.com*; *whore.org* had of course been taken since the dawn of cyberspace, so we had to make do with *omcroi.com*), and follow him across the bar. He stares at Chanya's dress on the stool and cocks an eye at me.

"Versace."

"Fake or real?"

Gingerly I hold it up, hefting the weight of the blood it has absorbed. "Unclear."

He grunts much as Maigret used to do, as if

7

absorbing a clue too subtle for my understanding, and we continue up the stairs, passing the bra without comment. I pick up the panties on the floor outside the room (almost weightless and apparently innocent of bloodstains—they are more a *cache-sex* than a proper undergarment, with the rear panel no more than a bootlace that divides the buttocks). I hang them over a stray electrical cable for now. Chanya was too stoned to lock the door, and when we enter, she blesses us with a rapturous smile from that awesomely beautiful mouth, before returning to whichever of the Buddha heavens she has escaped to.

She is quite naked, stretched out on the bed with her legs akimbo, her full firm breasts pointing at the ceiling (an exquisite blue dolphin is jumping over her left nipple), her long hair shining like a fresh black brushstroke on the white pillow. She has shaved her pubic hair save for the subtlest filigree black line, which seems to point to her clitoris, perhaps as a road sign for drunk and fumbling *farang*. The opium pipe, a classic of about three feet of bamboo with the bowl two-thirds of the way down, lies beside her. The Colonel sniffs and smiles—as with my mother, the sweet aroma of burned poppy sap holds fond memories for him, though of a radically different order. (He used to trade it up in Laos in the golden years of the B-52s.) The room is tiny and hardly big enough for the three of us when I bring two chairs and set them on opposite sides of the bed.

The sex goddess between us begins to snore while Vikorn dictates her statement:

"'The *farang* had been drinking even before he came into my club. He called me over to join him at his table and offered to buy me a drink. I accepted a Coca-Cola while he drank'—ah, let's see—'nearly a full bottle of Mekong whiskey. He did not seem to be able to take alcohol very well and seemed confused and disoriented. When he offered to pay my bar fine and take me back to his hotel, I told him he was too drunk, but he insisted, and my papasan, one Sonchai Jitpleecheep, asked me as a special favor to go with the *farang*, who was very big and muscular and seemed likely to cause trouble if I didn't.'"

"Thanks," I say.

"'He struck me as a man with many problems and talked rather abusively about women, especially American women, whom he called *cunts*. I think perhaps he had had a relationship that had gone badly wrong and that left him with very strong feelings of bitterness toward all women, even though he claimed to like Asian women, who he said were much kinder and gentler than *farang* women and more womanly. When we reached his room, I suggested to him that he was perhaps too drunk to make love and that it would be better if I went back to my club. I even offered to give him back my bar fine, but he grew angry and said he could fuck all night and pushed me into the room. He ordered me to undress, and I did so. I was

9

now quite frightened because I had seen a large knife'—do we have the murder weapon?"

"A large knife, as a matter of fact—looks like a military thing, solid steel with about a twelve-inch blade. I left it in the hotel room for now."

"'An enormous military-type weapon lying on a bedside table. He started to tell me what he would do to my body if I didn't gratify his desires. He stripped naked and threw me on the bed, but he seemed unable to get an erection. He started to masturbate to make himself big, then made me turn over onto my front. It was then I realized that he intended to sodomize me. I begged him not to because I never do that sort of thing, and his member now was so big I was sure he would injure me. Still he insisted, without using a condom or a lubricant, and the pain was so great I started to scream. He became very angry and grabbed a pillow to try to stifle my screams, where-upon I completely lost control of my mind because I was sure he would kill me. Luckily I was able to reach the knife, which I swung around behind me while he was still inside me. By chance I seem to have severed his penis. He went into shock at first and stood up, hardly able to believe what had happened. He kept staring at his penis, which was lying on the floor near the bed (it popped out of me and must have fallen off him when he stood up), then he let out a terrible bestial yell and jumped on top of me. I had turned over onto my back, and unfortunately I was still holding the knife in both hands in a vertical position, and it penetrated his lower abdomen when he landed. His struggles only made the wound bigger. I did what I could to save his life, but it took some time to push him off me because he was very heavy. I was too much in shock to call the police, until I realized he was dead and then it was too late. All I could do to show respect was to pick up his penis and put it on the bedside table. My dress and bra had been on the bed and were soaked in blood. I had to put them on before I could leave the room. When I got back to the bar, I stripped off my clothes and ran up to the comfort rooms, where I took a powerful tranquilizer and lost consciousness.

"'This statement was taken by Police Colonel Vikorn and Detective Jitpleecheep of Royal Thai Police District 8 while I was in full possession of my faculties. It is true to the best of my knowledge and belief, in testimony of which I hereby set my right thumb print.'"

I open the ink pad and roll her thumb over the ink, then onto the bottom of the paper. Vikorn, a consummate professional, has neatly ended her report without the need for a second page.

"Anything I've left out?"

"No," I say in awe. The statement is a masterly mosaic of several standard stories from the Game, artfully interwoven with great economy of language. Still more remarkable in a cop who carries his legal scholarship so lightly, he has laid the foundations for an impregnable defense to a charge of murder or even manslaughter: she used only such force as was necessary to save her life and did not deliver the fatal blow; when she saw how badly he was wounded, she attempted without success to save his life; and she expressed sorrow and respect by her sensitive placing of his severed member in a position of honor. The dead *farang*'s standard-issue hatred of the opposite sex arising from bitter personal experience of his own country-women provides a motive for his aggression and his sexual preferences. "I think you've covered everything."

"Good. Give her a copy when she wakes up, and make sure she memorizes it. If there's anything she wants to change, tell her she can't."

"D'you want to visit the scene of the crime?"

"Not really. Anyway, it wasn't a crime, so don't prejudice justice by calling it that. Self-defense is not illegal, especially when by a woman on a Saturday night in Krung Thep."

"Still, I think you'd better come," I say. He grunts irritably but stands up anyway and jerks his chin in the general direction of the street.

CHAPTER 2

The receptionist, already oozing servility thanks to the five thousand baht I gave him an hour ago, starts to stutter when he sees Vikorn, who is by way of being emperor of these *sois*. The Colonel switches on his five-thousand-kilowatt charm and hints at what a lucrative future awaits those who know how to keep their mouths shut at a time like this. (Positive-type stutters from the receptionist.) I take the key again, and we mount the stairs.

Inside the room the stench that invariably accompanies a competent disemboweling has grown stronger since my first visit. I switch on the air-con, which only serves to cool the stench without diminishing its potency. I can see Vikorn working himself into a rage with me for dragging him over here. "Look," I say. I take out the dead *farang*'s passport from the drawer where I found it earlier. I am not an expert on our occult immigration practices, but the form of his visa disturbs me. The passport is the property of one Mitch Turner.

It disturbs the Colonel too, for he grows pale as

he stares at it. "Why didn't you mention this before?"

"Because I didn't know if it was important or not. I didn't know what it is. I still don't."

"It's a visa."

"I can see that."

"Good for two years with multiple reentry thrown in."

"Yes?"

"They never give two-year visas. Never. Especially not with multiple reentry. Except in certain cases."

"That's what I thought."

The visa has deepened our sense of tragedy, the violent loss of a relatively young life so far away from home. "CIA or FBI?"

"CIA. We let in about two hundred after 9/11. They wanted to keep an eye on the Muslims in the south on the border with Malaysia. They're a pain in the neck because they don't speak Thai so they have to have interpreters." He looked at the corpse. "Imagine an overmuscled six-foot white *farang* with an interpreter trying to be incognito down in Hat Yai on a Friday night among our little brown people. Damn. I suppose it couldn't have been Al Qaeda?"

"But we already have a statement from the perpetrator?"

"She could be persuaded to retract. You didn't see any long black beards tonight?"

Is he serious? Sometimes my Colonel's super brain is beyond my poor faculties of comprehension. "I really don't see how that would help."

"You don't? Look, he's CIA—they'll lean on us from the top down. There are going to be footprints all over my shoulders, not to mention yours. They'll want their own doctors to examine Chanya—no signs of abuse, and we're in the shit. We could lose our most productive worker, maybe even have to close the club for a while."

"How would it help if it was Al Qaeda?"

"Because that's exactly what they'll want to believe. They're practically blaming the weather on Al Qaeda over there. Just say it's Al Qaeda, and they'll be eating out of our hands."

We exchange a glance. No, it's hopeless. It just doesn't look like a terrorist castration/murder. So what to do about Chanya? I did not examine her private parts, but somehow one doubts that any man would dare to abuse her. Speaking off the record if I may, she's as resilient as a wolverine and when cornered just as ferocious. I can tell by his expression that Vikorn shares my doubts. Whatever the truth of what happened in this room earlier tonight, it is unlikely to be on all fours with her statement, which she has not yet read. Now we are both staring at the *farang*'s face.

"Kind of ugly, don't you think, even for a *farang*?"

I had thought the same thing myself but lack my Colonel's fearless self-expression: an abnormally short neck almost as wide as his head, no chin, a mean little mouth—perhaps she killed him for aesthetic reasons? Vikorn's eyes rest for a moment

15

on the rose in the plastic cup. I know what he's thinking.

"Doesn't quite fit her statement, does it?"

Vikorn turns his head to one side. "No, but leave it. The key to cover-ups is to leave the evidence alone, make the story do the work. The trick is all in the interpretation." A sigh.

"Bodies deteriorate rapidly in the tropics," I suggest.

"They need to be incinerated as soon as possible for public health reasons."

"Having taken a statement from the perpetrator and thereby solved the case, with no identifying documents on his person—we'll have to lose the passport."

"Good," Vikorn says. "I'll leave it to you."

We both give the victim the honor of one more scan. "Look, the telephone cable has been stretched—the phone is on the corner of the bed. A last-minute emergency call?"

"Check with the hotel operator."

"What shall I do about that?" I point.

Sophisticated practitioners, we have not troubled ourselves unduly with the murder weapon, which is lying in the middle of the bed, exactly where one would expect to find it if Chanya had killed him in the manner Vikorn says she did. I see this as a lucky sign and clear proof that the Buddha is looking favorably on our endeavors, but Vikorn scratches his head.

"Well, keep it. She did it, didn't she? So her prints

are going to be all over it. What could they find on the knife except his blood and her prints? It all points to her statement being true. We'll give it to them as corroboration." A sigh. "She'll have to disappear for a while. Since it was self-defense, we don't have the power to hold her. Tell her to change her hair."

"A nose job?"

"Let's not exaggerate—we all look the same to them." A pause. "Okay, let's go back to the club. You better tell me what really happened tonight, just so I can take precautions."

CHAPTER 3

Students of my earlier chronicle (a transsexual Thai—M2F—murders a black American marine with drug-crazed cobras—standard stuff in District 8) will recall that my mother's commercial talent invented the concept of the Old Man's Club as a way of exploiting the hidden business opportunities of Viagra. The idea, which still fills me with filial admiration, involved blitzing every red-blooded Western male over the age of fifty (ideally, those most pissed by the options left them by their postindustrial utopia) with electronic invitations to screw his brains out in a congenial atmosphere especially tailored to the tastes of his generation. Photographs of Elvis, Sinatra, Monroe, the Mamas and the Papas, the Grateful Dead, even the early Beatles, Rolling Stones, and Cream still adorn our walls, and our music pretends to emerge from our faux juke box (chrome and midnight blue, with a billion glittering stars). The sounds come out of a Sony audio hard disk hooked up to one of the best systems money can buy.

My mother saw Viagra as the solution to the management problem that has beset the trade since time began: how to accurately predict the male erection. Under her business plan, an old man would come ogle the girls, choose one he liked, then book her by telephone from his hotel room when he had swallowed the Viagra. The drug takes almost exactly an hour to reach full steam, so the logistical problem originally posed by nature was thereby solved. It ought to have been possible to use a simple computer program to work out which of the girls would be occupied almost from minute to minute. (At the height of our enthusiasm project management software was discussed though in the event not installed.) And guess what? It worked a treat, save for one small flaw that really could not have been foreseen by any of us, not even Nong.

What we had left out of account was that these sexta-, septa-, octa-, and even nonagenarians were not old men of the serene, humble, and decrepit genre we were used to in the developing world. No sir, these were former rockers and rollers, swingers and druggies, ex-hippie veterans of Freak Street in Kathmandu, San Francisco (when there were beautiful people there), Marrakech, Goa before it went mainstream, Phuket when there were only A-frame huts to sleep in, the world when it was young and LSD grew on trees along with magic mushrooms and a thousand varieties of marijuana. Scrawny contemporaries of Burroughs and Kerouac, Ginsberg, Kesey, and Jagger (not to mention Keith Richards), these boys, doddering though they might appear, had once taken a tribal vow never to underdose. You're only supposed to take half a Viagra to enhance performance, but would they listen? The hell they would. Some popped as many as three or four. Only a half dozen suffered heart attacks, despite dire warnings on the bottle, and of those only three actually expired. (Desperate times when Vikorn's Bentley had to be requisitioned as an ambulance in the teeth of expletive-enriched objections from his irascible chauffeur, who doubted there was much Buddhist merit to be made in saving the lives of geriatric *farang*.) The others uniformly declared they'd gone to heaven without having to die first.

Now what was wrong with that? I'll tell you. Gentlemen, take a whole Viagra (or more), and you kiss your natural flaccidity goodbye for eight hours or longer. (Forget about urinating for a day; questions arise as to how to carry out basic chores with that broomstick between your legs. Many report nostalgia for detumescence. Poetic justice: there's nothing to do but screw, whether you want to or not.)

They wore the girls out, who started to leave in droves. My mother had promised full satisfaction and she hated to disappoint, which left us with no recourse but a relay system. One horny old codger could get through five or six healthy young women before the drug started to fade and he allowed himself to be carried back to his hotel in a condition best described as ecstatic catatonia (or

20

rapturous rigor mortis). Profit margins shrank to paper-thin.

Something had to be done. At an emergency board meeting it was agreed to delete "satisfaction guaranteed" from the advertising and to appeal to a broader market. Overworked young men suffering from stress-related impotence were favored. We continued to be the destination of preference for the Western raver on a pension, and at the same time the more traditional customer began to favor us (Western ravers with no pension, basically), but we had lost our market niche. We were hardly different from all the other bars and as such suffered the seasonal downturns, not to mention the recession in the West. Suddenly we were running at a loss in a bear market. It was Nong who suffered most, for the club was her pride and joy, her brainchild and the vehicle by which she was to prove to the world that she was not merely an exceptionally successful whore (ret.) but also a full-fledged twenty-first-century businesswoman of international quality. She grew unusually religious, meditated at the local *wat* every day, and promised the Reclining Buddha at Wat Po two thousand boiled eggs and a hog's head if he would save her business. Even Vikorn burned a little incense, and I went further in my meditation than ever before. With such mystic brain power working on our behalf, a miracle was inevitable.

Her name was Chanya, and I still remember the

day she walked into the bar asking for work. She spoke English fluently with a slight Texan drawl (but enough Thai in it to keep her exotic), having spent nearly two years in the United States until 9/11 forced her to come home. Post 9/11 was no time to be traveling on a false passport in America. You had to have grown up in the business to recognize her genius. My mother and I saw it instantly; Vikorn took a little longer to catch on. Within a week we were boiling eggs like crazy and taking them and the roasted hog's head to Wat Po, where the monks ate them or gave them to the poor. Let me explain.

First, *farang*, please dump those childish notions you harbor about our working girls being downtrodden sex-slave victims of a chauvinistic male-dominated culture; take it from me, there's nothing your media won't do to comfort you in your post-industrial despair to make you believe your culture is superior to ours. (Are they kidding?—I've been in Slough, England, on a Saturday night—I *know* what atomized basket cases you are.) These are all country girls, tough as water buffalo, wild as swans, who can't believe how much they can make by providing to polite, benevolent, guilt-ridden, rich, condom-conscious *farang* exactly the same service they would otherwise have to provide free without protection to rough drunken whoremongering husbands in their home villages. Good deal? Better believe it. (Don't look at me like that, *farang*, when you know in your heart that capitalism makes whores of all of us.) Most of the girls, being the sole breadwinners and therefore matriarchs, dispense the whole gamut of family business through the medium of the cell phone (generally in our staff toilet while changing into their working gear), from care of the sick to rental purchase agreements, from the chastisement of miscreants to the number of water buffalo to invest in this year, from marriages to abortions, religious duties, and grave decisions as to who to vote for in local and national elections.

But chemistry is at least as important for commercial sex as it is for the more art-house variety, which is where you start to differentiate between the supporting cast and the superstars. Here's the secret: your superstar *makes* the chemistry. She is a tantric master in a G-string, a topless sorceress, a dancing dervish with wicked allure. She knows how to turn herself into a mirror that reflects the many and varied fantasies of the men she seduces. Guess how many have come up to me to confide they've finally found *her* at long last, the woman of their dreams, the girl they've been waiting half a lifetime for, the one they are so sure of they will marry her tomorrow if only she'll agree, the saintly Chanya? Answer: roughly fifty percent of Chanya's customers. We have even employed a bouncer (known as the Monitor—like me, he doubles as a cop during the day) to protect us from attack by the brokenhearted. In short, Chanya saved our business, and we are not about to desert her in her hour of need. All genius has its dark side. In our preatomized society personal loyalty is still important, which is why even the wily Colonel Vikorn did not hesitate to interrupt his Saturday night in Bangkok (as the song says, it makes a proud man humble—and occasionally dead) when he realized our superstar was at risk. So here's what really happened.

I spotted him the minute he walked in the door. We are between mamasans at the moment, a lamentably common state of affairs, which means that as junior shareholder I have to fill in as papasan pending approval of a replacement by my somewhat demanding mother. (Like all ex-whores she has an inveterate loathing for mamasans and can never find the perfect one. I suspect her of manipulating to keep me as papasan.)

I have already described his face, which was not much improved when inhabited by his spirit. A nasty piece of work with the ridiculous arrogance of an iron-pumper. The girls all took the same view and kept away from him, leaving him isolated at a table on his own in a corner, growing ever more volcanic as he observed the girls favoring men older and less muscular than himself. He was drinking modestly (Budweiser beer, not Mekong whiskey, but one does not defile Vikorn's brilliant narratives with minor quibbles). I was loath to waste Chanya's porcelain talent on this earthenware vessel and really only intended for her to charm him out of our bar and into someone else's. We are fond of each other, Chanya and I, and understand each other. It took no more than a shift of my eyes for her to grasp what I wanted. At least (this moment in the narrative requires needlepoint accuracy) I *think* it was the shift in my eyes that sent her over to his table. Within a minute or so his mean little mouth was stretching itself into a smile of sorts, her hand draped lazily over one of his rocky thighs, and when she leaned forward to sip at her "lady drink" (a margarita with extra tequila), he fixated on her breasts. Yet another proud man was in process of being humbled.

He was the type whose libido required secretive intensity before it could switch to full alert. Chanya adapted herself in a second, and now they were talking conspiratorially (and intensely), almost head to head. To make matters worse, Eric Clapton was singing "Beautiful Tonight" on the faux jukebox. This irresistibly romantic song was the final straw. The iron-pumper's hand found its way to Chanya's nearest thigh. I checked the time by the clock on the fax machine. Less than five minutes had passed, and Iron Man was molten—something of a record even for Chanya. I decided to help her out by playing the Clapton song over again—or was I simply curious about the effect of an encore? Tiny tears appeared in the corners of his abnormally blue eyes, he swallowed hard, and the words "I'm so damn lonely" were recognizable as they emerged from that mean mouth, even at a distance of thirty feet, followed by the unbelievably inept "You look beautiful tonight, too."

"Thank you," says Chanya, modestly lowering her eyes.

Just then the rose seller came in. One admires this man's quixotic courage and that of his colleagues: the nut sellers and the kids who sell lighters. (Every bar tolerates them on the understanding they will be discreet and not stay long.) Can there be a greater optimism than a lifelong vocation of trying to sell roses to johns? I'd never before seen him sell a single flower, this rail-thin middle-aged man with a jaw deformed by a tumor he can never afford to have removed. Shyly, Iron Man beckoned him over, bought a single rose for which he paid far too much, and handed it to Chanya.

"I guess I'm gonna pay your bar fine, aren't I?"

Accepting the rose and feigning surprise mixed with gratitude (all the girls can do Oriental Humble on demand): "Are you? Up to you."

Exactly seven minutes, according to the clock on the fax machine, and she was about to score. By way of answer, he pulled a five-hundred-baht note out of his wallet and handed it to her. She put her palms together in a cute *wai*, then stood up to bring me the bar fine so I could record what was, now I remember, her second score of the evening. It was Saturday night, after all, and she was Chanya. The earlier customer had been a young man apparently without stamina, for she had taken less than forty minutes to return from his hotel.

The only unusual feature of the transaction with Iron Man was that she did not look me in the eye when she handed over the money and I made out her ticket. Nine times out of ten she winks or grins at me at precisely this moment, when her back is turned to the john. A minute later, and they were out the door. It didn't occur to me to fear for her safety; after all, she had clearly tamed him already—and she was Chanya.

"That's really the way it went, and there's no more I can tell you," I explain to Vikorn and my mother, back at the club. It is three-thirteen a.m. by the clock on the fax machine, and none of us are in the mood for sleep.

"She didn't look you in the eye when she handed you her bar fine? That is unusual. I've seen her, she likes you, she always looks you in the eye and winks. I think she has a thing for you." My mother has picked up on this rather female detail. Vikorn is clearly back in Maigret mode, on a plane of lofty strategy beyond our reach. Nong and I wait for the pronouncement. He rubs his jaw.

"There's nothing more we can do tonight. Tomorrow we'll send in a forensic team to take pictures—nothing too thorough, though. Sonchai will arrange for removal of the body. He'll get the authorization for immediate incineration from— well, I'll find someone. He'll lose the passport.

The *farang* was probably AWOL from some dreary little town in the South where he was supposed to be looking out for men with black beards wearing Bin Laden T-shirts, so the chances are no one knows where he is. She obviously got the opium from him and the pipe too, so it looks as if he's been in Cambodia. Looks like he was not entirely the weightlifting moron he pretended to be, either. He at least had the imagination to try a little poppy sap. It could be weeks before he's traced to here, though I expect they'll come calling eventually. I don't see any real risk, so long as we lie low and Chanya disappears for a month or so and changes her hair. I don't want them interrogating her. We don't know what she got up to in America." Turning to Nong: "You better talk to her, woman to woman, find out where her head is really at." Then turning to me: "Or maybe you should do that, since you two seem to get along so well. Try to get her in a good mood. We don't want you to wind up castrated, too."

My mother laughs politely at this incredibly tasteless joke—he is the major shareholder, after all. I go out into the street to call him a taxi because he doesn't want his limo to be seen again tonight on Soi Cowboy. All the bars are shut, but the street is now crammed with cooked food stalls, which invariably appear after the two a.m. curfew to fill the street with delicious aromas, serving exclusively Thai dishes to a thousand hungry hookers babbling to one another with stories of

28

the night. It is a peaceful scene and one I have grown to love, despite the serious religious misgivings I have about working in the trade and making money out of women in a way that is expressly forbidden by the Buddha. Sometimes our sins are a compulsion of karma: the Buddha rubs our face in it until we are so sick of our error, we would rather die than go that way again. (But if that is the case, why do I feel so good? Why is the whole street in a festive mood? Did the rules change? Is monogamy an experiment that failed, like communism?)

Believe it or not, I don't spend any of the money. Vikorn's accountant wires my modest ten percent share of the profits into my account with the Thai Farmer's Bank every quarter, and I let it stack up, preferring to live on my cop's salary in my hovel by the river when I'm not sleeping at the club. To be honest, I've promised the Buddha that when I get the chance I'll do something useful with it. Does that sound pathetic to you, *farang*? It does to me, but there's nothing I can do about it. When I tried to take some money out of the account to buy a fantastic pair of shoes by Baker-Benje on sale in the Emporium (only $500), I was prevented by some mystic force.

After helping my Colonel into his cab, I stroll down the street, now entirely empty of *farang*. Some of the stalls boast electric lights, powered by illegal hookups to the illegal cables that grow up the walls of our buildings like black ivy, but most use gas lighting, which hisses and makes the mantles burn brilliantly. I see many beautiful and familiar faces dip in and out of this chiaroscuro, every girl ravenous after her night's work. In between the cooked food stalls, fortune tellers have set up their minimalist presentations: a table and two chairs for the well-to-do, a shawl on the ground for the others.

Each turn of the Tarot cards causes a female heart to leap or sink: marriage, health, money, baby, an overseas trip with a promising *farang*? Nothing has changed since I was a kid. To add to the festive atmosphere, a blind singer with a microphone chants a doleful Thai dirge with one hand on the shoulder of his companion, who carries the loudspeaker on a strap as they make their majestic progress down the street. I toss a hundred-baht note into the box, then, remembering Chanya and the need for luck, chuck in another thousand.

Everyone knows me: "Sonchai, how's business?" "Hello, Sonchai, got a job for me?" "Papa Sonchai, my beloved papasan," in a tone of playful satire. "When will you dance for us again, Detective?"

I'm very happy that Vikorn has saved Chanya from that crude and undiscriminating justice they have in America where, if they extradited her, they would never make allowances for her youth and beauty, the stress inherent in her profession, or the ugliness of her victim. Nor would she be able to purchase indulgences in the manner of our more flexible system. That remark about not knowing what she got up to in the United States, though—it is clear proof of the superior vision of his mind, not to say the paranoia that is a professional hazard for a gangster of his stature. Me, for example: I have never given her time over there a second thought. Didn't she simply work in a massage parlor like all the others?

All of a sudden I experience a dramatic slowing of my thoughts, a draining of energy after prolonged tension. I'm totally burned out, about to crash. I walk slowly back to the bar and mount the stairs to one of the second-floor rooms to lie down. It is eight minutes past five in the morning, and the first signs of dawn have popped out of the night one by one: the muezzin chanting from a nearby mosque, early birdsong, an insomniac cicada, new light in the east.

We Thais have our own favorite cure for emotional exhaustion. No pills, no alcohol, no dope, no therapy—we simply hit the sack. Sounds simple, but it works. In fact, in survey after survey we have admitted that sleep is our favorite hobby. (We *know* there's something better on the other side.)

It turns out that the Mitch Turner case has disturbed me at some deep level, however, for in my sleep my dead partner and soul brother Pichai comes to me, or rather I visit him. He sits in a circle of meditating monks who exude honey-colored glows and at first does not want to be disturbed. I insist, and slowly he emerges from his divine trance.

Want to help? I ask. *Look for Don Buri,* Pichai replies, then returns to the group.

I wake up deeply puzzled, for *buri* is Thai for cigarette. *Don,* I think, is Spanish for *mister.* That's Pichai at his most gnomic, I'm afraid. I guess I'll have to rely on more conventional sources. Even so, the dream continues to replay in my head in the form of a question: *Who in the world is Don Buri?*

CHAPTER 4

By the time I finally get up, it's early evening and I feel guilty for neglecting Lek.

Lek is my new cadet, assigned to me by Vikorn himself. He's been training with me for over a month, and I try to take the responsibility seriously. Nong, though, sees him more as a family slave and insists that I educate him in the finer points of domestic service. Trying to strike a balance here, but submitting to her bullying nonetheless (there are reasons why he needs to get along with her), I call him on his cell phone and tell him to pick me up at the club.

Six thirty-five, and the city is still at a standstill from the rush hour. Lek and I sit in the back of the cab, the driver of which has tuned his radio permanently to FM97, or as we Bangkokians call it, Rod Tit FM (Traffic Jam FM). All over the city people imprisoned in vehicles without possibility of parole are using their cell phones to participate in Pisit's call-in radio program. The theme this evening is the scandal of the three young cops who proved conclusively that three young women were engaged in prostitution by having sex with them for money. "With cops like these who needs criminals? Call me on *soon nung nung soon soon nung nung soon soon.*" Now calls from the grid-lock flood in, mostly in a mood of hilarity. Lek, though, eighteen years old and only three months out of the academy, wrinkles his nose.

"Have you spoken to your mother yet?" He has managed to make his head lower than mine so that his delicate face is turned up to me like a flower, his hazel eyes oozing charm. In a feudal society everything is feudal, which is to say personal. I am not merely his supervisor, I'm his lord and master, and his fate rests in my hands. He needs me to love him.

"Give me time," I say. "With women the mood is everything. Especially with Nong."

"Are you going to speak to Colonel Vikorn?"

"I don't know. It's a judgment call." I have the cab stop at the junction of Soi 4 and Sukhumvit.

The story of our errand goes like this. Once upon a time, not more than five or ten years ago, every side *soi* on Sukhumvit boasted at least one stall that sold fried grasshoppers, but with the relentless blanket bombing of our culture by yours, *farang,* we grew somewhat self-conscious about this quaint weakness of ours, with the result that—in Krung Thep, anyway—our insect cuisine was driven underground. At the same time, though, avant-garde *farang* cottoned on to this culinary exoticum with the enthusiasm of the pretentious, so that now the one place where you *can* buy fried grasshoppers is the *farang*-dominated Nana Plaza.

We arrive at Nana just when the various hunting lodges, known as go-go bars, are shifting into top gear. "Handsome man, I want to go with yooo," a girl in black tank top calls out to me over the palisade of one of the beer bars, but Lek's star is far brighter than mine. Neither the girls nor the *katoeys* (transsexuals to you, *farang*) can take their eyes off him as we push our way past mighty Caucasian bodies in sweaty T-shirts and walking shorts, half drunk more with the sexual opportunities than with the alcohol, although everyone is knocking back ice-cold beer from the bottle. This evening every TV monitor, and there must be about five hundred, is tuned to a tennis match between our very own Paradorn and someone nobody cares about in the French Open. There's no commentary, however, because the ten thousand sound systems are all booming out the usual combination of Thai pop and Robbie Williams.

Finally we reach the far end of the plaza, which is dominated by *katoeys* who drool at the sight of Lek. In a serious breach of authenticity the stall owner at the back of the plaza has labeled his various products in English: waterbug, silkworm, mole cricket, ant mix, dried frog, bamboo worm, scorpion, grasshopper. I load up on grasshoppers for me, waterbugs, silkworms, mixed ants, and dried frogs for Mum. While the vendor is pouring ants into a paper cone, Lek and I spare a moment to watch a ritual that is far more ancient than Buddhism. Young women in short frilly dresses—this is a bar where the schoolgirl fantasy is intermittently and imprecisely invoked—are standing behind one another in a line with their legs apart while the girl at the front draws elaborate shapes on the ground with a large wooden phallus. When the luck god has been summoned, she sends the phallus skidding across the floor between the girls' feet, then bangs loudly on the door to the club. Straightening herself with the air of a job well done (*if that doesn't bring in the johns, I don't know what will*), she leads the girls back into the bar and the twenty-first century.

Back at the club I make sure that Lek carries the little bags of insects and hands them to my mother, who has not yet opened for business. (She was waiting for supper.) We all sit down in the bar to eat what, I suppose, is breakfast, and for twenty minutes there is silence save for the snapping of legs and the squirting of guts. When I've finished, I leave Lek with my mother while I climb the stairs with the last packet of grasshoppers.

Chanya is awake and beautifully rested after her prolonged sojourn in the arms of Morpheus. She is wearing an outsize T-shirt and nothing else, sitting in a half-lotus on the bed with her back against the wall. I offer her the open packet, and she delicately picks out a fat one to munch. She flashes me a comradely smile marred only by the remains of a hairy leg in the corner of her mouth, apparently suffering no ill effects from her killing spree beyond a touch of nervousness in her eyes as I hand her her statement. (The advantage of a culture of shame as opposed to one of guilt is that you don't start to feel bad until the shit hits the fan.)

She reads it carefully, then looks up. "You wrote it? This is your writing."

"The Colonel dictated. I simply wrote it down."

"Colonel Vikorn? He must be a genius. This is exactly how it happened."

"Really?"

"Every detail is correct, except he drank Budweiser, not Mekong whiskey."

"A minor detail. Let's not bother to change it. I'll corroborate Mekong if it comes to that. I was behind the bar, after all."

That iron-melting smile: "That's fine then."

I cough and try not to look too sadly at her long black hair. "Just one thing—you'll have to cut your hair and disappear for a while. Do something else, be someone else for a couple of months, until we can see how the land lies."

A shrug and a smile. "Okay, whatever the Colonel says."

"We'll bring you back to work as soon as we can. We have to know what the Americans are going to do when they find out *what'shisname* is dead. How heavy will they get? How valuable was he to them? You see the problem?"

"Of course. I'll probably cut it all off—I've always wanted to meditate in a nunnery. Maybe I'll do a meditation course upcountry somewhere."

"That'll be fine," I say, although the thought of her losing all her hair almost moves me to tears. A slightly awkward silence. "Chanya, you don't have to tell me if you don't want to, but if there's anything you did in the States when you were over there that you think we should know about . . ."

She searches my eyes. In hers I see only innocence. "I worked of course. The money was fantastic, especially in Las Vegas. It's a wonderful country, but a bit bland. I got bored after a while. I was planning to come home as soon as I had enough dough to build my own house in Surin, and enough to retire on, but 9/11 ruined my plans. I came home sooner than I intended and for family reasons I needed more money. I stayed here because you're a good papasan, and your mother's been a good boss. It's fun. I like your club."

The temptation to ask her exactly what happened last night is very strong, but my professional discipline, learned at the feet of my master Vikorn, enables me to resist. That was one hell of a disemboweling, though. Even for a Thai, her coolness is a little unusual, not to say downright scary. I fear my smile was just a tad alienated when I left her alone with her statement and the packet of crickets. I didn't even ask about the opium since that did not officially exist. I noticed she'd got rid of the pipe.

Downstairs my mother has Lek cleaning glasses. I check the time, then switch to the radio on the sound system to listen to Rod Tit FM. Every cop in District 8 will be listening at this moment, for Pisit has told us he has a scoop on the eternal and notorious battle between our beloved Colonel Vikorn and that blackguard General Zinna, who has just emerged unscathed from a court-martial in which he had to explain his apparent involvement in large-scale trafficking of heroin and morphine. His claim that he was framed by the police, in particular Vikorn, was tacitly accepted by the court.

Pisit begins by reminding us that this drug rivalry between the army and the police is not new. Every Thai has heard about, and some still remember, the great standoff up in Chiang Mai in the fifties when civil war seemed about to break out over a dispute between the two services as to who exactly owned a massive shipment of opium that the Kuomintang (with the connivance of the CIA) had sent into Thailand by train. The standoff lasted three days before a compromise was reached: the entire shipment would be dumped into the sea. According to legend, the dumping of the several tons of opium was organized by the Director of Police, who arranged for a ship to be in the way. Now the perennial battle seems to have fallen onto the shoulders of Vikorn and Zinna. What Pisit didn't tell us in advance is that his source today is none other than Zinna himself.

Pisit: General Zinna, it is a great honor to have you on this show. You must be relieved and exhausted after your ordeal.

Zinna: What ordeal?

Pisit: General, I was referring to the court-martial that cleared your name.

Zinna: Oh, that. I was framed by a certain police colonel, everyone knows that.

Pisit: But General, if this is true, it is dynamite. Any particular reason why this police colonel, whom we shall not name, or indeed any policeman, would desire your downfall?

Zinna: Simple—they're scared of exposure. Right now the police run Thailand. Look at the news every day, what do we find? We find naked, unadorned reports of police corruption throughout the country at every level of the police force, but not a damned thing is being done about it. Why? Because the government itself is scared of the police. The police have become the only cohesive power in our country. And they call this democracy. That particular police colonel we have already mentioned is always going on about democracy. It's all just a power play, of course. This is the problem with the West, it is childishly superficial. Create a system that resembles theirs, no matter how defective and corrupt, and they praise you. Create a different system, and they try to undermine you. So what the cops have so cleverly produced is a police state that looks like a democracy. No wonder *farang* love us. It's their system exactly.

Pisit: And the police are scared of the army because it is the only viable alternative to them?

Zinna: Certainly. And the only unit powerful enough to expose them and survive.

Pisit: Nothing to do with rivalry over income sources?

Zinna: What are you getting at?

Pisit: General, you just referred to reports of police corruption. I would guess at least fifty percent of those complaints are drug related.

Zinna: Of course. There has to be motivation for cops to run the country. Under the guise of democracy, of course.

Pisit: And if the army ran the country again?

Zinna: That is a very provocative hypothetical.

Pisit: What would you like to do to that certain police colonel who framed you?

Zinna: That is a private matter between him and me.

Lek, of the abbreviated attention span, has tried to follow but lacks the background that makes the interview comprehensible. "Would you mind telling me what that was all about?"

My mother and I exchange a glance. "The

Colonel's never been the same since his son Ravi died," Nong says.

No wiser, Lek turns his wide eyes onto me. "The army shot Ravi during the troubles in May '92," I explain.

CHAPTER 5

The landline rings. It's the forensic team in quite a tizzy. They want me over there at the hotel where Mitch Turner died right away. I think about taking Lek, but he's doing his professional duty as he sees it by ingratiating himself with my mother (they're discussing the finer points of mascara application), so I go on my own.

When I arrive, I see what they mean. In their zeal they turned the corpse over and left it that way. Now they are all staring at me staring at it. I'm not sure whether to vomit or simply scratch my head. I am too stunned to do either. My mind flashes back to Chanya and the way she was this morning: cool and bright, cheerful as a lark. Shaking my head, I lift the receiver on the hotel phone and tell the operator to get me Vikorn at the police station. For once he is actually in his office.

"The forensic boys turned him over."

"So?"

"He's been flayed. From shoulders to the top of his backside. The whole of the surface skin is gone. It's just a bloody mess."

43

A long pause, during which I think even Vikorn is stumped. Then: "Tell them to turn him back the way they found him. Have they taken photographs of his back?"

"I think so."

"Tell them to destroy those." A click as he hangs up.

While staring at the victim as they turn him over again, I am thinking *farang,* I'm thinking France, Germany, England, Japan, the United States, G8, I'm thinking *decadence.* In a single stroke the case has been taken out of Thai psychology, and I'm reduced to whatever cultural insights I acquired overseas. The poor, you see, murder honestly for passion, land, money, or superstition, so this brutal disemboweling/castration appeared at first glance as a common enough expression of rage, fear, or greed well within the grassroots tradition of every third-world country. (The severed penis, frankly, appeared to me as Thai as *tom yam* soup.) The flaying, though, that gratuitous extra, can only come from a society with a large, wealthy, and bored middle class. (It has *ennui* written all over it.) So what the hell did happen to Chanya in America?

The next day I spend with Lek on the tedious chore of disposing of the body. Although Vikorn has already primed the clerks at the morgue and arranged for a lightning autopsy for the sake of appearances (he died from loss of blood from an unusually extensive stab wound to the abdomen and stomach and his penis had been severed—surprise, surprise—no mention of the skin missing from his back), there are any number of forms to fill in, people to jolly along, and suspicious glances to deal with, and the guys at the crematorium are a real pain. Somehow they've heard that the cremation is not entirely on the level and want a bribe of a value I do not have the authority to grant, so Vikorn has to be reached on his cell phone. I take a certain pleasure in their changes of expression when he's finished with them, but it is a draining day, and I don't see Chanya again until early evening, just before I am ready to open the bar. I think her true vocation should have been actress, for I hardly recognize her. It isn't merely that her hair is short and spiky and mauve, or that she is wearing a different style of makeup; she has succeeded in changing who she is. She wears a long black skirt, a circa 1955 white blouse with lace, and flat-heeled shoes. She is doing the demure Thai schoolmistress type (plus dash of fragmented urban dispossessed), with fantastic attention to detail. When she takes out a pair of unfashionable government-issue spectacles, I shake my head in admiration. She has come to say goodbye. We hold hands for a moment and lock eyes. It does not surprise me that she has the capacity to read my mind.

"It's not the way you think, Sonchai. I want you to know that."

"Okay."

A pause. "I kept a diary all the time I was in the States. Maybe I'll show it to you one day."

She pecks me primly on the cheek, gives one last wink, and is gone with a promise to call me from time to time to see if the coast is clear for her return.

As it happens, my mother joins me in the bar just a few minutes after Chanya leaves. She takes a beer from the refrigerated shelf, and I sit down with her at one of the tables while she lights a Marlboro Red and I report on the progress of the case so far. When I'm finish, I say: "Mother, you know better than anyone, what makes a girl like Chanya freak like that?"

She squints thoughtfully as she inhales, then shrugs. "It can be a lot of things. A girl goes through many phases. She'll start out believing what the customers tell her and get on some ego trip, until one day all of a sudden she starts to wonder if the johns are not exploiting her instead of the other way around. Like with any service industry, nobody ever really knows who is bull-shitting who in this game. She gets past that stage and starts to take a professional pride in what she does—she wants to be a star, because there's nothing else to aim for." My mother exhales thoughtfully. "Then she realizes that time is passing, younger women are getting the atten-tion, a bigger star than her comes to work at her bar. Another rite of passage she has to cope with—a period of depression perhaps, before she comes to terms."

I furrow my brow. "But none of that seems to apply to Chanya."

"No, I know. She passed through those stages years ago. I've never seen such a pro. So it must be burn-out. It happened to me once. You become a victim of your own success. You forget one little thing: all you're doing is fucking for money. Your whole life turns on the male member, you become as obsessed with it as men are. Somewhere inside you a resistance builds up. Some women really freak. I myself had to stop for a whole year when you were ten—maybe you remember, we spent that year in the country with Grandma? Eventually we were running out of money so I had to go back, but it was never quite the same after that. I've been watching Chanya get closer and closer to that wall for a while now."

Why do I wish she were not quite so matter-of-fact? I am consciousness trapped in a pipe. Sometimes it's hard to breathe. Chanya?

"So you think she simply freaked?"

"Yes, I think so. Maybe he was particularly obnoxious, but she would have known how to deal with that. Thing is, a girl gets tired of using guile. Sometimes she craves a full-blooded showdown. I think that was his knife, not hers—and I think it gave her an excuse. She saw it in his room, and some demon possessed her. That's how I see it."

"If it was his knife, and what with him being so

big and muscular, no one was going to doubt it was self-defense, even without Vikorn's help?"

"Exactly. That's why I'm still mad at her. She must have thought about it, even calculated. She could have stopped herself. She could have done what I did—cool off for a while. She's rich, after all, she doesn't have a child to look after, she could have afforded to retire all over again. But she's addicted to the Game, you can see. It's the same in every profession: when someone finds they have exceptional talent, they can't stop. They need to score. It's the hunt by that time, not the money."

"In that case, how did she do it? That was a big guy."

A smile. "She's slim and strong—she would have been much faster than him. He was lumbering and muscle-bound. And she would have had the element of surprise." A quick glance at me. "I think she cut it off after she killed him. A kind of trophy."

"And the flaying?"

Mom stares at me, makes a gesture of incomprehension. We both look up as Lek comes into the bar from the yard where Nong has had him organizing the empty beer crates. He looks at me expectantly.

I don't really have the energy, but I accompany Lek to the *wat* near the police station. Put any Thai under a microscope, and you'll find an encyclopedia of superstition embedded in every

48

cell, but Lek's kind are the most extreme in that respect, and he's itchy with impatience after a day spent in proximity to death: he's already lived too many hours with this threat to his luck and spiritual health. We walk quickly to the temple and purchase lotus buds, fruit, and candles from the street sellers outside. Lek goes through the ritual with fastidious elegance, then sits back on his heels with his hands in a deep *wai*, eyes closed, praying rather than meditating, I would guess.

He takes so long, I leave him there and return to the station, where I'm told Vikorn wants to see me. I assume he wants to talk about the Mitch Turner case, but he wants to talk about Lek instead. In his office he sits under a photograph of the King and a poster from the Crime Suppression Division illustrating the hundred and one ways the police have found to supplement their income.

"Is he queer?" he snaps.

"No."

"He's very effeminate. I'm getting complaints from some of the men. If he's queer, I'll kick him out. I don't want you lying to protect him. This isn't the time for your bleeding-heart stuff."

"He's not queer. He's not interested in sex at all." Vikorn sits back in his chair to stare me into submission. I'm not really ready to tell Lek's story, but I guess I don't have a lot of choice. "He's from Isaan, from Napo village in Buriram province, not far from where you grew up." He nods. "When he was five years old, he had an accident. He was jumping onto the hind legs of a buffalo to spring onto the animal's back, the way you country people love to do, when the buffalo jerked his legs and sent him flying. He was lucky not to land on the horns and be gored to death, but when he hit the earth, he split his head open on a rock. They had no medical facilities, nothing at all. They assumed he was going to die. He looked dead already. Why do I get the feeling you know what's coming next?"

Vikorn's expression has altered dramatically. His eyes are glittering when he stands to pace leisurely up and down. There is relish in his words. "They called the shaman, who built a charcoal fire near the kid's head and blew smoke over the boy to assist the shaman's seeing. The parents were called. The shaman told them their son was as good as dead. There was one hope and one hope only: they had to offer their child to a spirit who would fill his body and bring him back to life. But after that the child would belong to the spirit, not to the parents." He cocks his brows at me.

"It worked, but in this case there was a downside," I oblige.

Vikorn raises a finger. "The spirit was female."

I hold my palms together and raise them to my eyes in a *wai* to acknowledge his penetrating understanding while he resumes his seat behind the big desk. "Will you help him?"

He makes an expansive gesture with both hands.

50

"Queers are a Western import. *Katoeys* are as Thai as lemongrass. I'll protect him as long as I can, but we've got to get him more suitable employment."

"He's going to start taking the estrogen soon. It could be tough."

Vikorn grins. "A male cop with tits? Is he going to have the full operation?"

"He's not sure. Anyway, he doesn't have the money right now."

"So why the hell did he become a cop?"

"Same reason I did. He didn't want to be a whore or a gangster."

Vikorn nods. "I understand. Has he found an Elder Sister yet?"

"No. He's asked me to talk to my mother about that."

A thoughtful pause. "I don't want him working the bars. Is he going to dance?"

"That's what he wants to do. He's looking for sponsorship. He practices all the time. He loves classical Thai, the Ramakien."

He turns his head to one side. "I had a cousin who was a *katoey*. He died of AIDS. Actually, he wasn't particularly promiscuous, but it was in the early eighties, before anyone knew about that disease. He was unlucky, I guess. Give young Lek one word of advice. If he doesn't have the operation, tell him not to use Scotch tape. It's unyielding and causes terrible sores over time. That woven elasticized plaster they

51

use in hospitals is much better. Okay, you can go."

As I stand up to leave: "Is there anything you're not an authority on?"

For my exit he offers a dazzling smile.

When I get back to the bar, I find that my mother, who is nowhere to be seen, has abandoned control of the sounds to one of the girls:

> I pinch you on the bum
> I pinch you on the bum
> You pinch me on the bum
> You pinch me on the bum

Challenging stuff. I quickly switch to Chopin's nocturnes and almost gasp with relief: real music is a taste I developed under the tutelage of a German who hired my mother for a few months in Munich when I was a kid—and who later ended up in our famous Bangkok high-security prison called Bang Kwan. My eleventh and twelfth years were crucial for me. My mother's trade was un-usually itinerant, and we spent nearly all the time abroad, in Paris and Munich where her sophisti-cated customers undertook duties as surrogate fathers. (I learned to love French cuisine and Proust, Beethoven and Nietzsche, Ermenegildo Zegna and Versace, croissants at Les Deux Magots and sunsets over the Pont Neuf in high summer, Strauss played by men in lederhosen while drinking steins of beer in a Munich *Biergarten*.) Unlike my mother, who loves the Doors (for reasons both sentimental and historic: *Apocalypse Now* is the only DVD she owns that is not a bootleg), I don't much like rock or pop.

I lie down on one of the benches and more or less doze off until my mother walks through the door looking fresh as a daisy. We sit down at one of the tables while she smokes a cigarette and listens to my chat with Vikorn about young Lek.

"He doesn't know any older *katoey* himself?"

"No. He's fresh out of the police academy, and before that he'd never left Isaan. All he knows about *katoey*s is what he's seen on TV and what he experiences of his own feelings."

Nong shakes her head. "Poor kid. That's a tough row to hoe. He won't survive without the right Elder Sister, someone to initiate him, show him the ropes, warn him. He's such a beautiful boy, too." A sigh. "*Katoeys* got hit the worst during the AIDS epidemic. I used to know thousands. We girls used to drink with them after hours in the old days—they can be hilarious, terrific fun, but totally chaotic. No attention spans at all, worse than girls. He needs a retired *katoey* in her thirties or older, someone who made the whole thing work for her, big time. I want his role model to be a big success financially—that's the only way to save him from what comes after the initial euphoria. We have to save him from the despair of those middle years. *Katoeys* don't age well without a lot of dough."

Mother and son exchange a glance.

My jaw drops. "You can't be serious?"

"Why not Fatima?"

"She's a killer."

My mother blinks. "What's that got to do with the price of fish?"

"But that's how she got her money, that's how she made it big, by killing her lover."

"By killing her lover and using her smarts at the same time. Exactly what your little angel needs for his arrival on earth."

CHAPTER 6

Breakfast time: the street is full of early-morning cooked-food stalls. I'm pretty hungry, so I choose *kuay jap*, a thick broth of Chinese mushrooms and pork lumps steaming with nutrition as the hawker dips and raises his ladle, a great writhing knot of *kuaytiaw phat khii mao* (literally "drunkard's fried noodles": a stir-fry of rice noodles, basil, chicken, and a crimson tide of fresh sliced chiles), a single fried trout with *naam plaa* (a transcendentally pungent sauce made of fermented anchovy—an acquired taste, *farang*), a glass of cold, clear nongaseous water from the world-famous Krung Thep faucets, a 7-Up—and I'm all set. (Dollar fifty the lot, no charge for ice and water.)

Back in the bar I see from our computer diary that we are expecting a tour group. That's what we've decided to call them, anyway. We don't accept clients in gangs anymore, but there are about a hundred who benefited from our former advertising and arrive every three months or so in clumps of aging punks. These particular guys I remember well as representing maybe the DDD level of the retiree market.

A call from Immigration at Bangkok International Airport: one of the officers wants to confirm a statement that I have booked hotel rooms for a group of twenty old men who have been giving the Thai Air stewardesses a hard time for the past fifteen hours. They are all drunk.

"Yes," I confirm.

"You think you can control them? Or d'you want us to refuse entry?"

"They'll be fine."

A grunt of disbelief, but he lets them through. A couple of hours later a bald, stooping sixtysomething giant in a black cowboy hat with silver studs, skintight stone-washed denims, and irrefutably genuine rawhide boots bursts through our swing doors, followed by a mob of similar rejects from the *farang* subconscious.

A whoop. "Sonchai, my man! Hey guys, here he is, Mr. Viagra himself. Gimme the coldest beer you got, kid." Leaning forward, whispering with urgency: "Score the dope like I told you in my e-mail?" A side whisper from mouth-corner to his closest aides: "What d'you say, fellas, a few beers before we get into the joints? Sonchai won't let us smoke on the premises, so we'll have to take it back to the hotel—or bribe him to let us smoke upstairs."

"Oh, he takes bribes? That's just like the cops on Freak Street in the old days."

"I don't take bribes," I say.

"That's right, behave yourselves and act civil,

this is a Buddhist country and Sonchai here is a yogi—he meditates every day." Turning to me: "So you got it?"

I reach behind the bar and hand over a package about three inches by two by one, wrapped in brown paper. My mother and I both decided that no way was the bar ever going to sell narcotics, not even ganja, but Colonel Vikorn, after his first glimpse of this gang, decided that any tranquilizer was better than geriatric freaks on alcohol tearing the place apart. The old giant hands over two thousand baht (Nong took over the pricing—that's roughly a thousand-percent markup), then grabs the package and disappears into the men's room, together with a few others in the know. I remember that Lou Reed is a great favorite with this crowd and send *Transformer* blasting through the sound system. In less than ten minutes the big cowboy and his cronies are emerging from the toilets. Lalita has just arrived and recognizes the gang from last time but cannot remember anyone's name. A brisk wave: "Hi guys, *sabai dee mai*?"

"Hey Lalita, just great to be here. Jeez, do you have to be so goddamned beautiful?" To Lalita with pleading eyes: "I'm suffocating over there, La, we all are. To be old and sick is bad, but suppose you ain't sick? Suppose all your bits are still in full working order, but you got a mug so craggy and out of date, people look at you like you're a Model T Ford?"

Now Om and Nat arrive, one in jeans, the other

in a black dress with arabesque trimmings that dips so deeply at the back, you can tell she's not wearing underwear.

Nat's dress has sent the tour group into fantasyland. "Hey, guys, time to score the Viagra?"

Now the rest of the girls arrive.

The first thing each of them does as she crosses the threshold is to *wai* the Buddha statue in the corner above the cash register. He's a little guy no taller than two feet with, according to my mother's grasp of Buddhist doctrine, a gargantuan appetite for marigolds and incense and is liable to turn the luck off pronto if we let him go hungry.

All the girls have worked this gang before and manage them skillfully as they squeeze past hoary groping hands on their way to the lockers. They are all taking signals from me that the evening is not to start too quickly. After Chanya's adventure there is an increased police presence on the street. The cops are all controlled by Vikorn, of course, but appearances are important at times like this.

The bald giant calls to me: "What do we do about the blue pills, Sonchai? They on the house again?"

"No, not on the house. You can get them from a pharmacy. Any pharmacy."

"Okay, right, boys, policy change. We have to go buy our own Viagra. How about we do that, freshen up, raid the minibars, smoke a few spliffs, and come back ready to rock and roll?"

Whoops of joy at this magic phrase. It is only

when they have all trooped out that I notice the stranger who must have slipped in when my back was turned. In his early twenties, big, broad-shouldered, long black pants, polished black shoes, stark white shirt, an intensity to his gaze that could be mistaken for a permanent frown. Not exactly a typical customer, especially when you take into account the black hair, pencil mustache, and brown skin.

All the girls have gone to their lockers now that the gang has left. He and I are the only ones in the bar. I switch the music back to Chopin.

The newcomer seems not to notice the distillation of high genius that emerges from the sound system in the form of infinitely tumbling and rising piano notes. He orders a can of Coke and sits on one of the stools at the bar. He looks at me, Thai to Thai.

"You're a pimp?" the stranger says in a tone of surprise, too innocent to be insulting. I do not bother to explain the technical difference between what I do and what a pimp does.

Despite the frown, he is a handsome fellow, somewhat thickset for Thai genes. He makes no secret of his contempt for those aging punks—or for me. He glances around at the pictures of Elvis, Sinatra, et cetera, with a sneer. I find it hard to meet the purity of his gaze.

"American," he says in a neutral tone. He knows I will not mistake his meaning.

I respond with a smile, raise my hands: what can you do?

He catches sight of the Buddha above the cash register and connects him to me with a sweep of his eyes. "They told me you were Buddhist—I mean a real one, not a superstitious peasant."

"Did they?"

He wants to say more (perhaps he is a little young for his age—his kind often are), but his silence is judgment enough. To tell the truth, I'm caught off guard. The last time I saw such religious sincerity was in a monastery, but this is no Buddhist monk. In the near-empty bar I find myself looking around with his eyes. Not particularly uplifting, I guess, a tad too earthy for a pure soul. (But then look what pure souls have done to the earth, I remind myself.) I refuse the unspoken invitation to repent, and we are in a kind of silent standoff that I do not believe he can win (my bar, my street, my country, my religion— I belong to the majority here), when he fishes in the pocket of his pants to pull out a piece of A4 paper, folded into four. He spreads it out on the bar, watching my expression carefully. It is a digital picture of the *farang* Chanya murdered. I'm not able to control the flash of paranoia that passes across my face. The Muslim notes and records my wild-eyed moment, but there is no opportunity for explanation or discussion because the rest of the girls have begun to arrive, one by one.

CHAPTER 7

Homer listed ships. Should I not similarly honor the vessels of our salvation on the wine-dark sea of market forces?

Nat: Most of the girls keep their work clothes in lockers at the back of the bar, but Nat likes to dress up before she arrives. She claims it's because she needs time to work her way into her role, but Chanya once told me she tries to find customers on the sky train on her way to work. It's true she calls in sick more than the others, usually just when she would have been on the sky train on her way to us. That's okay, every girl has her idiosyncrasies, which probably make her unemployable in most professions. Look at Chanya, for example. In the circumstances, what other employer would have been so forgiving?

Marly: At twenty-seven, Marly is one of our smartest practitioners. Like most true professionals, she sees repeat business as the best way of evening out the violent sine curves of the trade, and that means setting her sights on the middle-aged and older. The charms of younger customers are more than offset by gentleness, generosity, fatherly kindness, wealth, and a tendency in the aged to go to sleep early, thus leaving her free for a little moonlighting should she need the dough.

Lalita is in an asymmetrical YSL fake in black with dipping back and plunging cleavage, revealing her beautifully enhanced bosom—tastefully done by a skilled surgeon, nothing too exaggerated. She is very gifted and has already built a fine two-story house with carport on a piece of land in her home village. Last week her earnings permitted her to purchase two more water buffalo for her parents to rent out. Her opening line to all newcomers: "I loved you from the moment I saw you walk through the door." I still smile to myself at how often it seems to work.

Wan and Pat, close friends, are wearing identical hot pants with tit-hugging tank tops and high heels. They are not from Isaan, which is in the Northeast, but Chiang Mai province in the far Northwest, where the weather is cooler and the opium fresher. They come from a hill village belonging to the Hmong tribe, where they grew up expert in poppy cultivation. When compulsory crop substitution made them redundant, they graciously switched vices to enable their families to make up for the reduced income. They plan to open a beauty salon in Chiang Mai as soon as they've scraped the money together.

Om, with a naturally boyish figure, has cut off her denims at the crotch and leaves cotton strings wherever she sits. She is from Phuket, where tourism has made everyone rich. She grew up without want but got bored with the family mini-market and came to Krung Thep in search of adventure. For her, prostitution is mostly a sport in which the huntress uses charm, guile, and the power of sex. The object is for the john to voluntarily transfer the cash in his wallet to her purse without noticing what a sucker he is.

Ay is in a bikini and high heels, revealing the silver insert in her navel at the center of her flat brown stomach, not to mention the leaping sword-fish whose sword peaks just above her panty line. She is a true child of Isaan, where she grew up unlettered. As is often the case with the illiterate, she owns a photographic memory and never fails to recall a john's name, even if she hasn't seen him for a year: a powerful charm in this line of work.

Here is Bon. She is more global than the others. She uses us as a base but prefers the more lucrative destinations of Tokyo, Singapore, and Hong Kong. She is a visa expert and offers free advice to any of the girls thinking of relocating overseas. Her English is all but perfect, and I'm told her Japanese is not half bad. She runs her own web page, which brings her a certain amount of work and enables her to keep up with her foreign customers. Way ahead of the curve, she owns her own small business in her home village that her mother manages.

Ah now, here is one of my favorites. Urn is from

the poorest part of Isaan, next to the Cambodian border, a genuine country girl who will not defile her identity by learning to read and write or by learning English beyond the skeletal vocabulary necessary for trade. She is slightly flat-footed from a childhood spent in the rice paddy and likes to roll her trousers up to her calves as if she were wading through a swamp. She is reflexively super-stitious and never omits to *wai* the Buddha or to take her shoes off when she enters the bar—for which the others never cease to tease her. She speaks Thai with a hayseed accent and a maximum of vulgarity. She also owns an exceptional figure and a brilliant smile, so she does not starve.

Su: nothing special to look at, but both my mother and I are in awe of her true Thai indo-lence. As an experiment the other day, I sent a missionary over to her. (We get them from time to time: white shirt, black tie with tiny knot, the sad courtesy of the professional sin-buster, Bible in quick-release shoulder holster—I'm afraid they all look the same to me, the men and the women.)

Missionary to Su: "Whatever you earn, I'll pay you the same for cleaning my condominium every morning."

Su (threatened, conflicted, and distressed): "Couldn't we just fuck?"

Farang, tell your evangelists not to bundle salva-tion with the work ethic. It really doesn't play in the tropics. Even the Muslims and the Catholics know better than that, and we Buddhists have bagged ninety percent of the market by peddling inertia for two and a half millennia.

Sonja: she is not with us anymore, but in her day she was quite the most beautiful girl in the street, a small star-shaped scar on her left cheek notwithstanding. (Motorbike: ninety percent of the scarring on Thai flesh is due to taking a corner too fast while drunk.) Her life changed when she saw a B movie starring Ronald Reagan in which the heroine, also scarred, came out with the immortal line, which Sonja immediately committed to memory: "Oh, how can any man love me when I am so hideously disfigured?" The ploy proved so fetching, she had to produce a short list of suitors, which consisted of an Englishman, an American, and a Chinaman.

The Englishman: "But darling, it only makes me love you all the more."

The American: "Come to the States, I'll have someone take care of it."

The Chinaman: "I want a ten percent discount." Naturally, having been trained by my mother, Sonja chose the man most likely to make a fortune in this lifetime and went to live happily ever after in Shanghai with the Chinaman. (It's your system, *farang*.)

And so on. Not a one of them whose combination of calculation and naïveté could not defeat the hardest of asses—unless the hardass has God on his side, of course. The dark young stranger has

65

not ceased to squirm and sneer since the girls came trooping in. The moment is saved by the Australian, thank Buddha, who trips on the threshold with his habitual curse.

CHAPTER 8

Slim and wiry, about thirty-six, his inevitable name is Greg, and he has been a regular these past two months. He sits next to Ay, who immediately and expertly shifts on the stool so she can hook a leg over Greg's walking shorts. Greg appears not to notice.

"Gimme a Foster's, Sonchai." A cock of the head. "Thirsty weather, mate."

"You buy me drink," Ay says.

"Do I know you?"

"Yes."

"Better give her one, Sonchai."

The young Muslim is watching.

Ay finishes her tequila in one, then sucks on the salt-encrusted lime. Nobody knows what swarthy fellow in a sombrero first introduced our working girls to tequila (okay, it was probably a Chinese entrepreneur), but history will reveal this act of marketing genius in its true glory.

"You pay bar?" Ay wants to know, now massaging Greg's member, which has begun visibly to swell under his shorts. The dark stranger turns away in visceral disgust to stare at the wall.

"Let's go back to my hotel—at least there's enough space to turn around in." He takes a five-hundred-baht note out of his wallet and holds it up to the light. "Or maybe we'll have a few more, what d'you say?"

Ay plucks the note from his fingers with amazing speed and hands it to me. I raise my eyebrows in a question to Greg. "Yeah, may as well, the kid's right, I'll only be too shit-faced later, probably make an arsehole of myself." Looking at his fly. "Christ Ay, what you been doing down there while I've been having an intellectual conversation with Sonchai here?"

On his slim figure the protuberance is somewhat dramatic, drawing the interest of the other girls, all of whom want to measure the circumference and check for hardness. "Big banana," Lalita confirms among the oohs and aahs of the others. "I hope you gentle with her."

The Muslim grinds his jaw.

"What about me? I'm just a poor little Australian *farang* all alone in your big hard city."

"You hard, not city."

Greg bursts out laughing. "You can't win." A quick glance at the Muslim, then away. Greg catches my eye, I shake my head. Silence.

"I go change," Ay says.

We all watch her backside under the bikini bottom as she walks down the bar on her high heels. Except the Muslim. The atmosphere starts to congeal.

Fortunately, Ay's "dressing" was a simple matter of slipping on a skirt and T-shirt. Now she is back, and Greg has already paid for the drinks and her bar fine. "See you later," he calls out.

The Muslim watches the couple's exit with exquisite disdain.

Now the bald giant and his gang burst in, filling the bar. Hardly an improvement, I guess, from Allah's point of view.

"Hey, Sonchai, what you do to the sounds, man? That stuff is about a thousand years old."

I switch to the Moody Blues, "Nights in White Satin."

"Better."

I shift my attention to deal with this gang. They are in a fairly manageable state at the moment, but old men of this tribe require ceaseless vigilance. Fortunately more girls have begun to arrive—Marly, Kat, Pinung et al.—until there is one for each old man, who feels honor bound to show appreciation and virility by cooing and slobbering all over them. The girls, laughing, hardly have time to change. Their drinks are waiting for them when they return from their lockers, and I have to make a call to order more tequila.

Everyone knocks back their drinks except for me and the stranger, who purses his lips. He has refolded the picture, and I'm wondering why he remains sitting here when the old men so obviously get on his nerves. I'm deeply worried now, because I'm having one of my flashes.

I'll have to explain. We were teenagers when my best friend and soul brother Pichai killed our *yaa baa* dealer. Our mothers arranged for us to spend a year at a monastery in the far North, run by a highly respected abbot who happens to be Vikorn's elder brother. Pichai was killed in the cobra case (op. cit.) last year, by the way.

Twelve months of intensive meditation in that forest monastery changed both of us in a way that is impossible for nonmeditators to understand. Ever since, I have experienced flashes of insight into the past lives of others. Sometimes the information is precise and easy to interpret, but most of the time it consists of rather vague phantasmagoric glimpses of another person's inner life. This Muslim's is something else, something so rare in Bangkok, I'm in shock. I'm almost certain of it: we met at the great Buddhist University at Nalanda, India, oh, about seven hundred years ago. I have to admit he's kept his glow.

From the corner of my eye, I see him put some money down on the counter under his empty Coke can and disappear out the door.

Light dawns somewhere in the bald giant's brain. He remembers that Lalita knows how to jive.

"'Jailhouse Rock,'" he yells.

The girls all remember from last time. "Yeah, Sonchai, give him Elvis."

We start with "Blue Suede Shoes," go on to "Jailhouse Rock," "Nothing but a Hound Dog," and most of the others. A few of the old men pick their partners and start to jive. We're all clapping them on with plenty of oohs and aahs and whoops. Now the bald giant declares in a shout that all the old folk took a couple of Viagra each about half an hour ago. Screams of hilarity from the girls, who like to check and discuss the mysterious and creeping tumescence with their owners and with one another. The old folk's vacation has hit the sweet spot: *This is really living* beams on those craggy old faces.

When I return to the spot where the Muslim was sitting, I see he has left exactly the cost of the Coke, plus a card with a telephone number and address, plus that photograph of Chanya's victim neatly folded.

"Jai dum" is Marly's comment as she passes by the empty stool where the stranger sat and scowls at it. Black heart.

By now the playlist has progressed to the slow tunes. Elvis is singing "Love Me Tender," and the ex-hippies are holding their partners close, clinging more than hugging.

"Old men," Marly whispers to me in Thai. "Dead soon."

CHAPTER 9

At the beginning of this *kalpa*, three men traveled together, a Christian, a Muslim, and a Buddhist. They were good friends, and when they discussed spiritual matters, they seemed to agree on all points. Only when they turned their gaze on the outer world did their perceptions differ. One day they passed over a mountain ridge to behold a fertile and populated valley below.

"How strange," said the Christian. "In Village One down there the villagers are all fast asleep, whereas in Village Two they are lost in a hideous orgy of sin."

"You are quite wrong," said the Muslim, "in Village One everyone is in a perpetual state of ecstasy, whereas in Village Two everyone is asleep."

"Idiots," said the Buddhist. "There is only one village and only one set of villagers. They are dreaming themselves in and out of existence."

CHAPTER 10

The address on the Muslim's card is of an apartment building a few minutes' walk away, but there is nothing I can do while the old men are waiting for the miracle of medical science to rescue them from impotence, a period the girls see as a window of opportunity to persuade their increasingly ardent suitors to buy them more lady drinks. (The bar and the girls cut the profits of the drinks fifty-fifty—some girls prefer to make their money that way.) One by one the old codgers take their paramours to the rooms upstairs (we charge five hundred baht for two hours) or back to their hotels.

I'm now too preoccupied with the stranger's card and the photograph of Mitch Turner to think of anything else. It is ten minutes to midnight by the clock on the fax machine, but I decide to try the number on the card anyway. Someone lifts the receiver on the first ring. The salutation, in a dialect from the deep South, is spoken softly, almost in a whisper. Not the voice of the young stranger: there is power and age in the tone I hear now, and the habit of authority.

"This is—"

He switches to standard Thai: "Yes, we know who it is. We were hoping you would do us the honor of coming to see us."

A pause. "I'm scared."

"I understand," the old man says, somehow managing to convey compassion over the telephone line. "What guarantee can we offer that would reassure you?" Although obviously older than me, he uses a polite form of address normally reserved for youth when addressing age. In other words, he knows I'm a cop. Interesting and, in the circumstances, disturbingly subtle. Why do I get the feeling he's smarter than me? "Would you like to bring a colleague? Of course, you can make a telephone call to inform Colonel Vikorn where you are going. We don't really mind, although we would prefer not."

I feel like a man in a blindfold: is the next step an abyss or merely level ground? I take a long time to reply. "No, it's okay. I'll come now. Shall I come to the address on the card?"

"Yes, if that's all right. And thank you."

I call my mother to tell her to come mind the bar. She is in the middle of watching a soap (a family of wizards who live in a mysterious region above the earth and intervene in earthly affairs from time to time, especially in the love life of the lead couple, who are perpetually pursued by a light-stepping human skeleton—we like realism in our entertainment). My argument is compelling, however, and she arrives in about fifteen minutes in her Chanel business suit and her discreet perfume by Van Cleef and Arpels, dripping in gold. Some of the girls are returning one by one from their romantic trysts and, surprised to see the matriarch herself behind the bar, give her deep, respectful *wais*.

The apartment is close to Soi Cowboy, and it takes me only ten minutes to walk there. It is in Soi 23, a street famous for its restaurants, which cater to every conceivable taste (fussy French, flaky Chinese, Vietnamese, British, German, American, Japanese—we call it the "street of the hungry johns"). As I stroll up the *soi*, I have frequently to step off the pavement to avoid bumping into romantic couples, most of whom consist of middle-aged white men and Thai women in their twenties. (Cultural note: look closely, and you will see the girls are flinching away from embraces, despite what they are about to do, or have recently been doing, in private: a matter of *face, farang*.)

A modest building guarded by a few guys in security uniforms with handcuffs and night sticks hanging from their belts. Two of them are sitting at a makeshift table playing Thai checkers with bottle tops. I flash my ID and take the lift.

A door like any other opens onto something quite different. I count eight prayer rugs (richly colored in greens and golds, geometrical patterns only) laid out in parallel at an odd angle to the room as the young man from the bar lets me in. Something in his manner suggests an ancient Arab tradition of hospitality (he has suspended the heavy judgments for the time being, even morphed into gracious host), and he manages a *wai,* which I return. I'm distracted, though, by the other person in the room, a man in his sixties with a long robe and a skullcap, who rises from a chair to *wai* me mindfully. I *wai* back. *Wais* are more than just a matter of placing your hands together and raising them to your face, however; they are a social semaphore with a whole alphabet of meaning. Let me be frank, those who embark on the spiritual path have ways of recognizing each other's rank, and this imam impresses me immediately. (Thin and straight, there is depth and fire in those coal-black eyes.) I raise my pressed palms as high as my forehead and pause there for a moment, a form of homage that pleases and impresses the young man. (Under the rules a Buddhist cop need not show such reverence to a southern Muslim, however senior.)

"Welcome, stranger. Our house is your house." The old man offers the traditional welcome in that power whisper I recognize from my phone call. He nods to the young man.

"My name is Mustafa Jaema," the young man says, "and this is my father, the cleric Nusee Jaema."

I do not disguise my surprise. Although rarely photographed, Nusee Jaema is often in the news these days as a moderate voice in the far South, respected by Buddhists as well as his Muslim followers. There are those who believe that he alone holds back the threat of insurrection—for now. I know he lives in a town in the far South called Songai Kolok.

"I am Detective Sonchai Jitpleecheep," I say, "but then you already know that."

"Let us sit," says the imam, elegantly descending to one of the prayer rugs and tucking in his feet. His son and I do likewise.

"Please do not be afraid," Mustafa says.

The imam raises a hand. "Forgive my son, he is thinking of the American, Mr. Mitch Turner." To Mustafa: "The Honorable Detective is not afraid, his intuition is too good, and anyway there are only the three of us." To me: "We asked the others to leave us in peace. I'm afraid that too many Muslims in one room these days sends shivers down Buddhist spines. Is that not so, Detective?" I shrug. He studies me for a moment. "I give thanks that Allah has blessed us with a man tonight." Darting eyes from his son. "Let us cut to the chase, as Americans love to say. Why are we here? Why have we invited you? Mustafa, tell the Detective everything."

In the presence of his father, Mustafa has become self-conscious. He garbles his words. "As you know, Songai Kolok is on the border with Malaysia, where half the world's computer components are made." A glance at the old man. "We were eavesdropping on the American. We followed him here."

A sigh from the old man. "It is in the nature of youth to begin at the end and work backward. The beginning, Mustafa, if you please."

I watch Mustafa compose himself. "We knew Mitch Turner. Everyone in Songai Kolok knew him. That was his problem. Our problem too." I half-expect the old man to interrupt again, but both are questioning me with their eyes. Do I understand? How smart am I? Smart enough to be trusted?

The old man coughs. "I think I do not need to bore a man of your discernment with irrelevant detail. Will it suffice to say that our people called my attention to his presence the minute he arrived in our town?"

"My father has organized an intelligence network," Mustafa says proudly. "It is necessary."

"You guessed the American's profession," I supply. "Perhaps not all of your fellow townspeople were hospitably inclined toward a *farang* spy?"

"Exactly," from the imam in a tone of relief. "He was a source of great anxiety to me and my supporters. Can you guess the rest?"

"Word spread locally, then down into Malaysia? Perhaps as far as Indonesia?"

A profound nod from the imam. "I cannot control all the young men in Southeast Asia. We received many requests, some more polite than others, some barely disguised demands with menaces . . ."

"For assistance in killing him?"

"Yes. And with the escalation in violence in our

78

part of the country—the somewhat heavy-handed way the government is dealing with it—it was becoming difficult to continue to protect him."

"*You* were protecting *him*?"

Gloomily: "Who else? His people could not even protect their own skyscrapers."

The harsh irony takes me by surprise. I stare at the old man. "You feared a backlash from the government if he were assassinated?"

"Let us be frank, he was CIA and looked like every young fanatic's idea of an arrogant American predator. If he were murdered in the South, Washington would be sure to put still more pressure on Thailand. We were terrified of an Internet beheading. More pressure, more backlash, and so the vicious circle continues until we are all rounded up and placed in camps. This was my fear. When we were told yesterday that he had been murdered—you are not the only one who can bribe a receptionist, Detective—I knew I had to come to Krung Thep to assess the situation."

My eyes flick to Mustafa: serious, intense, a young man with a mission quite free of troubling nuance. There could hardly be a greater difference between him and his subtle father. The old man reads my mind without effort.

"Oh yes, my son also is tempted by the world of black and white. Of course, everyone who enters that tunnel believes they are on the side of the white. Is that not so, Mustafa?"

"I have always obeyed you, Father."

"Obeyed without understanding. And when I'm dead, will you remember my wisdom?"

Mustafa looks away, then back to me. Adoration of his father may be the most human trait in this stern young man. "Have you any idea how much the Muslim majority did not want the United States to make a total asshole of itself and encourage the radicals? My father's position is very difficult."

I say: "What d'you want me to do? I should probably take you in for questioning. After all, you seem to know a lot about the murder victim."

A stiffening from Mustafa, but the imam is not perturbed. There is a twinkle in those old eyes: "But that would upset your Colonel's cover-up, would it not? We understand that one of your, ah, employees was responsible."

I nod. "I understand. You want to make sure nobody blames a Muslim?"

"Would that not be both a fair and truthful result?"

I want to play every cop's game of *I ask the questions,* but there is a higher calling. I accept the old man's challenge to look into his eyes. "Yes."

"Then a man of your integrity would want to be sure that justice was done?"

I raise my hands in an extravagant shrug. "You must know it is not up to me."

Mustafa shifts on his rug. "Your Colonel is well known throughout the country. He is very wily. If things go wrong with his plans, he will start blaming us for sure. He has no morality at all."

"If he does, what can I do?"

"Warn us," Mustafa says, "that we may prepare."

A long silence. The imam's concentration is unwavering as he looks at me.

"We want you to come down South to see us." He makes a curious gesture with his right hand, as if he is caressing an invisible creature. "You see, we knew Mr. Turner quite well. He was here to spy on Muslims, of course. Now he's dead, murdered. That in itself is sufficient for the Americans to feel justified in whisking some of my people away to unknown locations, interrogating them, perhaps torturing them, using up years of the lives of innocent men—husbands and fathers upon whom their families depend. I cannot simply wait and do nothing." He studies me.

"I see. That's really what you came for? You think all it takes is for you to show up in Krung Thep, call me over to your apartment, and get me on your side for the sake of a God I don't believe in?"

The old man winces. "Not for Allah—who cares what name you call him? I see that in the language of your prophet the Buddha you are an awakening being. You cannot allow yourself to be the instrument of a serious defilement that may cost many lives. For you that would be impossible. Within your belief system, how could you even contemplate the endless lives of suffering you would have to endure? We want you to come see us in Songai

Kolok—I'm sure your Colonel will agree. After all, a certain amount of background will prepare you for when the CIA arrives, will it not?"

"But what do you get out of it?"

"Your integrity. We ourselves could not hope to persuade the Americans that, far from killing Mr. Mitch Turner, we were exerting ourselves to save his life. But coming from a Buddhist policeman who has conducted an inquiry and made a written report—"

"Something to wave at the media or a judge?"

The imam surprises me with a broad grin. "Is this not the way wars are won in the modern world? And of course, look how much merit you will make."

"You seem to know a lot about Buddhism."

"I'm Thai. My mother was Buddhist until she converted at my father's insistence. I am not a fanatic. Educated clerics know that Islam did not suddenly appear from nowhere. It bears many influences, some of them surely Buddhist and Brahminic. It is the youngest of the great religions, which is why we see it as the perfection of a spiritual path as old as man himself."

Who could not be moved: this rail-thin old man who must loathe Bangkok and all it stands for, on a pilgrimage with his son and a group of disciples for the sake of peace; the shrewdness to understand the political implications of Mitch Turner's death; the naïveté to stake everything on a five-minute assessment of my character. But there is more here.

"Exactly how well did you know Mitch Turner?"

Mustafa turns to his father. This is a question they anticipated. "We asked him to leave, once," the old man says with a sigh. "Unfortunately, our visit to his apartment had the opposite effect. The Western mind is wild and unpredictable, devoid of center. He came to see me several times after that, and I offered what solace I could to an infidel. You Buddhists have your nirvana, we have Allah, even true Christians have a path of sorts, beset though it is by childish miracles. But what of these products of capitalism like Mr. Turner? Human souls locked out from God forever. One hears their screams of anguish even while they drop their bombs, these young people who have no idea who they are. They think they are killing others. They are killing themselves. I warned him of his death wish, but a good part of his identity had already been annihilated. He was a collection of cover stories."

A long pause. "Now I understand better," I say. "In any investigation it will be discovered that you knew him, that he came to see you, that you were able to eavesdrop on him. You're right, it won't look good."

"Come," Mustafa says in a voice of such urgency I think for a moment he intends to take me out of the room. "Come to Songai Kolok. We know about you. You are a complex man, but truthful. You take your Buddhism seriously. If you make your report early, exonerating us, it will be difficult for anyone to contradict later."

"But how can I justify a report when the case is closed?"

Impatiently: "Your Colonel will not fool the CIA. We don't know the details of the cover-up, exactly, but it will certainly be a pack of lies. The Americans will be sending agents very soon, and everyone knows how dishonest they are. Would people who invade sovereign countries on false pretenses stop at anything? There are many interests in the West who benefit from wars with Islam."

I shake my head, glance from one to the other. "So now you've made it my problem?"

I may be mistaken, but I do believe I glimpsed a smile pass over the old man's lips.

CHAPTER 11

I'm wearing my earphones, listening to Rod Tit FM at the same time as wondering what to do about the noble imam and his son. I'm of a mind to call Vikorn, who has flown up to his mansion in Chiang Mai for a few days. Subtext: to be with his fourth *mia noi*, or minor wife, a spirited young woman who doesn't take any nonsense from the gangster—and won't have his kids either, a revolutionary form of mutiny that Vikorn has never had to deal with before. My mind flits to Pisit, who is nattering in my ear about how superstitious we Thais still are. He is taking his rage out on a *moordu*, a professional seer and astrologer whom Pisit clearly despises.

Pisit: Take the current trend to buy lottery predictions.

Seer: Yes?

Pisit: I mean, how pathetic. Thais are spending more on these little pamphlets that you see all over the newsstands than we spend on pornography.

Seer: Is it your point that pornography would be a superior superstition?

Pisit: My point is that pornography is not a super-stition at all. In other countries newsstands make money from honest lust, not medieval mumbo jumbo. Do you have any input into these predictions?

Seer: No, I'm not qualified.

Pisit: Oh, so there's a branch of your profession with special qualifications to predict next week's winning lottery numbers?

Seer: You could say that.

Pisit: And could you tell us what is the success rate?

Seer: It depends. Some have a high degree of accu-racy—they can improve one's luck by as much as fifty percent.

Pisit: Just by someone like you staring into a crystal ball?

Seer: Not exactly. You see, someone pays a bribe to the lottery operator, then they make a profit by selling the information to the pamphleteers. They have to pretend it's mumbo-jumbo, as you put it, and dilute the success rate, or someone will get suspicious. It's not as risky as bribing an operator, then winning the lottery outright. People get caught that way.

I finally summon the courage to call Vikorn, who hates to have to deal with business when he's at his retreat in Chiang Mai. He listens, though, and I note a catch in his voice when he says: "Nusee Jaema is involved? You're sure?"

"Yes. You know him?"

"Of course. He's the main moderate influence down there. He set up a network, which his son runs. He's walking a tightrope. If he cooperates with us, his people might see him as a traitor. If he doesn't, he might be seen as a militant."

"What kind of network?"

"Information. You better go down there, see what you can find out."

There's nothing for it, it seems, but a trip to the benighted South. But back at the bar next morning I am distracted, not for the first time, by an e-mail message on a computer monitor:

> Michael James Smith, born in Queens, City of New York, Social Security Number: 873 97 4506, profession: attorney; marital status: divorced (five times); children: three; financial position: wealthy; criminal record: none, successfully avoided conviction for substance abuse a number of times, by hiring an expensive lawyer. Military service: enlisted for Indochina War, 1969-70, rank of major; served with honor (Bronze Star and Purple Heart); believed to have attended detox program for alcoholism during March/April 1988; active member of Veterans Against the War.

The e-mail comes from one Kimberley Jones, an FBI special agent who worked with me on the cobra case. The karmic reward I continue to enjoy from refusing to sleep with her, despite a campaign of threats, bribes, cajoling, and tantrums on her part, is that she has become a friend for life. (The karmic price is that she still won't give up—this particular message is unique in that it is entirely free of sexual innuendo, declarations of undying lust, or the legendary fury of a woman scorned.) I am now inestimably in her debt, for she has adopted Thai ways to the extent of putting personal feelings before abstract duty and used the FBI database to illegally obtain these precious details of Michael James Smith, attorney, Vietnam war veteran, former user of Thai prostitutes (at least one, once), and father of at least four children, not three. My cell phone rings even while I'm staring at the screen.

"You got it?"

"Yes."

"You're reading it right now, aren't you?"

"Yes. How did you know that?"

"Love intuition. How do you feel?"

"Terrified."

"Going to get in touch with him?"

"I don't know."

"Going to tell your mom?"

"I don't know."

"You mean I went to all this trouble and risked my career just so you can do your Thai thing and think about it for the next three lifetimes?"

"I want to thank you. You've done something no one else could have."

"Thank me with your body next time I'm over there."

"Okay."

Silence. "Was that a yes?"

"Yes. How could I refuse?"

"But you don't really want to?"

"Don't be such a *farang*. I owe you, I'll pay, you'll enjoy."

Whispered: "Promise?"

"Promise."

"Have you any idea how horny this is making me? How am I going to get back to sleep now?"

"Thanks."

"I'm going to hang up, Sonchai. This is doing something to my head, I don't know what."

"You can say heart if you like."

"Yes. Right. Heart. I said it. Bye."

She hangs up. Now I'm alone again with Michael James Smith, the Superman who came in from the war one fine night to find his destiny waiting behind a bar in Pat Pong. The man I mythologized long before I knew his name. The bastard whose bastard I am.

I'm shocked that his name is really Mike Smith. I extracted it from my mother after three decades of cajoling and begging, but I was convinced she was lying. The name and the Vietnam record and the approximate age were all Kimberley Jones had to go on, plus the likelihood that he had become a lawyer and was born in Queens. I never asked her to do it. She must have thought about it for months before compromising herself. I guess that means a lot in *farang*-land, no?

What to do about him? While I am pondering this most challenging of questions, I see that I have received a new e-mail. When I check, it is from Kimberley again:

> You kind of threw me just then. I guess I hadn't really thought through what it must mean to you. I was holding out on one thing, but I guess if we're going to be lovers I'll have to share it with you. Just be careful how you use it and try to cover the trail: mikesmith@GravelSpearsandBailey.com.

Ah, the immediacy of modern communications! I think I would have preferred the age of sail, when letters took months to travel from one continent to another and one might easily have died of cholera or heatstroke before knowing how one's heart has been treated by the special correspondent on the other side of the world. But this is the twenty-first century, after all, and when in Babylon, one must do as the Babylonians do. A couple of clicks brings up our standard advertisement for the Old Man's Club. I add the single line *Hello from Nong Jitpleecheep and your loving son Sonchai,* before zinging it off to Superman alias my biological father. I guess it's the kind of early-morning message every middle-aged man with those kinds of skeletons in the cupboard least wants to receive. We'll never hear from him, right?

I call my mother and tell her about Kimberley's e-mail, keeping to myself for the moment the fact that I've just taken the irrevocable step of sending him a message.

A long silence. Whispering: "She really got those details from the FBI?"

"Yes."

"It's been thirty-three years, Sonchai. I don't know if I can handle this." A muffled sound that could have been anything—surely not an un-controlled sob? But she does hang up immediately, which is not like her at all.

Now I'm alone with him again. Hero and substance abuser, successful lawyer, lousy husband, absentee father (at least in my case). Lost soul?

My cell phone is ringing again. "Would you mind telling me what you intend to do?"

I confess that I've sent Superman her cyber-version of "Hello Sailor!" with our family name attached. A gasp. "Have you lost your magic tortoise? Sonchai, you could have at least discussed it with me. Don't you have any respect?"

"He's my father."

She hangs up again. I shrug. When I call Bangkok Airways, they tell me there are nine flights per day to Hat Yai, only two a week to Songai Kolok. I book the next flight to Hat Yai.

CHAPTER 12

FYI:

Roughly translated, the full name of our capital means: "Great city of angels, the repository of divine gems, the great land unconquerable, the grand and prominent realm, the royal and delightful capital city full of nine noble gems, the highest royal dwelling and grand palace, the divine shelter and living place of reincarnated spirits."

Phonetically it goes like this: "Krung Thep mahanakhon bowon rattanakosin mahintara ayuthaya mahadilok popnopparat ratcha thani burirom-udomratchaniwet mahasathan-amonpi-man-avatansathrisakkathatityavisnukamprasit."

There's no Bangkok in it.

PART 2
THE SOUTH

CHAPTER 13

On the flight to the deep South I sit next to two young sex tourists who are chuckling over a familiar chestnut:

"So I paid her bar fine and took her back to my room for an all-night, and when I went to use the bathroom in the morning, canyabelieveit, she's actually been squatting on the seat—there are foot marks all over it."

This particular story always annoys me. I think it does illustrate the cultural gap though, not because the girls are used to squatting, but because Westerners find it so important and shocking. I guess the toilet is right at the center of the *farang* mind, just as Buddha is with us, no? I'm afraid I could not resist an intervention.

"Recent research shows that people who squat rarely if ever suffer from cancer of the colon," I tell the young fellow next to me (headscarf, nose stud, three-quarter walking shorts, and T-shirt).

A quizzical look. "That right?"

"Yes, soon you'll all be squatting over there too. It'll take a while to catch on, there'll be squat-ins, everyone will have to go to classes, there'll be how-to best-sellers with illustrations, talk-show hosts will demonstrate how it's done, missionaries will be dispatched to other countries."

"Huh?"

Isn't universal education a wonderful thing? I turn away to stare out the window at weightless white puffs, still irritated, until I remember the venerable Monsieur Truffaut, who hired my mother for a few months in Paris when I was young. There was a squatters' toilet even in his *cinquième arrondissement* apartment. My mother always respected him—and the French—for that. Actually, my mother and I both prefer to squat. Neither of us has ever suffered any kind of bowel disorder in our lives, by the way, *farang*.

In Hat Yai I catch a cab to the railway station.

Train: I think we must have bought our rolling stock from the British in the heyday of empire; I imagine an Edwardian in worsted wool somewhere in the English Midlands calculating that if he left out the upholstery, he could fit in one more native per seat. After half an hour the slats have imprinted themselves on my bum, which I am sure must resemble a wicket.

Scenery: Small black violin-shaped birds sing in unison on telephone wires, a silver-gray buffalo with long horns blunders across a field, naked kids play in a stream, the grass is the same green as a card table, in flooded fields the first frail shoots of this year's second rice harvest; everything distorts with heat. You could say the landscape

96

changes dramatically from Hat Yai on south, though not for any reason of geography. All of a sudden the women working the fields are wearing Islamic headscarves and long skirts. Many are in black from head to foot. It is not in the nature of our women to cover their faces or affect prudishness, but the statement is unambiguous: this is another country. The men, too, wear Islamic headgear, either the skullcaps that so resemble those of their Hebrew brothers, or flowerpot-shaped things that cling to the sides of their heads. It is early evening, just before sunset, and the cries of invisible muezzins calling the faithful to invisible country mosques haunt the gathering dusk. Fear settles on my shoulder for a long haul. Anything can happen down here.

It's dark by the time the train reaches Songai Kolok, and my instinct is to check the town out first, before contacting Mustafa.

It looks as if every second building on the main street is a form of rentable accommodation. I toy with the idea of using one of the seedier ones for old times' sake (I could produce an encyclopedia of the dives Mum and I stayed in overseas, when she was commuting between johns) but decide against. I will have a Muslim guide to massage, after all, so I choose what looks like the biggest and best. It's called Gracious Palace in Thai, Malaysian, and English and manages to be big, expensive, dingy, overlit, and sleazy all at once. At reception they issue me with towels, soap, and three condoms. Well, you can't say they're not taking HIV seriously.

Half an hour later I have showered and changed my clothes (generic black shoes, black pants, white shirt as usual); I am strolling through the town and beginning to get the picture. What I like best is the police station. It's a big, even majestic building encircled by a perimeter wall, on the outside of which there are maybe three hundred little bamboo huts leaning against it and a girl or two in each hut. The huts are not brothels, of course—they're too small for that. They pretend to sell food and drink, and some of them even have small fridges with beer, but there's no mistaking the point of the exercise.

The girls are not usually local Muslims; they tend to be Buddhists from all over Thailand, especially the poor North, who have decided to specialize in this niche market. It doesn't pay nearly as well as the *farang* market in Bangkok, but it's a lot more reliable. Every weekend and most weekdays great hordes of pious young Muslim men from Malaysia cross the border here and leave their piety on the other side. They come in expensive four-by-fours, on cheap Honda motorbikes, in buses or minibuses. Some even come by bicycle. Some come on foot. Right now, for example, the town is flooded with them. The girls have all learned Malay, and the ringgit is an accepted currency. Young men are standing or sitting in every one of the huts, purring while the girls charm them. In a way they can be more civilized than *farang*. They don't come just to get laid—they want the full debauch, including alcohol and a huge cavernous disco with karaoke. The sex comes at the end of the evening, so long as they're still sober enough.

With my professional eye I spy one beauty who owns an elegance you do not generally see outside of Krung Thep. She surveys me with a blink almost imperceptible to a nonprofessional, sees my Thai style of dressing, and discards me as a possibility. It says a lot that a woman like that is working here. It doesn't say nearly as much as the police station, though. No one familiar with Asia can doubt that the cops charge the girls rent for the use of the perimeter wall against which to lean their huts.

As I walk, my orientation acquires ever greater accuracy. The flesh trade is everywhere, it is the economy of this town, there is really nothing else. I think of Mustafa: what an affront it must be to him; what torture to his pure soul to walk through this town day after day. In every hotel lobby, every café, restaurant, and street corner, there's a huddle of women somewhere between twenty and thirty years of age. Usually they look past me, for they have trained themselves to specialize in Malays, but most seem amenable to persuasion, should I weaken. Not exactly a hotbed of Islamic fanaticism: I think any Al Qaeda evangelist would be laughed out of town. Muhammad himself couldn't incite these local guys to a jihad: they're in Islamic heaven already.

I try to think of the *farang* Mitch Turner hanging out here month after month. Well, it seems he bolted for Soi Cowboy at least once. I can see why. Prostitution aside, this is a small, claustrophobic town.

Out of the corner of my eye I see a young Muslim man pull out a cell phone and speak into it. Did I imagine that involuntary jerk of the chin in my direction? While he is talking, I pull out my own cell phone and call Mustafa: engaged. That would prove nothing to a properly trained cop, but to a third-worldy working on intuition, it's pretty conclusive.

As soon as the young man closes his phone, I call Mustafa again: it rings.

"Sonchai, where are you?"

"You know where I am."

A pause. "I'll come now."

He arrives on foot within ten minutes. I'm seeing him in context now, *his* context, this serious young man of Islam. I want to observe his reaction to the prostitutes who are responsible for the town's economy: *his* town, *his* economy. But he seems hardly to notice them. A mission of some kind has usurped his imagination. He looks grimly ahead, walking tall, straight-spined like his father. There is no denying the beauty of his surrender to Allah—no serious meditator could fail to approve—but the Buddha gave us the middle path;

I see no golden mean in Mustafa's. Without his father's restraining hand, he could clear the town with a bomb and hardly notice. We do not *wai* each other; without the old man our recognition is neutral, like enemies who find a common purpose for a moment, before resuming an ancient feud.

"I have the key," he says, not looking at me and fishing in his pockets.

"Not on the street, Mustafa," I say. I guide him into a café, where I order a 7-Up and he drinks water. He is uncomfortable here, even though the café does not serve alcohol. I think he would be uncomfortable in any surrounding designed to induce congeniality. I see it in tantalizingly vague and elusive mental images from many centuries ago: even then he was impaled by that same single-mindedness that is a form of tunnel vision. Buddhism was too subtle for him then, as it is today. To the evolved mind of the Gautama Buddha, any desire was an obscene distortion, even the desire for God. Mustafa is one of those passionate souls who were made for Islam, the warrior religion.

"Relax," I tell him. "Open your mind. I need information."

"What information?" He is startled and defensive. For him, our meeting here was circumscribed with a beginning, a middle, and an end. He has no idea how Western this quaint shrinking of reality is.

"Well, how about the address?"

A blink: "I was going to show you, but you insisted on coming in here."

"Good. In a minute you will show me where Mr. Mitch Turner lived. That is the future, Mustafa. Let's stay in the present. Don't you like it here?"

He looks around and shrugs. "It's just a café."

I cannot penetrate this iron skull. But I was his teacher once, and he loved me with the very same fierceness, the same passion, the same blindness. "Mustafa, let me tell you something: you are brilliant at what you do. It's really not that easy, even in a small town like this, to have someone followed, to know where they are minute to minute. But your network has been on my tail since I arrived. I didn't notice myself until I saw one of your people with his cell phone, and even then it was just a hunch on my part."

"So? My father has to know what is going on at all times. I told you that in Krung Thep. It is his network, not mine. He says—" He breaks off, scared of saying too much.

"What? What does your father say?"

"He says there is nothing more threatening to the modern world than a moderate Muslim. The fanatics hate us because they think we are heretics and cowards, and the West hates us because we have a morality it lost a long time ago—many *farang* are converting to us, especially in America. I have to protect my father."

"So you run the network that he put in place?"

"Yes."

"So you probably know more about Mitch Turner than anyone on earth. At least, the Mitch Turner who lived here in Songai Kolok for however many months."

"More than eight months." He catches my eye and allows the faintest trace of a smirk. "Eight months and two weeks."

"Your people followed him wherever he went, didn't they?"

"My father told you, we were trying to keep him alive. The only way to do that was to keep an eye on him."

"Did he know?"

A shake of the head. "He was very stupid." He looks me in the eye. "No, that is not the word, but he was a typical *farang*, lost, confused, pulled in a thousand directions like a man consumed by demons. He lived in his head and saw very little of the outside world. I could have had ten men following him in a line, and he wouldn't have noticed. Of course, being *farang* he thought he was the only one doing the spying. He deteriorated after the first month. A whore came to see him from Bangkok from time to time. He used drugs. He went through a bad patch, he thought he was undergoing a religious conversion. That's when he went to see my father. But it was just his Western psychosis. Why do *farang* think that God loves crazies? Allah loves men of steel."

"A whore? D'you know who?"

"No. She never stayed long enough for us to find out."

"You didn't get a picture?"

"No."

"Why not?"

"We didn't need to. He kept a picture of her in his apartment. If you had not insisted on coming into this café, you could have been looking at it right now."

Oh Mustafa, I want to say, *you haven't changed at all.*

"You searched his apartment regularly?"

"Not regularly." The question has thrown him a little.

"Mustafa," I say. He looks me in the eye. "If you want me to conduct a full investigation and produce a convincing report, you will have to tell me everything."

Reluctantly: "One of our electronics experts from over the border gave us a device, some gadget that recorded the keystrokes of his computer. Naturally, we had to get into the apartment to fix it in place, then again to take it away."

I can hardly control a smile and find some solace in the grin that is building on Mustafa's face. He controls himself immediately, however.

I maintain an admiring smile while I speak: "The device recorded the first keystrokes he used whenever he went online, didn't it? His access code, in other words. That's why you only needed the device to be in place for a short time. You got into the CIA database?"

"Not at every level. After access, there are many different checks. We never got beyond the gossip." To my raised eyebrows: "That's what we called it, because that's what it basically was. Just a lot of junk, the kind of crap they love to talk about."

I had decided to wait until morning before trying Turner's apartment, but absent getting laid, there is really nothing to do in this town, and anyway the setup has begun to intrigue me. I think of my spacious but seedy hotel room and decide to stick with Mustafa.

Mitch Turner's local address turned out to be just around the corner from where we were sitting. It is a five-story apartment building, very close to the police station. When we enter, the concierge, who lives and works in a small room with a single bed, a television, and a view of the entrance, turns away from Mustafa with a stony look.

"A Buddhist. One of yours," Mustafa explains.

"You intimidated him to get the key?"

"I didn't do a thing." A pause. "Didn't need to."

I'm breathless by the time we reach the top floor and sweating in the night heat. Mustafa seems unaffected by the climb. When we enter the apartment, what hits me immediately is the view over the police station, the perimeter of which is dense with young men and women and cacophonous with a thousand cheap stereo systems all blasting out a mixture of Thai and Malaysian pop.

I share a glance with Mustafa, who nods toward the master bedroom. I first see a small stack of books, then: there it is, in a place of honor next to the single bed: a silver-framed picture of Chanya.

She has to be in the States because she's wearing a padded parka coat and looks just about as cold as a Thai can get in those northern climes. She looks happy enough, however, and that amazing smile of hers shines through. Even though you can see nothing of her figure under that parka, you just know that that is an exceptionally attractive woman staring into the camera lens. Come to think of it, there *is* something special about that picture. I think it was taken by a man in love.

What a terrific exercise in perception I'm experiencing, like something out of a Buddhist manual. I replay that moment in the bar when Chanya seduced a sullen, dumb, weightlifting, whore-mongering moron and substitute a highly intelligent, educated, sensitive man who already knew her and obviously adored her. *I'm so damn lonely,* he told her. *You look beautiful tonight.* So why did she kill him? Why did she mutilate him? Why did she skin him? I check Mustafa's eyes, but they have glazed over. No curiosity here about the *farang*'s love life. I wonder what Mustafa does with his mind in those moist moments that even fanatics experience. Do they all simply postpone, pending paradise?

"You know who she is?" I ask him.

He shrugs. What does it matter? She was just a whore from out of town, of no more consequence to him than a ball of fluff. She was not part of any war that interested him. I allow myself the luxury of dwelling on her face (that smile) for a few moments: no way Mustafa is going to read my heart, which I have to admit has sunk just a tad. I pull open the picture frame and take out the picture of Chanya, which I pocket.

Unable to follow up on the mystery of the picture, I examine that small stack of books on the bedside table. *Huckleberry Finn,* a black Bible, the biography of the FBI spy Robert Hanssen by Norman Mailer and Lawrence Schiller, a translation into English of Dante's *Inferno,* a copy of the Koran in English, *The Encyclopedia of Arachnids, Advanced Spider Keeping,* and *Problems in Identification and Classification of Asian Arachnids.* I flick through the vivid color plates: scorpions luminescent under ultraviolet light. I raise my eyes to Mustafa.

"He collected them, I forgot to tell you. At first we thought he was genuinely insane. We used to watch him crouching in dark alleys with some kind of little net and a bottle."

The rest of the books are in Japanese script, indecipherable to both of us. One includes pictures, though, lithographic prints of samurai dueling with their famous curved swords. As I flick through the book, I see it is some kind of manual. There are photographs of samurai swords and diagrams that seem to show how one is made.

107

"He was fluent in Japanese," Mustafa explains. "We think that was his main qualification, what got him into the CIA. He had Japanese friends."

Finally, Mustafa gives way to the disgust that has been building since we entered the flat. "How can children like this hope to lead the world? Look at the books, at his life. This was a thirty-year-old teenager, a consumer kid taking culture off a supermarket shelf: samurai stuff from Japan, a whore from Bangkok, a little Christianity here, a little Islam there, when he wasn't hunting for spiders or smoking opium." He looks about to spit.

"Smoking opium?"

He grunts, unwilling to say more.

I follow him around the rest of the flat while he throws glances of contempt into odd corners. We find the terrarium on a shelf against a back wall in the spare bedroom. Mustafa peers at it, then shakes his head. "Nobody fed them." I peer into the rectangular space behind the glass: dried corpses of hairy tarantulas, a scorpion with babies on her back, other spiders dead in their webs as if in the aftermath of a cataclysm.

In a cupboard Mustafa finds a cheap telescope of the kind that can be bought in department stores. Our exchange of glances is a classic example of telepathy. If Mitch Turner needed a good telescope, he would have persuaded the CIA to supply a state-of-the-art model. So he used this one for what?

"Checking out the action around the police station," Mustafa grunts.

There doesn't seem to be anything else of immediate significance, nothing that would explain Mitch Turner's violent death anyway. I observe that there is no laptop, but Mustafa says whenever Turner left the apartment for any length of time, he took a laptop with him, probably following standing orders to check it into a bank vault or safe-deposit box. Well, there doesn't seem to be much more we can do tonight, so we leave the apartment and Mustafa locks the door.

Out on the street the night is in full swing. The whole town is alive with disco music and flashing neon signs from cheap hotels. A tall and very thickset Malay in his late thirties is ushering three girls into his hotel as we pass. Three? I shoot a glance at Mustafa, but he's in whatever space he uses to block out unacceptable aspects of reality. I wonder if he saw them at all, those three very attractive girls who seemed to be enjoying themselves? I guess that within his superstition those women would be seen as pure evil, seductive emissaries of Satan. Well, looks like that Malay and those girls are going to be merrily rolling in it for the next few hours, after which all participants will retire satisfied and sleep the sleep of the just. I do not explain to Mustafa that in the Game women often prefer to share their labor—they may even see it as a kind of perk in that they demand extra for doing less. It's more fun, too, if you have a friend or colleague to chat with in your own language while you're working the john. For country girls there's an echo from the rice harvest, when everyone has to pitch in, and there's a lot of chatting and flirting and you tell jokes to pass the time, hardly noticing what your hands are doing. I think of the big dark Malay laid out like a rice paddy while the girls work him and discuss the dollar-baht exchange rate across his erection. I pity Mustafa, who so resolutely rejects the simple dance of life, the humor. At the same time I wonder how Mitch Turner, the confused American spy, took it all.

There don't seem to be any cafés with spare tables and chairs, not with any privacy anyway, so we end up in the lobby of our hotel, which has been transformed into a kind of anteroom for a gigantic brothel. Girls are sitting on all the sofas, and as we watch, dark-skinned young men with pencil mustaches approach one or another. They are different from *farang* in that the deal is done so quickly, usually within five minutes. No romantic buildup, more an Asian-style business deal. The woman is happy enough with that, since it might mean she can fit in more than one customer tonight. Some of the couples start immediately for the lifts, but most wander out into the street in search of a disco, where the young gallant can demonstrate his expertise in karaoke and the lady will applaud with adulation in her eyes.

Mustafa doesn't want to look at it, so we find

an empty table in a corner. He still has some explaining to do, so I give him the silent treatment.

"You are wondering why we took such interest in one individual, when there are hundreds like him in Thailand?"

"Yes."

"You must ask my father for a full explanation. According to him, the *farang* Mitch Turner was a fascinating product of the West. He said that just as intelligence agencies like to take terrorist bombs apart to see how they are made, so we should look into the soul of this strange fish, this human bomb, to see how it was made. After all, he didn't invent himself—he was a creature of his culture."

"His naïveté, confusion, lack of center?"

"All those things, but what most interested my father was his spiritual agony. You must understand that although my father is very learned, he hardly ever meets *farang*, especially not American spies. My father is a great imam, which is to say a connoisseur of souls. Mitch Turner interested him a lot. Until he met Turner, I think he doubted that *farang* had souls. When he saw what a mess Turner was in, what he called the 'great howl of agony' at the center of this man, he felt he'd understood why the West is the way it is." A ghost of a smile. "It was as if he'd cracked a code and now could read the Western mind." Staring into my eyes: "He told me he would never have believed it was possible for a man to be so tormented and still live, still function." Excited now, sharing a passion with me for the first time: "He also said that without a war, America would descend into total confusion and would have to turn itself into a police state to survive, because its people no longer have any internal structure. Americans can never be defeated by war. It is peace they find intolerable."

"He reached these conclusions on the basis of one specimen?"

"Why not? True knowledge comes from Allah. It does not need scientific method, only a clue, a hint for the spirit to follow."

As he speaks, I note that he is watching the action in a totally unseeing way, like a show in a language he does not understand. For me, though, it is impossible not to take a professional interest in what is going on all over the rest of the lobby: the young men approaching the girls, the big ironic smile on the faces of the women; the man's complex mixture of shyness, courage, arrogance, urgency, and anticipation, the woman's searching eyes, trying to guess what sort of lover this one will be while they negotiate; the mutual relief that is almost a kind of orgasm when they reach a deal; the abrupt change of body language when they put their arms around each other and make for the lifts or walk out into the night. I know that Mustafa, if he sees anything of interest at all, sees only sin, which will no doubt be eradicated sooner or later by Allah—along with a whole range of other activities that I consider merely human.

When I tell him I'm going to sleep, he stands up immediately, like one who has been released from a dirty job.

CHAPTER 14

B ack in my room I made the mistake of drinking a couple of Singha beers from the minibar. They knocked me out for a few hours, and now I'm awake with quite a thirst and a slight headache. (Drink Kloster or Heineken, *farang*, when you come for your vacation—they're cleaner brews.) The worst of it is, I'm fully conscious, and when I use the remote to switch on the TV, I see from the information bar that it's four-thirteen in the morning. As I lie on the bed I remember my dream, in which Chanya came to me. The quality of light, the expression on her face, the whole atmosphere of the dream, tell me it was a communication from her of some kind, though I cannot decipher its meaning. She and I occasionally discussed Buddhism. She was a keen meditator herself, and our backgrounds were so similar we often speculated that we had known each other in previous lifetimes, perhaps a great many. We were too shy to say it, but we both wondered if we were not soul mates of the kind that meet up lifetime after lifetime. Only when karma is very favorable do such soul mates succeed in having a full-blooded relationship; after all, that would be the next best thing to enlightenment itself. More often we look out for each other from a distance, like guardian angels. I feel I'm her guardian at the moment, but in the dream it seemed the other way around. Restless, I pull some clothes on and go down to the lobby.

All the girls are gone, except for five who are hanging around on a couple of the sofas. From their snippets of conversation that I overhear, it seems that only two of them had customers tonight; the other three have not been lucky and are moaning about the number of women in town. There just aren't enough men to go around. At the reception desk the clerk is asleep in his chair, his head resting on his folded arms on his desk. He starts when I try to wake him and gives a sullen shake of the head when I ask to use the business center where there is Internet access. I offer money, but still he refuses. The business center doesn't open until nine in the morning. I'm in a stubborn mood and toy with the idea of threatening to bust the whole joint, but that would not be playing the game. Instead I cajole him, make him laugh, offer some cash again, and this time he consents to let me use the hotel's Internet access from behind the reception desk.

I'm so keen to check my e-mail because I want to know if I've got a reply from Superman. When I check the list of new messages, I feel a dull, bruised sensation in my heart because there is nothing from

Mike Smith, even though with the eleven-hour time difference that is hardly surprising. I take a couple of minutes to scan through the usual business stuff (another gang of unruly old men who had such a good time six months ago, they want to come back for Christmas), before I notice the new correspondent: chanya@yahoo.com.

Her message is very brief: *Sonchai, here is the diary I told you about. Chanya.*

The attachment, on the other hand, is more than five hundred kilobytes, nearly as long as a novel, and of course it is in Thai script. As I start to read, I'm impressed by the clarity and simplicity of the writing. Only a noble soul writes like that. I am also totally absorbed. When the clerk starts to get restless, I have to bribe him again to let me print out the whole of her diary, which I take upstairs to my room and spend the rest of the night reading. I'm hollow-eyed by the time I meet Mustafa in the hotel lobby in the morning.

Out in the street, on the way to Turner's apartment, Mustafa's cell phone rings; well, actually, it makes no sound, merely vibrates in his pocket, and he fishes it out in an instant. A few words in the local dialect, and he closes it again and slides it back in his pocket. "They're here already."

"Who?"

"Who do you think?"

As we turn a corner into the street where Turner's apartment is located, he nods toward the building. Two *farang* in tropical cream business

116

suits, white shirts, and ties are on the point of entering the building.

"You see what I mean?" Mustafa says. "It is more arrogance than stupidity. They might as well have 'CIA' stamped on their jackets, but they cannot believe we're smart enough to work out what they are."

Maybe he has a point, but we'll have to abort our examination of the apartment. Not at all sure what to do next, we stroll a little closer to the building and find a café with a view of the street. I order a 7-Up, and Mustafa orders water. We're both wondering how two *farang* in business suits are going to negotiate their way past the concierge.

Not easily, it seems. Within minutes they're leaving the building with frowns on their faces. Worried frowns, it seems to me. Mustafa looks at me with a touch of insolence: *Okay, cop, now what d'you want to do?*

"Watch," I say. I go to the door of the café and call out in English, "Can I help you?" as the two men pass. They stop in their tracks, a little surprised but pleased to find a fluent English speaker in this remote town.

"You guys look a little lost," I say, using the kind of smile that's supposed to go with words like that. (I can't decide on my accent—I can do British or American. Generally one uses Brit when talking to an American and vice versa: the two cultures seem to intimidate each other quite well. On instinct, though, I use American with Enthusiastic

Immigrant coloring, and in a flash they decide I have Green Card written all over me; obviously, I'm the best they can hope for down here.)

They start to talk. Now we are all doing Sympathetic American Abroad, a specialized genre in which the superiority of *farang* culture, the stupidity of the native population, and the poor health standards and the appalling state of the plumbing are all expressed subliminally, without a single politically incorrect word passing anyone's lips. Using basic cues, I give the impression of a native son—Buddhist, not Muslim—who has returned from the United States on vacation and despises his hometown. Mustafa has retreated into a psychological shadow and throws me hostile glances from time to time.

While we're talking banalities, I take in the two Americans. The older is in his mid-fifties, slim and wiry, a military fitness about him, a short spiky haircut, and intelligence of the ruthless variety about those thin lips. And something else that I cannot put my finger on. Something not quite American. Or human. Does it surprise you, *farang,* that a good ten percent of the entities you see walking around in human form are not human at all? It's been going on for a few hundred years now: immigrants from the Outer Limits, with their own agendas. Call them Special Forces from the Other Side. The final conflict won't be long now.

The other is young, perhaps not as young as he looks. To a tropical type like me, that blond hair and simplified Nordic face—you've seen that jawline in cartoons—looks maybe seventeen, but I suppose he must be mid- to late twenties.

All of a sudden I am key in the Americans' pursuit of happiness. Big smiles and an obscene parody of Oriental humility and deference as they introduce themselves properly, shake hands, enter the café, and sit down at the table. Well, at least they're smart enough to be polite.

"Like I say"—I still have that smile plastered all over my face—"I'm just here on a discover-my-roots trip. I was born here, but Mom and Dad escaped stateside when I was still a kid, thank God."

Unable to resist this patriotic call, the younger one gives a sincere smile, while the older one simply nods.

They order Cokes. Their body language indicates they're quite ready to lose Mustafa, who remains silent as if enveloped in an invisible chador and clearly makes them nervous.

Making it up as I go: "I'm thinking of doing a trip down south myself, planning to take that jungle train the books talk about. Supposed to be quite something."

"Is that right?" Politely, but sharing glances with each other.

"Yeah. What are you two guys doing here? Going south yourselves, or have you just come up from there?"

Sharing that glance again: "Oh, well, we're here on business, actually."

119

"You are? In a town like this? Well, I'm not going to ask, but I can't imagine what kind of business an American could have here. Hell, it's all Muslim, you know. Except at night when it's all sex, ha-ha."

Sheepish grins. "Yes, well, we only got here last night. Took the plane to Hat Yai from Bangkok, then a four-hour taxi ride. We didn't really know what to expect. Neither of us has been here before. Actually, we're looking for a colleague of ours."

"Oh yeah? An American?"

"That's right. I wonder if we could, ahm . . ." The hint is for Mustafa to lose himself, but he doesn't take it. One more glance, and a nod is exchanged. "Look—ah, frankly we're a little worried about our friend. We haven't heard from him in a week now, and well, to look at he's pretty obviously an American, and this is a very Islamic town."

"Oh, that's too bad." I give them a big worried shake of the head. "How awful."

"Yes, well, we don't know if it's awful or not, but we were wondering . . ." It seems it's hard for them to say exactly what they were wondering with Mustafa sitting at the table.

"Would I be right in thinking your colleague lives in that apartment building over there? The one I just saw you come out of?"

"Correct. That's what we were wondering, if there might be an informal way of taking a look at the apartment, without necessarily getting the

120

police involved, just to check that there's been no foul play."

"Informal?" I'm frowning with my head to one side.

Coughs. "Yes, look, we're not all that familiar with your country, and the last thing we want to do is to cause offense, but if there were some way in which a person of influence could talk with that concierge . . . You're from around here, you speak the language. Maybe he has a key? We just want to make sure our friend's okay."

I'm still frowning uncomprehendingly, but I've added that special gleam of Third World Greed.

"Oh, we'd be willing to pay for your time, wouldn't we?"

"More than willing. A quick glance into that apartment would be worth quite a lot to us, I'd say." I raise my eyebrows. "Oh, we'd make it worth your while."

"Keep your money," I say with a smile. "Let's just wander over and see what we can do, shall we?" I frown in concentration. "But just in case the authorities get involved, I ought to know exactly who you are. Do you have your passports with you?"

"Passports? Sure."

"Could I take just a quick peek at your visas?"

Two blue passports with eagles on the front appear. I see they are both holding business visas. The older one is named Hudson, and the young blond is Bright. I hand the passports back. "What is your business? Are you working in Thailand?"

Their command of their mutual cover story is really quite smooth. It seems they are executives in the telecommunications industry, more on the infrastructure side than marketing. Mitch Turner is stationed down here to get a general impression of the political situation right on the border. Nobody wants to invest in heavy engineering costs only to find that civil strife or terrorism has ruined the project.

"So he's a kind of industrial spy?" I ask.

The word does not faze them at all. No, not a spy, that would be overstating it, let's say the advance guard of a feasibility study.

"I see," I say. "And you think our local Muslims might have taken a dislike to him?"

Deep frowns. I seem to have hit a nerve. "That would be the worst case. It could be anything. He could be in his bed right now suffering some kind of seizure. He could have gotten hit by a truck. Until we get inside his apartment, it's going to be hard even to hypothesize."

The four of us cross the street together. Mustafa finds a way of guiding me into the concierge's office, then out again triumphantly holding the key. "Money talks around here," I explain.

Up three flights of stairs with everyone sweating in the tropical heat, then we're in Turner's apartment. A quick look, and it is obvious that Mitch Turner is not here. They seem to be on the lookout for something specific, which I would guess to be Turner's laptop, and don't take much interest in anything else. Mustafa and I watch them rummage around in a wardrobe. They pay some attention to the empty silver picture frame but soon give it a shrug. Finally the older one, Hudson, gives me a brief smile. "Well, he's not here, and there are no signs that he left in a hurry."

Mustafa, though, has stationed himself by the front door, blocking it with his big shoulders. A mean look has come over his features. "They palmed something," he snaps at me in Thai. "Something they found in that wardrobe in the bedroom."

I'm doing Disappointment and Consternation when I take up a position next to Mustafa and engage Hudson's eyes. "Come on, guys, we saw you palm it."

An exchange of glances between the two. "I'm afraid we can't do that," says Bright, the younger one. He makes a face of muffled triumph: Clark Kent has disrobed. Hudson seems less sure. I think he's seen through me, at least to the extent of not making any assumptions.

"I brought you here in good faith," I say. "I can't let you steal anything."

"Well, you see," Bright begins, but is silenced by a gesture from Hudson.

"We're here on government business," Hudson says in a reasonable tone. "U.S. government."

Bright checks my face: isn't that enough?

"How do I know that?"

"You don't," says Bright. "You'll just have to take our word for it."

"Oh? Well, the Royal Thai Police might have a different view." I take out my police ID to show them. Bright is nonplussed in the way of Caucasians: he turns crimson, his mouth makes strange shapes, and he throws repetitive glances at Hudson, who is carefully studying my ID. "Nothing will be removed from this room."

Hudson and Bright do an eye-shift, which means I don't know who I'm dealing with (i.e., *the most powerful blah blah blah . . .*), so I go into Thai Malicious. My suddenly cynical expression says that Third World Revenge starts here: sure you can invade, but then *whatchagonnado*? This tar baby just gets stickier and stickier, and you really don't want to spend even a week in a Thai jail, much less the year or so I have in mind. The threat of *quagmire* focuses Hudson, who nudges Bright, who takes the cue and fishes something out of his pocket and hands it to me. *(We'll get it back once we have your ass kicked by someone who understands who we really are.)* I still don't know what the hell it is. It's a kind of slim oval about two and a half inches long, three-quarters of an inch wide, half an inch deep in smooth gray plastic, with the words SONY MICRO VAULT stamped on the end.

The atmosphere is strained as I lead the CIA out of the apartment and let them watch while Mustafa the dark-skinned Muslim locks the door to Turner's apartment and pockets the key with a proprietary air. It occurs to me that this incriminating move is the last thing his father would have wanted, but it has discomfited the two spies. We find ouselves out in the street, where the vehement heat and Islamic costumes further disorient them. They walk away without saying goodbye.

CHAPTER 15

It's lunchtime, but Mustafa and I have different tastes. He leaves me to go off to a Muslim restaurant, while I seek out a Thai canteen that is famous for the heat of its *grataa rawn,* a sizzling variety show of marine life. Actually, I could just as well have eaten some lamb with Mustafa, but I wanted to be alone for a moment. I pull out the picture of Chanya while I'm waiting for the *grataa rawn.* I would almost have preferred the simple case I first assumed it to be: an irrational outbreak of violence from an overstressed whore. Now the complexity seems infinite and infinitely impenetrable. I really have no idea what's going on or where it all will lead.

I'm in a pretty somber state of mind when Mustafa arrives at the restaurant in a pickup truck. It's a Toyota four-by-four with three young men in the back. I guess from the bulges they are armed guards. Mustafa and I sit in the front of the truck with the driver while the guards, scarves covering their heads and faces against the dust, bump up and down on a bench in the open back.

The road out of town leads northeast, and we soon leave the paved highway for a rutted track. There is no air-con in the cab, so we drive with the windows open. The heat down here is always a few degrees higher than in Bangkok; it doesn't sound like much, but when you live at the upper limit of what the human frame can tolerate, it makes a difference. When we slow down to accommodate the rutted terrain, I feel like we're in a mobile oven. The terrain is lush, though, even for Thailand, because they have a lot more rain down here. When the driver finally stops the truck and we get out, the intensity of the silence hits us all between the eyes. We've been rattling up and down in a noisy vehicle for more than half an hour; suddenly there is only a single cicada with the energy to rub its legs together.

Mustafa beckons to me, and I follow him down a footpath that leads into a tranquil valley in which the only buildings are a large wooden house on stilts and a tiny mosque, apparently made of wood that has somehow been fashioned to produce a dome. He tells me to stay with the guards while he checks on his father. He emerges from the house with joy in his face and beckons for me to climb the stairs to join him. Inside the house the old imam with the fire in his black eyes welcomes me with his usual hospitality. We sit on mats drinking peppermint tea. My report is brief but welcome. Of course, in light of the photo-graph of Chanya in Mitch Turner's bedroom in

Songai Kolok, no responsible cop could avoid the conclusion that Chanya killed Mitch Turner, for whatever reason. They knew each other; she went back to his hotel when he came to Bangkok. Whatever happened in the hotel room, only she came out alive.

The imam has been examining my face while I speak. "But your Colonel is strangely keen to protect this prostitute. Why is that?"

"She's a key worker. These things happen from time to time. I guess he's just protecting the club and its reputation."

"You will put your report in writing?"

"I can't do that without permission."

Silence. Mustafa looks angry.

The old man says: "If Colonel Vikorn changes his mind under pressure from the Americans, will you warn us?"

"Yes," I say. "Okay." A long shot comes to mind. I'm shy to ask the question, considering its mystic origin, but what the hell? "Does the name Don Buri mean anything to you?" Blank glances.

The interview is over, and I go back to town in the truck with Mustafa, who is wrestling with some karmic obsession and says nothing throughout the journey. Indeed, he hardly manages to say goodbye.

Back in my hotel room I call Vikorn with my heart in my mouth. "I'm just about finished down here." I tell him about Hudson and Bright, the picture of Chanya.

"So?"

"I'm convinced Chanya did it."

Impatiently: "Well, what else is new?"

"So it wasn't a Muslim assassination."

A pause. "I hope you're not resurrecting that bleeding heart of yours?"

"It's not a bleeding heart, it's practical politics. If we try to blame Al Qaeda, it could have repercussions down here."

Even more impatiently: "Nobody's blaming Al Qaeda. You wrote her fucking statement yourself. Chanya acted in self-defense."

"She knew him from the States. He had a picture of her in his apartment. She sent me a copy of the diary she kept when she was over there. They were longtime lovers."

A longer pause. "You better get back here."

"I think I should make a written report—"

"No."

"If the CIA find out that she knew him, the cover story won't work, and you'll start blaming Muslims. That's your B plan, isn't it?"

"Get back here."

"If the Americans put pressure on us and our government gets clumsy, there could be war down here."

"War or no war, people die. They're always causing trouble in the South. Don't you want to save Chanya?"

"I don't want to be responsible for an insurrection."

"Then tell Buddha it's all my fault. Obedience is part of the Eightfold Path; you tend to forget that from time to time. Read my lips: *no written report.*"

CHAPTER 16

Rebirth, *farang* (in case you're wondering): You are lounging on a magnificent balcony open to the starry sky, divine music is playing with such exquisite perfection you can hardly stand it, when all of a sudden something terrible occurs: the magical sounds break up into an obscene cacophony. What is happening? Are you dying? You could put it that way. That awful noise is the first scream of an infant: you. You have been born into a human body hardwired with each and every transgression from the last time around, and now you must spend the next seventy years clawing your way back to the music. No wonder we cry.

PART 3

THE ZINNA DISTRACTION

CHAPTER 17

*F*arang, I humbly offer an apology. I had intended, on my return to Krung Thep, to reread Chanya's diary and share it with you (honestly), but duty—and ambition—compel me to postpone. Just now, while I was unpacking in my hovel by the river at about six this morning (the flight from the South was delayed, I didn't get in until after midnight), the cell phone rang. It was Vikorn's formidable female assistant, Police Lieutenant Manhatsirikit, known, not inappropriately, as Manny.

"The Colonel's not around and I can't get hold of him, so you'll have to sort this out on your own. It sounds like a nice little Trance 808 at the Sheraton on Sukhumvit. The general manager's scared shitless about the publicity, so you'd better get over there. Take someone with you."

"Why me?"

"I think it's X file."

"Zinna?"

"Must you be so indiscreet over the phone?"

I call Lek, whom I extract from the depths of sleep by dint of persistent ringing on his cell

135

phone. He is all deference, though, as his mind clears and I tell him to be waiting outside his housing project so I can collect him in the cab.

At the Sheraton the general manager, an elegant but anxious Austrian (one of those European men who spend a good chunk of their time in this body trying to persuade a slick of hair to cover a bald patch—he was a woman last time around: vain, snobbish, and French; as is often the case when we switch genders between incarnations, he is having trouble adjusting: *bald* was never an issue last time; on the contrary he kept a magnificent head of hair all the way to his—actually *her*—deathbed), is waiting for us.

He ushers us into a lift, which takes us to the floor of suites near the top of the building. Outside room 2506 he produces a key to let us in. "Room service found him early this morning when they went in to collect a food trolley from last night. No one responded to their knocks, so they assumed the suite was empty. No one's been inside since."

In the room Lek takes one look at the corpse, then falls to his knees to *wai* the Buddha and pray that we will not be contaminated by death or bad luck, while the manager looks on in amazement. I tell the manager to wait outside.

The Japanese, dressed in smart casual, is slumped sideways on the sofa with that telltale professional hole in his forehead. I note that rigor mortis has set in but have forgotten exactly what that means in terms of the time of death. Lek, fresh from the academy, can't remember, either. I undo the buttons on the shirt to check if there are any other wounds, in the certainty that there will be none.

"Not a mark on him," I confirm, mostly to myself. There won't be any other clues, either, of course, so why waste time looking for them? I call the manager back in.

"It's a very professional hit. One small-bore slug between the eyes. How long has he been staying here?"

"He wasn't staying here. He must have been invited by the guest, who has disappeared, of course. Why the hell they had to choose this hotel I can't imagine."

My cell phone rings. It's Vikorn. "What are you up to?"

"I'm on a T808 at the—"

"I know where you are. Get out of there."

"But Manny said it's X file. Zinna."

"That's why I want you out of there. This is needle, pure provocation, I'm not taking the bait. Let the fucking army deal with it. I don't want any record that you were there at all. I'll needle him back with silence, while I think up something better." Despite the restraint in his strategy, he is boiling with rage.

"Oh." Somewhat crestfallen, I take another look at the corpse. "This is the General's calling card?"

"He's just letting us know he's back on form, after that court-martial."

Out of the corner of my eye I watch Lek

137

posturing in front of the long mirror opposite the sofa. He can stand on one leg and pull the string of an imaginary bow with extraordinary elegance. I'm wishing I hadn't allowed the manager back in.

"So who's the stiff?"

A grunt from Vikorn. "The victim is a muckraking journalist based here and employed by some Japanese environmentalist group with an ax to grind about Japanese destruction of forest lands in Asia. He was investigating a Thai-Japanese corporation that intimidates peasants off their lands in Isaan so they can plant eucalyptus trees. Eucalyptus soak up the whole of the water table and destroy all other forms of vegetation, making the land useless for generations, but they grow fast and keep the Nips supplied with disposable chopsticks. Why the fuck they can't use plastic chopsticks, I just don't know. If the Chinese used disposable wood, there wouldn't be a tree left on the planet."

"So what's in it for Zinna?"

"The dear General owns a thirty-five percent stake in the Thai-Nippon Reforestation and Beautification of Isaan Corporation. His men do the intimidating."

"He's never done this on your patch before."

"The little prick's showing off, making a point, breaking all the rules. He got off that court-martial, and now he's rubbing my nose in it." The Colonel can hardly speak for indignation.

"You're going to let him get away with it?"

"I'm hardly going to knock heads with Zinna

for one little T808, am I? Because that's exactly what he wants me to do." A pause dominated by his dragon breathing. "There's always more than one way of skinning a snake."

"What shall I tell the general manager?"

"That there won't be publicity. That's all he needs to know."

I close the phone and lock with the manager's anxious eyes. "It's taken care of," I say. He checks my expression to see if I mean what he wants me to mean, then grunts with relief. "What about the corpse?"

"Army specialists will take it away later today."

"*Army* specialists? Why would they deal with this?"

"Because we won't, and they can't just leave it here. Someone will call them. Don't worry about it—it's one of those funny little Thai things."

"How much do I owe you?"

"I don't take money. Save it for the army."

"Look," Lek says as we are about to leave. I'd left the corpse's shirt undone. Lek is pulling it open again. "Isn't that the most beautiful butterfly you've ever seen? I mean, it's just gorgeous."

I pause to study the tattoo, which in my haste I had disregarded. It's true, the workmanship is magnificent, the colors both subtle and vivid. Come to think of it, it's a minor masterpiece.

"I've never seen one as good as that before," Lek says.

★　★　★

In the cab on the way to the station, stuck in a brooding jam at the intersection between Petburri Road and Soi 39 (on the other side of the glass: carbon monoxide laced with air), Lek says: "Did you know that according to Buddhism there were three human beings at the beginning of the world?"

"Yes."

"A man, a woman, and a *katoey*?"

"That's right."

"And we've all been all three, over and over again, going back tens of thousands of years?"

"Correct."

"But the *katoey* is always the loner."

"*Katoey* is a tough part of the cycle," I say as gently as I can.

"What's a Trance 808?"

"The murder, love. It comes from the number of the standard homicide documentation: T808. Vikorn called it *Trance* 808 once, and it caught on."

Back at the station Manny (she's five feet tall—just—and so dark she's almost black, with the intensity of a scorpion) commands me in her most severe tone to go see Vikorn. "Don't take him with you," she adds, not rising from her desk, jerking her chin at Lek. In a meaningful glance at me, she adds: "The old man's been looking at the Ravi pictures."

I turn pale but say nothing.

Upstairs, I'm standing all alone on the bare wooden boards outside his office. In response to my knock, a bark: "What?"

"It's me."

"Get the fuck in here."

I enter gingerly, in case he's waving his pistol around, a common adjunct to Vikornic rage. Well, actually he *has* taken it out, it's lying on his desk, but the signals are even worse. In a single timeless locking of eyes, I see that he's been playing those old memory tapes again; wallowing. There's a near-empty bottle of Mekong rice whiskey next to the gun, and an album of photographs in a large plastic cube showing his son Ravi at key moments in his short life. Ravi's corpse dominates the montage.

For everyone in District 8, the story is fundamental to our mythology. None of us were there at the time, but each of us has lived every moment. A few snaps from the photo album will be enough for your astute understanding, *farang*:

Snapshot 1: Ravi at age zero. Vikorn, husband to four wives, father to eight girls, holds his only son as if he were holding the meaning of life.

Snapshot 2: Ravi aged five, playing kiddie golf in a lush garden with the lovestruck Colonel.

Snapshot 3: Ravi at age sixteen bearing the symptoms of a seriously spoiled brat (smirk; gold Rolex; Yamaha V MAX motorbike; a beautiful girlfriend he was in the process of destroying with cocaine, sex, and alcohol; the old man making up the threesome with an obscene beam).

Snapshot 4: Ravi in his early twenties in Gucci casual standing in front of his scarlet Ferrari in Vikorn's country estate up in Chiang Mai.

Snapshot 5: Ravi dead from a wound in his chest, his shirt soaked in pink blood fresh from the lungs.

The riots of May 1992 took everyone by surprise. It was supposed to be just another army coup (we've had thirteen since our first constitution in 1932, nine of them successful), but something had changed in the common people. General Suchinda, our prime minister of the month, was totally wrong-footed: the downtrodden were actually *marching for democracy*. A few bullets should do the trick. The order was given from on high. Zinna, no more than a colonel at the time, was one of those officers who believe in leading by example. (Perhaps he doubted his men would fire on their own people?) He raised his own gun, a large pistol, and fired just as he gave the order for his men to do likewise. Fifty died in the un-Buddhist bloodbath. Outrage and democracy swiftly followed (it was that or civil war), but Ravi, it seems, had never intended to join the march; he had simply been forced to abandon his Ferrari because the demonstrators were blocking the street and he got caught up in their rage. (The autopsy revealed white powder all but blocking Ravi's nasal passages; he had died with a half-empty bottle of Johnnie Walker Black Label in his left hand, and the alcohol level in his blood was high.)

No mention is made of Ravi in the final report of the commission of inquiry into the riots, but every Thai understood what had gone on in Zinna's mind when he selected his one and only target. Ravi, you see, *looked* like a rich man's child, even from a distance. Perhaps Zinna didn't know who he was, but he understood very well *what* he was, and by all the rules of feudalism he should have held his fire. But Zinna, an upwardly mobile soldier-gangster of humble origins with chips on both shoulders, saw no reason for special treatment and fired deliberately at the arrogant, spoiled, drunk, drugged product of the system he served. Or did Zinna indeed recognize the son of his greatest rival? This is Vikorn's firm belief, for Zinna had purchased his commission with the fruits of his own substantial trafficking. Only Zinna knows what was in his mind when he pulled the trigger, but certain it is that with one fatal shot, he started a feud to last a lifetime. An unexpected consequence has been Vikorn's passionate conversion to democracy. He saw that the people were the only stick big enough with which to beat the army.

There have been many skirmishes in this war, for Zinna is no mean adversary. Deciding eventually, like all great narrators, that truth is best expressed through fiction, Vikorn one day last year had a truck dump a pile of morphine bricks onto Zinna's land in his country hideout up in Chiang Mai, then tipped off the local police chief. The scandal almost sank the General, but with his usual resilience he mounted a spirited defense at his court-martial, during which he supplied video shots taken from a security camera. The film showed a truck inexplicably arriving across a field, then two young men wearing black lace-up boots unhooking the back and pulling the gray brick-sized contents onto the land. Close-ups indicated the boots were not army but police issue.

The minute he saw that Zinna would survive his trial, Vikorn began another tack. Rather than micromanage Zinna's downfall himself, he has instead guaranteed promotion and a hundred-thousand-dollar reward for any cop in District 8 who finally nails the General. In addition, he has placed a trusted subordinate in charge of the file (if you can call it that, for nothing is ever written down in this inquiry), with the standing instruction to work on it whenever there's nothing more pressing in the in-box. Vikorn's choice of subordinate in this case was shrewd in the extreme: how did he guess that buried among my most secret defilements was a passion for promotion?

"He dropped the mark on my patch." Vikorn glares at me.

"Not the best party manners."

"Don't give me your fucking supercilious *farang* back-chat."

"Sorry."

"D'you realize what this means?"

"Maybe I'm missing the finer points."

"Maybe you're missing the main fucking point. Would you come to my house and drop an elephant turd on my Persian rug?"

"Your what?"

"That's the level of insult. It doesn't get worse than this. No one, I mean *no one,* not even your army fuckups, does this. It's the main rule. Without it we'd have—we'd have—"

"Anarchy?"

He looks at me but does not see me. In this case *blind rage* is no metaphor. He stops abruptly, goes to his desk, and picks up the gun to examine it curiously, as if unsure of the crimes it is about to commit, then with great care lays it down again next to the photos. I breathe a sigh of relief, for I have seen this before: the white heat of his fury slowly but surely mastered by a Herculean determination to use his great intellect for the purpose of spite. He looks at me again, eyes still glazed somewhat, but brighter. "Yes, anarchy. Do *farang* really suppose that our society could survive one minute without rules? Just because we don't follow the written ones doesn't make us third-world bums. No *jao por* wastes a mark on another *jao por*'s patch. It just doesn't happen. This could take us back to the stone age."

"I understand."

"Good. You understand. Well, that's all that fucking matters, isn't it? In the whole fucking universe, what really makes the stars shine and the planets orbit is whether Sonchai Jitpleecheep understands or not."

"I didn't—"

"Didn't what? You're in charge of the X file—you were supposed to protect me from this."

"Huh? You never said anything about protecting you from Zinna's provocation. You said keep an eye out for opportunity—"

A scream: *"Don't you see I've got to respond? And it has to be even worse than what he did to me?"*

I refrain from saying: *That's not a very Buddhist point of view.*

Heaving, but resuming self-control. "Give me a report. How many major drug busts since Zinna got off?"

"Only two. They were both attempted exports to Europe."

"And?"

"The first was a minor player, a mule. She's pleading guilty. There's no obvious connection to Zinna—it was heroin, not morphine."

"And the other?"

He looks at me, causing a great quaking in my guts. "Sorry, I forgot to follow up."

"You what?"

"I was distracted. They brought him in a few days ago, looks like a heavy hitter, but we got focused on the *farang* Chanya wasted, and then I made that trip down south."

Glaring: "We still have the junk?"

"It's with the forensic boys."

146

"Morphine or heroin?"

"Looks like morphine."

Screaming: "*Do what you need to do. I want to know where that morphine came from. I know* he took my dope back from the army after the court-martial."

Exiting with a high *wai:* "Yes, sir."

I'm out in the corridor making running repairs to my psyche after the Vikornic onslaught. Look at it this way: for the Colonel to guess what Zinna will do next, he merely has to consult his own psychology. If *Zinna* dumped a hundred kilos of morphine on *Vikorn's* land, what would Vikorn have done? Do I hear: *Sold the dope, of course?* In the event (not, when all was told, unlikely) that Zinna found a way of wriggling out of the frame-up, would the General miss an opportunity of making twenty million dollars or so out of the product that his arch-enemy so generously supplied free, gratis, and for nothing? Do wounded bulls charge red rags?

Back at my desk, my first call is to Sergeant Ruamsantiah.

"That *farang* with the morphine last week. What was his name?"

"Buckle. Charles, but he calls himself Chaz."

"The Colonel is taking an active interest in the case."

"Why would he do that?"

"Because it's morphine. How many times do we see morphine these days?"

"Hardly at all. It gets synthesized into heroin before it leaves the Golden Triangle."

"Exactly."

A moment of silence, then: "Wow! Vikorn, that cunning old bastard! He knew Zinna might get off the inquiry, persuade his army chums to sell him back the confiscated dope, and export it, right? So now Zinna has to get rid of more than a hundred kilos of morphine in a hurry before someone blows the whistle on him. All the heroin labs are inconveniently located up north, so he's not going to have time to synthesize."

I say nothing.

"So anyone caught with morphine at this moment has a better-than-even chance of being a courier for Zinna?"

"Correct."

"Amazing. I never would have thought of that." A pause. "It's like they say: with the Colonel it's the B plans you have to watch for."

"You got that right."

All enthusiasm now, with little bubbles of ebullience punctuating his speach: "I'll go check on Buckle myself—he's downstairs in the cells. I'll call you back in five."

"Great."

While we're waiting for the good sergeant, *farang*, let me revisit the Buckle bust with you. It happened about a day before Chanya killed Mitch Turner.

CHAPTER 18

F lashback: I was having a quiet morning pottering around the Old Man's Club when my cell phone started ringing. It was Lieutenant Manhatsirikit at her least glamorous.

"Get over here, pronto."

I showered quickly and grabbed a cab, only to discover when I arrived that it was not a shoot-out or an investigation by the Crime Suppression Division (our anticorruption bureau: everyone's worst scenario) but an interpretation job. I'm the only one in the station who speaks English worth a damn, so they tend to drag me in whenever there's a *farang* who needs terrifying. (Hard to convey the finer points of intimidation if the perp doesn't understand a word you're saying.) This guy, though, was something else: the kind of shaved skull like a pink coconut that belongs on the end of a battering ram, a fat round face bursting with Neolithic fury, small eyes, ironmongery hanging from his pincushion ears, short and incredibly muscular arms and legs, a frown characteristic of the intellectually deprived, tattoos on both forearms screaming of his inextinguishable love for Mother (left forearm) and

Denise (on the right, in indigo, from elbow to wrist), and puncture marks in all major veins. On the bare wooden table in the equally bare interrogation room: two suitcases, open to show plastic-wrapped gray blocks about six inches by four. Ruamsantiah handed me a British passport: Charles Valentine Buckle. The sergeant explained that Buckle had been caught at his hotel in a combined police/customs operation after a tip-off, bang to rights.

"Tell me if he's as stupid as he looks," Sergeant Ruamsantiah ordered me.

"And if he is?"

"Then we better start looking for Denise."

Ruamsantiah's intuitive approach to law enforcement is famous throughout the station. I myself would have preferred a more thorough investigation, in which the stages of detection are more clearly defined, but his conclusion that this sack of testosterone:

1. was too stupid to arrange for the purchase, transportation, and export of $500,000 worth of morphine on his own;
2. must therefore be within the control of another person of superior intellect, who on the evidence of his tattoos and macho-slave posture was likely to be a woman;
3. whose name, on the balance of probability, was likely to be Denise,

was hard to fault. I noted, with admiration, that the *Denise* tattoo was darker and fresher than the other, which virtually proved Ruamsantiah's hypothesis. Indeed, the more I looked at him, the more convinced was I—as was Ruamsantiah—that he would not make a move without Denise. Yep, Denise done it.

"His mobile?"

Ruamsantiah took a rather outdated Siemens from a drawer under the table and handed it to me. With considerable pride I was able to locate both his telephone address book on the sim card and the list of numbers recently dialed and calls received. (You don't work with whores without learning mobiles, *farang.*) There was a predominance of one particular number, which looked like another mobile. When I checked with the address book, I saw that it corresponded to the number under the single letter D. The Pink Coconut was watching me with increasing fury, which expressed itself in recurring bursts of sweat with which his face and shaved pate were covered, just as if he'd come in from a tropical storm. (There was a periodic seeping and an unpleasant odor characteristic of consumers of dairy products—you don't get that sort of stink with lemongrass.)

"D is for Denise, right?" I snapped.

I did not, myself, consider this as evidence of forensic brilliance on my part, but Charles Buckle was clearly impressed. "Yeah." Then he clammed his mouth shut in an odd kind of way, fearing he'd said too much.

"Let's see if she's awake, shall we?"

I used the autodial feature to call the number under D. Twelve rings before a British accent that had been dragged from the bottomless pit of sleep answered. "Chrissake Chaz, what the fuck d'you want now?"

"Good morning," I said. "This is the Royal Thai Police Force, and Chaz is going to jail for the rest of his life, assuming, that is, that he avoids the death penalty. We would like to ask you a few questions concerning—"

Neither the sergeant nor I was ready for it. Arrested persons in Thailand are hardly ever violent for cultural reasons: the cops would shoot them. Indeed, a second after Chaz charged at me, apparently discounting the wooden table between us, Ruamsantiah was on his feet reaching for his service revolver, which he had stuck in his belt at the base of his spine, but Chaz, mad as a hatter, had launched himself across the table, apparently in a desperate but chivalrous attempt to protect the subject of his right forearm from implication in international drug trafficking. The table had other ideas and moved with him, creating the impression (as I and my chair went down under it) of a kind of four-legged land raft on which the lone sailor was making an adventure tour of the interrogation room, while Ruamsantiah prepared to take a shot at him and I rolled out of the way, spilling the Siemens as I went, which exploded into its various components. The suitcases followed me to the floor, and a few of the blocks burst their packing and crumbled, increasing the net value of my khaki open-neck shirt and black pants by maybe $50,000 as I rolled in their contents. I think Ruamsantiah would not have resisted the temptation to shorten the case with a bullet through that pink coconut had not the coconut itself made violent contact with the opposite wall, leaving its owner groaning in a heap along with what was left of the table. A flimsy third-world piece of furniture, it pretty much disintegrated when it hit the wall, unlike that robust first-world cranium, which suffered no more than a dramatic increase in its pinkness. Still, Ruamsantiah agonized over every cop's dilemma in such circumstances: shoot the bastard or merely beat the shit out of him?

Reluctantly, but perhaps bearing in mind the mountain of paperwork that invariably accompanies the death in custody of a *farang*, Ruamsantiah opened the door of the interrogation room and called for reinforcements. Before long the room was filled with vigorous and enthusiastic young men in black lace-up boots who were quick to see a cure for boredom. Coconut began to squeal as I left the room with the remains of the world-class narcotic smuggler's mobile in my hands.

I had to go to the latrines to dust off my shirt and pants, where I used the occasion to reflect on the fragility of human values: this gray poison, for which people risk life and liberty, was now worthless dust on the floor of an old police toilet. There is no constant in life but change. I also wondered what would happen if I encountered one of our sniffer dogs from the narcotics unit before I had the chance to go home and shower. To the dog, of course, the heroin would remain the most valuable commodity in the universe, since without it he'd be just another unemployed mutt wondering where his next meal was coming from: there are no more enthusiastic supporters of the war on drugs than our sniffer dogs.

Downstairs the forensic boys were too involved with their MP3 project (WAV to MP3 is no problem, but transferring Windows Media Player format into MP3 is quite a challenge, they explained) to check the sim card immediately. They pointed out that in view of the screams from the interrogation room, it did seem as if a confession was imminent, so what was the hurry? They'd get back to me.

Down in the canteen I tucked into a chile-intensive breakfast with a 7-Up before returning to the second floor, by which time the screams from the interrogation room had ceased.

At the top of the stairs one of the young cops in heavy black boots came out to tell me the Coconut wanted to confess. At least, they thought that's what he wanted. When I entered the room, I was quite pleased to see no blood, bruises, or broken teeth. Whatever they did, though, was amazingly effective. The Neolithic fury had quite dissipated, and the fat face was flabby with surrender and exhaustion, revealing the soul of perhaps a five-year-old yearning for Mother as he lay supine on the floor with a cushion thoughtfully placed behind his head which they propped up against a wall. With most of the buttons on his shirt popped, I saw what a gift he had been to various body artists over the years, some more talented than others, though all with the standard addiction to indigo.

When I asked him if he wanted to confess, he licked his lips and nodded. Now we hauled him to his feet and dragged him to a chair, revealing the telephone book he was lying on. The telephone book is the interrogator's best friend in these parts. Inserted between boot and perp, it prevents all signs of physical abuse without detracting too much from the point of the exercise.

Ruamsantiah shook his head in wonder. "He's tough, I'll give him that. They've been going at it all the time you were having breakfast, and they only just broke him. I've never seen anything like it—incredible pain threshold. The ugly bastard must be made of concrete."

Now he mentioned it, I noticed that all the young men were sweating and some were still breathing heavily.

Somebody brought a Dictaphone so Chaz's confession in English and my simultaneous translation into Thai were both recorded. Chaz was commendably brief (Him: *I done it.* Me: *Done what?* Him: *The dope*), so much so that Ruamsantiah told me to tell him that if he didn't think up some convincing details, he was in for another round, this time without the telephone book. Chaz seemed to want to comply but was inhibited by some mystic force that had the power to banish fear.

Ruamsantiah: "What happened with the idiot's mobile?"

I explained that it might be a while before our musically inclined geeks were able to retrieve Denise's telephone number from the sim card.

"I'll get it myself," said the sergeant, who made for the door. By now about twelve young men were all licking their lips. I was not sure how long I could hold them off; nor was I sure if I *should* hold them off. Maybe if they gave Chaz Buckle a really good going-over while he was still weak from the first beating, he'd see the light and get his sentence reduced by giving us details of Denise's smuggling ring. If I used my influence to save him from a further beating, on the other hand, he would almost certainly get the death penalty. A man whose main crime was a room temperature IQ would rot on death row while the mastermind Denise went free. Properly understood, karma is more complex than a weather system, but fortunately I was saved from the need to intervene in this man's destiny by the sudden and triumphant return of Ruamsantiah, who had, he explained, grabbed back the mobile and simply clipped all the bits together again. It seemed to be working, indeed was that very minute receiving a text message: *Chaz, where the fuck R U and ? is going on?????*

I confirmed the message originated from the same number as Denise's mobile. Ruamsantiah's eyes flicked between Chaz and the mobile. He nodded at me, and I pressed the autodial button. This time only a couple of rings were required. A cautious tone: *Yes?*

"It's me again. He's in a Bangkok police station getting beaten up after being found with two suitcases of ninety-nine-percent-pure morphine, which he has confessed he was planning to smuggle out of the country. He has named you as an accomplice—"

A great bull yell from Chaz, who tried to attack me again, but this time everyone was ready. Two of the cops sat on him while others held his arms.

A contemptuous tone from Denise: "Leave it out, sonny boy. My Chaz wouldn't grass on me for all the tea in China. What kind of rank fucking amateur are you?" She closed the phone, leaving me stranded in perplexity. When I tried her again, I got a busy signal.

I looked thoughtfully at Chaz. Whatever doubts I might have had concerning Ruamsantiah's rather precipitous conclusion that Denise was behind the racket had now been cleared up. But our evidence against her, although intuitively compelling, could be argued away by an expensive lawyer. Indeed, it could be pretty effectively laughed out of court by a cheap one, since it consisted entirely of that tattoo on his right forearm. Even a Thai court might hesitate to condemn her to death without more to go on.

The sergeant and I shrugged at each other. Ruamsantiah seemed to feel sorry for this great pink baby, who would probably not actually be executed (because he was pink, not brown, the King would pardon him eventually after a few decades on death row) but who would certainly be ground down by our prison system until he was no more than a toothless shade on slopping-out duty. Well, there was nothing more to be done for the moment.

"I guess we better check that it really is morphine in the suitcases," I said to Ruamsantiah, who blinked. What else could it be?

And there it was left, *farang*, because the next day, before I'd had a chance even to consider what the morphine might signify with regard to Zinna, there was the problem of Mitch Turner to deal with and then that trip down south to Songai Kolok.

End of flashback, *farang*.

CHAPTER 19

Ruamsantiah, still in awe of Vikorn's low cunning, calls back slightly breathless: "I've just been in the cell with him."

"How's he doing?"

"Bad. Really bad. The jailer had to use restrainers."

"Withdrawal?"

"Cold turkey with extras. He's strong, he was bashing his head against the bars."

"Is he in interrogation mode?"

"He could be, with a little help. You'll have to do it—the brute hardly speaks a word of Thai."

"I'll be down. By the way, did you get his record from Scotland Yard? I'll need it before I question him."

"I've got the fax, but I couldn't read it because it's in English. I'll send it up to you."

The sergeant sends a young constable, who arrives on the double with Buckle's British record sheet. He started in reform school, after which he began a five-year career as a moderately successful burglar, followed by jail, where he addicted himself to heroin and began an apprenticeship as a small-time trafficker. After the first serious drug bust he developed an increasing sophistication in his MO and is now suspected of large-scale trafficking from Southeast Asia to the U.K. via Amsterdam in a well-organized ring. Said to have developed a serious reluctance to go back to jail, which has resulted in greater caution in the way he does business. Despite numerous detox programs, he has never been able to kick his smack habit.

I meet Ruamsantiah at the steps down to the cells, and we walk with the jailer to cell four. For once the jailer has exercised compassion in that he has used padded, hospital-style restrainers instead of his usual chains. We stare through the bars. Chaz is in poor shape, shivering and groaning, with some nasty cuts and bruises on his forehead. "Self-inflicted," the jailer defensively reports.

"Is he on anything?"

"Only tranqs."

The jailer selects a key from a sparkling chrome chain as long as infinity, then opens the door. Ruamsantiah and I enter the cell, dank with one man's total despair. I say: "Chaz." There is only a flicker of recognition, then a return to his compulsive shivering.

"Maybe we can help you."

Again, a brief flicker of recognition, but this is not the same man as the one I interrogated last week. Thwarted craving shows us our darkest places, our deepest fears, our basic cowardice. "Denise didn't get you out of here like she promised, did she, Chaz?" I am using Paternal Concerned with plenty of saccharin and just a dash of menace. He stares at me, then lets his head down again, shivering and shuddering.

"You weren't any ordinary courier, were you? You're a pro, Chaz. I've seen your record sheet— you're not just some dumb mule like the other losers who hang around Ko Samui and Pataya, waiting to be used, those *other* ugly dumb tattooed bastards who'll risk anything for a fix. You were the boss's main man, her lover, weren't you? You didn't have to worry about a little thing like a bust, because the boss is so rich and influential and so damn well connected, she could get you off of anything anytime. That's why you had the nerve to jump me, remember? This is Thailand, and all she needs to do is bribe the forensic lab—throw money at it, as they say—and you were going to be walking the streets again, shooting up on the best stuff money can buy, right? That was the plan, you talked about it many times, she told you how special you were, how powerful she was, didn't she? But you were way too experienced to take her word for it. There had to be more to it than this, she had to show you her influence. Her connections. You'd been east enough times to know what connections mean over here. According to your passport you've made twenty-five visits in the last five years. Connections are wealth, power, happiness—connections are *everything*. And even

Denise is just another lost *farang* if she doesn't have them. So tell us, who is *her* main man?"

This time he doesn't even bother to look up. I nod to Ruamsantiah, who produces a small glassine bag with white contents from one of his pockets.

"Chaz," I say softly. A sudden flick of his eyes, which fix on the bag in Ruamsantiah's left palm, then down again to stare at his navel. "I can relieve your suffering, Chaz." I finally have his full attention. Suddenly his eyes are pleading. "It's okay, Chaz, you can trust me, I'm a cop, ha-ha. No, really, I give you my word. We'll let you come down slowly, reduce the dose a little every day till you're clean, maybe even find you some methadone. That's the humane way to do it, isn't it?"

He gulps, opens his mouth, stares at the packet, and shuts his mouth. In a whisper: "I can't do cold turkey, it's killing me." Our eyes lock. This is a confession straight from the soul. He just can't do it. He *really* can't do it. Oh, how he would love to play the macho martyr immune to all weakness, but the dope dragon is too powerful.

"Of course, you'll have to help us nail that bitch and her supplier."

A quick look, a nod, and then he bursts into tears. In a sob-drenched whisper: "Gimme the smack, I'll tell you what you want to know."

Ruamsantiah and I exchange a glance. "Better get him some gear," I tell the sergeant. "Make sure it's sterilized."

While the sergeant is gone hunting for syringe,

oil lamp, and other accessories, I use Coaxing Voice on the perp: "You're small fry, Chaz, a mule, a dummy. She used you, then she let you twist in the wind. But she's not such a big fish, not really. She's just another middle-aged fucked-up *farang* on her last life, isn't she? She moves nothing, shakes nothing, she just hangs around the table with her tongue hanging out. So her crumbs are bigger than your crumbs, but at the end of the day it's still crumbs. Because over here the trade is owned by the locals, right? There are no *farang jao por*, Chaz, no *farang* big bosses, they're all Thai—but you know that. Now tell me, who did Denise produce to convince you that she had the connections to keep you safe? That's what it takes in your game, doesn't it, for a wise guy like you to take a risk, even if you *were* screwing her. She had to show her credentials, didn't she?"

Ruamsantiah has returned with a disposable plastic syringe still in its germ-free packet, a small oil lamp, and some aluminum foil. He lays it all out on the crude wooden table at the back of the cell, while Chaz watches intensely. Ruamsantiah lays the packet of smack next to the syringe. Now the sergeant and I are both looking at Chaz.

"A Thai army general," he says in a broken voice.

"Name?"

"Zinna."

"Tell me more about General Zinna. How many times did you meet him?"

"Once."

"She produced him just the once to convince you she was kosher?" A nod. "You must have been impressed."

"He came in uniform, with soldiers."

"Where did you meet him?"

"How do I know? She took me somewhere, I wasn't paying attention."

"Describe the place."

"Big house, three stories, lot of land, dogs, monkeys."

When I translate, Ruamsantiah stares at me. "He's talking about Khun Mu."

Chaz Buckle has recognized the name: "Yeah, Mu, that was it."

I nod. "Can you manage to cook on your own, Chaz, or shall we get someone to help you?"

"I'll do it."

I watch while the sergeant drags the table over to where Chaz is taped to the bars by his ankles and wrists, then releases Chaz's wrists. He immediately hunches over the table, pulls off a strip of aluminum foil, and starts to shake out the smack from the packet, oblivious to all human emotion, including his own shame. I leave him with Ruamsantiah.

CHAPTER 20

In a jam at the intersection between Asok and Sukhumvit—that black hole where time gets lost—I ask the driver to switch off his Thai pop CD so Lek and I can listen to Rod Tit FM. Pisit has invited none other than my mother on the show in her capacity as Thailand's most famous, and vociferous, ex-prostitute.

These are sad times for sleaze, *farang*. Our government is going through one of its puritanical phases and has decided to impose an earlier curfew. Starting next month, all the bars will have to close at midnight. Naturally, the flesh industry is outraged, the whole of Soi Cowboy has been mobilized, no *farang* is allowed to pass by without signing a petition. Pisit's first guest is a *katoey* who works the bars. Lek listens, riveted.

The *katoey* with deep voice maintains that she intends to sue the government for the cost of her operation and the ruination of her life. She had the whole shooting match cut off for purely commercial reasons. She grew up as a boy in Isikiert, one of the poorest regions in the poorest part of the Northeast, with five sisters and one brother. Her

165

mother is blind from cataracts, her father's health is broken from rice farming in the tropical heat twelve hours a day, her sisters are all mothers of infants by drunken Thai men who don't pay child support, and anyway none of the girls were likely to make a fortune in the Bangkok flesh trade for aesthetic reasons. Her only brother suffers from Down syndrome and requires constant supervision. As the cutest of the brood, she was nominated (unanimously) as the one to solve the family's financial problems in the big city. Borrowing as best they could and pooling everything they had, they just about scraped enough together for the operation that turned her into one of the sexiest-looking whores on the Game. It was a onetime, high-risk capital investment that, after a painful lead-in period, is finally beginning to yield a reasonable return, and now the government is sabotaging the fledgling cottage industry with this early-closing nonsense. Everyone knows the major part of the business of the Game is conducted between midnight and two p.m., when the johns' resistance has been properly ground down by alcohol and the attentions of near-naked young women (or *katoeys*). What maniac in government had this bright idea? Obviously they care nothing for the poor. If she has no money to send home, is the Interior Minister going to take care of her family?

Pisit turns to my mother, who needs little launching:

The government isn't merely killing the goose that lays the golden egg—it is ruining the only wealth-distribution system we have in this feudal society. This government has no common sense at all. Do they seriously think we'll get rich by becoming as sterile as the West? I've been to Paris, Florida, Munich, London—those places are museums populated by ghosts. The bottom line is that for more than three decades the people of Isaan have been kept alive by what little cash their daughters in Bangkok have been able to send home. There are whole towns, roads, shops, farms, water buffalo, cars, motorbikes, garages—whole industries that owe their existence to our working girls. These courageous young women are the very essence of the female genius for sustaining, nurturing, and honoring life with life. They are also everything that is great about the Thai soul, with their selfless devotion and sacrifice. They ask for no help or gratitude, they don't expect admiration, they gave up looking for respect decades ago, but they are the heart of our country.

Pisit: How much of our government's attitude is influenced by Western media, do you think?

Nong: Well, I must say I don't know what the Western TV networks would do without a brothel in Southeast Asia to point their cameras at. Of course our government is influenced, but it's just a question of the TV networks improving their ratings. They never trouble to really understand us. What can you do? This is the ersatz morality of the West.

Pisit: Does this crackdown spell the end of the sex industry in Thailand?

Nong: I don't think so. After all, it's been illegal for nearly a hundred years, and look what we've achieved. Also, there's a lot of investment from the West these days because the upside potential of investing in a well-run go-go bar is much greater in my view than, say, investing in General Motors. Our girls charge far less per hour than in most societies, yet at the same time they are among the most sought-after women on earth. Rates have not increased in real terms since I myself was active.

My heart swells with pride at my mother's mastery of a vocabulary usually reserved for the ruling classes, but the taxi driver twists his head around. "That's your mom? She must have been a real goer in her day."

"You may go back to your Thai pop CD now," I instruct.

When the jam finally starts to ease, Lek says: "Have you seen the new stuff from YSL? It's in the Emporium; some amazing dresses."

"I haven't kept up with the fashions this year."

"Armani and Versace still have the best colors, though."

"Italians have the best eye for color."

"But I still prefer the Japanese designers. Junya Watanabe's stuff this season is out of this world. Dusty grays in satin and velvet. Such a shock at first, you know, then you think: perfect. So did you speak to your mother?"

I swallow, then cast a glance at his ink-black hair, the hue of youth still on his flesh, the buttery glow in those high cheeks, the innocence still in those eyes. I've been mulling the thing over in my mind for days, wondering if my mother's wisdom had deserted her in middle age. It seems almost against nature to introduce this angel to Fatima. Then it clicks. *Initiation* is the word. My mother is right, as usual. Not only will Fatima be good for him— she is exactly what he needs for experience and survival. Also, Fatima is very rich. If she decides to adopt him, he'll be set up for life.

"Actually, she suggested a friend of mine who I'd just not thought of in connection to you. I haven't seen her in over a year, but it won't be difficult to look her up. I'll see what I can do."

Lek beams happily and throws me one of those grateful swooning looks of his. "Remind me again, where are we going?"

"We're going to see Khun Mu, Lek."

CHAPTER 21

Take a poor Thai girl out of her third-world village, throw money at her, and what is the third thing she wants, after the three-story wedding-cake mansion and the lurid Mercedes? Louis Quinze furniture in acrylic tones, as a rule. Even beige is garish at this level of light reflection, and the green carpet is like something you might play tennis on, but Khun Mu somehow fits the decor.

A word about Mu. Before Vikorn shot him, her husband Savian "Joey" Sonkan used to boast that he'd spent more money renovating her body than he'd spent on the house and the five-car garage, but Mu began sculpting her body before she met him. She was what was known as a late developer. Most of her friends left the Isaan village at around eighteen to work in the big city, and many of them returned for holidays to boast about the money they were making out of dumb *farang* men who hired their bodies for ludicrous prices. (You could buy a fully grown buffalo for what those guys spent in a night at the bars.) For years these stories seemed not to affect Mu overly much, until one fine day

170

she stole the family savings from under her parents' bed and blew everything on silicone breast enhancements and a new wardrobe, then fled to Krung Thep to make her pile. As luck would have it, she found her destiny not with Western men (the rigid echoing bosom and the pink body stocking proved resistible, despite assurances from her consultants) but with a home-grown *jao por*—a young drug baron who appreciated a woman whose taste was as bad as his own.

Joey didn't just deal drugs—he lived with them. After my Colonel took him down, we found whole cupboards full of *yaa baa,* the matrimonial mattress stuffed with heroin, bales of ganja in the garage. Vikorn, who had long grown out of shoot-outs with desperadoes and would have been happy to come to some arrangement (say, a modest seventy percent tax on Joey's gross profits), never wanted to kill him, but Joey's other passion, apart from drugs and modifications to his wife's body, was chase movies, the more violent the better. He wanted to die like Al Pacino in *Scarface,* and after years of provocation Vikorn finally granted his wish.

My dead partner Pichai was there at the stakeout, as were I and half the cops from District 8, not to mention all the TV networks. Joey appeared unarmed on the bedroom balcony, insulting Vikorn's manhood and goading him into a duel, while Vikorn crouched behind one of the police vans clutching a hunting rifle with infrared aiming device, which he fired before Joey finished proposing his rules of engagement. Maybe Joey had expected some such foul play, for he had placed himself at the very edge of the balcony, thus providing for a telegenic fall, including a backflip before the final splat. A few minutes later Mu appeared on the balcony waving a frilly Louis Quinze white handkerchief and smiling for the cameras. She held no grudges, she explained, beaming. After all, the house and cars were hers now, not to mention the furniture. A couple hours later at the station we discovered, to our astonishment, that the dumb moll who could hardly read and write possessed total recall. She was also apparently fearless and listed a total of three hundred and twenty-one names of her husband's business associates (a selective list even so: none of them were cops), while maintaining the same eager-to-please smile on her face and pointing her pyramids at us. With very little encouragement (well, an offer of immunity from prosecution, to be precise) she was able to confirm that, despite appearances, Joey had been secretly (and invisibly) armed and that Vikorn was correct in claiming he'd shot in self-defense, thus silencing bleeding-heart critics in the media. Her negotiating skills also proved superior to those of her late husband. Before she left the station, she pointed out to Vikorn that her life was now worth maybe one baht and that if she didn't have protection for the rest of it, she had as good as committed suicide by giving us that list of suspects.

"You need money" was Vikorn's response.

"Exactly."

"Okay," Vikorn said. Mu took this single foreign word as permission for her to continue to trade with the army. He also let her keep about ten percent of the drugs in the house. After all, the remainder was more than ample for the ritual photo-op with Vikorn standing in full Pol Colonel uniform smiling before a table laden with heroin, morphine, meth, and ganja, the street value of which was enough to buy a fleet of airliners.

All that was a few years ago. We still consult Mu now and then. Vikorn is no mean negotiator himself, and part of the deal was that she should remain an informant—particularly against Zinna, who was Joey's principal supplier. To keep her alive, our visits to her are restricted to no more than one a year, and total anonymity is required.

Money and time have shown her to be by nature neither a whore nor a crook but a true-born eccentric. Despite the security risk, she has refused to vacate the mansion, the grounds of which she has turned into a refuge for stray dogs and monkeys, which she feeds personally three times a day, usually in a blinding pink housecoat, except on anniversaries of her husband's death, when she wears mauve, Joey's favorite color. (One of the Roll-Royces is also mauve.) Armed and uniformed (mauve) security guards are everywhere and constantly patrol the perimeter of the grounds. There is even a sentry box where I had to flash our IDs, and a digital camera that enabled her to examine my and Lek's faces before letting us in.

Now we're standing on the tennis-court carpet in the main reception room while she sits on a glittering beige five-seater sofa, fondling a young and very sleepy female Dalmatian. I happen to know, for Vikorn likes to keep tabs, that she has no regular lover, unless it is one of the security guards, which is unlikely. She is like a billionaire nun with a weakness for animals. The solitude has all but dissolved self-consciousness, and the unrestricted play of emotion across her face, from sad to gay and back again, is quite childlike.

Lek is in shock at the vulgarity of the decor and stands rooted to the spot.

Mu says: "I remember you. You are the half-caste who was at the shoot-out. Did you kill my husband?"

"You know very well it was Colonel Vikorn."

"Ah, yes. At least, he took the credit in the media, but he's a very cunning man. Perhaps it was you or one of your colleagues who pulled the trigger." I say nothing. "Would you like to see him?" I cough. "Come along, I'm sure he'll be delighted." She lays the Dalmatian down in one of the lounge chairs, then casts a glance at Lek. "Is the beautiful boy coming?"

In a room adjacent to the lounge, Joey is embalmed *à l'américaine* in a characteristic pose from life, sitting in a director's chair holding a mobile to his ear, a cigar in the other hand, an open-neck

Gucci shirt and jacket, smart YSL slacks, and multi-colored loafers. His huge smile, acrylic in intensity, perfectly fits the house theme. In a neat melding of cultures, Mu has surrounded him with gold images of the Buddha in his various postures, and electric imitation votive candles flicker everywhere. The decor is the house standard, and the dominant color—you guessed. She changed into a mauve housecoat before entering the shrine. I have the disturbing sense that there is nothing but modified naked body underneath.

A finely manicured hand flits to her mouth. "You know, every time I think of that day I feel awful."

"We really didn't want to do it," I explain. "Vikorn would have made a deal if Joey hadn't wanted to die."

"I know. But afterward. At the station. You must have thought me so stupid, so naïve, so much the typical country girl out of her depth in the big city."

"Not at all. We were all pretty impressed, actually."

"You were?" A deprecating laugh. "Don't sweet-talk me, Detective. You were all laughing behind my back."

"Why should we have done that?"

"The silicone, of course. Joey was always so busy making money, he never inquired about proper enhancements. Look."

She pulls open the housecoat, and there they are. For the first time Lek shows an interest in

175

the case. I feel it will be a load off her mind if I follow her directions and examine them, although I've already seen the point. The stiff silicone is all gone, replaced no doubt with saline bags or collagen, which, I can report, yield nicely to the touch, bounce and swing beautifully, and really are more or less indistinguishable from the real thing, although a purist might complain they belong on a woman ten years younger.

"Can I?" Lek asks. Mu smiles and nods. With great reverence he handles both breasts, as if examining art objects that he soon will own himself. "They're amazing."

"Yes," I say, "excellent. You must be very proud."

"Yes," as she does up the coat with a quick glance at Joey. "Now, what d'you want to know? About once a year Vikorn sends someone to me, but I'm really very out of touch now."

"In front of Joey?"

"Of course not. Let's go upstairs—I like to look at the animals."

The bedroom is so large, it is like the bedding department of a great store. Everything is high schlock. For a moment my tortured eye rests with optimism on a modest set of bookshelves. I'm impressed that the books are all Buddhist; my heart sinks, however, when I see they are all the same book.

We three sit demurely on a window seat, which I think must be her favorite in the house, and look out onto the courtyard, where a monkey is riding a Great Dane, just like a jockey, even using his long arm to urge him forward. All is going well—even the dog seems to be enjoying the privilege of transporting a higher species from place to place, when another monkey, a chimp I think, somewhat older and shrewder looking, wants to hitch a ride.

"That's Vikorn," Mu explains.

Vikorn's first thought is to swing from the tail, which has the effect of halting the dog. Now he jumps on his back, joining his colleague, while other monkeys gather round. Mu pronounces their names softly from time to time. The whole of District 8 is here, it seems.

One by one Mu names the dogs. They are all well-known drug dealers. "That's how I remember people. I think which of my dogs they most resemble. Unless they're cops, then they have to be monkeys. The monkeys are smarter, but they're not very happy. There's always a problem with them, but the dogs are pretty content unless the monkeys start giving them a hard time."

"Is there a dog named Denise?"

She flicks me a glance. "Denise?" Pointing to a female bulldog: "Yes, there she is. Is she the one you want to know about?"

"If you don't mind."

She hesitates. "Is this authorized? Vikorn is supposed to keep me alive."

"We took precautions, came in a cab; I'm sure we were not followed."

Agitated, she gets up to fetch a Chanel handbag

and a large hand mirror in silver frame. Without a hint of self-consciousness she opens the bag, takes out a silver box that might have been designed for snuff, drizzles a line of the white contents onto the mirror, scrapes it all together with a razor blade, leans over, presses one nostril with her left index while sniffing through the right, switches nostrils, and rises again to replace handbag and mirror on a nearby table, all in a seamless movement. Catching Lek's eye: "For my nerves."

Flicking me another glance, she sighs. "There are more *farang* women in the business than there used to be. Denise has been around quite a while now. At first she was a minor player, quite scatty. The British intelligence people, MI6, were spying on her in Ko Samui and Phuket. She never carried herself but used men as mules—a variation on the usual method. The men were always clapped-out white men, mostly Brits and Australians with no brains, beach bums with habits to feed. More than half of them got caught, so her reputation suffered, and everyone who knew anything about the business was afraid to carry for her. Somehow she made contact with the army and reinvented herself. But she had to convince the mules that she was properly connected in Thailand. One of Zinna's men introduced her to me."

"You arrange her credibility sessions?"

A smile. "You could put it like that. She became very careful about the men she used. They were still stupid but much more experienced. They weren't the usual bums, they were part of the industry in their own countries, usually they had done jail time, but at least they knew the ropes. The last one, Chaz Buckle, knew a lot about Thailand and how the system works. He knew that the best way to leave the country with a suitcase full of dope was to have one of the authorities on your side. Cops or army."

"He was her lover?"

"Yes. They usually are. She uses sex like that—I think it's the way she gets her kicks."

"He has her name tattooed on his arm."

She shrugs. "Tattoos—what do they mean? They're like T-shirts. But maybe they had a real thing going. After all, she introduced him to Zinna himself."

"Why would Zinna agree to that?"

Locking eyes with me. "Because he suddenly found himself with more than a hundred kilos of morphine that he needed to move in a hurry. I think you know where the M came from. It's the same stuff Vikorn used to try to frame him in that court-martial. He wanted to get rid of it right away because he knew Vikorn would be on to him. He needed the carriers to take as much as twenty, thirty kilos at a time—you can't do that with amateurs; you have to use people who know what they're doing. And such people want security. In Thailand they want to know someone big is on their side to ensure a smooth passage out of the country. They tend to be wise to the scam that uses a small-time carrier as a sacrificial decoy while the big shipment goes undetected."

"The meeting took place here?"

"Yes. I'm the neutral ground."

"Zinna came with some of his men?"

"Of course. It was quite a show. The *farang* carrier Buckle was very impressed." She glances out the window, then back to me.

"Thank you," I say. "That's what I needed to know."

She smiles politely and gets up to lead us downstairs. Clearly this is as much risk as she can take. The interview is over. Outside, on the magnificent pillared porch, she rests her eyes on Lek. "Can you really take care of him? He's too beautiful, too innocent." Reaching out, she strokes his hair as if he were a dog. "Poor darling hasn't been wounded yet. I do hope you survive."

In the cab Lek controls himself for as long as he can, then blurts: "So when do I get to see Fatima?"

"I've got to prepare her. She may not want the responsibility. Give me a week or so." Softening my words with a smile: "I'm quite busy, you know."

CHAPTER 22

I'm feeling pretty good, *farang*. In fact, I'm feeling like a *farang*. Truth be told, I cannot recall ever carefully preparing a watertight case and generally going the whole investigative nine yards. I must admit it's not something I'd want to do more than once in a while, it's so damned time-consuming (I mean, nine times out of ten you know *whodunit* so you grow the evidence accordingly—it's one of those efficient Asian techniques you'll have to adopt as global competition heats up—can't have your law enforcement potting fewer perps per cop than us, can you—especially now you've dumped the rule of law in all cases where it proves inconvenient, right?), but Vikorn wants it done by the book this time. We're going to leak the evidence to the media and run it on the Internet, so the judges will have to nail Zinna or risk impeachment themselves—there will be no funny business behind the scenes like last time. So I'm sitting at my desk making one of those lists cops like me never make:

Evidence

1. The dope. Well, it's definitely morphine that Buckle was carrying, our forensic boys did all the tests, and Ruamsantiah called them on the telephone this morning: *Of course it's morphine—is the Dalai Lama a Buddhist?* They're happy to go into print, we'll have the report by this evening.

2. Chaz Buckle, with a little chemical inducement, is ready to sign off on his increasingly detailed revelation of the Denise operation and her connection to Zinna.

3. Khun Mu, with a guarantee of security from Vikorn and a sum of money that he won't discuss (but will have to be enough to buy Mu a new identity and a new life with no loss of amenities: I reckon well over a million dollars has changed hands), will testify that the meeting between Zinna, Denise, and Chaz Buckle did indeed take place on her land.

All I have to do is find Denise and bang her up for a week or so until she's ready to confess all she knows about Zinna in return for a dramatic reduction in what would otherwise be a death sentence. It doesn't get much neater and more satisfying than that, and I'm ready to concede there are times when your system has its merits, *farang*. (Promotion, here I come.)

Except that my mobile is ringing, and I'm having one of those gloomy glimpses into the immediate future. I see from the screen on the phone that the call is from Ruamsantiah.

In a depressed tone: "We had to let the *farang* Chaz Buckle go."

"Huh?"

"Our forensic boys decided the stuff he was carrying was just icing sugar after all. They claimed the first tests used contaminated instruments that misled them."

"Zinna paid them off?"

"Is there another explanation? The General sent some high-powered lawyer to explain to us that we have no legal right to hold Buckle. Then the Director of Police called Vikorn to tell him to let him go."

"How's Vikorn taking it?"

"He's in his office waving his gun around."

I close on Ruamsantiah and take a deep breath before I call Vikorn on his mobile.

Vikorn: "You've heard?"

"Yes. We had to let him go."

"Have you any idea what this is doing to my face?"

"Yes."

"I'll be a laughingstock."

"Not necessarily. We can call for a second

opinion on the dope, maybe send it to a *farang* agency overseas."

"So then we end up with two conflicting forensic reports. That's all the wriggle room he needs."

"You can't give up now."

"Thais laugh at losers. I'm looking like the loser here. I frame him, he gets off. I grab one of his couriers, he springs him."

What can I say? This is all true.

"Be careful—he hasn't finished yet," Vikorn says despondently, and closes the phone.

I'm back at the bar in the evening. It's quite a slow night, and I'm thinking of closing early, when my mobile starts to ring. It is the colonel in charge of the Klong Toey district. It seems that a squat, muscular, unusually ugly, and tattooed *farang* has been found dumped in the river. Someone told him I might know something about it. I call Lek to tell him to pick me up in a cab.

CHAPTER 23

At the junction of Ratchadaphisek and Rama IV, Lek says: "I've never been to Klong Toey before. Is it as bad as they say?"

"Pretty much."

"You don't mind about going there at night, just the two of us?"

"We're cops, Lek."

"I know. I wasn't asking for myself. I feel so safe with you. You're like a kind of Buddha for me—just being with you banishes fear."

"You have to stop talking like that."

"Because it's not macho cop? But I love you for what you're doing for me—I can't deny my heart." I sigh. "Would you mind telling me when we're going to meet my Elder Sister?"

"When we're ready. You and me."

The truth is, I've still not found the stomach to introduce Lek to Fatima. Every time I pick up the phone to call her, I have a vision of her eating the kid alive. "Look, Lek, remember what you were telling me the other day, about the path of a *katoey* being the toughest, loneliest path a human being can choose?"

"I didn't choose it. The spirit who saved my life chose it."

"Right. And maybe that spirit has chosen Fatima—but I need to be sure. I feel like I'm holding your life in my hands here."

Lek stretches out a hand to rest on my knee for a moment. "The Buddha will give you enlightenment for this. You're so advanced, you're almost there."

"I don't feel advanced. I feel like I'm corrupting youth."

Lek smiles. "That only shows how holy you are. But I have to follow my path, don't I? This is my destiny we're talking about. My karma. My fate."

"Right."

"Will you lend me the money for the collagen implants in my buttocks and chest?"

I groan. "I guess so."

Klong Toey: grave crime at its most poetic. The *talat* (market) is the emotional center, a square acre of green umbrellas and tarps beneath which chilies lie short and wicked on poor women's shawls; chickens cram together dead or alive; ducks grumble in wooden cages; every kind of crab mimes death agonies in plastic bowls or gasps in the heat (both fresh- and saltwater, soft shell or hard); open-air butchers chop up whole buffalo; jackfruit, pineapple, orange, durian, grapefruit, bolts of cheap cotton, every kind of hand tool for the third-world handyman (generally of such

inferior steel, they give out during the first hour—
I have a personal vendetta against our screwdrivers,
which bend like pewter—they would drive you
totally nuts, *farang*); and so on. There are even
some corrugated iron shacks nearby from the
skulduggery school of architecture, joined clan-
destinely by precarious walkways that cry out for
a chase scene, but most of the buildings surrounding the square are three-story shop-houses
of the Chinese tradition. The sidewalks provide
good clues as to the business of the shops: whole
automobile engines pile up outside their ateliers
dripping black oil; air-conditioning ducts of all
dimensions stand proud outside another; CD rip-
offs on stalls, the latest boom boxes block the way
outside the stereo store. There are no *farang* here
(either they don't know, or knowing, they stay
away), these slow-moving crowds of brown folk
are as local as *somtam* salad, common as rice.
The point: Klong Toey district includes the
main port on the Chao Phraya river, where ships
have unloaded since the beginning of time. (There
are sepia pix of our forefathers in traditional three-
quarter black pants, naked to the waist, their long
black hair tied back from their fine foreheads in
magnificent ponytails, unloading by hand in the
impossible heat, many emaciated from your opium,
farang.) A couple of streets away: a fine big customs
shed and a complex of buildings belonging to the
Port Authority of Thailand. The river itself is no
more than a stone's throw away, and many of the

original inhabitants of this seething township have built their shacks on stilts on the other side of the water. Medieval riverboat men ferry the poor to and fro for twenty baht a trip in their modest hand-built canoes (with Yamaha outboards and millionaire bow-waves). In short, everyone knows the main industry is pharmaceuticals, for there is probably nowhere in Thailand where dealers, kingpins, addicts, cops, and customs are so conveniently massed together in one square mile of business-friendly riverfront real estate. Inevitably spin-off industries such as contract slaying, loan-sharking, and extortion have moved their head-quarters here. I'm a little surprised that Colonel Bumgrad is troubling himself with a mere Trance 808. I was afraid of hostility on his part, for he is one of Vikorn's many enemies, but he's the in-carnation of charm as he greets me when Lek and I get out of the cab.

They've laid Chaz Buckle out on the dockside under a blanket. The police launch is tied up to a capstan between two gigantic container vessels. The view is blocked in every direction by looming bows, rusting sterns, and iron gangplanks. Impenetrable marine shadows cast darkness over the poorly lit footpaths. Bumgrad nods to me, and I lift the blanket: a single shot in the back of the head, with exit wound that blew out his left eye. He is soggy from time spent in the river, but the assassination is recent. Even if I did not recognize the ruined face, the tattoos would have been identification enough.

"We haven't checked his pockets yet," Bumgrad murmurs. "We thought maybe you would want to do that."

I lean over the body, then jump back as a small blind eel wriggles from out his mouth. His pockets are undulating. Lek, watching closely, puts a hand over his mouth. When I rip open his shirt, I see that his stomach, too, is in perpetual motion. There is a faint *pop*, and a blind white head with mouth full of tiny teeth emerges from his belly button. I snap my head around—is this some kind of joke?—but Bumgrad and his men are gone, disappeared into the black maze of the dock. Lek steps back, stifling a squeal. Eels are burrowing out of the corpse, desperate to find a way back to the river. I also take ten paces back.

A whoreshriek from the bows of the container boat—sailors are a specialized market that my mother and I don't touch—then silence, save for the ring of iron-shod heels. A short stocky uniformed figure with ramrod back and voluminous chest emerges from the dark beyond and marches toward us until he is standing in a pool of light shed by a small lamp hanging from a ship's cable. I slowly get to my feet, close my hands in a *wai*, and raise them to my lips.

"Good evening, General Zinna," I say, carefully maintaining the *wai*.

Without replying, the General walks slowly toward me and stares down at the corpse. "Someone exercised compassion," he says in a whispered baritone.

"They killed him before they shoved the eels up his ass. That way he didn't feel them eating his guts out. I doubt I would show such restraint toward someone who really irritated me. Know what I mean?" He raises a hand, and snaps his fingers once. There is a sound of running boots; now more than a dozen young men in black sweatshirts and army haircuts are emerging from the shadows at a jog. They stand behind him in military formation until he nods to two of them, who go over to Chaz to shine a flashlight on his belly, which is now quite eaten away with a tangle of white writhing worms. The General walks over, picks one of the eels out of Chaz's guts, deftly kills it by whipping its head against the capstan, and returns to me.

As he slides the dead eel into my trouser pocket, in hardly more than a murmur: "Tell Colonel Vikorn he's gone too far. He framed me, I got off, now the dope belongs to me. He doesn't get a second shot. I'll have his guts, one way or another." Casting a contemptuous glance at Lek: "And I'll have your bum boy, too."

He and his men turn and leave. We are alone in marine darkness with a corpse full of hungry eels. As if sensing the coast is clear, the girl at the bow of the ship shrieks and laughs again with impressive professionalism calculated to make her sailor feel powerful, predatory, irresistible, charming, and horny. It seems a secret party is under way, for a couple more girls cry out, laugh, make vulgar jokes in Thai while their men shout in Chinese.

Three female faces appear over the bows, then immediately disappear.

Sudden quiet, in which the soft padding of a large rat can be heard. Far off someone is crossing the river in a long-tail boat. I decide to save the man I once interrogated from further forensic indignity, but it is not easy. He's heavy and elusive in the way of corpses. Grasping his wrists and signaling for Lek to help me, I drag him to the side of the dock, twist him around, then try to push him in. Lek leans over from the hips, elegantly failing to grasp the cadaver's feet. I'm sweating in the night heat and experiencing an irrational reluctance to make contact with the eels, which are still feasting. With a foot on one shoulder, near the neck, I give a mighty shove. His arms still outstretched, the tattoos *Mother* and *Denise* are the last of him to slide over the edge and into the river with the most discreet of splashes.

I reach into my pocket and throw Zinna's dead eel after him. Where's Lek? Frantic for a second (I experience a vision of rape and degradation at the hands of Zinna's men), I catch sight of him a little farther down the dock, in a pool of light.

The most classic of all our classical dance derives from the Hindu *Ramayana,* in which the god Vishnu incarnates as Rama and gets into a fight with evil over the life of his bride Sita. Lek is playing Sita on her knees pleading for her lord and master to believe in her eternal fidelity.

191

I put my arm around him as I lead him away.

"He called me a bum boy."

"Don't worry about it."

"I'm not a bum boy, I'm a dancer."

"I know you are."

He turns his big hazel eyes onto me, merciless in his trust, love, and expectation.

When we pass the spot, we hear the ferocious churning of fish and eels that the T808 is feeding. For a tantalizing moment I see his life disperse into its many components, which spin away from one another into the night. The composite problem that was Chaz Buckle is now resolved.

CHAPTER 24

It seems, though, that other composites are resolving into dust and spirit this violent night. Just after I've dropped Lek off at his project, Lieutenant Manhatsirikit calls me on my mobile.

"The Colonel's at Khun Mu's house. Better get over there."

There's nothing much to say, *farang*, that you have not already guessed. At Khun Mu's house all the dogs and monkeys are dead (gutted), the guards executed, mostly by bullets to the skull. Khun Mu, naked, is wrapped around Joey's embalmed corpse in an obscene position, her throat cut. And there is a fat dead *farang* woman in her mid-forties slit from gut to chest, lying on the king-size bed in the great bedroom, wearing only a huge pair of shorts.

"Denise?" I ask Vikorn.

He nods. "She lived in a million-dollar mansion overlooking the Andaman Sea in Phuket. He kidnapped her and brought her here just to show that he could." A shaking of the head. "Just to make a point." Looking at me: *"All our witnesses are dead."*

Vikorn walks over to the sofa by the window and

sits heavily. I've never seen him so despondent. "We've been going against him symmetrically," he mutters, "that's the problem. We can't beat him on violence. He's the army, for Buddha's sake." A quick glance at me. "I'm sorry, Sonchai. I'm taking the file away from you."

"You have someone better?"

"It needs nuance, a woman's touch."

"Manny? She's not exactly subtle."

He shrugs: no comment. He is huddled on his seat, shrunken, the very image of defeat; there are even tears in his eyes. I feel a great wave of pity—but wait! Somehow his projection of despair, frustration, misery, near-senility is a little too pat.

"Someone's come up with a Plan C, haven't they?"

He looks at me blankly as if he has no idea what I'm talking about.

At the station the next day, it is revealed that Vikorn spent the morning watching international news on his TV, which is normally dedicated to Thai pool. (He runs the main gambling syndicate.) When I go in to see him, I find him fixated by the monitor. It seems there has been a terrorist bomb in some remote village in Java, Indonesia, five Indonesian Hindus dead, about twenty more hospitalized. No one doubts the culprits are from an extreme Muslim faction, particularly because one of them died in the blast. Bits of his skullcap and beard, some fingers, a leg, and other body parts have been recovered. It is anticipated that his identity and that of the particular splinter group to which he belonged will soon be known. Naturally, the Western intelligence agencies are interested and only too willing to lend assistance.

I have no idea why Vikorn, who is hardly a fully globalized world citizen (I'm not sure he could identify France on a map), should be so interested, but when I cough with a view to attracting his attention, he raises a hand. When the news program has exhausted its real-time coverage, he lifts his telephone and—to my amazement—tells Lieutenant Manhatsirikit to get him on the next flight to Jakarta. While he is on the way to the airport, she is to make arrangements for him to meet someone senior in the Indonesian police, with a view to "mutually beneficial information sharing." I am staring open-mouthed while he rummages around. In all my time in District 8, my Colonel has never once left Thailand's sacred soil. Now Manny arrives and scowls at me before telling him that an interpreter has been located and this person, who is fluent in whatever language they speak down there (Vikorn keeps calling it Indonesian, but both Lieutenant Manhatsirikit and I have our doubts), will meet him at the airport tomorrow. When she has left, he checks his watch. Seven p.m. "We're going to eat," he tells me, and presses an autodial number on his mobile to call his driver.

In the back of his Bentley, with "The Ride of the Valkyries" screaming from the sound system, his driver with his usual supercilious expression plastered all over his mug, my Colonel places a hand on my shoulder. "You're going to forget last night. It never happened. You're going to concentrate on the Mitch Turner case."

"At least tell me what your Plan C is."

"You might not want to know. Anyway, it's classified."

I can hardly believe my generosity of soul. I'm actually *pleased* he's still fighting Zinna, even if I have missed my promotion (and the hundred thousand dollars). I don't want to let him off too lightly, though; this is quite a letdown I'm dealing with. I look out the window of the Bentley as we speed along Rama IV. "For a moment I thought you were getting old."

He spares me a contemptuous glance. "You think that's all it is? A primitive vendetta between two old men?" Leaning toward me to prod me in the gut: "What I do to keep the brakes on Zinna isn't just for Ravi. It's for the country, too. Let the army run the drug trade, and you get rich generals. Rich generals get big ideas and stage coups—that was the whole problem with the opium trade. Before you know it, we're back to military rule. And what do Thai army generals know about the global economy, human rights, the rule of law, the welfare of women, the twenty-first century in general? Next time you vote in a more or less straight democratic election, think about it. Thai police may not be the world's finest, but we're not military. Under us there are free elections. No *farang* would understand, but I expect better from you."

He still hasn't finished. In fact, he is digging me in the ribs. "Who knows, under democracy the country might flourish until it's worthy of a refined fellow like you. But if that happens, it will be because badasses like me kept the army snout out of the feeding trough, not because some monk manqué rescued a few dumb dogs off the street."

I shake my head in wonderment. He always has an answer. His dexterous use of the word *manqué* is particularly irritating; in Thai the word has exactly the same quality of supercilious pretension and is just the sort of thing I come out with when I want to irritate *him*. Who told him he could say *manqué* and get away with it?

I brood for a long moment. His driver stops at the beginning of Pat Pong, our most venerable— and famous—red-light district. There is no way the limo is going to squeeze down this crowded street at this time of night. Vikorn and I get out and walk while his chauffeur takes the car away. The Colonel is in plain clothes and looks like just another Thai man, somewhat on the short side by Western standards, indistinguishable from the other middle-aged Thai men who work this street, virtually all of whom are pimps. Vikorn seems to suffer no threat to his ego, though, when a young white tourist in cutaway singlet and walking shorts, regulation nose stud and eyebrow pin, asks him where the Ping-Pong show is. Vikorn stops in midstride and, with a smile expressive of deep greed and sympathetic lechery, points to a small sign on an upper terrace: *Girls, dirty dancing, ping-pong, bananas* . . . "Great," says the young *farang*, mirroring Vikorn's smile.

"Fuckee, fuckee," says Vikorn with a dumb grin.

The street is crammed, not only with horny white men but with greedy white women too, for some of the best designer rip-offs in Asia are on sale at the stalls that fill the center of the street. Tear aside the veil of conventional morality—see with a meditator's eyes—and the looks on the faces of the women are not so different from the men's:

"Only two hundred baht for Tommy Bahama jeans—that's just over three quid." Eyes bulging: "You can't get a gin and tonic for that in Stoke Newington."

"See this fake Rolex? Look, the second hand goes around all smooth without jerking, just like the real thing. It's only ten pounds."

Examining it with wonder: "We could buy a few and sell them—even at a hundred quid it's cheap."

"Would we tell everybody they're fakes?"

Thinking about it: "Have to, really, they're all going to know we've been over here."

"But they don't know what they cost in Pat Pong, do they? I mean, we could be buying at ninety and only making a ten percent markup?"

Nodding thoughtfully: "For all they know."

★　　★　　★

The Princess Club is in a side *soi* that is jam-packed with people. We have to squeeze past big Caucasian bodies, then into the bar, which is also packed. The mamasan recognizes Vikorn instantly, and a quite different expression appears on her face, in contrast to the tough/dumb look she wears for the customers. The Colonel is not merely immensely rich and the owner of the club, he is also her liege lord, the man who provides her, her aging mother, and her teenage son with food, lodging, and dignity. The relationship is complex and goes beyond money. (Even after her retirement he will keep her in food and pride—the bondage works both ways.) She *wais* him and makes a little curtsy; he nods at her and smiles; face has been exchanged across the sea of pink drunken mugs, most of whom are watching the girls on stage.

Whether the girls are allowed to dance topless (or naked) in a particular club depends entirely on the whim of whichever police colonel is running the street. This is not Vikorn's street, but no one is going to interfere with his bar, so here the girls are all topless. They don't bother to put their bras on when they come down to the floor to mix with customers, and yet they always seem in control. Strange how these wild-looking young *farang* men, who with their tattoos and body piercings and alcohol abuse might be barbarians on a break from sacking ancient Rome, don't dare to grope any of those oh-so-tempting young mammary glands as they wobble and swing past their eyes—not without a franchise from the owners, anyway, which always costs a couple of drinks.

The mamasan points upstairs, and we manage to squeeze past the wild hordes to the far end of the bar, then up two flights to a reception room, where they have prepared Vikorn's supper. We sit cross-legged on the floor, as we were both brought up to do, at a low benchlike table that is already laden with *yam met ma-muang himaphaan* (yam with cashews), *naam phrik num* (a northern dish consisting of a chile and eggplant dip), *miang kham* (ginger, shallot, peanuts, coconut flakes, lime, and dried shrimp), Mekong whiskey with *chut* (ice, halved limes, and mixers), and some *phat phet* (spicy stir-fry).

No sooner are we seated than two of the dancing girls appear, wearing T-shirts and bras now, to ask what we want to drink in addition to the Mekong. Vikorn orders a couple of beers, to be followed by a cold white wine from New Zealand. (This is all my fault. I started him on wine a few years ago, and now he cannot eat his *kaeng khiaw-waan* without it.) I ask between mouthfuls if he has any idea how exactly Mitch Turner died.

He looks at me as if I'm a particularly slow-witted fellow who needs help. "What does it matter how he died? We're dealing with theater, not reality. *Farang* gave up on reality when they invented democracy, then added television. What matters is what we tell the world. Handle it right, and we all live happily ever after. Handle it wrong, and . . ." He opens his hands, indicating just how tragically unpredictable life can be for nonmanipulators. The girls arrive with his green curry with extra chili along with the wine in an aluminum ice bucket, stir-fried mixed vegetables, *tom yam,* Chinese kale, a spicy duck salad, mouse-shit peppers, and some shredded *kai yaang* (grilled chicken).

"So how do we handle it right?" I ask, humbled, irritated, and relishing the feast all at the same time.

He makes a gesture with his left hand that might appear obscene if one did not know its country origins. What he is actually doing is tickling a fish—fishing by hand was his favorite sport as a boy. It takes a quite incredible patience—merely getting close enough to the fish to tickle its belly is only the beginning—fools make a grab and lose the catch—only the cool stay the course long enough to mesmerize the fish, *then* grab it. All you need is a heart as cold as the fish's.

"What do you want me to do?"

"Just concentrate. Our friends from the CIA will come calling very soon now. Follow the road signs and keep your mouth shut. Or do you want them to drag Chanya off to Guantánamo Bay?"

"They wouldn't do that."

"Why not? Turner was CIA checking out Muslims. He was murdered. She did it. They could leave her to rot over there for the rest of her life, or until she's totally insane."

He is using Piercing Eyes to stare at me. I know he's playing three-dimensional chess and probably has me mated on every level; but he needs something, that's why he's taken me to dinner.

"If you're a good boy and stick to the Mitch Turner case, I'll tell you why my Indonesia trip will protect Chanya." I gasp at his ruthlessness. He leans forward. "You think you're so smart? You've been in love with that whore since the day she came to work for us. I know it, your mother knows it, *she* certainly knows it, and so do all the other girls."

I fall strategically silent. Then with what I think is fine timing and a not-bad display of low cunning, I say: "So how's the *mia noi?*"

Feigning indifference: "Which one?"

"The fourth one who lives in your mansion in Chiang Mai."

"Oh, her." Frowning. "She's fine." For a moment I'm foolish enough to believe I've hit a nerve, but this is Police Colonel Vikorn—he doesn't seem to have any. Flashing me a grin, he launches into a brilliant parody of his paramour, mimicking perfectly her screechy voice when in the throes of a tantrum: *"'You shit, I'm giving you the best years of my life, and you don't appreciate it, you keep me cooped up here in this hick town when I could be in Bangkok, what d'you want me for, some kind of trophy? You haven't fucked me for a month, my body's going to waste, I'd rather be on the Game than your personal property. What d'you think this is, the fucking*

Middle Ages? Why don't you give me some decent money at least? Just because I don't want your kids, you're punishing me with exile from everyone and everything I love, as if you haven't got plenty. You've got more dough than twenty Chinamen, you have. I'm going to have an affair with one of the security guards, that's what I'm going to do. I'm a young woman, and you're a miserable old fart who can't get it up. I'm going to have the biggest tattoo on my ass and a silver ring in my pussy whatever you have to say about it. I could have men crawling at my feet, I could . . .'"

What can I do? I'm doubled up and coughing from laughing too hard. It's as if she were here sitting at the table with us.

In the Bentley on the way back to the station, Vikorn gives me an unusually tender tap on the shoulder. Reaching into the door pocket on his side, he brings out a small satchel and hands it to me. I peek inside. It is a Heckler and Koch machine pistol. I gulp.

"It's just a precaution. Keep it with you when you can, especially at night. Take this too." It is a piece of paper with a number on it. "Plug that into your autodial numbers, so you can call it just by pressing one button. There won't be a reply, but I'll bring some of the boys to find you, so make sure you're either in your apartment or in the club. Nothing's going to happen before I get back from Indonesia."

"Zinna?"

"What you're calling Plan C—I'm afraid he may not take it too well." Vikorn has to concentrate to wipe the grin from his face. He catches his driver's eye in the rearview mirror. The driver is stifling a guffaw.

CHAPTER 25

Thus have I heard: the faithful Ananda one day asked the Finest of Men: Lord, how is it that in the animals we see all the gods represented—the ferocity of Kali in the tiger, the strength and endurance of Ganesh in the elephant, the cunning and strategy of Hanuman in the monkey—but nowhere do we see an animal that reflects the Buddha? With a nod the Tathagata gazed over the world with an omniscient eye, then described to Ananda an animal living on another continent that was the size of a monkey, owned only three toes on each foot, and was capable of hanging upside down from the treetops for weeks on end; that ate only the leaves rejected by other mammals; that had a metabolism so slow, it took a week to digest each meal; that put up with pain and indignity without complaint; and that was constitutionally incapable of haste.

Tell me, *farang,* can there be greater proof of enlightenment than that the man with the universe at his feet chose the three-toed sloth as role model? If he so completely extinguished ego, why cannot I?

In other words, all of a sudden I find myself quite cured of the defilement of ambition. I worked on it over the weekend, meditated my way into tranquillity, swam for as long as I could in the ocean without a shore—and smoked a couple of joints. It was a struggle, but I got there. No, I don't want promotion anymore, I don't want the hundred thousand dollars, let *her* have it (the bitch). If she wants to defile her soul by serving Vikorn's sordid (and largely irrational) vengeance, so be it, but let her watch out for karma. Next time around Lieutenant Manhatsirikit will be my pet goldfish. (It still hurts that she's closer to him—and smarter—than me: what could the Plan C consist of?)

Back at the club, with nothing better to do, I make that call to Fatima.

She drawls into the phone: "Darling, it's been so long."

"I'm sorry."

"I was beginning to think you were ashamed of me."

"Never. You're way out of my league these days. I'm intimidated."

"Don't lie, darling. Nothing intimidates you. But you must want something, no?"

I explain to her what I have in mind for Lek. I'm quite pleased with her momentary hesitation. "An Elder Sister? Me? You know, I've never done that for anyone. I've never wanted to. It's a tough

206

path." A giggle: "I'll do it if you beg me to. I want you on your knees in drag."

"I can't beg. I don't know if it's the right thing or not."

"Darling, don't start talking like a *farang*. There's no right or wrong—either young Lek is a natural or he's not. If he is, and he certainly sounds like it, then a whole army could not stop him. Bring him to me. I'll know what to do the minute I set eyes on him."

"When?"

"Now."

"But it's past midnight."

"Can there be a better time?"

I call Lek, who gasps with awe, excitement, and fear. We take a cab to Soi 39, where Fatima owns a three-story penthouse apartment in one of the city's most prestigious developments. On the way I'm seeing Lek the way Fatima will see him; he's just too damn beautiful for his own good.

Bastard son of a Karen bar girl and a black American GI she's never met, Fatima is tall and chocolate brown. Of course she is ravishing in her favorite kimono (crimson with a great white sash), her long tragic face, scrubbing-board stomach, long finely manicured hands, exaggerated mascara, and eyes that have seen the very depths of desolation. She stands at the door holding Lek at arm's length. I'm already an irrelevant spectator. How to explain to the spiritually sightless the extraordinary event that takes place when Lek's guardian spirit recognizes this ancient soul? Fatima leans against her doorjamb; behind her: a vista of rare art objects, mostly priceless jade items on pedestals, leading to a floor-to-ceiling panoramic window filled with city lights and a yellow moon.

"Oh Buddha," she says, still holding Lek's hand. I cough. "You can leave us now," she whispers hoarsely, without taking her eyes off Lek.

When I get back to my hovel, I can't sleep. I have lived and worked in the heterosexual division of the sex trade all my life, I have seen all the things that men and women do to each other—and none of it approaches the intensity of *katoeys*. I don't want to worry about Lek anymore, or what Fatima might do to him. He'll have to follow the complex rules of his new world. By contrast, the assassination of Mitch Turner seems a more penetrable mystery—almost mundane, but no less compelling for that. I take out the fat wad of A4 paper I collected in Songai Kolok and start to read Chanya's diary all over again.

PART 4

CHANYA'S DIARY

CHAPTER 26

Chanya begins her diary thus: *There are two Chanyas. Chanya One is noble, pure, and shines like gold. Chanya Two fucks for money. This is why whores go mad.*

She refers to herself in the third person, a permissible device in spoken and written Thai and very common in the humbler classes: *Chanya has always wanted to go to Saharat Amerika.*

I seriously thought about translating the whole thing word for word for you, *farang*, but the style didn't fit with the rest of the narrative, and I know how you love congruity (I also got frustrated because I couldn't stick in any comments of my own), so I've opted for an impressionistic rendering of the kind deplored by all true scholars, if that's okay?

America was a dream that infected her soul via a television screen while she was still a child. Starting with the Empire State Building and the Grand Canyon, her mind had collected a million brilliant images of a nation with a genius for self-promotion. One fine day, when she had saved

211

enough money to keep her parents for a few months, and had paid for her sister's college fees for that semester, and had bought a piece of land in her village near Surin where she would build her trophy house on her return, and had bought a laptop with Thai word processor, she contacted a gang who had a reputation for honesty and reliability. Their fees were high—nearly fifteen thousand dollars—but they provided the full service, including a genuine Thai passport with a genuine entry visa to the United States, a return air ticket good for one year, a minder who accompanied her as far as Immigration in New York to make sure she did not freak out at the crucial moment and blow the whole operation, and a room and a job in a massage parlor in Texas.

In return for her working in the massage parlor for six months, the gang reduced the fees by five thousand dollars. Of course, she would pay this back by swelling the profits of the massage parlor, which would contribute to the gang's overheads. She would have to make her own money those first months through tips and by turning tricks on the side, but she knew how to do that and had no illusions. She would use that time to perfect her English, get to know more about American men, and work out which was the best city in which to practice her profession for maximum profit.

The way she saw it, she would be at the top of her game in a country that paid better than any other. When she finished, after a couple of years, she would still be under thirty years old. She would retire to her brand-new house with carport and giant wide-screen TV, decorated internally with photographs of *Chanya in Amerika*. The whole village would be proud of her and give her face. She would be a queen, and everyone would approve of the way she took care of her family. Maybe she would have a baby? Unlike most of her friends, she had not fallen pregnant to a Thai lover at age eighteen. She was childless and went along with the more recent fashion in that she liked the idea of having a half-*farang* child, who tended, according to the latest fad anyway, to be more beautiful than Thais and with lighter skin. She had no particular desire to marry, although a Buddhist ceremony was not out of the question. She knew enough about *farang* men to know that the father of her child was unlikely to stick around. Indeed, the chances were he would disappear the day she told him she was pregnant, which was fine by her. The function of a husband was to provide. If a woman had money, what did she need a husband for? She could satisfy her sexual needs anytime she liked, although she had always practiced Buddhist meditation and expected to become more devout once her working days were over. She would probably give up sex altogether once she retired. It was a very long time since she had enjoyed it or even thought about it other than in a professional sense. Come to think of it, she wasn't sure she ever had felt any real passion for a man. Sex was boring. It was paytime that made her heart skip a beat.

She has insisted on a window seat in the Thai Airways 747, and her first view of America is the New England coastline. The gang chose for her to fly west, with a short stopover at Heathrow Airport in London, so for most of the journey, there has been only blackness out the window as they fled the sun. Now, though, the sun has caught up, and eight thousand feet below, the New England coast looks as pristine as when the Pilgrims first arrived. She had no idea that America could be breathtaking in its natural beauty, so it's quite a surprise to behold that aquamarine lazily lapping at a jagged line of rocks that reflect the morning light with the brilliance of diamonds. She has never been out of Thailand before, never seen a northern landscape. It looks so pure and unspoiled.

The big moment comes when she reaches the immigration booth and a tall, stern *farang* in uniform checks carefully through her passport. The minder from the gang is in a parallel line, watching, ready to jump her if her nerves let her down. *(Oh, solly, solly, mister, my sister she very emotional, I take her go sit down over there.)*

But her nerves do not fail: *Chanya rides this dragon. Chanya owns big pair mighty balls.*

Here is the benefit of choosing the right mafiosi and of generally knowing what you are doing.

Plenty of girls get caught at this stage because the passport is poorly forged, or there is something wrong with the visa. Not with these guys. Although he seems to try quite hard (when he pierces her with those cold blue eyes, it is obvious he knows what she is, but she keeps her cool and gazes steadily back), the immigration officer cannot find anything wrong with her papers and lets her through. Now customs wants to search her bags because she has arrived from Bangkok. Here again many girls get into serious trouble because the gang has slipped something into their luggage, trying to run two scams at once, but not this group. The only item the customs officer examines closely is her secondhand laptop, which she bought in Bangkok mostly so she could send e-mails to all her friends and family, especially her sister at Chulalongkorn University, but also because part of her American plan is to keep a diary. The officer lets her through, and all of a sudden she's *in the country*. There being no Buddha statue to *wai* to in this pagan land, she places her hands together near her forehead, facing in the direction of Thailand. Translated directly from the Thai: *Say good morning to Chanya, Amerika.*

She and her minder take one of the shuttle buses to catch the connecting flight to El Paso. He watches her pass to airside, then disappears. Another minder, not Thai but Texan, meets her off the plane in El Paso. He is red-faced and balding with bad skin, and a sour odor seeps from his body, but she can tell he's a professional by the way he discounts her charms and gets down to business. On the way to the massage parlor he explains that the advantage of jet lag is that she'll be fresh and alert in the middle of the night, so she'll start working the graveyard shift in a few hours. Better get some sleep. He lets slip that she is the first Asian woman to work for this particular outfit.

The first Spanish word she learns is *coño*. It means "cunt," a word women of her trade employ a lot, including in Thailand, but the Mexican women in the massage parlor use it all the time. It punctuates everything they say and sounds unspeakably filthy. Most of them are bilingual in Spanish and English but prefer to speak in Spanish. They tend to have families on the other side of the border and to know one another from Ciudad Juárez, where they have boyfriends and husbands who work as grunts in the narcotics trade. Chanya has mentally prepared herself for any kind of American man who hires her—she really hadn't thought that the other women would be a problem. She sees at once it's a cultural thing but has no idea what to do about it. She was lovingly brought up by poor but devout Buddhists, and she herself never violates any of the strictures except one. The Buddha requires of his followers that they find "right employment." Chanya made a decision to postpone complying with that one because prostitution offered better money than any other work and made it easy for her to comply with some of the other Buddhist strictures, especially the ones that dealt with showing respect to one's parents. In the Thai interpretation that meant providing for them if they were too poor or old to provide for themselves. It also meant providing for her siblings until they were old enough to work, an event that could easily be delayed indefinitely. Chanya never steals, hardly ever tells lies, cultivates good thoughts and lovingkindness, never takes drugs, doesn't drink too much alcohol at this stage in her life, tries to see the best in people—including her customers— and most important of all keeps her mind as free as possible from defilements. All of which, together with her outstanding good looks and fantastic figure, infuriate the hell out of her colleagues, especially when more and more men ask for her services.

After a week she has made her first important decision: *Whores here all demons.*

In other words, they are impervious to compassion or any Buddhist salvation. When they die, they will return to the hells whence they came and remain there for tens of thousands of years before getting another crack at the human form, which they will probably make a mess of all over again. "Idiot compassion" is a novice stage in Buddhist doctrine. Chanya passed that phase a long time ago. She encloses herself in an impermeable mental shield that translates as aloofness but gains her some respect. The demons had seen her as something frail and pathetic, a tasty morsel dangling at the very end of the food chain. Now they see she is something else, a different animal entirely. *Coño*. She pays no attention to their religion, which seems important to them but strikes her as a barbaric product of one of the lower hells, full of torment and anguish that lead nowhere: *Chanya fucks demons.*

After less than a month the offers of marriage start to come in. It amuses her that the Texan male courts in a way that would be instantly recognizable in the East. He tells you how much money he's got, shows you around his "spread" just like a bird showing off its plumage, and treats you like a princess in a cage. Some even had the sense to feign humility: "Aw, you know, it's just a li'l ol' spread, I ain't rich exactly—but a' course any woman takes me on full time is gonna get half sooner or later. I'm getting on a bit, you know."

The frontier between marriage and prostitution was as hard to pin down in the United States as it was in Thailand, apparently. Some of the spreads were gigantic in the Texan tradition, but she doubted the owner had any real intention to share. As her fame grew, more and more red-faced men from out of the jungle (she is still very Thai; for her, anything that is not city or suburb is jungle) arrived in the massage parlor's parking lot in big

SUVs. Her boss doubled her fees and told her the five thousand dollars would be paid off in three months instead of six, when she would be free to leave. He was an experienced pro and realized she was just too hot to keep. The feds would be around sooner or later to take a more expert look at her passport, maybe check with the ID database in Thailand on which fingerprints were recorded.

Marriage, she now decides, is not out of the question, but she sees through the men. She sees the meanness behind the charm, their assumption of a future of unchallenged dominance that arises from her being Asian, serene, and eager to please. For her part, if she is looking for anything in particular in a man, it is a Thai sense of fun. Money is important, but without fun life simply is not worth living. Although she enjoys a laugh and a joke with some of the customers, she isn't having a lot of fun, not with the Mexican women developing a homicidal rage toward her. The boss sees it too and hints that she should probably leave as soon as the three months are up—those women have mean connections. Anything can happen in El Paso. Maybe she could leave even sooner—he increases her hourly fee again. Within a record two months of her arrival, she is free to leave.

Vegas is the place to go for a woman like her. She knew this even in Bangkok. When she first sees the town from the Greyhound bus, she recognizes the vibrations. Using her connections within

America's Thai mafia, she has no difficulty finding a job with the biggest of the city's agencies. The agency is so well organized, American style, it even holds an induction course. Chanya sits in a seat in a conference room of a large hotel, along with about fifty other young women, most of whom are not Caucasian.

She has often heard prostitution referred to as an industry but has never seen it treated like one before. The platinum blonde who stands facing the new recruits is a masterpiece of modern surgery: tit enhancements, stomach tucks, nosejob, face-lift—the lot. She is over forty, though—way past active service—and has surely been shunted over to the human resources side of the profession. No surgery could do much about her voice, which is sandpaper and steel:

"It's like this, and in this order. I don't want to hear about any of you getting the order wrong, so if you have a learning disability or poor English, write it down. I provided paper and pencil on each desk."

1. The john arrives in Vegas. He has heard about our services and asks the cab driver how he can contact us on his way from the airport.
2. The cab driver has one of our cards like this. [It shows a lurid Asian girl with huge bare breasts on one side, the telephone number on the other.] You

will notice that there is a code number on the card. Each individual card has a different one.

3. The john calls the number, and the operator asks for the code on the card. This helps ensure it's a real john and not a cop. It also means a payoff for the cab driver.

4. The john states his preferences, i.e., race, breast size, height, blow job only, hand job, vaginal intercourse, anal intercourse, special services, all of the above, etc.

5. The operator takes down his hotel details and calls him back in his room to make sure he's really there.

6. If he is where he says he is, the operator tells him the price and usually adds that the girl will be there in twenty minutes.

7. The operator calls the girl on her cell phone and tells her where to go. She also calls one of the bodyguards to meet her in the lobby of the john's hotel. This is important. You do not go to the john's room or even call him until the guard is in place. You tap the guard's cell number into the autodial feature of your own cell phone. If at any point there is a problem, you press the autodial number, and the guard will

be up at the room in double-quick time.

8. You make contact with the guard and then call the john on the hotel phone to come down to meet you. You do not go straight to his room.

9. The john tells you what he is wearing. You and the guard both check the john when he appears, but he will not see the guard. You approach, you will call him either honey or sweetie, you will not use any other term of endearment.

10. The john takes you up to his room. He must now pay you the base fee of two hundred dollars. You do not make a move until you have pocketed the cash.

11. You now tell him to take out his cock. This is important. If he is an under-cover cop, he will not take out his cock. If he refuses, then you leave the room. If he is not a cop, he will take out his cock, which you will work on for a few moments.

12. You then tell him to lie on the bed while you strip. After you have stripped and he has ogled you, you explain that the price given by the agency was merely for turning up and stripping. If he wants more, he has to pay. You will have your own scale of fees for serv-ices, starting with hand jobs and going

all the way up to ass-fucking. What you charge at this stage is up to you—obviously the young and stunning will charge the most. In any case, you are advised not to begin your service until you have got your dough.

13. The rest is up to you and your creativity, but always use a condom for oral, vaginal, and anal sex. From time to time we plant men on you to check for quality control. Any girl who does not roll her own condom on the john will be fired.

14. An elegant exit is always a good idea. Be polite at all times, but a good exit gives the possibility of repeat business. A repeat customer simplifies things, and of course you know by this time he is not a cop.

At first she feels much less isolated than in El Paso. There are plenty of Asian women on the Game here—Japanese, Korean, Vietnamese, Chinese, Thai, Filipino, Malay, Indian, Pakistani—more or less every Asian race is represented. If they are less popular than blondes, that doesn't seem to matter, there is plenty of work to go around. Here the men are all tourists from other states—the whole of Nevada is a revolving door, millions are flown and bused in every week. Every customer comes with those bulging, moist, expectant eyes of a man who has escaped from his prison for a week or two—or a day, or an hour.

Almost all the other women are American citizens, though. Many were born there, others have immigrated and stayed long enough to take the oath of allegiance and generally behave exactly like other Americans. Practically every one of them is on drugs. The white women tend to claim, perhaps truthfully, that it was drugs (mostly coke, crack and meth, sometimes heroin) that drove them to the Game in the first place. They needed the big bucks to feed their big habits. The Asians and the blacks often claim it was prostitution that drove them to drugs. Everyone agrees that to survive on the Game in America, you more or less have to be on dope of one kind or another. Pretty soon Chanya understands what they mean. The men hardly trouble to ask her name, there is no repartee, no fun—even less fun than in Texas. To her it makes no sense at all, since imposing a layer of misery has no effect on the popularity of the trade. On the contrary, it may be the puritanical monotony of the working week that drives the men to seek relief in Vegas: not raging bulls, exactly, more like cows waiting to be milked.

She becomes a production-line worker, if a highly paid one. It is exactly what the men expect. They really *need* to be disappointed—she can see them starting to tell themselves how sorry they are as they put their pants back on, how they will try to live better lives and buy their wives a new dress. Her good looks and superb figure are only minor advantages—generally the men are too rushed and furtive to notice.

She starts to drink regularly, usually a couple of tequilas at the end of a session to keep her head level. She stays more than six months, long enough to save thirty thousand dollars, then takes a bus to Washington. One of her friends from Bangkok has called her. Wan arrived in America soon after Chanya and found work in a Washington, D.C., hotel where the Game is very well controlled. There is a sauna and massage spa attached to the hotel where Chanya can work.

In Washington it takes Chanya a week to realize she has dropped into a whore's paradise. The hotel where Wan works owns five stars, which means diplomats, high-rolling secretaries, heads of security, and others stay here. But before Chanya has time to apply for a job, her friend introduces her to a Thai diplomat named Thanee, a light-skinned man in his mid-forties with obvious Chinese genes who belongs to one of maybe a dozen very wealthy families who control Thailand. Chanya has heard of his family, who are often in the news in Bangkok. The patriarch, who is still just about alive, made a lot of money in the opium trade while it was still legal, or semilegal, but his eldest son showed true commercial genius by investing his share of the family fortune first in electronics, then in telecommunications. Thanee is a second grandson who showed no interest in business but demonstrated a flair for diplomacy. With his connections it was inevitable that sooner or later he would land a plum job in Washington. He is part of a permanent lobbying group looking after the interests of the Thai economy—well, the interests of Thai patricians, actually.

The negotiations are very short, and he and Chanya close the deal with hardly more than a smile. Wan finds an excuse to leave them alone after about five minutes. It is such a relief to speak her own language and to be with a man who understands where she is coming from, she almost loses her professionalism.

There is no hurry to get her to bed. He takes her to a Thai restaurant off Chinatown, where he urges her to choose her favorite dishes. He orders a bottle of white wine to go with the raw prawn salad, and a bottle of red for the duck. He makes her laugh with some Thai jokes, but at the same time his sophistication is pretty intimidating. He not only speaks English perfectly; he owns a kind of smoothness that seems to impress, even frighten, the waiters. He is a master of both cultures, something that leaves her almost speechless with admiration. Best of all, they understand each other perfectly: there will be no misplaced passion and no offers of marriage with this guy. They will proceed back to his apartment at a leisurely Thai pace, their private party will begin with her massaging him slowly with aromatic oil, little by little intimacy will develop, he will not force the issue but will wait for her to signal she is ready. She will stay the night, they will breakfast together, perhaps they will have sex one more time before he pays her generously. She will allow herself to fall in love with him in a very controlled way. They are as far apart within the Thai class system as it is possible to be, so neither of them is going to develop unreasonable expectations. On the other hand, both of them will greet each other with affection and a degree of relief at their next assignation. She will almost certainly become one of his *mia noi* or minor wives in Washington.

Which is exactly how it happens, except that she quickly becomes his favorite *mia noi*. Indeed, Wan tells her he dumped all the others the same week he met Chanya.

Thanee's wife number one, Khun Toi, the matriarch herself, spends most of her time in Thailand with their two children and only rarely comes to Washington. Of course, she knows about Thanee's various *mia noi*. She would have laughed out loud if anyone had told her he was faithful to her. She herself, having been educated in the West and being as liberated as any woman in her own Thai way, has a regular lover in Bangkok whom Thanee knows all about. It is not out of the question that Thanee will introduce her to Chanya on her next visit. Everyone would know the rules: Chanya would show great deference toward Khun Toi, and Khun Toi in return would develop an affection for Chanya.

Which is exactly how it happens. Khun Toi stays for ten days, she and Chanya get along marvelously and go shopping together. Khun Toi buys Chanya some fine new skirts and dresses with the best designer labels, Chanya carries all their bags to the waiting limo. At the end of the ten days Khun Toi tells her husband how it is to be: Chanya is far too beautiful and valuable to be left to the mercies of the local sex trade. Thanee is to pay her a stipend every month, enough to live and dress well and to accompany Thanee from time to time on those few social functions where Americans will not raise too many eyebrows. Chanya will be invited to Thanee's Asian-only soirées. They will not live together, and Chanya will be discreet about coming and going from Thanee's penthouse apartment. Thanee must give her a key so as to make her comings and goings smoother. For her part, Chanya will dedicate herself to Thanee and not take on any other clients. That will take care of the risk of disease, which has been worrying Khun Toi for quite a while. Not that she and Thanee have sex very often these days, but she doesn't want him to get sick and die.

"Three quarters of my money would go back to my parents," Thanee explains to Chanya in front of Khun Toi. Everyone laughs, Thai-style.

Chanya thinks maybe Khun Toi gets off on arranging her husband's naughty fucks. I could smell her when she hugged me tonight. She's making him screw her while I'm writing this. She's going to make him tell her what Chanya's like in bed, what he makes me do. Well, we do everything, honey.

At first Thanee is too canny to give Chanya more than the tiniest glimpse of his professional life, and such glimpses as she is allowed come out of small talk among her new lover and his Thai friends. But although she left school at the age of twelve and has never spent a minute thinking about geopolitics, Chanya catches on fast. She is astonished and even a little dismayed at the unofficial view of this *Saharat Amerika* she spent so much time and effort to reach. According to Thanee and his Chinese friends, the world's only superpower and its biggest economy is also old, gridlocked, overtaxed, overgoverned, more over-armored than *Tyrannosaurus rex,* and too hidebound for any dramatic expansion. Modern China is a young country that began life in 1949. It has only just entered the great period of wild entrepreneurs and robber barons, enjoys just the right balance of corruption and law and order that allows the strongest and most ferocious of its businessmen to cut through the red tape, while lesser citizens are kept under control. It approximates to the golden age of the Rockefellers, Joseph Kennedy, and Al Capone. China is also very close to Thailand. When the present phase of road-building projects in Laos is completed, there will be direct land routes all the way from Beijing and Shanghai to Bangkok. This seems to excite Thanee and his closest associates, both the Chinese and the Thai. China is already dominating the economies of Southeast Asia. Within twenty years it will be the world's largest economy and the most important country in the world for anyone living in Thailand. With two billion natural capitalists, its potential for expansion is incalculable.

Understanding the subliminal message, Chanya realizes with sadness that she is Thanee's last Washington luxury. He sees that she has understood. Perhaps he has deliberately allowed her to overhear certain conversations—he's certainly smart and devious enough for that.

Career moves take planning, though, and with Asians an awful lot of wining and dining. He is out most nights in his tuxedo. The occasions to which he is able to invite her are few, but he buys her three evening gowns just in case. She causes a sensation in her long gowns with her shining black hair plaited and pinned up and the gold necklace he bought her glittering against her brown skin, large single gold-set pearls in her ears. She sees that not a few Chinese and Thai men intend to inherit her after Thanee's departure. And so they might have done, were it not for a curious move by Thanee himself.

★　★　★

Chanya thinks she will puzzle for the rest of her life about why exactly Thanee introduced her to the *farang*. For quite a while she will think of the tall, muscular, and rather unattractive man as just that: the *farang*, probably because since she took on Thanee, she has hardly met any white men at all. Why did Thanee invite her to lunch with the *farang* at 7 Duck on Massachusetts Avenue (wicker and pillows everywhere, the penne pasta with seafood would have been a lot better with more chiles), on exactly the day that he broke it to her that he had been posted to Beijing and would be leaving in two months? Sometimes she thinks it might have been a kind of malice, not toward her but toward the *farang*. Perhaps the subtle revenge of an Asian diplomat who has not failed to notice how even his smoothness, charm, intelligence, and perfect English still do not qualify him as an equal of the Americans who believe they run the world? If that is the case, then it is a stroke of malicious genius on Thanee's part; anyone could have foreseen how hard the *farang* was likely to fall.

Mitch Turner cannot keep his eyes off her all through the lunch, to the extent that it becomes embarrassing and Thanee makes signs of irritation too subtle for Turner to notice. Chanya has to keep dropping her eyes so as not to lock with the *farang*'s. Sometimes she slips rather rudely into Thai, in the hope the American will be offended, but he seems not to notice. Those blue eyes simply burn into her skin. He cannot stop staring at her.

This is not entirely surprising. She has been in Washington for five months now and for most of that time she has been kept by Thanee, who is not a man to begrudge a woman when it comes to clothes and cosmetics. She is wearing a fawn Chanel business suit, and her creamy brown skin has benefited from endless visits to upmarket beauticians who also know how to emphasize the mystery in those Oriental eyes, but best of all, her natural poise convinces everyone that she is a young diplomat herself, the product of the best education money can buy. Surely no peasant girl who began her working life by minding water buffalo barefoot in the paddy could possibly know to sit like that? And to be so relaxed it is almost intimidating? That is the word Mitch Turner will use later, when they know each other better. That whole lunch *he* feels intimidated by *her*!

On this day at least she is saved by neo-Puritanism. Normally Turner permits himself only half an hour for lunch, and this one has gone on for seventy minutes. When he can take his eyes off her, he gets into a cryptic conversation with Thanee that she cannot follow. Now Turner must get back to the office.

Thanee and Chanya exchange signs of relief undetectable to non-Thais, order champagne as soon as he's gone (of course Mitch Turner never drinks at lunchtime—and very little at other times), and slowly seduce each other for the thousandth time. When they eventually arrive at Thanee's apartment, she automatically goes to the bathroom to change into a bathrobe to begin his massage. When she finds him on the sofa, also in a bathrobe, he gives her a box finished in crimson velvet. Inside is a heavy gold chain with a Buddha pendant. When she takes it out, she sees the chain is very chunky and not especially beautiful. It is twenty-three-karat gold and alone worth maybe five thousand dollars. The Buddha pendant is in gold and jade and worth double that. The chain does not really suit her, it is too hefty and ostentatious, but she knows that is not the point. This is Thanee's Thai way of taking care of her. The gold is her insurance in the United States—or anywhere else, for that matter. If she ever gets herself in serious trouble, she can pawn or sell it. Thanee is saying goodbye, in other words. For the first time in her life, Chanya bursts into tears over a man. She recovers quickly, though; only a stubbornness around the jaw tells how hard she is fighting to control herself.

He comforts her and makes love to her in a way he has never done before. His tenderness says it all. He loves her too, more than she dared hope, but neither of them is so dumb as to suppose they can run off to a desert island somewhere. The rules of the Thai feudal pyramid are etched into both their hearts. He could not possibly take her to Beijing, that would be broadcasting their intimacy in a way that would damage his wife's face, and in the East nothing is more important than face. This last party of pleasure is the best they can do, and they make the most of it. He forbids her to come to the airport when he leaves. She understands. The news of his assignment to Beijing has got out, and the press will be all over him. The airport will be no place for a *mia noi*.

We Thais do not set great store by the compulsive amplification of emotion through that distortion of the facial muscles so beloved in the West. When they say goodbye for the last time, it is in the parking lot of Thanee's apartment building. His chauffeur, a Thai, will take her home. Both are dry-eyed and solemn at the last kiss. Both know they will never meet again.

At exactly the moment when Thanee's plane takes off, Mitch Turner calls her in her apartment, where she is watching TV.

"Hello," he says, his voice dry and unnaturally high. "I hope you don't mind my calling. I guess you didn't expect to hear from me, but, ah, I did hear over the grapevine that Thanee flew out just now, and I was afraid—ah—you might be feeling a bit down. Maybe you have a lot of other things to do, but if not, I wondered, could I buy you a drink or a bite to eat? I certainly would like that very much."

"Get lost," Chanya says, and hangs up. She goes back to watching *The Simpsons,* the quirky humor of which she has only recently begun to understand.

★　★　★

The *farang* is certainly stubborn. He does not actually stalk her, he knows better than that, but he carefully chooses moments to simply show up. Thanee told her Mitch Turner is CIA undercover, ostensibly another Washington staffer taking care of lobby groups and visiting dignitaries. She wonders if he might not be abusing his professional privileges, so uncanny are the occasions when they almost bump into each other. A Thai man in that state of towering lust (her word; she doubts Turner would have called it that) would certainly start to make threats sooner or later; Turner could easily check her passport and visa on the CIA database and threaten her with deportation if she didn't give him what he wanted. She allows him points for doing no such thing. He behaves, in fact, like a gentleman in love. Quietly persistent, from sidewalks, carefully chosen tables in her favorite cafés, the odd telephone call: "Just checking you're okay, no need to feel threatened. Want me to get lost?"

"No, it's okay. I'm sorry I said that, it was a bad moment. Thanks for calling."

"Sometime when you're over him?"

"Maybe."

She puts the telephone down with a wan smile. The romantic *farang* thinks she is moping over Thanee. Well, she is in a way, but there are many ways to mope. When you've been brought up by subsistence farmers, lovesickness can be something of a luxury, and Chanya has a problem. Thanee paid three months of her rent on her small apartment and has left her with ten thousand dollars on top of all the gold and expensive clothes. In addition, she still has the thirty thousand dollars she saved in Las Vegas. But when the rent and the money run out, she will be back to ground zero as far as making a fortune in *Saharat Amerika* is concerned. A week after Thanee leaves, she calls Wan to ask her if there are any places vacant at the sauna of the hotel where she works.

Wan fixes her up with an interview with the boss, a Hong Kong Chinese, who sees her potential instantly. Samson Yip makes sure she understands that this is the United States, not Asia, especially not Thailand: feds are everywhere. They are especially interested in Asian women who work in massage and sauna businesses. Some of the men who come for massages are FBI hoping to sting the joint. The slightest hint of soliciting for work on her part would be a disaster not only for her but for him, Samson Yip, too. Yip is short and fat and does not share her reluctance to sport huge quantities of gold. His own necklace is even chunkier than hers, and a lot uglier. As a Thai, she is familiar with the Chinese mind. He is ruthless and greedy but straight. He will not try to cheat her. In return, she better not try to cheat him if she wants to stay in America. Understood? Good, so this is how it is.

More than half the men who come for massages or to use the sauna baths are foreigners. Some are sophisticated Europeans, especially French and Italian, with whom a certain understanding is possible. Many are Asians, especially Japanese and Chinese, who generally know how to play the game. Samson Yip tells her she can use a certain very limited amount of discretion in such cases. Americans, on the other hand, are strictly off limits unless he personally gives her the go-ahead.

After a week he sees he's been wasting his breath. Chanya is far too smart to make a false move. Yip tells her never to take a customer back to her apartment. He supplies a room in the hotel. The room changes from day to day, sometimes from hour to hour, so she will not draw too much attention. Of course, certain employees in the hotel know what is going on. Keeping them quiet is part of his overhead.

Within two weeks he has doubled her hourly rate. Within a month she is his star worker. It isn't merely her good looks and physical charms; those three months with Thanee have polished her natural talents. Diplomats especially appreciate a certain subtlety in her approach, a new charm to her conversation. All the men like the way she makes them feel special. It is almost like not being with hired flesh, more like having found the woman of your dreams waiting for you in a sauna bath.

So when Mitch Turner shows up for a full-body massage, she gets the shock of her life. She's been so careful, tried to make sure he is not following her when she comes and goes from the hotel. She has only a very limited understanding of the difference between FBI and CIA. She hasn't heard from him or seen him for more than three weeks, so she assumed his passion was spent and his mind flipped on to some other obsession in the feckless way of American men. But here he is, with a white towel wrapped around his loins, lying on the massage couch, waiting for her.

She makes no sign of recognizing him, simply treats him like any other customer, except that she is especially careful not to do anything that might be misconstrued. Her massage technique has improved somewhat, although to tell the truth she has never exactly been of professional standards. In his case she carefully leaves out upper thighs and buttocks. She has to admit he owns a superb musculature, one that is obviously the product of many hours pumping iron. Neither of them says anything personal or gives any sign they know each other, until half an hour into the massage, when she tells him to turn onto his back and their eyes lock. She turns her face away to speak to the wall.

"Why are you here?"

"Because I'm obsessed with you."

"I don't want you to come here again."

"How can I stop myself?"

"I'll leave, go to another city."

"I'll find you."

"I'll go back to Thailand."

"I'll find you."

"I'll cut your dick off while you're sleeping."

"That's the most Thai thing I've ever heard you say."

She hadn't considered he might be familiar with Southeast Asia.

When she's finished with his massage and he's left, Samson Yip calls for her to go see him in his office. He asks her about her last client. She tells him truthfully all she knows. Yip looks grim, in a state of shock almost.

"He knew everything. Every damned thing. Even the numbers of the rooms we use. He must be FBI or CIA. He'll close me down if you don't do what he wants. It's up to you—you can run away, or you can see him. He claims he only wants to get to know you better, have dinner a few times, no sex, just give him a chance. He's weird enough to actually mean what he says. What will you do?"

"Tell him I'll have dinner with him once. That's all. No sex. If he wants more, I'll run away—or he can have me deported if he wants. Up to him."

Yip nods, his big oval face of many chins concentrated in puzzlement. "Just tell me one thing. He seems like a good, clean-living American with a strong career—the kind of man women like you come to this country to marry. Why do you keep rejecting him?"

Chanya looks into Yip's face and sees only money, greed, stupidity. "Because I'm a whore."

Yip nods again. He isn't so stupid after all. He

is just testing to see how smart *she* is. "You're right. An American like him could never forget or forgive. Once the first months of passion were over, he would torture you with it for the rest of your life."

"Worse than that, he would torture himself."

The Chinese grunts. He's worked with whores all his life. The way they are able to read men at a glance still astonishes him from time to time.

Mitch Turner takes her to a Thai restaurant in Adams-Morgan, just off Columbia Road. She is impressed that he knows not to take her to an upmarket Thai place, where the chile is diluted and the food virtually tasteless. This one is budget to mid-range and frequented by Thais. The food, although not quite the standard of a Bangkok food stall, is not at all bad. One of the waiters happens to be a young Japanese, and for the duration of the evening she is convinced Mitch Turner brought her here to show off. When she gets to know him better, she will revise that view, but she is impressed. He looks so totally American, the kind that might boast he doesn't own a passport, but his fluency and obvious familiarity with Japanese manners causes her to revise her estimation upward. What she likes most is his deference to the young waiter's background, even to the point of bowing. Very few *farang* can call on such courtesy. She allows him one of her more generous smiles. He is as delighted as a schoolboy.

There is no need to sleep with this man to have him in the palm of her hand—he is safely nestled there already.

He hardly drinks at all, which disappoints her a bit. Thanee taught her to enjoy a bottle of wine over dinner, and the tension in the air could certainly do with some help from alcohol. Unfortunately, he seems afraid of it. She settles for a single glass of red wine; Turner drinks mineral water.

Another surprise: he's not bad at small talk. Not as good as Thanee, of course, who could talk amusingly about soap bubbles—there is a self-consciousness in the way Turner chats about Washington, this and that—but he's not nearly as heavy as she feared. In return she confides how much she loves *The Simpsons,* in the enthusiastic tone of a recent convert. He smiles. Giving nothing of his profession away is clearly second nature to him, however. The meal is almost over before he comes to the point.

"I'm sorry I put the heat on Yip. I was desperate. Now you've done what I wanted, and you're having dinner with me. I'm a man of my word—anyone who knows me will tell you that—so I won't be bothering you again. If you say no next time I ask to see you, I'll take that as final. Just do one little thing for me. Read this." He hands over a book-sized package that she has already noticed. "It's in Thai. If you don't have a lot of time, just read the New Testament, especially the four gospels."

She looks at the package in bewilderment.

When he drops her at her apartment building, he says: "I don't want to sleep with you. Not till we're married. I just want to see you from time to time." A painful smile. "I want to court you. I'm very old-fashioned."

She stares at him, holding the book in one hand, her Chanel handbag in the other. She admits that for a full minute she is seduced by the prospect of a simplified, safe, clean, scrupulously moral existence with a strong, honest, devout man who will never let her down, who will provide for her and their children and generally enable her to live happily ever after. Then she realizes she's thinking about soap opera, not life. His timing has certainly added to the unreality. Is it part of American culture to virtually propose on the first date?

Her revised opinion is that this is a very dangerous relationship for one of them. As an illegal immigrant, she can only suppose the victim will be her. Nevertheless, she acknowledges that he has won this round. She will not refuse to see him again. But there is one thing he has to understand: "No way am I going to get close to you without sex. Whatever your God thinks about that, you better tell him: no courting a Thai girl without a lot of sex. Tons of it, till it's coming out your ears."

She ignores the pained expression on his face as she turns to walk to the lifts. She had decided not to turn again to look or wave at him, and he is quickly obscured by a concrete pillar. When she reaches the lift doors, she stops in her tracks. The voice of Homer Simpson calls out: "Chanya, say Chanya, I got tickets for the Springfield Isotopes game next Saturday, wanna come?" She turns quickly, even tries to search for him in the parking lot, but he is gone. She is gaping in wonder. That was not merely the mimickry of a gifted amateur, that was a perfect, professional-quality imitation, and more than a little eerie.

As she ascends to her apartment, she is thinking:

> Chanya catches strange fish this time. Twenty minutes in bed with him, and Chanya will know everything. His face not so bad, but he's ashamed of it. Wants to be pretty American boy. Something unreal, like movies. In Amerika everyone in the movies. Maybe he can't get it up?

What a disaster that would be, to marry a man only to find out he's useless between the sheets. But why has she decided to see him again at all? Financially she's doing extremely well at the sauna, and she could hook any number of Asian men whom she knows in the diplomatic corps and who are constantly calling her, all of whom would understand her so much better than the *farang*. Karma is a weather system too complex to analyze.

Once in her apartment, she dumps the Bible on a table, still in its package, and forgets all about it.

★　　★　　★

243

So who is Mitch Turner? Chanya would have been surprised to know how many people have asked themselves this question. She realizes after the first supper that he has told her nothing personal about himself at all. Even the Thai translation of the Bible, which could seem a charming and intimate gesture by a pious man, was clearly a contrived event, something not quite what it seemed, as if the piety were all in the acting.

He waits a whole three weeks before asking her out again, this time to the Iron Hearth near Dupont Circle. No chiles here, it's high-end romantic, with lamb chops in paper garters at finely laid tables around a blazing fire. Did he realize he was setting himself a trap? It is not the kind of restaurant where you can decently not drink wine. He makes a good, knowledgeable choice of a Napa red, which is fine by Chanya, but he hardly takes more than a couple of sips from his glass. Halfway through the meal the bottle is three-quarters empty, and Chanya puts down her glass to stare meaningfully at him. She has done almost all the drinking but is only slightly tipsy. Self-consciously he takes three or four sips, then puts his glass down. She continues to stare. He picks the glass up again to drink a little more. She doesn't let him off the hook until he has drunk all of it. Apparently satisfied, she allows the waiter to empty the remains of the bottle into her glass.

"Isn't she the most beautiful goddamned thing you ever saw in the whole of your life?" Mitch

244

Turner, red faced, suddenly demands of the waiter, who shares an astonished glance with Chanya.

They skip dessert, and she has to fend off his advances in the cab all the way back to her apartment. His greedy, strong, needing, famished hands are everywhere. When she threatens to slap him, he giggles. "It's coming out my ears, Marge," he whispers in that perfect—and eerie—imitation of Homer.

Once in her flat, she takes him in hand whore-style: a shower together first, when she carefully washes his private parts in cold water, with no effect on his impressive erection. Softly humming to himself, he covers her breasts with liquid soap and tries to write his name in the bubbles. In bed he comes alive in a way she could never have predicted.

In fact, he's amazing. Twenty-five minutes in, and he's still pumping away and she is bucking and humping under him, sustained mostly by professional pride. To his very tender "Did you come, darling?" offered in a French accent, she is compelled, as a truthful Buddhist, breathlessly to admit: "Three times."

"Me too." He chuckles and goes on humping. By the fourth climax she is reconsidering the Christian Bible. Maybe there's something in it after all?

Even after he's finally finished and she's taken him to the shower again and they are lying side by side, that single glass of wine is still working its magic. He lies there spilling his guts like a schoolboy. After his life story (he went to a strict religious school in Arkansas, Yale, studied in Japan), he starts into Washington gossip of the most virulent kind.

It seems that Mitch Turner was brought up by strict Southern Baptists, and his father was a senator. He has a sister to whom he is very close, and two brothers, both successful businessmen and near billionaires in the telecommunications industry. But it is his strange repertoire of accents and voices that holds her attention and astonishes her with the accuracy of the mimickry. His rendering of the large range of different characters that seem to inhabit his body is so precise, she has to cover her mouth from the sheer weirdness of his theater. When he leaves, she can only shake her head. A strange fish indeed.

In her diary Chanya admits to a certain irresistible callousness concerning Mitch Turner and alcohol. She will see it work over and over again, that most amazing metamorphosis. Turner is thirty-two and loses about half of those years every time he drinks. The mysterious process renders him useless for all social purposes, but in private he's a big, hyperhorny sixteen-year-old with a dozen different identities and a lot of fun. From now on she always keeps a bottle of red wine at home. The ritual never fails. He enters guilt-laden, tense, serious, taciturn, heavily mysterious, hinting that he doesn't know how much longer he can go on sinning with her. She gives him a glass of wine, and within minutes he's peeled off the whole of his adult personality and turned into a big, groping, babbling baby. After sex he invariably unloads, psychologically. The problem, though, is that this unloading involves a number of increasingly contradictory stories. In some variants of his personal history, his beloved sister disappears and is replaced by a lovable but wayward brother whom Mitch is perpetually saving from ruin. Sometimes his mother is a Catholic from Chicago. Quite frequently his father is a wastrel who abandoned the family when Mitch was four years old. (Mitch got to where he is today by dint of brilliance and scholarships.) In yet other variations, his father was a diplomat who was stationed in Tokyo for years; hence Mitch's fluency in Japanese.

Another woman might have seen danger signals, but experienced prostitutes are used to listening to men tie themselves in knots. She assumes he has a wife and family somewhere and does not credit Chanya with enough intelligence to detect the contradictions. Slightly amused at the extent to which his prejudice has led him to misjudge her, she admits she looks forward to his visits, to witnessing his dramatic personality change, the extraordinary sex, and best of all the funny, wild, infantile babbling-in-many-voices that in her humble opinion makes him a kind of genius. Let's face it, she's known one hell of a lot of men, and not a single one ever made her laugh like this. True, it's the laughter of astonishment, of disbelief, but isn't that what men in love are supposed to be able to do to a girl? She hasn't had this kind of fun since she was in Thailand.

The detached Buddhist side of her also notes that his dependence on her is already a little scary. Twice he has admitted that he feels reborn. Or to be accurate, born for the first time. Now that he's known fun, Thai-style, he can see just how totally fucked up his childhood was (his expletive). Or was this simply American bullshit?

She is fascinated by the extent to which he has underestimated her and likes to trick him into ever more glaring inconsistencies.

"Mitch, tell me the truth now. Was your father really a senator?"

"Dad? Sure, one of the finest on the Hill, a fine upstanding American, the kind you'd trust your fortune to, or your wife."

She gazes at his glass. Recently she has subtly increased the dosage. She bought two balloon-sized wineglasses that can hold half a bottle each. She has poured maybe a quarter of the Napa red into his, and he has sipped maybe a third of that.

He grins. He knows she is waiting for him to drink some more and go through his metamorphosis. Slightly tipsy already, he sniggers a bit. She smiles. He takes a gulp. Of course, he is thinking about the sex they are about to enjoy—another marathon for sure—while she is waiting with her usual fascination for the personality change. A couple more sips, and here it comes. His face flushes, a new light comes into his eyes.

"So what was he like really?"

"A total shit, a twenty-four-karat asshole," Homer Simpson says.

She has doubled up on the sofa. It's the dramatic shift of consciousness, so total and so blatant, coming without warning or apology. To her it's the most literal illustration of the truth of Buddhist doctrine, which explains that there is not one personality but a million modes of consciousness. Properly understood, an individual can choose any one of them at any time, although the enlightened choose none at all.

"An asshole?" She's laughing so hard, she can hardly get the word out.

Her laughter—the laughter of a beautiful woman whose charms, to him, have grown to mythic proportions—is highly contagious. She can see this clearly enough. (Whatever else is fake, his obsession for her is authentic, or she really has lost her knack for reading men.) He joins her on the sofa, where she is still laughing from deep in her gut, an abandoned belly laugh. "You know, once he turned the TV off because it was showing two dogs fucking?" That really sets her off. She winds up on the floor helpless for a full five minutes. But is it true? What are they both laughing at, exactly—theater or reality? Perhaps the contradictions are deliberate after all, to see if she would play this game by his strange rules. For a moment she thinks she understands: this is a variant of a kind of sex play common in men who visit whores: her function is to enter into some long-suppressed world of childhood, which is the only place he feels alive. As if to confirm her suspicions, he begins an extraordinary and hilarious five minutes when he mimicks brilliantly every TV personality whom she names.

In the middle of the hilarity, he suddenly stops laughing. She has not seen this before, although it will recur with greater frequency from now on: a hole has suddenly opened up somewhere in his mind, he is swallowing nervously, and his face is racked with some complex emotion, whether guilt or resentment or plain old fear is hard to say, and he gives no explanation. Perhaps he is unaware of his own change of mood? She reaches to his glass on the coffee table and hands it to him. He drinks greedily, finishing the glass. Within seconds the hilarity is back. She steers clear of dangerous themes and lets him undress her. She makes a note never to ask about his parents again.

What exactly is his attraction for her, outside of the belly laughs and the sex marathons? Why does she put up with him when she could get the same money from a hundred other johns? Any whore would understand: this strange man has shared his complexity with her. In a career that has already spanned nearly ten years, all she has known of men is the oversimplified commercial transaction, a pasteurized, time-limited congress uniquely appropriate for the modern West if only they would change their hypocritical laws. The way she sees it, Mitch Turner is her real introduction to *Saharat Amerika*. Maybe it *is* love that brings a smile to her face when he stands in front of the mirror, admiring his triceps and worrying that he isn't going to the gym often enough anymore. In a handsome man this vanity might be embarrassing, but in him it's a form of charm. Like a woman, he is constantly working on improvements. For a long time he has been planning an epic tattoo on his back but cannot find the right body artist here in the States, where most tats are so lurid. Next time he goes to Japan, he'll seek out the best. Japanese tattoos—*horimonos*—are a genuine form of art and can be quite exquisite. Maybe one day he will summon up the courage to spend a month in Japan to undergo a full-body *horimono*.

On her one and only visit to his apartment (his personal sense of security is extreme) she finds that it is exactly a reflection of him. At first glance everything seems to be under control, all items in their proper places, as if his ménage is permanently in a state of combat readiness; then she finds the gigantic terrarium full of big, hairy, and exotic spiders, and his bedroom walls covered with photographs of naked Oriental women elaborately tattooed. The porn doesn't bother her half as much as the spiders. Is this a normal hobby for a grown *farang*?

251

One evening, when she is in a somewhat hostile mood toward men (a spot of trouble at the sauna bath, which drew a reprimand from Samson Yip), she breaks her own rule and confronts him with the most glaring of his contradictions so far:

"Mitch, just level with Chanya for a minute. Your father was a senator, or he left you all when you were young, or he died in a traffic pileup when you were twelve?"

There's no doubting the speed of his mind: "It's all true. The man I call my father, the senator, was actually my stepfather, who my mother married after Dad deserted. Dad did abandon us when we were all young, and he did die in a traffic pileup when I was twelve—but none of us had seen him for more than eight years by that time."

"And your mom: a Baptist from Texas or a Catholic from Chicago?"

"Mom? Well, she was both. She was born a Catholic in Chicago, but when she married the senator she converted. That was the one stipulation he made—after all, he was giving her one big leg up the social ladder by marrying her."

"And your beloved sister Alice?"

A cloud passes quickly over Turner's face as he changes the subject. "Want to know about my childhood, really? It was hell, as simple as that. Hell as in the kind of deliberate, planned, petty-minded torture of a concentration camp. Why have you brought this up? You know it upsets me."

"Okay, okay. Why you study Japanese?"

The question brings another furrow to his brow. He does not answer for quite some time. She thinks he is wrestling with another of his astonishing and very Western demons and waits in anticipation. Finally he says it: "An old World War II vet introduced me to Japanese pornography." She gasps in astonishment. He explains.

Then as now the Japs were way in advance of the West in this important industry, and by the age of thirteen, thanks to the vet, Mitch Turner was already a connoisseur of the genre. He and his best buddy kept a virtual library of mail-order magazines from all over the world. It took Mitch and his pal a month of intense analytical research to confirm empirically that Japanese quality control won the day, in porn as in so many other industries. You could practically feel the quality of the girls' flesh, almost hear the moans, just by looking at the magazines. When they got into video, the difference was even more obvious. With their very artistic tattoos, the highly inventive situations so far in advance of the women-in-school-uniform cliché of the Western model, the sheer variety of the S&M, you could see why the Jap economy was doing so well. Turner saw futon after futon occupied by naked and artfully tattooed young women, all the way from Fukuoka to Sapporo.

"So why you join the—ah—thing you joined, the Company?"

Mitch Turner suddenly grins: "They wanted spies who were fluent in Japanese. At the time there was concern the Japs were stealing American industrial secrets in a government-sponsored program. And I'm a genius at passing exams, so I got through the recruitment stuff no problem." A condescending smile: "I have a photographic memory and an IQ of a hundred sixty-five—genius level."

"So you can be anyone you want?" She is aware how provocative this question might be and deliberately locks eyes with him, in a kind of challenge. She watches his confusion carefully, until he seems to decide on a new direction. With a thoroughly convincing beam: "You know, I don't think I could live without you, now that I've found you. You're the only woman in the world who has ever understood me."

But the alcohol is wearing off, Mitch Turner's metamorphosis is going into reverse, and soon the guilt and the responsibility will claim him all over again. Chanya thinks there is time for one last innocent question: "So you screwed your brains out while you were in Japan?"

Too late, the chemical reaction has reversed itself, the impermeable Outer Layer is creeping over him like rust, protecting that bizarre inner core from further oxidation. "No, I didn't."

"Why not?"

A shrug in which there is more than a little contempt all of a sudden, even revulsion. "There are better things to do during your short time on earth, Chanya. I hope you'll see that someday. I do wish you would read that Bible I gave you. How much do I owe you for today's massage?"

She has grown used to it. At the end of every session, even when they have spent the night together, he will suddenly pretend that he hired her for a simple no-sex massage and insist on paying her whatever she asks. She has learned to play up.

"For the massage? Five hundred dollars." When he has paid up in crisp new bills, which he must get from the bank every time especially for her, she says: "When will I see you again?"

A somber shake of the head. "I don't know. I'm not sure we should continue with this. It's wrong. It's not good for either of us, and I really do need to think about my responsibility to you, about what I'm doing to your soul. I don't think we'll be seeing each other again for a while."

She agrees, making the appropriate expression of regretful acceptance. *She* knows he'll call again in a day or so, but does he? How lost between two minds is he?

This is a question she will not be able to answer until it is way too late. She is all alone in a big rough country, after all, and as tough as she is, there are times when a big lonely hole opens in *her* mind, too. Once, not thinking, she rang him at his office to tell him about that episode from *The Simpsons* when Marge got breast implants. She had his number because he'd made a point of giving her his business card when he was drunk.

("I want you to call me every hour on the hour, I want to hear your voice, I want to talk dirty with you for hours and hours": of course she knew better than to use it when he was at work and sober.) Now, suddenly cognizant of what she has done, she holds her breath, not sure how he'll react. Maybe she's gone too far and he'll break it off for real this time? A long pause, then: "Marge didn't mean to get implants—it was a screwup at the hospital." A pause. "I'll take you to lunch. Where do you want to go?"

"Jake's Chili Bowl?"

"That's black, not a good idea."

"Oh yeah, that's right."

"Tell you what. Dress up for business, and I'll take you to Hawk and Dove, up on the Hill. I'll tell everyone you're part of the Thai ecology delegation. They're here for two weeks to try to stop Americans from buying up huge chunks of their nature reserves. Ad lib if anyone comes up to talk to us."

Chanya has not had a chance to be a real human being since Thanee left. She doesn't realize how much she's missed playing the exotic Oriental trade delegate until Turner mentions Hawk and Dove, which Thanee took her to twice. The Thai diplomat bought her a black business suit of American cut (pants, not skirt), which she now wears for Mitch Turner, along with the big chunky gold necklace with Buddha pendant that she has never worn outside her apartment. With her hair pinned up and her mascara cunningly applied in the way taught in the beauty salons, black high heels and a serious expression on her face (Thanee once taught her how to do American Grim, advising that it was the best facial expression for getting things done in the United States), the combination of severe trouser suit with extravagant Oriental gold makes her look not so much part of a lobbying group as a member of the Thai aristocracy.

Context is the most magical of powers. In Hawk and Dove, sitting on a stool next to the very serious Mitch Turner, who never does anything but Grim while on duty, it is clear that staffers who serve the needs of members of Congress assume she is a foreign dignitary of enormous importance and treat her with a respect she didn't know her soul craved. She decides she loves Hawk and Dove and will extract frequent visits there from Turner as a price he has to pay for the deepening of intimacy, even though at this very minute he is experiencing something of a crisis, not believing he's had the reckless balls to take her there at all. Surely there are customers of hers among the clientele?

She looks around with a studious expression on her face. Nope, no man whose cock she's serviced, as far as she can remember. Mitch Turner's flesh turns gray, and he orders a bottle of wine.

In her diary Chanya tells us no more about this lunch, or by what process they wound up back at her apartment, where they proceeded with the usual ritual. The lunch has had an effect on him, though, that neither anticipated. In bed afterward Turner, still high from his medicine, reflects on the wisdom of introducing her to his parents. She does not ask which set of possibly fictional mothers and fathers he has in mind. Obviously, they are playing a variation of the usual game. The mood is light and careless, and Chanya is caught unawares.

"Not a good idea, Mitch. I'm Thai. Thai women have reputation, you know."

Pensively: "But you did so well at lunch today. I could always tell them that you're here on some kind of trade delegation. They won't know the difference. You'll have to meet them sooner or later."

"No, I won't."

Watching that hole open up in his mind is more than a little scary. Surely only children experience such lightning mood swings? His face is contorted with fury, quite suddenly, without warning. But what world are they in, exactly? Which parents are they talking about? The senator and the sister disappeared from view weeks ago; in the most recent version he was brought up by an eccentric aunt.

"You're saying you're not going to marry me?"

The incredulity in his voice says it all: *What, a third-world whore passing up the chance of a lifetime?*

"I don't want to talk about it."

"*I* want to talk about it. Chanya, I'm sorry to

have to say this, but I can't go on any longer, I really can't. I don't think you realize how much I'm compromising here. You haven't even read anything of that Bible I gave you."

To shut him up: "Okay, I'll read the Bible, then we'll talk."

She has no idea why her reading the Bible should be a precondition for discussing marriage—after all, he has not shown the slightest interest in Buddhism—but she wants at all costs to do something about his sudden black mood. This is the first time she really admits to herself that alcohol may not have a totally benign effect on this *farang*.

When he leaves, she makes an effort and reads the four gospels in the Thai translation, then goes to the beginning and reads Genesis before losing concentration. She can truthfully say she has never heard such infantile mumbo jumbo in her entire life. Christianity, it seems, is a miracle religion, with the blind being restored to sight, lame people suddenly walking, the dead raised, and to top it all that enigmatic fellow who talked in riddles managing to resurrect himself and walk around with the holes from the crucifixion still in his body. And what about the God himself, who happens to be male of course, who started it all? What a jerk to plant those two trees in paradise and then tell Adam and Eve not to eat their fruit. In her mind the whole book is a kind of extension of Mitch Turner's fantasy world. *The Simpsons* is more compelling.

Fed up with being the recipient of condescension, she gives him her view of the Christian Bible straight, without pulling any punches, and waits for the reaction. Strange expressions pass across his face; his forehead is alive with furrows; then: "Actually, you're probably right, Christianity is total bullshit. See, I'm going into politics one day, and in this country you need a church to get anywhere in public service. You've shown me I have a ways to go. I should thank you for that."

Frowning, she asks a question that would never have occurred to her prior to exposure to Washington. "You're going to run for president one day?"

Mitch's face turns grave, as if she has hit a personal truth too deep for discussion. He makes a tolerant smile but does not reply.

Chanya is not amused this time. This man is simply a tangle of tricks, a lightning-fast but disembodied mind spitting out explanations that change from moment to moment. Maybe politics is the one profession where he really will excel?

Chanya's diary shows that their relationship began to deteriorate from that moment on. She sees that alcohol is having a negative effect, indeed he begins to be an increasingly nasty drunk, and she stops giving him wine. He, on the other hand, has started drinking at home for the first time in his life (he claims). She seems wearied by the continual conflict and does not trouble to record their arguments except one in which Mitch Turner takes the side of feminism.

Chanya: "So here all the women are men. You have only men in this country. Half have pussies, the other half have dicks, but you are all men. Women walk like men, talk like men, call each other assholes and cunts just like men. In other words, two hundred and eighty million people are looking for something soft to fuck." She flashes him her most brilliant smile. "No wonder I make so much money."

He flinches, searching for a way to guide the conversation. (She thinks it is his future political personality he's airing here.) Quietly and sincerely: "Women gained their independence. Maybe they exaggerate a bit, but the way they see it, they were dominated by men, almost to the point of being slaves."

"So now they're slaves of your system. The system doesn't love them or treat them well, it only fucks them. They have to slave all day in offices, work work work to make somebody rich. After work they're exhausted, but they go off looking for men. How is that an improvement?"

"But you prostitute yourself for men. So you're a slave to money."

"When you say money, you give it *farang* meaning. When I say it, I give it Thai meaning."

"What's the Thai meaning?"

"Freedom. I turn trick lasts maybe an hour, two hours, if I want I can live on the money for the rest of the week. I'm not dominated by man, and I'm not dominated by system. I'm free."

"You're still prostituting yourself. You're still working."

"Ah, you see you contradict yourself. I'm working just the same as other women, you just said it."

"But you sell your body. How's that being a good Buddhist?"

"You don't understand. I only prostitute part of the body that isn't important, and nobody suffers except my karma a little bit. I don't do big harm. You prostitute your mind. Mind is seat of Buddha." Shaking her finger at him: "What you do is very very bad. You should not use your mind in that way."

"What way? I use my brain for my work. That's not prostitution."

"Thanee told me many times Washington professionals like you don't agree with the president, the way he's doing things. He's very dangerous, could have whole world hating America. You told me he has to divide the world into good and evil because he can only count up to two. But you work for him, let him use your brains for schemes that will bring trouble on whole world. That's prostitution. Could be very very bad karma for you. Maybe you come back as cockroach."

Mitch Turner bursts out laughing. He seems to admire the wacky ingenuity of her argument.

Chanya in a fix, don't know what to do about this guy.

She thinks that probably the affair would have continued to deteriorate in the way of such affairs, they would have gone their separate paths, perhaps she would have had to leave Washington, perhaps she would have gone back to Thailand after a few more months, for she had really done exceptionally well and already had enough money to retire on. But the date of this last conversation was September 10, 2001.

Curiously, it is on this very day that Chanya, feeling depressed and exhausted from their argument, records one of those revelations that come to everyone who spends a long time in a foreign country. On the corner of Pennsylvania and Ninth she is overcome by nostalgia for her homeland. She is experiencing a revolution in attitude.

From the start something very specific has impressed her about Americans, even the humblest: it is the way they walk. Even bag people walk with purpose and energy and with total certainty about the direction they want to go in, which is a lot different to the way Thais walk in Bangkok or Surin, where the need for purpose and direction has not much penetrated the collective mind. Now she has seen quite a lot of the country, and in the process a germ of awareness has slowly grown.

They don't know where they're going, they just know how to look as if they do. They walk like that because they're scared. Some demon is whipping them from inside. Chanya will never walk like that.

For a moment she feels she understands everything about *Saharat Amerika;* it coincides with a decision to go home to Thailand sooner rather than later. She doesn't want to marry a frightened man who has perfected the art of going nowhere with such zeal and determination. To admit that you are lost seems closer to enlightenment and a lot more honest. More adult, even.

Mitch Turner calls her around three p.m. the next day, when the whole country is in turmoil. He is playing the impeccable, responsible professional, which is the character he uses for work.

"You'll have to get out." He knows, of course, that she is an illegal immigrant, has checked her out on the CIA database, perhaps even checked with his contacts in Thailand. "I don't know where in hell this is going to lead, but you can bet everyone with a foreign passport from anywhere east of Berlin is going to come under scrutiny. They're already talking of arrest without trial. You could get caught up in something that could take away years of your life."

She doesn't need to be told twice. As soon as the airlines are working again, she gets on a plane.

She is back in her home village near Surin on the Cambodian border by the twenty-second of that month. The first luxury item she buys is a Sony flat-screen TV, on which the images of 747s crashing into the twin towers are replayed over and over again, no matter the channel.

That's the end of Chanya's diary, *farang*.

PART 5

AL QAEDA

CHAPTER 27

It's early afternoon by the time I reach Soi Cowboy and open the bar. I'm keen to check with Lek after his evening with Fatima, but first I need to discuss Chanya's diary with Nong.

I *wai* the Buddha as soon as I've switched the lights on. The important thing, always, is to keep the beer and spirits replenished. Most customers drink Kloster or Singha or Heineken, and the girls of course make half their money through lady drinks, a fact which is never far from my mother's mind. She has left a message telling me to order more Kloster and tequila from the wholesalers as soon as I get in. The tequila is not a problem, in the worst case we can always buy a few bottles retail, but the Kloster is dangerously low.

When I look up at the Buddha statue, I finally understand why I'm feeling so edgy. The little guy is fresh out of marigolds. Out in the street I find a flower vendor, from whom I buy as many garlands as I can carry. (Wherever you go in my country there will be a flower vendor, her stall laden with Buddha garlands: it's a sure bet in a land populated by sixty-one million gamblers.) As

269

soon as I've smothered him in flowers, I light a bunch of incense, which my mother keeps under the counter, *wai* him mindfully three times, and stick the incense in the little sand pit we keep for that purpose and beg him to switch the luck back on. The minute I've finished, my mother Nong arrives with her arms full of marigolds.

"I was so busy yesterday I forgot to feed him," she explains from behind all the flowers. I don't say anything, merely watch while she takes in the garlands I've just hung all over him. "Oh. Well, he'll forgive us now." A beam. "We should be in for some really good luck. How did you get on in Songai Kolok?"

I make a face and tell her to sit down at one of the tables. I tell her about the diary and the all-important fact that Chanya knew Mitch Turner in the United States. Had a passionate affair with him. Nong gets the point immediately. "There could be evidence linking her to him? If the Americans investigate, they'll surely find out he was seeing a Thai girl in Washington. Even though she was traveling on someone else's passport, they might find out who she really is?"

"Exactly."

I gaze up at the Buddha and make a face. How many marigolds will it take before he forgives us for neglecting him? Nong follows the direction of my gaze, goes up to him, lights a bunch of incense, and *wais* mindfully, with rather more piety than I was able to muster.

"I'm sure you didn't *wai* him properly," she scolds. "It'll be okay now."

Now "Satisfaction" is playing on my mobile. It's Vikorn, wanting to know how I got on in Songai Kolok. "You better get over here," he tells me, and closes the phone.

The public area of the station is crowded with the usual collection: beggars, whores, monks, wives complaining about their violent husbands, husbands complaining about their thieving, lying wives, lost children, the bewildered, the ruthless, the poor. Everyone here is poor. Vikorn's corridor is empty, though, as is his room apart from him. He listens while I tell him more about Chanya's diary and the CIA men Hudson and Bright who turned up in Songai Kolok. He stands after a while, then walks up and down with his hands in his pockets.

"Look at it this way. You're a brilliant scholar with at least a Ph.D. in something hideously complicated. While still an idealistic student, you decide to serve your country by joining the CIA, which eagerly recruits you. Ten years down the track you are no longer a naïve student. Everyone you knew at college is earning twice your salary and having fun spending money. Men and women who were twenty percent dumber than you in school are now captains of industry, technology billionaires—maybe they've retired already from their first careers. *They* don't have to worry about what they do and don't say to their wives and families, *they* don't need to think that the

271

order could come from on high any minute for them to pack their bags and spend four or five years of their lives in some godforsaken dump like Songai Kolok. *They* don't suffer polygraph tests every six months, random drug tests, electronic eavesdropping. You, on the other hand, are snared in the organization. Promotion is the only hope, the only way out of an incredibly frustrating trap. Now, spying is just the same as soldiering in one respect. What you need is a nice big war to open up the promotion prospects. Since 9/11, there is only one way anyone in the Agency is going to get promotion, and that is by nabbing a few Al Qaeda operatives. Tell me, how did they strike you, those guys you met who were sniffing around Mitch Turner's apartment?"

As usual, my master has effortlessly demonstrated his strategic genius, the superiority of his mind, his encyclopedic grasp of human weakness in all its guises. "The older one, Hudson, was exactly like that," I admit.

"Middle-aged, frustrated, desperate for promotion, sick to death of the tedium of small-scale spying, wondering what the hell he's doing in the third world when he expected to be driving a nice big desk in Washington at this stage in his career, ideologically jaded?"

"Yes." It does not seem appropriate to mention Hudson's extraterrestrial origins at this moment.

"And the other one?"

"Typical socially immature *farang* male with big

ideas and tendency to walk into elephant traps." There seems no need to go into the poor boy's antecedents; people simply do not realize how boring most past lives are. Like so many of our species, Bright has been a herd animal for more than a thousand years, getting himself honorably killed in most of history's great battles. Doubt did not enter his soul until he lay limbless and dying at Da Nang, when he entertained the unthinkable: *Had he been misled?*

"Hmm." Looking at me brightly: "The great weakness of the West is that it has nothing with which to inspire loyalty except wealth. But what is wealth? Another washing machine, a bigger car, a nicer house to live in? Not much to feed the spirit in all that. What is the West but a gigantic supermarket? And who really wants to die for a supermarket?" He stares at me. I shrug. "It's simply a matter of being careful." He makes that obscene fish-tickling gesture and grins.

When I check on Lek, I find he has called in sick for two days. Nobody knows where he is. When I call Fatima, she doesn't know, either.

"Should we be worried?" I ask her.

"Darling, it was his moment. I had to kick him out of his comfortable little nest. Did he fly or not? There are no rules. If he survives, he'll be back. He can't do without me now."

"You didn't even check on him?"

"Don't be a child, darling."

*　*　*

273

Chanya in my dreams again last night. An artificial lake of the kind only seen in Rajasthan, a perfect square with a temple apparently floating on a white raft in the center. On shore, a line of forlorn young men. Each pilgrim is ferried out to the island for an interview with a Buddhist monk who resides there. When it is my turn, I find I cannot look into the monk's eyes. My hand holds out a photograph of Chanya. I wake up in a sweat.

The dream has shaken me. I don't think I'd admitted to myself how desperately I wanted her, and now I'm going through that disgusting form of anguish that is so entertaining when it happens to someone else. Having Vikorn make snide references to my emotional life is one thing, but to be outed by the transcendent is quite a different kettle of *pla*. Even so, I take a good couple of hours before I open my mobile and flick through the names until I reach C.

"Sonchai?" she says in that designed-to-melt tone that makes you want to kill her when she uses it on other men.

"I was just wondering how you were getting on."

"Were you? Did you read my diary?"

A hoarse whisper: "Yes."

"I suppose it's not that interesting, really. I just thought you would want to know the background, in case . . ."

"Sure. I understand. There are a couple of things, though, maybe we should talk about."

"There are? Like what?"

"Hard to talk over the phone, don't you think?"

"In case we're being listened to? Is it that bad already?"

"Ah, maybe, we just don't know."

"What d'you want to do?"

"Maybe we should have a bite to eat?"

CHAPTER 28

Forget it, *farang*, I'm not telling you what happened at supper. Let's say I made a total needy, clumsy, nerve-racked asshole of myself (there's a reason why love is female in all responsible cosmologies, it turns men into clowns), but the steamed bass with lime was excellent, the cold Australian white out of this world, and my uncompromising kiss smack on the divine lips when we said goodbye better than both. (If she didn't know before that I was gaga, she does now.) I'll leave it at that for the moment, if you don't mind. I'm taking it as a manifestation of cosmic compassion that she's not working anymore. No, of course I didn't tell her about the dream.

It is about ten in the evening when I return to the Old Man's Club, where my mother has been in charge. She is nowhere to be seen, but many of the customers are wrinkling their noses in judgmental style.

I trace the aroma to the covered area in the yard where Nong is sitting. She does something furtive

276

with her hands when she sees me, but it is too late.

"I thought you were on a diet."

"I am. It includes fruit."

"I'm sure it doesn't just say fruit. I bet it says citrus fruit or something. You were eating apples only a few days ago."

"Fruit is fruit. What's the difference?"

I decide to play this delicate moment artfully and put on a charming smile as I approach. Despite her suspicions, she responds to my affectionate peck on the cheek and is too slow to stop my left hand as it makes a grab for the odiferous yellow splotch on her plate.

"Thieving brat."

I munch cheerfully. Ah, durian, its exquisite melancholy decadence, its haunting viscous sensuality, its naked raw unashamed primeval pungency, its triumphantly morbid allure—oh, never mind, *farang*, no way you'll understand durian without spending half a lifetime out here.

"It's got to be the most fattening fruit in the world. Whatever *farang* concocted your diet has probably never even heard of it."

"There's an e-mail," she says, not without a tone of relief. "He's going to be delayed at least another week. Some case he's got to be in the States for."

May Buddha forgive me, I'd forgotten all about Superman. I rush to the PC and check the e-mail.

My dearest Nong and Sonchai, I'm so terribly sorry, but I'm going to be delayed. The Court of Appeals just informed me that they've moved one of my big three cases forward for hearing over the next few days. I'm representing one of the firm's biggest clients and there's just no way I can avoid being here for it. I'm going to come as soon as it's over—and I mean as soon. I'm keeping a bag packed and I'm going straight from the office to the airport the minute the case ends. I'm burning up about you two. My god, Nong . . . My god (I love you too, Sonchai, even if we've never met).

I'm mulling this over (he said: *I love you*, but then he added *too*) when all of a sudden everyone freezes because two strangers have walked into the bar.

Well, not strangers exactly. America is certainly a tribal society, isn't it? The effect they have on the old codgers in the bar makes me think of a couple of Cheyenne coming around a turning in a forest to find a band of Crow having lunch. Hudson and Bright and all the customers hitch their pants simultaneously. Hudson turns away from the wrinkled hippies with a sour look and stares me in the eye.

"Hello, Detective. Remember us?" Hudson says, almost without moving his lips, as hard, gaunt, and haunted as ever.

"Songai Kolok. You were businessmen at the time."

"And you were an American resident with a green card. Let's cut to the chase. You know why we're here?"

Wordlessly I lead them out back. Hudson wrinkles his nose, and Bright sniffs ostentatiously. *(That's a third-world stink if ever there was one.)*

"Mother, these are the two CIA spies I met in Songai Kolok, when they were pretending to be businessmen in the telecommunications industry," I explain in Thai.

Have I told you before that in our primitive society we still have courtesy? My mother takes my introduction as a signal that these two men are higher up the pyramid than she. She stands and *wais* them mindfully. Hudson, I think, wishes he had a hat to lift, and Bright is confused. He thinks about a *wai*, then gives up.

"You mean they lied to you?" my mother asks, still maintaining the polite smile.

"Lying is what they do. They're spies."

"How disgusting." Nodding politely at Hudson. "Do they speak Thai?"

"Not a word."

Returning Bright's respectful nod with a beam. "Does the Colonel know about them? Are we going to bump them off?"

"Mother, please, that would not be a good idea. The CIA is quite powerful."

"I don't like the way that young one keeps sniffing

279

at my durian. Maybe I'll bump him off myself if he keeps doing that." In English: "Gentlemen, do sit down, my house is your home."

I see that Bright is not at all certain that it would be safe to sit in a place with such a pervasive odor. Bravely he pulls up a chair, though, and Hudson does the same. Hudson has not failed to notice that he is in the presence of an attractive Thai woman of about his age group. (I see a terrible bitterness that he would be prepared to melt down and recycle for the right lady, maybe a womanly Asian with courtesy and gentleness? Could this be her?)

"The older one fancies you."

"D'you want me to seduce him, find out how much he knows?"

"You're supposed to be retired."

"The young one really thinks he's the bee's knees, doesn't he? Shall we set one of the girls onto him? I don't think he'll look like that when we show him the video of his performance with his pants down."

I have an expression of filial adoration on my face. "That's really not a bad idea. Is room ten still rigged up?"

"Yes it is, despite your puritanical objections."

Explanatory note: Dear Nong has never forgiven me for refusing to join a syndicate that broadcasts pay-by-the-minute porn over the Net, usually without the consent or knowledge of the erection owner. The secret digital camera was all rigged up and ready to go when I found out and put a stop to it.

"Who shall we ask? What is his profile?"

"Easily aroused, good basic performer with not much imagination, probably can keep it up for the full twenty minutes if he needs to, a jaw-grinder on the home stretch, a triumphalist, resents it if the lady doesn't climax. We don't want submissive, he'd only get arrogant and contemptuous. Someone smart and subtle who will drive him crazy: *Oh, I hope you'll return soon, I get so horny when I don't come, shall I get you some Viagra next time?*"

"Nat?"

"She's so flighty, but I agree she's got the talent. In the right mood she would be perfect. I'll see if she's around." In English: "Excuse me, gentlemen, I must get back to work."

"We'll put our cards on the table," Hudson says in a flat, neutral tone as soon as my mother has gone. "You have information about the disappearance of one Mitch Turner. We think he was murdered in a hotel not far from here. We think he was with one of your workers at the time." He looks at Bright. "Have I left anything out?"

Bright looks me intensely in the eye. (He *really* intends for me to *really* get what he's saying.) "See, we're Americans at war, and we don't leave our dead in the field, no matter what. It's as simple as that. We just don't do it. So it's in everybody's interest to cut the crap, cut out all the—ah—little cover-ups and conspiracies and cooperate, get the

281

thing over and done with and bring the perp to justice, because we *will* get to the bottom of this, one way or the other." Out of the corner of my eye I see that Hudson has the grace to wince. "I hope you understand what I'm saying, Detective?"

I am obliging with Third World Fear and Awe when Nat appears with a smile to ask if anyone would like something to drink. Bright does not appreciate the distraction and snaps "Water" in the same tone of Stern. He flicks his eyes up at her. She is wearing a knee-length white cotton dress of relatively modest cut, although it does dip quite a bit, and she doesn't seem to be wearing anything underneath. His eyes do not ransack her body, but the very pleasing contrast of stark white with her creamy brown legs and shoulders is hard to ignore. Contact the first.

"I'll take a Coke if that's okay?" Hudson says with considerable courtesy. (I think he was hoping for Nong to return.)

I shake my head with a smile, and Nat makes a cute *wai* to Hudson and Bright. Bright wrestles with distraction and wins. "Maybe the detective can confirm that we're all agreed."

"On what?" I ask with a smile.

"Yeah," Hudson says, "you lost me a bit. What are we agreeing on here?" Why do I sense that these two partners are not enjoying a totally satisfactory relationship?

Bright goes—well, bright crimson. "I was just trying to—"

"I know what you were trying to do. Thailand is probably our greatest ally in this part of the world. If the president wants to screw up every international friendship we have, that's up to him, but you're not the president." He looks as if he is about to say something more, then changes his mind. I am expecting Bright to turn volcanic, maybe shoot Hudson with a Magnum, but instead he makes a face of childish pique. Hudson leans forward a little, engages my eyes rather gently, even gives his own a slightly pleading hue. "Detective, look, we know what probably happened. You know who we are. Why are we here? We are here because the organization we work for is not going to rest until the disappearance of Mitch Turner is accounted for. Until then, officially no one can say if this is a case of international terrorism, a case of domestic violence, a mugging that went wrong—or what? See what I'm getting at? If something happened between Turner and one of your girls, if that's all there is to it, if there are mitigating circumstances as there probably were, after all he was a big, strong guy—we think he disappeared on a Saturday night—he was known to have a very low resistance to alcohol—he shouldn't have been in Bangkok at all—you see where I'm heading? If there are grounds for reducing the charge to manslaughter, maybe even entering a plea of self-defense, we would be able to make the prosecution listen to you, maybe cut a deal. We just need to clear the thing up one way or the other. Americans are very tidy minded. We just can't have an open file with *Unsolved* stamped on it, not in a time of war, not in the case of someone like Mitch Turner. We would like you to help us. Please."

Nat returns with the water. By leaning over Hudson to pour, she reveals much of her upper body to Bright, who is now ripe for distraction after the reprimand from Hudson. He catches himself in a stare, looks up, and finds her eyes on him. He blushes all over again. Contact the second.

"I see," I say, wondering what to do. This whole situation cries out for Vikorn's skills. What does a monk manqué know? Are we playing three-dimensional chess or two-card brag? "The thing is, it's not in my hands."

Now Hudson is distracted. He is no fool, and Nat's skills have not escaped his notice. He and I both watch with clinical interest as she leans over Bright to pour his water. There is nothing flirtatious in her manner, but she does pour the water with unusual slowness. It's a very hot night under our crude strip lights in the yard. Everyone is sweating. Almost drop by drop the pure, clear ice-cold water fills the glass, which turns opaque with condensation. The moment seems to last forever. Nat shows no mercy while Bright concentrates on the glass so as not to glance sideways at the two brown young breasts hanging very near his face. He looks swiftly up when she is done, says *thankyou* in a gruff tone. She makes a cute little bow, keeping her face serious. Contact the third.

Farang, I'll bet you Wall Street against a Thai mango he'll be back, if for no other reason than to play the card of virile youth against Hudson's superior rank and thus restore his ego after that humiliating reprimand. Hudson thinks so too. He turns away with a mixture of amusement and irritation. (Why did they have to send him a boy?) Now he is waiting for me to say more. I don't. A sigh. "Okay, whose hands is it in? This Colonel Vikorn character? He has one hell of a reputation, and it's not for being an honest cop."

"A sleazebag," Bright mutters, avoiding Hudson's glare.

I make a submissive face. "Shall I tell him you want to make a treaty?"

Bright is not at all sure if I'm being sarcastic or simply inept in my use of English. He oscillates between rage and contempt with a bias toward contempt. Hudson covers his reaction with a cough. "Yeah, tell him we want to talk. I'm sure we can work something out. It would help a lot if we were able to speak to the last person to see Mitch Turner alive. That would impress us considerably."

They both finish their water in a few gulps, then stand up to leave. I follow them through the club to the front door, keeping my eyes on Bright. Yep, there it goes, that scan of the room he told himself he wasn't going to make. Nat, of course, is nowhere to be seen.

As soon as they're safely into a taxi, I call Vikorn.

He's silent for a full minute, then: "What's your instinct?"

"We're the Indians, they're the cowboys, they want to make a treaty. They want Chanya at the meeting, Colonel."

He coughs. "Tell them to come to the bar tomorrow night. We'll close it for as long as the meeting takes."

"Will Chanya be there?"

"I don't know."

In the dead of night my mobile rings. It is Lek at last. A desperate tone (he sounds as if he's dying): "You have to help me."

Lumpini Park (named for the Buddha's birthplace) at night: love at its cheapest, but the incidence of HIV is said to be over sixty percent. In the darkness: furtive movements on benches and on the grass, muted moans and whispers, rustlings of large animals in heat, the intensity of the atomic fusion (highly addictive, they say) of sex and death. It is past midnight in this tropical garden. At the edge of the park, I have to call Lek on his mobile to find out his exact location. He is standing alone by the artificial lake, staring at a reflection of the moon in the water. When I touch him, his body seems half frozen.

"She told me to come here," he whispers after a while. "She insisted that I see it at its worst."

"She's right. That's exactly what a good Elder Sister is supposed to do."

"I feel dreadful. She totally destroyed me."

"She's just testing you. Better you see the worst before you take the big step. You have to be sure you won't end up here."

"Half of the whores here are *katoeys*," he blurts. "They've lost everything, even basic humanity. They're just . . . just creatures. I've seen them hanging out on the benches, waiting for customers, just like starving demons. Some of them have lesions. *They service taxi drivers.*"

"What did Fatima say, exactly?"

"She said she would help me if I would drink the full cup of bitterness. She said the path of a *katoey* is sacred, only *katoeys* and Buddhas really see the world for what it is. She said I had to be strong as steel, soft as air."

When I put my arm around him, he bursts into sobs. "I don't think I have the strength. I only wanted to dance."

"You think dancing is easy?"

Looking up at me with those big eyes of his: "Thanks for coming. I had a moment of weakness. I better stay here for a while. I need to see it all, don't I?"

"Yes." There's really nothing more to say.

CHAPTER 29

The Old Man's Club would not, under normal circumstances, be anyone's choice of venue for such grim negotiations, but it is the best we can do. The CIA, who are not officially here at all, do not possess an office, nobody wants to do it in a hotel room, and the District 8 police station is hardly appropriate. The only reason I am present is because Vikorn needs an interpreter whose discretion can be relied upon. The only reason Chanya is present is to take the opportunity to prove she didn't do it. (She spent the whole of yesterday locked up with Vikorn in his office.) The only reason my mother is here is that it is her club and no way is she going to miss out.

Although both Hudson and Bright have read it many times before, they take a minute to study Chanya's confession, the one that Vikorn dictated and I wrote, which they have in English translation as well as the original Thai. They both look up at the same time, and it is the young and ferociously eager Bright who speaks first. I am surprised he begins by addressing me not as the official interpreter but in my capacity as humble scribe.

"You were present when this statement was taken, Detective?"

"Yes."

"You are the one who wrote it down?"

"Yes."

"While Colonel Vikorn was present?"

"Yes."

"And these are the true words of Ms. Chanya Phongchit as spoken at that time?"

"Certainly."

"Did you think anything odd about her story?"

"No. You have to remember—"

A peremptory wave of the hand. "I know, I know, this is Bangkok, and these kinds of things happen all the time. Let me cut to the chase, Detective." He leans forward, thighs pried open by the pressure of magnificent balls (obviously). "Detective, have you ever had sexual intercourse?"

A baffled pause. "It has been my good fortune from time to time."

"And have you ever had the good fortune to do it from behind? Never mind what part of the lady's anatomy is most interesting, let's just concentrate on the position."

Chanya inexplicably covering a grin, my mother frowning and staring at me, then from me to the Colonel. I think she has seen the drift quicker than anyone. The Colonel has not understood a word.

"Yes. It's not my preferred—"

Another peremptory wave. "Spare us the comment, Detective. Let me ask you this. When you exploited your good fortune in this way, did you notice that the front of your thighs were really rather close to the backs of the lady's? Putting it bluntly, Detective, unless you have a two-foot dick, your body would have been pressing against hers most of the time for the purpose of maintaining penetration?"

My heart sinks, and my mother looks away in disgust, I think, that the Colonel and I (her son of all people) should have committed such a gaffe. Only Chanya is unperturbed. On Vikorn's order I translate the interrogation so far. To my astonishment, he also is unperturbed and responds with an avuncular smile. I should add that since the arrival of the CIA he has scrupulously and impeccably maintained the part of every *farang*'s idea of a crumpled, corrupt, incompetent, and less-than-intelligent third-world cop who only dimly grasps what is being said and who lost the plot some time ago. A slight shaking has been introduced in his left hand—a subtle addition, artistically done—and he has a half-empty bottle of Mekong whiskey on a table next to his chair. He has not shaved this morning; gray stubble catches the light nicely. A few deft touches, in other words, and the master has transformed himself—an astonishing achievement when you consider that in actual fact he *is* a decadent sleazebag third-world cop, but of an entirely different order. Any fool can play his opposite, but to play the character who is only a couple of shades away from the person you really are—now that shows real talent, in my humble opinion. Bright has been ignoring him with exaggerated contempt. This is exactly what he expected from us. Hudson so far is carefully noncommittal in his body language. Bright grinds relentlessly on, his voice rising through the full gamut of triumphalism to find its level in an excited squeak.

"Any woman who decided to castrate you from such a position, even if she had the muscles of an Olympic weight lifter, would have to cut off one of your thighs first, wouldn't she?" Just in case he is not being explicit enough for my poor understanding, he stands up, folds Chanya's statement I suppose as representing the knife, bends forward, and swings backward with his hand a couple of times. "It's the one position where a man need fear no attack at all," he adds with a triumphant smile, "not even if the lady had access to a samurai sword," and sits down.

I translate for Vikorn, who has been watching the performance with a twinkle in his eye and who, to everyone's astonishment except Chanya's, bursts out laughing and clumsily claps a few times. Bright is seriously taken aback.

"Please tell our American colleagues how smart I think they are," Vikorn instructs, his left hand shaking as he reaches for the whiskey bottle. When I have done so, I see that Hudson has finally decided to take an interest in Vikorn and stares at him for the next few minutes. "They saw this obvious flaw immediately, on the first reading I am sure." A sip from his shaking glass. "What were we thinking that we produced such an amateurish statement? How could anyone hope to fool the CIA?"

I translate. Bright is lost now and checks with Hudson, who does not take his eyes off Vikorn.

"But what were we to do, gentlemen?" Vikorn raises his hands helplessly, an impotent old man caught in something way too big for him. "Chanya, my dear, please tell them exactly what happened."

Chanya looks at me demurely. "Should I speak in English or Thai? My English isn't really that good."

I've had no warning about this development and do not know how I'm supposed to reply. "Your English is fine," I say testily. She gives me one of her smiles. I disgust myself by melting and smiling back. She speaks in Thai, I translate.

"I always wanted to tell the truth about what happened to Mitch, but I was firmly instructed that for reasons of security I should keep my mouth shut."

"That's quite correct," Vikorn corroborates.

"As soon as we left this bar that night, Mitch became certain we were being followed."

"Oh no," from Bright when I translate, who buries his head in his hands and shakes it from side to side. "Wouldn't have been two men with long black beards, would it?"

"Shut up," Hudson tells him, and nods for Chanya to go on.

"I didn't see their beards until later—only Mitch saw them at that point. He said he'd been followed before, down in Songai Kolok, that he was sure his cover was blown and that maybe there was some kind of fatwa on his head."

"I just can't believe they're even trying—"

"Will you shut it?" from Hudson. An *I'll get even* glare from Bright.

"We thought about running away, but Mitch said that wouldn't do any good. The worst would be for them to catch up out in the street. He was sure they wouldn't have guns. He thought that in his hotel room he would be able to handle them." Bright is staring incredulously, making a great drama of holding his head, rocking from side to side.

Hudson interrupts, looking at Chanya. "Okay, I get the picture. You went back to his hotel, they burst in with at least one knife, slice him up, and cut his cock off. You're embroiled in the battle, but no one wants to hurt you, so you end up covered in blood but unharmed. Let's say all that is a given. Why in hell would you have concocted that statement?"

I translate for Vikorn, who takes up the story. "Think about it, gentlemen. What has your government been saying about the security risk here in

Thailand from Islamic fanatics? And what has that done to our tourist trade already? How much worse could it get if there's a report of a genuine terrorist atrocity, right here in Bangkok? This was not something I'm qualified to deal with myself. I had to go to the highest levels of government, to the chief of our homeland defense."

Hudson sighs. "So you're saying you were told to cover up?"

"Yes. What else were they going to say? The entire story depended on the evidence of a whore."

A pause. "That's all you've got?"

"Well, there's the knife. The murder weapon."

Now Bright's jaw has dropped, but Hudson's thin lips have opened just a tad. "Right. We were going to ask you about that. You have it here to show us?"

"It's in the fridge," says Chanya, and stands up to bring it. It is carefully preserved in a plastic bag, which Hudson holds up to the light. He seems to be wrestling with a smile as he hands it to Bright, who also holds it up to the light. He shakes his head and hands it back. "I still don't buy it. So they found some frizzy black hairs to stick on it. What does that prove?"

"Anything else?" Hudson asks Chanya.

"Well, Mitch fought very bravely, and at one point he managed to get the knife off them."

"He did?"

"Yes, and when one of them tried to grab it, he

sliced off two fingers before they overwhelmed him again."

Hudson's gaze is steady now, and the smile has gone from his mouth, but there is a subtle difference in the way he is looking at her. "Kept the fingers, did you? In the fridge, by any chance?"

Chanya walks to the fridge and comes back with another plastic bag and hands it to him. Bright is trying to follow Hudson's lead, but Hudson isn't giving anything away at all. He examines the frozen fingers in the bag, then hands them to Bright. "And when we send the knife and fingers away to the lab, the lab will confirm that these fingers produced some of the prints on the knife, right?"

"I'm certain of it."

"So they found some fingers and some hairs from a black beard—you're not gonna—"

All Hudson needs to do is stare at him this time. Things have taken an unexpected turn, after all, and Bright is no longer so sure of his cynicism. He closes his mouth and leans back on his chair, thighs splayed: *Okay, wise guy, it's your show and your funeral if you screw up.*

Hudson stands and beckons to me to join him at the bar. In a whisper: "Please ask your Colonel to join us." I beckon to the Colonel, who is in the process of pouring himself another drink. Vikorn joins us, bending forward and holding his lower back. Hudson says: "Just ask him one question, please. If he were to place a bet on these hairs and fingers turning out to have DNA that the CIA database will confirm is that of a known Islamic terrorist, perhaps one who died recently—if I were to open a book on it, how much would he place?"

"Three million dollars, even money," Vikorn says brightly, forgetting his backache. "Want to?"

"No," Hudson says slowly, "we don't have that kind of cash to play with. Certainly not on a stone cold loser." He gives me a nod, surprisingly friendly.

"What will you do about your colleague?" I ask in my most polite tone. He doesn't answer except with a subtle alteration in his facial muscles. I'm not an expert on encryption, but I think that look might translate as: *Bright doesn't want to spend the rest of his career in the field either.* I say sotto voce: "Would a video help?"

A true pro, he takes in my meaning with lightning speed and shakes his head. "Keep it as backup."

"He's a jaw-grinder on the home stretch," I report, still deeply in awe of my mother's detailed knowledge of the male rampant.

A quick grin builds around Hudson's mouth and is as quickly wiped off by professional discipline. "She could tell that just by looking at him, couldn't she?"

I have a feeling Hudson will be back.

"Well," says Hudson in a louder voice, indicating to Bright to stand up, "obviously, this evidence isn't something we can afford to ignore. At the same time, our government is sensitive to any economic damage Thailand might suffer if this sort of thing hits the news." A look at Bright. "Frankly, this is going to take a while to sort out. There will be top-level meetings, Homeland Security will be involved, it'll go to the Joint Chiefs, probably the president. Any officers associated with it will attract attention." A smile. "Hopefully of a positive kind."

Bright nods thoughtfully. Perhaps he deserves his name, for his change of posture is instant and very convincing. He shakes Chanya's hand, calls her and my mother *ma'am*, and generally demonstrates courtesy all around, even gratitude as he makes for the door.

When they have gone, I confront Vikorn. "You've put the blame on Muslims. You could start a war."

He shakes his head. "Grow up, Sonchai. I took your delicate little heart into account and fingered the Indonesians. None of your new friends in Songai Kolok is implicated. You should be pleased."

When I call Mustafa, I make the same point. "But he blamed Muslims," he says, and hangs up.

CHAPTER 30

In case you didn't get it, *farang*, that was the end of the Main Plot. (You remember, the Cover-up—but don't worry, I feel a Coda coming on.) Vikorn did not, of course, expect to be believed with his cock-and-bull story, but as we all know, that is not the way the intelligence industry operates. Belief is for choirboys. What you need (apparently) is a fantastically complicated and enticing distraction that will make it quite impossible for anyone to draw a conclusion one way or the other but at the same time will offer itself as a vehicle for promotion. (I don't need to tell you this, *farang*. I think you invented this game, no?) I guess Chanya is safe for a couple of decades while they mull it over. Doesn't Vikorn just take your breath away sometimes?

As a consequence, things are a little slow here, but just at the moment I'm rather fascinated by the homely family atmosphere that has been developing at the club this past week, thanks to Hudson and Bright.

Bright first. Nat reports to my mother, who reports to me, that he's quite a good boy really.

Nat's challenge to his virility punched a nice big hole through his ego, and with the ensuing flood of light we now have a brand-new picture of dear Steve, who fell apart immediately after coitus on the third date and confessed that he's not the great tough larger-than-life patriot he appears to be (*You're not?* exclaimed Nat with an expression of shock; *No,* he admitted in a tone that recognized that some people would find that hard to believe); *au contraire,* as Truffaut used to say, the poor young fellow is all bent out of shape from a particularly ugly divorce in which *she* made the usual baseless allegations of abuse in order to get the house, the car, and the bank account and full custody of his toddler daughter, with only supervised access for him.

We watched while he went through a schizophrenic period when he was not at all sure whether he should keep up appearances or not (or *whom* he should keep them up for; I myself was treated to a testosteronic strut and a sad droopy shamble in the space of an hour), but I'm happy to report that thanks to Thai therapy, he did not take more than a week to return to the human family and now he arrives every night on the dot at eight, pays Nat's bar fine, and takes her upstairs, where she rewards him with an orgasm including all bells and whistles. (We can hear her in the bar if we turn the system down. Bright knows this, of course, because Hudson told him, but cured of hubris by my country and my women, the dear lad reappears after his heroic coupling with no more than a grateful beam on his square Nordic features.) Nat asked me to ask Vikorn how much American spies get paid these days.

But Hudson, of course, is a different kettle of fish. Talk about many-layered (and multifaceted). I have to be humble here and admit I don't know any Asian who could keep a column of oiled billiard balls in the air from day to day the way he does—or who would want to. In the finer points of mental self-abuse, *farang* lead the world. He does it all by remaining close-lipped and secretive, of course, which provided a challenge for my mother, the courting of whom has been so unobtrusive—and secretive—that no one knows if they've actually done it yet—or even if he is actually courting her or not. (Nong turns uncharacteristically coy whenever I challenge her on the point, which is more than academic to me considering how close we are now to the visit from Superman. I wouldn't put it past her to use Hudson in order to get back in form for Dad—or vice versa, depending on what sort of shape Dad is in after all these years. She hasn't resumed her diet yet, which is certainly a clue of some kind, if indecipherable at the time of writing.) No, my mother has been no use at all in the Hudson study, and I have had to build on what I've been able to glean during those very brief and few moments when he has let his guard down. See if you can work it out, *farang*. He:

1. Brightened once when he heard Wan and Pat talking in their native tongue, which is Lao;
2. Spared a glance which was neither negative nor judgmental when one of the old codgers inadvertently flashed a large bag of dope in the bar one night;
3. Has found it necessary to interview Vikorn unaccompanied by Bright or any interpreter on numerous occasions, which seemed to leave both he and Vikorn in good spirits;
4. Is fifty-six years old;
5. Joined the CIA in his early twenties and was sent to Laos after graduating from the academy.

Oh, and there's a sixth point. In a quiet moment in the bar one evening, when I was forlornly checking the e-mail for signs of Superman, he leaned over my shoulder.

"Want to do a deal? I'll tell you something you need to know if you put in a good word for me with your mum."

"Fuck off. I don't pimp for my mother."

"Sorry, that's not at all what I meant. I admire her, I respect her. She makes me tingle in places I thought were dead. So I'll tell you anyway. Listen. D'you really think Mitch Turner sat twiddling his thumbs all day down there in Songai

Kolok without making any contribution at all to our glorious Agency?"

"I did wonder about that."

"Of course you did, you're a first-class cop in your own very unique way. So think about it. What do all members of the secret world have in common? We're compulsive gossips, that's what. And who can we gossip to? Only each other. Security clearance can be a pain in the ass. You've no idea what total junk most so-called intelligence really is. Now with encryption and e-mail, a guy with Turner's clearance can listen in to every damn piece of trivia that our bugs and agents pick up all over Asia. An American woman mugged in Nepal, a dumb Yank gets into a brawl in downtown Tokyo, an American child abducted in Shanghai—stuff that shouldn't be part of our work at all but still flashes across our screens."

"Turner sat reading that junk? It doesn't sound like him."

"He had no choice. Intelligence sifting was part of his job. He would have to give an opinion on it all: valuable or not, if valuable how many stars? The whole game is basically as dumb as that. Because of the need for security clearance, guys with Ph.D.'s do stuff a schoolkid wouldn't find challenging." That thin smile of his starts to build. "Drugs too, of course. We still have to do a lot of narcotics work, the DEA are such dummies."

I stare at him, not having the faintest idea where he's going here.

He leans a little closer. "What the hell do you think she was doing with herself while he was stoned out of his brain on the opium she brought him? All she needed was his log-in code. He probably told her the number himself when he was on the dope. Opium can do that—you see the world from a whole different perspective, one hundred and eighty degrees different. Yes, I've had my moments." I've stopped working the mouse. "She's a very very smart lady. For supersmart street sense, Chanya's the finest I've ever seen." He lets the smile spread some more. "Put in a good word for me, and I'll tell you more."

"I don't care."

A chuckle as he grasps my shoulder in a manly grip. "You're a lousy liar, and I love you for it."

With the CIA apparently on my side, I take the opportunity to ask that question that never seems to go away: "Does the name Don Buri mean anything to you?" He looks convincingly blank and shakes his head.

Later that night, with Hudson gone and the bar almost empty, Su emerges from one of the upstairs rooms with something in her hand.

"Know what this is?" Su asks when I'm half in, half out of the bar, fishing something out of her handbag. Instantly I step back in, breaking into a sweat of excitement and relief, for it is

303

none other than the Super Secret Sony Micro Vault. You wondered about that, didn't you, *farang*? You said to yourself: where is that damned Micro Vault he made such a fuss about chapters and chapters ago, surely that was a Road Sign if ever there was one? Well, the embarrassing truth is that I lost the damned thing, and I've been searching all over for it ever since. Of course Hudson and Bright have been grinding on at me daily forever (nag, nag, nag: *Has he found it yet? Nah: how typical, dah dumb third-world cop lost dah Micro Vault*), but I wasn't going to put that on record out of sheer shame. I've practically turned the club upside down—now our laziest whore is holding it in the palm of her hand.

"The john was humping me so hard in room five a couple of hours ago, I had to hold on to the mattress, and this thing dropped out. I thought maybe it would vibrate, but it doesn't."

"No," I say, taking it and stepping behind the bar, "it doesn't."

"So what is it?"

"It's a Micro Vault."

"Oh."

She leans over me while I slot it into the computer and double-click with bated breath. Su and I exchange an astounded glance.

"It's a man's back," she explains, drawing on deep experience.

"I can see that."

"Pretty muscular, damned good bod, actually. What are all those green lines?"

"It's a kind of grid."

I click and click, but there really is nothing more to it.

CHAPTER 31

One night, after the two a.m. curfew, the bar is empty save for Hudson and me. He is drunker than I've seen before, though still more or less in control. Sitting on a stool, he starts to talk, as if continuing a conversation, probably with himself.

"Freedom? What kind of dumb all-purpose Band-Aid is that?" With pleading eyes: "I mean, what are we selling exactly? *Money* is the state religion of the West. We pray to it every waking minute—and we're gonna make damned sure every last human on earth gets down on their knees with us. All our wars are wars of religion." A pause. "Want to know why I'm still here, at my age? I'm just a few hundred miles away from where I was thirty years ago in Laos. Look, I've made no progress at all, not financially, professionally not much, romantically not at all, not even geographically. Why am I still here?"

I shrug.

"Same reason the other guys couldn't go back. All over Southeast Asia there are American men who never go home. We *simply can't*. Because when we look into the eyes of your people, we see something, call it what you like. Soul? The human mind before fragmentation? Something sacred we *farang* habitually amputate like tonsils because we don't understand its function? Maybe it's your damned Buddhism. But we see *something*. Now tell me this, Detective. When you look into the eyes of *farang*, what do you see?"

When I fail to reply, he sniggers. "Yeah, that's what I thought."

Three days after this conversation, everything changed. Hudson and Bright arrived at the bar that evening, looking gloomy. They ordered a couple of beers, which they took to a corner table, where they whispered together. Finally, Hudson came over to the bar with his news.

"Your Colonel's little game worked too well. Maybe he's a kind of a genius. Well, we'll see. They're sending the Boss."

CHAPTER 32

I've been summoned to the police station, and I'm on the back of a motorbike listening to Pisit, who is on the warpath over a Hollywood film star who headed a campaign to stop a factory in the north of Thailand from employing underage children. She put pressure on a certain sportswear retailer, who canceled orders to the factory, which had to close down. Now the parents of the newly unemployed kids are having to sell their daughters into sex slavery in Malaysia because of lost revenue from the factory:

> Anyone out there with information on those algorithms in the English language that make its native speakers so self-righteous, or indeed on the psychopathology of crusading in general, give me a ring on soon nung nung soon soon nung nung soon soon.

I pull off the headphones as we near the station. There was something in Vikorn's tone when he told me about this meeting last night. Apparently yet another CIA has arrived, supposedly to kick ass. The alleged Al Qaeda connection has got Langley salivating. Things are not looking so good today.

She is tall, close to six feet, slim with a military bearing, a fit and handsome fortysomething, although her face and neck suffer from that drawn quality characteristic of those beset by the vice of jogging. Her hair is very short, gray and spiky: I wonder if she and Hudson share a barber? She does not waste time or money on cosmetics; her hygienic odor includes carbolic references. The suit is iron gray with baggy pants. We are in Vikorn's office, but it might as well be hers.

Vikorn, diminished, has let her take over, at least for now. A woman was the last thing he expected. (But I think he's working on a plan.) She keeps her hands in her trouser pockets, thoughtfully pacing up and down as she talks. There is about her the restrained superiority of a senior librarian with access to secret catalogs. Hudson sits uncomfortably, perhaps even resentfully. Bright has not been invited. Nobody interrupts. I translate for Vikorn in a whisper, so as not to disturb her concentration. She has been trained to smile frequently—and inexplicably—perhaps on the same course where she learned unarmed combat?

"This is serious intelligence. Detective, I want to thank you and your Colonel for bringing this evidence to us. This is a new direction for Al Qaeda, and a surprising one. We've never seen a castration theme before, but it makes a lot of sense from their point of view." She pauses, frowns fussily, continues. "And of course there might be a revenge theme from the Abu Ghraib fiasco. How does the world perceive America, especially the Muslim developing world? As some kind of Superman caricature—with emphasis on *man*—an overmasculine society obsessed with its power and virility. If they start cutting off our male organs, it will send one of those crude, potent messages that the young, ignorant, and fanatical tend to embrace. Actually, exactly the same technique of intimidation was used by the Ching emperors, who invariably cut off the testicles of prisoners of war, which certainly wore down the enemy's morale. It's smart. Very smart. We cannot let it go unanswered."

Hudson grunts. She pauses, leans her butt against a wall, and gives Hudson a cool but collegial nod before turning to me. "Did that all get translated? Am I going too fast? I'm sorry I don't speak Thai. Standard Arabic, Spanish, and Russian are my only foreign languages."

I pass the question on to Vikorn, who looks her in the eye for the first time, then turns to me. "Ask her where she is on the U.S. Army pay scale."

She allows a quick, patronizing smile at this typical third-world question. "Tell your Colonel I'm not in the army."

"I know she's not in the fucking army," Vikorn retorts. "They're paid on the same scale. What is her equivalent rank? That's what they never stopped talking about in Laos. Has she gotten above the warrant officer grades? Is she on the O scale or not?"

She flicks a glacial glance at Hudson. "It's quicker to just answer the question," Hudson advises, staring at the floor.

"It doesn't work like that anymore," she explains to me. Slowing her speech and with still more careful deliberation: "Your Colonel is referring to thirty years ago, when the Agency was running a secret war, so the pay scale was roughly equivalent to the military pay scale. Nowadays we tend to be paid according to the Federal Government General Schedule."

"Okay, the GS," Vikorn says, fishing in his desk drawer. "The military scale is based on that anyway. What grade is she?" He takes a sheet of paper out and studies it.

She absorbs this covert attack effortlessly, as a professional boxer might absorb a punch from an amateur, and raises her eyebrows to Hudson as the man on the ground who understands the local peasants.

"He didn't like the way you were walking up and down his office. He's checking that you understand the rules of trade. Best give him what he wants."

"I see," she says with a decisive nod. To me: "You can tell him I'm Grade Eleven if that will help."

I translate. Vikorn checks with his sheet of paper. "What Step?"

"Grade Eleven Step One." Horizontal wrinkles appear in her upper forehead while he traces her position on the scale with his fingers. "But the GS can be misleading," she adds, taking control by appearing to help, in accordance with the manual. "You get extras for locality, risk, that kind of thing."

Vikorn raises his eyebrows at Hudson. "Grade Eight Step Ten," Hudson confesses.

"So she starts at a base of $42,976 before locality, while he starts at $41,808. There's hardly any difference." Vikorn is beaming.

When I translate, she shakes her head, then closes her eyes to enforce patience. In a somnambulant voice (the subject may be close to her heart despite its spectacular irrelevance): "There's a drive to change the whole package, make it more result-oriented, more competitive, more like the private sector."

"There's a lot of resistance to the proposed changes though," says Hudson. "The BENS report is not so popular."

"You read it cover to cover?"

"Yeah, there are some practical challenges, like how do you measure results in the intelligence community? The greatest successes are things that didn't go wrong. How do you give credit for that?"

She shakes her head. "It's a problem."

"You see," Vikorn says when I've translated, "nothing has changed. They were moaning about the same stuff in Laos, until they learned how to make deals with the Kuomintang and the Hmong.

They only took a ten percent cut for transporting the dope, though, in their Air America transport planes, which the Hmong thought was terrific considering what the Chiu Chow Chinese and the Vietnamese and the French used to take. It was the increase in revenue thanks to the CIA that enabled the Hmong to go on fighting for as long as they did. That was one of the most successful CIA operations. Capitalism at its best. Actually, the only successful operation in that theater." I translate.

She smiles with glacial grace. "Let's take the excesses of Laos as read. I'd like to get back to the matter in hand. Does the Colonel have any questions about that?"

"Ask her if Mitch Turner was the deceased's real name."

After a pause: "It was one of them."

Vikorn smiles and nods. "Now ask her who he was."

Slowly, deliberately, politely: "Classified."

Vikorn nods again. Inexplicable silence. She turns to Hudson.

"People can be subtle in this part of the world," Hudson explains. "He has just pointed out that in his scheme of things, which you might call feudal capitalism or realpolitik depending on your point of view, we are both underpaid slaves whom he could buy twenty times over without noticing, who are engaged in an investigation into the death of someone who probably entered the country on a false name and who, for the purposes of police investigation, may not even have existed. In other words, we may not have a lot of leverage."

I have to admire her lightning adaptation to the situation on the ground: she finds a chair, pulls it up to Vikorn's desk, and sits on it. Leaning forward with a half-smile: "*Mitch Turner* was one of the names used by a nonofficial cover operator, a NOC, who was based in the south of this country who was murdered in a hotel room and who was somehow found by the detective here. I never met him myself." A glance at Hudson.

"Me, either. He was too new. They threw him at me while I was stateside. I was supposed to meet him for the first time the week he died."

"From what I've been able to understand, he was a brilliant officer, maybe too brilliant. There are remarks in his file to suggest he would have been better used in research. He had zero resistance to alcohol, which could be a security risk, and a tendency to confuse his cover stories. I've been sent over here not because he was murdered but because of the Al Qaeda connection, which your Colonel so effectively demonstrated with those fingers and black hairs."

"He confused his cover stories? I didn't know that." From Hudson.

"I'm afraid so." To me, as if I matter (but at least I speak English): "It's an occupational hazard, especially for people with a precarious sense of identity. You stay under cover long enough, you become the cover. There are some research papers on it. Sometimes a previous cover intrudes into the present cover—after all, identity is just a repetition of cultural triggers. He also had a dysfunctional personal life, but so does every NOC. They crave intimacy, but how can one have intimacy when one is a state secret? Some of the sacrifices we require are too much for our less stable officers. And then he had an intermittent religious streak, which didn't help. I am told we took him on because of his Japanese and his high IQ, but he wasn't going anywhere in the Agency. He was seen as a potential liability and a candidate for early retirement. The kindest thing to say is that his mind was too broad, he was an intellectual, a born liberal, he probably joined us as part of his romantic search for self. Speaking off the record, his death at the hands of Al Qaeda is more important than he was. Can we get back to that now?"

"Of course," Vikorn says with a patronizing smile.

The CIA woman—she told me her name is Elizabeth Hatch, but who knows?—nods a *thank you*. "Al Qaeda killed Mitch Turner because they knew what he was, but we don't have any record of him contacting them. His few attempts at recruiting down there seem to have been futile. Are we looking at a kidnapping or a recruitment attempt that went wrong? Or are we looking at a sincere attempt to join them, which they didn't believe in?

We were eavesdropping on his communications. He was going through a personal crisis. We need to know what he was thinking, what his true intentions were, minute to minute. You're the only one we have who might be able to help. And there's this."

With marvelous cool she takes a photograph out of her pocket to show to me. I jump, show it to Vikorn, who also jumps. It is Mitch Turner's corpse, taken after they turned him over, clearly showing the bloody mass of skinless flesh where someone flayed him.

She's played her trump card with considerable finesse, without a touch of triumphalism. In a level, glacial tone: "Don't ask me how I obtained it, and I won't ask you why you suppressed it." She looks at the pic curiously. "I don't know why you did that, exactly. It *does* rather complicate the whole thing doesn't it?" Nodding at me. "Perhaps that will do for now. You are our man in the field, I think you'll be wanting to go south again soon. Would a written report be feasible this time? If your Colonel doesn't mind, I would like you to report to me directly."

"Do I have to do this?" I ask Vikorn.

He nods reluctantly. "It's a deal. They've promised to leave Chanya alone, so long as we play ball."

That night, before going to bed, I smoke a big fat spliff, kneel before the Buddha image that

I keep on a shelf in my hovel, and form an intention to contact my dead soul brother Pichai. Everyone's personal rituals are hedged about with idiosyncrasies and customized talismans, which I won't go into. Casting aside all padding, my appeal to Pichai's superior forensic insight could be translated: *Where the fuck do I go from here?*

Sure enough, that night he comes to me exuding his usual golden glow. We stand together on a high mountain over which clouds are passing at amazing speed. There is a cosmic roar in the background caused by the intense energy of this location. Pichai points to a cloud formation, which immediately takes on the crescent shape of a gigantic beaked fish leaping over a wave. Pichai is urgently trying to tell me something, but his voice is drowned by the roar of the universe . . .

Next morning I make Chanya stand before me in one of our upstairs humping rooms, stripped to the waist. I do not resist the temptation to handle her left breast, over which that particularly elegant dolphin continuously jumps.

"Where did you get it?"

She shakes her head petulantly. "I'm not telling you."

I rub her nipple between thumb and forefinger as if it were money, causing it to swell under the dolphin. "The workmanship is fantastic."

She pushes me away. "Get lost."

"If I don't find out who really killed Mitch Turner, those morons will start another war."

"I said get lost."

Well, maybe it wasn't Chanya's dolphin Pichai had in mind. Maybe it wasn't a dolphin at all, but it's the only lead I've got.

PART 6

TATTOO

CHAPTER 33

Bored with Pisit today, I switch to our public radio channel, where the renowned and deeply reverend Phra Titapika is lecturing on Dependent Origination. Not everyone's cup of chocolate, I agree (this is not the most popular show in Thailand), but the doctrine is at the heart of Buddhism. You see, dear reader (speaking frankly, without any intention to offend), you are a ramshackle collection of coincidences held together by a desperate and irrational clinging, there is no center at all, everything depends on everything else, your body depends on the environment, your thoughts depend on whatever junk floats in from the media, your emotions are largely from the reptilian end of your DNA, your intellect is a chemical computer that can't add up a zillionth as fast as a pocket calculator, and even your best side is a superficial piece of social programming that will fall apart just as soon as your spouse leaves with the kids and the money in the joint account, or the economy starts to fail and you get the sack, or you get conscripted into some idiot's war, or they give you the news about your brain tumor. To name this amorphous morass of self-pity, vanity, and despair *self* is not only the height of hubris, it is also proof (if any were needed) that we are above all a delusional species. (We are in a trance from birth to death.) Prick the balloon, and what do you get? Emptiness. It's not only us—this radical doctrine applies to the whole of the sentient world. In a bumper sticker: *The fear of letting go prevents you from letting go of the fear of letting go.* Here's the good Phra in fine fettle today: "Take a snail, for example. Consider what brooding overweening self-centered passion got it into that state. Can you see the rage of a snail? The frustration of a cockroach? The ego of an ant? If you can, then you are close to enlightenment."

Like I say, not everyone's cup of miso. Come to think of it, I do believe I prefer Pisit, but the Phra does have a point: take two steps in the divine art of Buddhist meditation, and you will find yourself on a planet you no longer recognize. Those needs and fears you thought were the very bones of your being turn out to be no more than bugs in your software. (Even the certainty of death gets nuanced.) You'll find no meaning there. So where? Ah!

Back to the case.

Where does a smart man hide a leaf? the great Sherlock Holmes once asked. In a forest, of course. Where does a smart detective start looking for a talented tattooist with the eye of a Zen watercolorist? Not in Songai Kolok, that's for sure. Soi 39, Sukhumvit might be a better bet. The clubs are all Japanese. Since we still enjoy freedom of speech over here, the notices on the door make explicit the management policy of not allowing entry to non-Japanese. I dress up in my Sunday best (it is nine-thirty on a Friday night) and stroll down the street until I come to an elaborate Buddha shrine bedecked with marigolds. I raise my hands in a *wai* and silently ask for guidance.

Trying for maximum emptiness, I stroll up and down the street a few times, then, guided by nothing at all (always the most reliable source), knock on a scarlet front door. A hatch opens, an overdressed Thai mamasan scowls, and I explain why it is in her and her boss's interest to let me in. She tends to agree.

Within minutes I am in one of those hybrid sets so beloved of the pornography industry: dungeon from de Sade, papier-mâché rock formations (with plastic chains) from Disney, costumes from Geisha (let me be frank, our girls don't wear them that well—they tend to resent the restrictions), whores from Isaan. I am led discreetly to the back of the club, where I discreetly observe the various states of passionate undress of both customers and girls on the benches all around.

The girl chained to the papier-mâché rock (a dragon lurks in a hole nearby) is quite naked and trying not to look bored while they whip her and drop hot wax onto her breasts. She smiles at me with a face serenely incapable of debauchery (she will sell mangoes from a market stall tomorrow with exactly the same happy smile) and with her eyes asks if I want her. I am about to signal *no* when I notice the serpent coiled around her navel. The club is gloomy, too gloomy to examine a work of such quality. Confident that I am not the first to make the request, I call for illumination. The mamasan obliges with a flashlight (Hitachi, rechargeable battery). Up close and without the need for a magnifying glass, I confirm my deepest forensic suspicions: this is a very superior snake: emerald green scales of *variegated shades,* an ink-blue forked tongue ravishing her belly button, brilliantly designed wings. (Not the huge clumsy things you see Saint George grappling with, but the delicate, diaphanous propellants of Oriental myth: I know I'm on to something here.) I demand that the damsel be released from her bonds immediately.

Once I confirm that I am willing to pay, the girl, whose name is Dao, slips out of her chains without need for assistance. She recognizes no social imperative to put any clothes on, so now she and I are sitting on a padded bench at the far end of the club, situated not far from other benches with other bodies in perpetual motion. The mamasan would clearly be happier if I conducted my interrogation while at least going through the motions of seduction, and Dao rescues me from professional restraints by taking my right hand and cupping it over her left breast, where I gently pull off the wax flakes. She checks my cock to see if her body is having the usual commercially desirable effect on my body (no comment), while I whisper my question lyrically into her right ear: *Where in Thailand did she get such a marvelous tattoo?*

She smiles gratefully, as if I have complimented her on a new dress, and reveals there is another. Kneeling on the bench and turning her back to me, I see that a couple of dragons (lightly done with considerable humor, hardly more substantial than clouds, masterpieces of the body artist's craft—if I were to have dragons competing for my private parts, I would certainly choose these) are fighting for possession of the dark prize. "Fantastic," I confirm as she happily straddles me and places my left hand directly on her vagina, which she informs me, in case I hadn't noticed, is quite wet.

"But the tattoos?"

"Stroke me and tell me what you want me to do. I work much better when I'm horny."

There is (let's face it) a primeval signal sent to all parts of the male nervous system when direct contact is made in this way. It's quite a wrench to pull consciousness out of the crotch area and shove it a little higher up the spine.

"It's okay, you can fuck me here if you want. The boss is a rich Japanese—he pays off the police. We can do anything you like."

"But the tattoo?"

"Ask me while we're doing it. You've got me really horny."

"I can't—I'm shy."

"Oh, you want to take me somewhere?"

"No, I . . . I can't get it up."

"You kidding? That's one hell of a stalk."

"I like to just pretend."

Disappointed: "Oh."

"Just go through the motions. That's right."

"What turns you on?"

"If you would just talk about the tattoos, that would be great. I'll pay you just the same as if we were doing it."

"Tattoos, huh? And you're not even Japanese. A customer made me have them," she confesses into my ear, working her loins with a feline motion I'm rather fond of. "He was Japanese, of course. He said he liked my body, but I was too naked without tattoos. He said he would want me much more if I had them, and then he'd pay me double, so I said okay. It worked. Without the tattoos he hardly lasted more than a couple of minutes. With them he could go on and on for ages. Every time he got tired, he would make me stand up so he could study them again and get horny. He said they were the best he'd seen outside of Japan—the guy who did it was a master."

"What was his name?"

"You like the dragon who is licking my cunt from behind?"

"Very much."

"That one took ages. He had to come back every day for a week. He sort of sketched it out first, then did the coloring. He had to be really careful—you know, to avoid infection."

"Was it painful?"

"Not too much. He used some long Japanese bamboo needles that he had a special name for. I was terrified, but actually he was very gentle. He sort of turned me on in a weird way."

"What was his name?"

"The customer?"

"No, the tattooist."

"Can't remember. Ishy something? Ikishy? Witakashi? Or maybe it was Yamamoto—I really can't remember. Can you talk dirty some more? I'm losing concentration."

"What was the customer's name?"

"Maybe Honda. Or Toshiba."

"Okay, you don't want to tell me, that's okay."

"Them's the rules. Talk dirty, will you?"

Talk dirty? Oddly enough, considering my vocation, this is not an art I have ever had occasion to master. Furthermore, ever since my incarnation in the great Buddhist university of Nalanda, sex has often taken me in an odd way. With all due respect, *farang*, I have to say you've wasted the past two thousand years with your weird tendency to suppress it. That was never the purpose of celibacy; no sir, *au contraire*, the point is sublimation. Stoke up that fire, build it into an intolerable heat, a boiling cauldron of unendurable intensity, then let it take you up through the chakras all the way to the thousand-petaled lotus in the head. I always think about mathematics at this stage—Buddhist mathematics, of course. At Nalanda it took me only five short lifetimes to work my way up from slopping-out-untouchable to the abbot's favorite disciple. With the Mogul hordes clamoring at the gates and slaughtering monks all over India, five of us worked serenely to restore the zero to its pre-Vedic dignity as the numerical symbol of nirvana (it is the number of *om*, if that helps); as such it not only represents Nothing (an obvious enough discovery, hardly worth all the credit the Arabs demand for stealing it from us) but also Everything and, naturally, every shade of value between those two extremes. My discovery was that when trapped in an equation, so to speak, it constantly changed value, thus solving the problem and re-creating it at the speed of thought. Transcendental math may not be much use for the household budget, but it remains the essence of narrative.

"What was that you were whispering?" Dao wants to know.

"Nothing. Everything."

"You're a romantic? I haven't had a romantic client for ages. Would you like to have me with another girl? Do you have a wife? You could take turns dominating me."

"I'm not married."

"Or with another man—I like that. You can

exploit me with both your cocks at the same time. It wouldn't cost double—say, fifty percent more than for one."

"Did he have a shop?"

"Who?"

"The tattooist."

"No, he came to my customer's condominium every time. There was something special about him, you know, he wouldn't have had a shop."

"What was special?"

"What are you thinking about now?"

"*Om.*"

"That's your wife's name?"

"I told you I'm not married. Did he tattoo any of the other girls?"

"No. He was sort of special for my customer. All the other Japanese men were jealous when they saw my tats, but he wouldn't say who did them. They really turn you on, don't they?"

"Umm."

"Tell you what. Carry me over to the other bench, then you can look at them in the mirror."

Why do I get the feeling she's done this before? I note with forensic zeal that as she works her buttocks the two dragons, now in full view thanks to the mirror, are performing a kind of dance, a systole and diastole, clearly a reference to the inhalation and exhalation of the cosmos.

Dao, breathless, slowly eases herself off me. "Look at me, I'm sweating. You got me all worked up, and you haven't even opened your fly."

"Sorry, I was sublimating. Just sit on my knee so I can check your belly dragon again. I really would like to have one like that. It's amazing the way it keeps its integrity even when you're doubled over."

"You want me to try to find him?"

"Could you? Do you have anything to go on?"

"The customer went with another girl—someone called Du. She hangs out at the Rose Garden. I heard he made her have a tat from the same guy. That was before me, though—he dumped her because she hit twenty-seven. Those Japs don't like old ladies."

"You must at least be able to remember what his tattoos were like."

"The tattooist? Oh yeah, that's easy. No tattoos on hands, face, or feet. The rest, well, you know, total body. He was like a walking comic strip, no part of him left uncolored. He liked to work in just a pair of shorts, so I saw everything. Then one day I asked if I could see him naked, so he dropped his pants. I tell you, his body surface was ninety percent ink."

"His cock, too?"

"Especially that. He told me that when it was hard, you could see some famous Japanese naval battle with the Americans, but I only saw it all small and wrinkled. It wasn't such a big one. I told him he could have me for two thousand baht if he wanted, and I wouldn't tell the john, but he said he didn't like women that way. I just wanted to see the naval battle."

"He's gay?"

"He didn't say that. He just said he didn't do it with women. You know how weird Japs can be."

"Anything else?"

"He had this dreadful stutter. At first I thought he couldn't speak Thai at all, but then I realized he was fluent, except for the stutter. He seemed incredibly shy, like he'd been working in the jungle all his life and didn't know how to relate to people."

CHAPTER 34

Rose Garden: the women here are all free-lancers. You could say the semiliterate Thai owners of the bar showed the kind of commercial foresight for which business school graduates pray: they decided to allow single women to sit at the bar or at the tables all day and most of the night for the price of a single coffee or an orange juice. The standard travel books duly warned of a small army of impecunious, unscrupulous whores—not all of them young, either—not disciplined by employers or pimps, untraceable and unaccountable should the john wake up in his hotel room in the middle of the night to find both woman and wallet gone. Naturally, the result was a somewhat larger army of curious *farang* men who spent a great deal of money buying themselves and the women drinks in their earnest desire to find out just how unscrupulous these girls really were. Within a couple of years the result was a roaringly successful cooperative enterprise housed in a barnlike compound upon which the owners lavish nothing in the way of decor, although the Buddha shrine is one of the largest in the entertainment industry.

Now here is Salee making her way toward me through the dense fauna of men in the forty-to-infinity age range, squeezing past women spectacularly well turned out in those designer rip-offs your government is so hysterically upset about. (In the karma of crap the fakes are indistinguishable from the originals.) Creedence Clearwater Revival are playing "Have You Ever Seen the Rain," only faintly audible against the great mating chorus all around. As I gaze across this heaving global marketplace, I note that more and more women are streaming in through the doors. Charm is automatically switched to full alert as they make their way through the crowd. Salee, though, has been here for a few hours and has grown a little despondent. She has been a freelancer since my mother sacked her last year for getting outrageously drunk and dancing naked on the bar before passing out on one of the benches. Like all great bar owners, Mum has a puritanical streak.

"How's business?" I ask with a smile, automatically ordering a double tequila.

Salee makes a face as she downs it in one. "I'm getting old, Sonchai. I'm twenty-nine this month. These younger girls are doing two, three, sometimes four tricks a night. That's about a hundred and fifty U.S. dollars just for lying down for twenty minutes four times a night. Thing is, they're not like my generation. They don't just turn a trick,

then go get drunk with their mates in a Thai bar—
they come back here again and again, so each
girl can account for four johns. They're not
like whores, they're young businesswomen, and
they're cleaning up. Some of them have web pages,
the john sends them e-mails, and they meet him
at the airport. They've got the whole business sewn
up. It doesn't leave anything for the rest of us. It's
not fair."

"Want me to ask Nong to take you back? She
will if I tell her to."

I order another double tequila, which she quickly
drinks. Shaking her head: "No, frankly she was
right to sack me. I'm at that age, you know, when
I'm not going to get along with any mamasan or
papasan. You really need to be freelance by the
time you hit thirty. It's not just the wrinkles around
your eyes or the way your tits start to droop, it's
the whole way you hold yourself. Even the
dumbest john gets the message: *This is not a girl,
this is a woman.* And they come for girls."

"How long since you had a customer?"

A sheepish grin. "This afternoon." Laughing:
"But that just proves what I'm saying. I can't
compete with the younger women, so I have to
get here around midday, while they're still asleep."

"Any Asian men come these days? I don't see
too many."

She makes a quick scan of my face but decides
not to ask: "A few. Koreans come from time to
time, and just recently there have been two

Vietnamese men—big guys with tons of muscles, I guess they're half American, from the war. They were here earlier—they took out two of the girls. Maybe they'll be back."

"No Japs?"

"Very, very few. They tend to go for the Japanese clubs on Soi 39—but why am I telling you that?"

"I'm looking for an unusual Japanese male, late twenties to mid-thirties—a tattooist." A shrug. "He has a stutter but speaks Thai. Probably a serious loner."

Another shrug. "I'm not the best girl to ask. Asian men don't like me—look, I'm tall for a Thai. You know the golden rule."

"Always be smaller than the john."

"Want me to ask Tuk? She's petite, Asian men love her. I think she does Japs from time to time. I don't know if she's with a john or not right now, though."

Surreptitiously, I pass Salee a hundred-baht note. She squeezes my hand and slips off the barstool. I order another double tequila and let it sit on the counter, waiting for her. There are women sitting on the stools to my left and right, but they are with customers whom they have begun to mesmerize with expert strokes to the crotch—just like Vikorn catching fish.

The crowd is so dense, Salee has disappeared in less than a minute. When she ceases to surface, I assume she has been distracted by a john and start to gaze about for a better contact. Then suddenly two hands are tickling me from behind. Salee is standing grinning with her friend Tuk. I order another tequila for Tuk, who downs it in one in synchronization with Salee.

"A Japanese tattooist," I explain again, "with a stutter. Maybe one of those Japs who can't talk to people—a high-tech type?"

Tuk really wants to help. She frowns in concentration. "A tattooist? Does he have tattoos himself?"

"Full body except face, hands, and feet."

"Including cock?"

"I don't want to go off the subject," I explain, and order more tequila.

"I don't know if it would turn me on or not," Salee muses. "You'd at least want to make it big, just so you could see the picture. It must be a bit like a video game."

I finish my beer and order another. The alcohol must have loosened something in my brain, which finally remembers how to be indirect.

"Know a girl called Dao? She's on the Game."

"I know about a dozen."

"She has very unusual tattoos—dragons across her navel and two dragons on her backside."

Tuk stares at me. "That Dao? Sure, I know her. I used to share a room with her—there were five of us so it was pretty crowded, and I saw her undress every night. Amazing tats. Some of the other girls wanted the same, but she wouldn't say who did them. She was going with a Japanese john who made her have them. She charged him twice as much afterward—four thousand baht for short time, eight thousand for all night."

"Did you ever meet the john?"

"No. It was very secret. I think he worked here in Krung Thep, you know, and probably had a wife and kids as well."

Suddenly Salee breaks into rapid Isaan, the language of the far Northeast, which is closer to Lao than Thai. I'm unable to follow and watch while light dawns on Tuk's face and both girls begin to giggle. When they stop, they stare at me, then start to giggle again.

"Sorry," Salee says. "It's a bit embarrassing. You know the Game, Sonchai, you know how working girls go crazy from time to time—I mean, *crazy*?"

She is being coy, and I'm trying to discern her meaning. "I don't follow."

"Sure you do. You must have seen it thousands of times. A girl gets tired of being the sex slave—she wants a sex slave of her own from time to time. Last Christmas, Tuk and I made a lot of money out of some big fat Germans who were pretty domineering and ugly too, so we decided to splash out on a couple of pretty Thai boys from the gay bars off Surawong. It was to compensate and get our own back, you know how it goes."

Tuk takes up the story. "We went to about five bars before we found a couple of boys we wanted. We took them back to our room and shared them—we smoked some *yaa baa* so we could make

337

them work all night and get our money's worth, but that's not what you want to know about. While we were touring the gay bars, we saw an awful lot of tattoos—"

"And in one bar there were a few rich Japanese women, and the weirdest thing was, they seemed to like tattoos as much as male Japanese do. I mean, these are very artistic people, right? Like us, the women were there to hire cocks, but they wanted tattoos—"

"Especially on dicks."

"So in that one bar they had a kind of tattoo parade."

"And the winner was a Jap in his mid-thirties. They kept using this word *donburi, donburi,* which we thought was about *buri,* you know, cigarettes, but it turned out *donburi* means 'total body tattoo' in Japanese."

I rub my jaw and stare at her. "It does?"

"Yes, and he won the contest—they were really great tats. But he wouldn't go with any of the women. He said he wasn't for hire; he only came to parade his tats."

CHAPTER 35

L et's call him Ishy. Never mind how I found him—yes, I visited most of the gay bars off Surawong but uncovered no more than his cold scent, so to speak. It seemed the Jap with the shocking tattoos and still more disturbing stutter was no more than an intermittent extrovert who used the bars as his shop window—he sold no flesh, only his art. Now here he is in a Japanese restaurant on Soi 39. You don't want a list of every link in the chain—each shopkeeper, whore, bar owner, bouncer, bent cop, mamasan, security guard—that led me here.

You have seen such restaurants in movies about *yakuza* mobsters: underlit, with booths in dark wood, warm sake in tiny stone jars, a secretive, whispered inebriation in which soul brothers share male truths, serving girls in frilly aprons who curtsy (when they probably should be bowing: they're Thai); it is permissible to pass out from alcohol poisoning but not to talk loudly. He sat alone in a booth in front of a pint bottle of the finest sake from the renowned distillery of Koshino Kagiro. His stutter, though appalling when sober, dissolved into a passionate loquacity when the warm alcohol infused his brain. In accordance with the *yakuza* tradition of honor and initiation, the last segments of the pinkies on both hands had been severed. He merely grunted when I sat opposite him in the booth, as if my arrival were somehow inevitable, and called for a second place setting that I might share his bento boxes of sashimi, yellowtail, bream, and tempura shrimp. He ordered miso soup for me, stared into my eyes with a kind of impersonal hostility, then said: "Put the salmon on the rice, pour some green tea over it with some miso and shredded nori."

Oddly enough, he is a tall, handsome fellow whose social skills have been irrevocably crippled by his graphic genius. How can a man indulge in small talk when his inner eye sees great epics on the smooth surfaces of his companion's flesh? When he offered to do a full-size Laughing Buddha on my back for free if I would submit to those foot-long *tebori* needles rather than a Western tattoo gun, I began to understand his speech impediment. When we were both drunk enough, we migrated from the booth to the stools at the bar.

When not full of ink and body art, his conversation debauched into the *yakuza* gangs of Tokyo and Kyoto, stories that to me owned the sadism and gigantism of an alien cosmology. It seemed, quite suddenly, that he was sharing his autobiography. Here too only the *horimono* mattered. How to persuade a thug, a failed sumo wrestler

340

(say) with room temperature IQ, that he really doesn't want that ugly blue dagger in indigo from knee to crotch on both thighs, but rather a sinuous, elegant rose bush with each petal a masterpiece of detail? The cities of Ishy's Japan fairly burst with cutthroats swarming out from Underground at dusk (each with at least one pinkie missing), masters of mutilation, intimidation, and murder, of whom he was able to save only a few from the degrading clichés of his trade and then only at the risk of his own life. Nonetheless his fame grew: in Japan even thugs have culture. Senior mobsters called upon his services, he dined and drank at famous and famously discreet men's clubs where accomplished geishas entertained him and his clients; sometimes he was asked to tattoo the women with something elegant on the lower back or stomach. With enough sake in him he was able to overcome his inhibitions and attempt to bring enlightenment to the dull minds of the *yakuza* godfathers: his art was not an offshoot of graffiti (for which he had an abiding loathing) but part of the great ink-drawing tradition of Hokusai and his predecessors.

One karma-laden night he talked that giant godfather Tsukuba out of an M16 on both forearms and into a view of Mount Fuji, snow and all. Granted, Tsukuba was extremely drunk, as was Ishy.

"Do it now," demanded Tsukuba.

"Where do you want it?" the body artist inquired.

341

"On my forehead," yelled the don, provoking a chorus of admiration for his daring. Next day, sober, Ishy knew it was time to leave his homeland for good. A very powerful mobster with a brilliant picture of Mount Fuji on his forehead was baying for his blood. Natural destinations for one of his calling would have been Hong Kong, Singapore, Los Angeles, San Francisco—which is why he chose none of them, for surely Tsukuba would be looking for him there. Bangkok was the place to hide, with its small and discreet Japanese community and the countless tattoo-hungry hookers. He kept a low profile, rarely worked from home, accepted commissions only from trusted clients (Japanese businessmen mostly, who seemed to spend much of their waking lives dreaming up erotic *horimono* with which to decorate their favorite girls, having pretty much exhausted the vacant spaces offered by their wives' bodies). From time to time, though, the artist in him craved a deeper recognition. Much of the work on his own body he had done himself, but from the start he had known that his destiny lay with *donburi:* total body tattoo. Where even his resourceful *tebori* needles could not reach, he created detailed blueprints for a trusted apprentice to follow. The result was a beautifully integrated tapestry in which the themes that dominated his life were interwoven and explored like melodies in a Mozart concerto: Mount Fuji, a Toshiba laptop, a geisha in full regalia, the first

Honda moped, a dish of Kobe beef, Admiral Yamamoto in full dress uniform, five drunken samurai in traditional body armor, each of the positions for copulation recommended by the *Kama Sutra*—and so on. In Bangkok he started parading himself at gay bars, just to exhibit his work.

Drunk together after more bottles of sake than I can remember, Ishy finally undid his shirt, then took it off. The *donburi* was like a silk T-shirt of quite fantastic quality, with a subtle symphony of colors composed on a precise pyramidal structure that, if I am not mistaken, was a clear reference to Cézanne. Thai waitresses all came to admire. "You can take off the rest of your clothes," one of them told him. "No way you're going to look naked."

So he did, and there it was, though I refrained from studying it too closely for fear of being misunderstood. The girls were less inhibited, however, and one of them worked his member, the better—she explained—to appreciate his art. Fully tumescent, his penis provided a unique and very Japanese perspective on the Battle of Midway.

Apparently most comfortable in his designer skin, Ishy poured more sake and shared his inner life.

"I was one of those, you know?"

I had learned by now that much of his conversation assumed clairvoyance on the part of the listener. "High tech from the start?"

"I never really learned to talk to people. It still

feels weird to me, which is why I stutter so much. I played games on a pocket calculator from the age of four onward. When the first personal computers arrived, I knew why I had incarnated at this time. After a while I couldn't leave my bedroom. My mother used to leave food at the door, and my dad left books. Once they had a doctor come to examine me. He said I was nuts. There was no cure, half my generation had the same problem. One day my dad left a book of *horimono* illustrations along with some Hokusai prints—he was at the end of his rope with me." Ishy paused to swallow sake. "It was like a religious experience. Actually, it *was* a religious experience. I asked my father for more art books and, above all, more *horimono*. He obliged with a virtual library. Above all others the great Hokusai stood before me clothed in his gigantic talent. Even today I could sketch a perfect copy of each and every one of the *ukiyo-e* woodblocks, and I know every stroke of 'The Breaking Wave' as another man might remember the words of a favorite song."

Ishy paused to swallow more sake and spared a moment to stare curiously at one of the serving girls who had brought a friend from the kitchen and, crouching in front of him, was stimulating his member once again.

"It was as though I was remembering a previous lifetime. I directly *experienced* the excitement of the first woodblocks: to be able to make unlimited prints: what a breakthrough! And Moronobu's genius in seeing that *ukiyo-e* was the perfect subject! I followed *ukiyo-e* from these beginnings, through Masanobu, Harunobu, Utamaro, Hiroshige, and ultimately the incomparable Hokusai. But like any good apprentice, I perceived my master's weakness. No, that's too strong a word—let us say every generation must reinterpret reality in a form most suitable for them. This is the age of immediacy, is it not? How many kids have the attention span to even visit a museum or an art gallery, much less meditate on the wonders therein? But a Hokusai indelibly etched into the fabric of your own skin, now *that* speaks to the twenty-first century, *that*— I knew—even the dullest Japanese, even a mobster, would be able to appreciate. As soon as I could, I moved into a microscopic apartment in Shinbashi, the old red-light district of Tokyo. It was exactly like coming home." To the serving girl: "You only have to make it hard, darling, you don't have to make me come."

"It's amazing."

"Thank you. Another bottle, please."

I confess I could not resist watching while, suddenly bereft of care and attention, the great battleships sank into flaccidity. But it was four-fifteen in the morning—the Japanese manager of the bar, apparently in awe of Ishy and his tattoos, had allowed us to stay long after he locked the front door—but now the serving girls were in jeans and T-shirts. Having exhausted the power and wonder of Ishy's *donburi,* they were ready to go home to bed. I myself could not think straight, otherwise I would never have made the blunder that still haunts me as I write.

"Mitch Turner," I mumbled, hardly able to remain on my stool. The name slowly penetrated Ishy's drunken skull, light dawned, and he stared at me in horror, then slid off his stool onto the floor. I wanted to assist but fell down myself. The manager helped me into a taxi. I gave orders that Ishy was to be taken care of, his address obtained if necessary by going through his pockets. It had taken a week of hard footwork to find him—I didn't want to lose him. But I fear my instructions lost much of their original clarity to the alcohol that twisted my tongue. It had been an extraordinary night. I needed to pass out.

At about ten in the morning I woke up in a panic from an alcoholic coma. In my dream Pichai had come to me again: *Why didn't you arrest the donburi?*

Staring wide-eyed into cosmic darkness: *He got me drunk. I think it was the tattoos. Who in hell is he?*

Pichai's voice cracked up as with a defective satellite connection: Renegade . . . naga in human form . . . Nalanda . . . way back . . . tattoos . . . powerful magic . . . try decoy—stakeout . . .

From my bed, head splitting with the worst hangover I can remember, I called the Japanese restaurant. Only the cleaning staff were on duty. Using Intimidating Voice, I persuaded the woman who answered the phone to get me the boss's home number. When I rang him, he denied knowing anyone called Ishy. No, he had never met a Japanese of that bizarre description—was I sure I had the right restaurant?

CHAPTER 36

Now you find me in familiar mode, *farang*, sitting in front of a computer monitor in my favorite Internet café, scrolling through various entries in the online version of the *Encyclopaedia Britannica*. You need not feel inferior, I don't know what the hell *ukiyo-e* is either. Here we are: *These depicted aspects of the entertainment quarters (euphemistically called the "floating world") of Edo (modern Tokyo) and other urban centers. Common subjects included famous courtesans and prostitutes, kabuki actors and well-known scenes from kabuki plays, and erotica. Ukiyo-e artists were the first to exploit the medium of woodblocks.*

The coincidence strikes me as almost grotesquely literary. Now Vikorn calls me on my mobile. I am summoned to the police station, where I am ushered into Vikorn's office. Hudson is there, somewhat wild-eyed, pacing up and down. The impression of a mind unraveling is quite strong. Or to be more accurate, the Alien Within is clearly taking over. I suspect an Andromedan, although I'm not an expert.

"Progress?" Hudson asks.

I tell a tall tale of tattoos and whores, a drunken night with Hokusai's posthumous apprentice, the effect that the two words *Mitch Turner* seemed to have, although in the circumstances it was hard to be sure.

"I need the Islamic connection," Hudson barks, staring at Vikorn. "That bitch is gonna have all our balls if she finds out about that little trip of yours to Indonesia." Swallowing: "I also want that fucking laptop."

Vikorn is hard to read at this moment. Is he actually intimidated by Hudson, or is he merely being obliging? My intuition discards both possibilities. Something is going on here, some drama long suppressed reaching back to before I was born. Vietnam/Laos: what is my karma here? My father? It is disturbingly easy to see Hudson as the source of the seed that became me, even though he is not Mike Smith. As Hudson turns his gaze to me, Vikorn stares at Hudson in a way I've never seen before.

"Forget the fucking tattoos," Hudson is saying. "Forget the whole Japanese connection. It's a red herring. Follow the Islamic trail. *No Victory but Allah's.*" He hesitates for a moment, then recites what I take to be the original words from the Koran in Arabic. To me his accent sounds impeccable; there is relish in the guttural tones. Defensively (catching the look on my face): "I'm a good American, I'm entitled to my schizophrenia."

He paces, goes to the window again, stares out, then begins to speak in that narrative voice that might belong to a different man, or at least an earlier version of this one. There is heavy metal in the midtones.

"Most people don't stay in the Agency very long. It's like any other job in the States—Americans get restless, bored, enraged that their talents are not properly appreciated. We move on. *We move on—* change the view every ten minutes, and you can convince yourself for a while that you've escaped the treadmill. But not forever. After a certain specific moment in life, you start to look back. You discern a pattern. Something ugly, manic, cramped, tortured, and repetitive. That pattern is what you are, what your culture has made of you. But that's not a reason for giving up. It's not a reason for becoming a Mitch Turner. It's not a reason for changing sides. You got to soldier on, right or wrong. How you ever gonna know how wrong you are, how you ever gonna learn your life's lesson, if you're just a feather in the wind? You gotta suck it all up—there's no other way."

He resumes his seat as if nothing unusual has happened. "I want you to go back down south. Stop frigging around with mad Japs and crazy Bangkok whores. Stay there for a month, a year if you have to." He passes a hand over his spiky short hair as if to enforce patience. "And I want that fucking laptop." Another pause, then: "Before *she* gets it."

I raise my eyes to Vikorn, who nods.

But I really don't want to go back down south on a wild-goose chase. A brief prayer to the Buddha does the trick. I have no sooner stuck the incense in the sandbox than my mobile starts twanging.

CHAPTER 37

T hat's exactly how I found him when I came this morning," Nat whispers, hoarse with horror, sharing wide eyes with Lek (to whom I had to talk sternly before he would get out of bed; he apologized in the cab, the estrogen is upsetting his system, he's starting to feel moody even though his nascent breasts are hardly noticeable). "I stayed with him every weekend. He gave me a key." She shows me.

We are standing in a rented two-room apartment on Soi 22, Sukhumvit. Stephen Bright had a beautiful body; its youth and sinewy texture are apparent still even though its internal organization has already failed. At this very moment cell walls are breaking down, bacteria are burrowing into previously forbidden zones, the composite has lost all integrity. The entity that played Bright for twenty-seven years is frankly relieved to be rid of its chemical prison and at the moment of writing is having a lot more fun in a gentler, kinder galaxy. He did all he could to avoid yet another early death by violence but, having performed his duty as he saw it, now looks forward to a long period of rest and recreation. He hasn't totally rejected our solar system but will probably favor Venus for his next visit. Looking at it with terrestrial eyes, though, his body, minus the penis (discarded in a cheap wastepaper bin), with a great gaping gash in his gut, purple tubes hanging out like bunches of grapes—well, what can one say? It's a mess. This time I am the one to turn the corpse over. Yep, afraid so.

Lek covers his mouth, shares another very female glance of terminal terror with Nat, then finds a carpet to kneel on while he *wais* the Buddha. Seeing this, Nat immediately joins him. (Over here it's not death but the dead who send the green balls down our trouser legs. Believe me, there's nothing more depressing than a clinging ghost on your back for life.) I wait while the two of them, palms joined in high *wais,* silently inoculate themselves with a potent mixture of magic, superstition, and customized Buddhism. Nat is the first to stand up, followed by Lek, who cannot resist a second glance into the wastepaper bin. He involuntarily touches his crotch area. (I've resisted this reflex myself, but only just.) Nat reads his mind. "It's different for you—they'll use an anesthetic, and anyway you don't need yours."

"I've always hated it," Lek agrees, "but I'm used to it, you know?"

I am watching Nat closely. The horror is genuine. So is the sorrow. She catches my eye. "Stephen Bright proposed to me a couple of nights ago. I thought maybe I'd finally got lucky. I mean, he was a serious boy, and I think he actually loved me. He'd suffered so much, you know, and he was always so grateful when we made love. He said I was a very generous lover. Actually, I didn't do anything I didn't do with other customers—he was just so grateful all the time." She bursts into tears.

"His back?"

She shudders. "That was my fault. I have this thing about tats, you know, and I kept asking him, wouldn't he like something on his back? He said he'd look into it. Then one night he surprised me with it. It went all the way from his shoulders to the top of his backside. It wasn't at all what I expected but it was amazing, I mean really superior."

"Did he tell you who did it?"

"He said it was a Japanese who was known to the intelligence community. That's all he said."

I have decided to bypass Hudson, not out of mistrust—his commitment to the meaningless is surely unimpeachable—but because I don't think I can quite stand his Arabic at this moment. The female CIA seems an oasis of sanity in comparison.

"Hello?"

"It's me, Detective Jitpleecheep."

"Yes, Detective?"

"You'd better come." I give her the address, then I tell Nat to take Lek back to the club. She puts her arm around him in a sisterly gesture, hugs him.

"I don't know if I'm really going to go through with it," Lek moans as they leave. "Maybe I'll just use tape. Lots of dancers do."

"You really want to be half and half all your life?" Nat asks gently at the door.

"No."

The female CIA arrives, with Hudson. I watch her while she stares silently for several minutes at Bright's corpse; were she not a seasoned professional, I would describe the succession of expressions on her face as emanating from deep prurience. She composes herself eventually; it's like watching someone get dressed after an orgy: "You see, they severed his penis, just as we suspected they would. And look at his back."

Hudson and I follow her directions. There is hardly any difference between him and Mitch Turner in this respect—the whole of the top layer of skin has been peeled away, from shoulders to lower back, leaving the subcutaneous blubber to seep.

"Well, at least we don't need a homicide detective to tell us these deaths are linked." She looks at Hudson. "But the ones who assassinated Mitch Turner died in that explosion in Indonesia, am I correct? So this is a brilliantly coordinated, centrally planned, high-level Al Qaeda atrocity: different hitmen deliberately copying the first murder, so as to demonstrate corporate identity. The intention is to intimidate all Americans everywhere." Biting her lower lip: "This is big. Much bigger than I thought. It's the psychology of terrorism honed to a remarkable level of sophistication. If this gets out, Americans will be more afraid than ever to travel overseas. If these kinds of killings show up in the States, as I'm sure they will sooner or later, the whole of the American mind will be held for ransom. It's brilliant, it's evil." To me: "Any crinkly black hairs? I want the best forensic investigation you can manage on this apartment. If you need any special support— for example, a kit to lift prints off flesh, analysis of microscopic fiber samples—let me know. I'll have them ship whatever you need with some skilled operators on the next plane." Looking curiously at Hudson: "This really is starting to look like war."

Hudson stiffens at this holy word.

An hour later Vikorn and I are standing together in Bright's apartment. The situation, as much as the corpse, has begun to give me a headache.

"I just don't see any way out of it," I tell him.

Vikorn is strangely unperturbed. "It's okay. I still have a few of those hairs left. No fingers, unfortunately."

"Are you crazy? Those hairs belong to a terrorist who's known to have been killed before the murder. You'll blow the whole scam."

He shakes his head at my obtuseness and at the same time takes an airmail envelope out of his pocket. He rips it open and begins shaking it around the room. Crinkly hairs fall out like black snow.

"You'll never understand them. You present dedicated *farang* with contradictory evidence, and they'll use their infinite ingenuity to mislead themselves even further."

CHAPTER 38

Elizabeth Hatch has summoned me to a private evening interview, and here I am in the back of a cab on the way to the Sheraton on Sukhumvit. In a jam at the intersection between Silom and Rama IV, opposite Lumpini Park, the driver and I listen to Pisit, who has been on the rampage all day, having finally woken up to the injustice in the way the government has ordered the police to slaughter about two thousand presumed drug traffickers, on a quota basis. The problem, as Pisit sees it: How do we know any of these people had anything to do with drug trafficking in the first place? Isn't that what trials are for? And isn't it a strange coincidence that all of them are small-time dealers, if they are dealers at all? Shouldn't a crackdown on drug trafficking at least try to include the kingpins? He's found a retired Crime Suppression Division officer to interview.

Pisit: Why aren't any *jao por*—kingpins—included in the slaughter?
Former cop: Excuse me for saying so, but that is

not a very intelligent question. If it was possible to simply kill jao por, their enemies would have done so ages ago. By definition it is very difficult to kill jao por.

Pisit: So the government has taken an executive decision to kill non-jao por and suppress crime the easy way?

Former cop: It's logical isn't it?

Pisit: Might we take the logic one stage further and have the cops kill people with no connection to crime at all?

Former cop: Are you trying to be clever?

Pisit: No.

Former cop, after ruminative silence: Actually, that's probably exactly what's happening. After all, if all you need is the appearance of a crackdown, it doesn't really matter who you kill.

Pisit: You mean this is government-by-spin Thai-style?

Former cop: You could say that.

I am curious that the CIA has chosen the hour of nine p.m. to see me. Still more interesting is the way she is dressed: a splendid navy trouser suit by Versace with white lace blouse. I find it shocking that her wrists are a-wobble with elephant-hair bracelets, and she has discreetly dyed her hair a couple shades darker. The lipstick—wet-look crimson, thinly applied—perhaps gives the game away, along with a haunting perfume by Kenzo. Is there a single

CIA officer who will not reincarnate as a chameleon?

"I felt the need for some on-the-ground experience," she explains when she meets me in the lobby. "One must resist isolation on this kind of case."

"Dancing?"

A quick look: "Is that your recommendation?"

"Traditional Thai?"

"Perhaps not."

I follow her trail of hints from the girls in bikinis dancing around aluminum poles in Nana Plaza, to the topless ones at the Firehouse on Soi Cowboy, to the naked ones at the Purple Pussycat, also on Cowboy, until we finally reach the upstairs bars in Pat Pong. It is dark in this club except for the pool of light where the star of the show is performing her act.

I've seen the banana show too many times not to be bored. Elizabeth Hatch is riveted. Suddenly, in a whisper, as if she wants to bond with me, or perhaps reward me for indulging her tonight: "One bomb in this place will be all the message they need: support America, and we'll break your economy. You don't have the intelligence operators or the security forces to protect your country, and we can't protect you either. So what kind of ally are we?" A thin, pitying smile followed by a prudish tone: "Are those really razor blades? I read about that in one of the guidebooks, but I didn't believe it. How on earth does she do that without cutting herself to ribbons?"

"It's a trade secret. D'you want me to call the mamasan over?"

"Let her finish. That is one very beautiful body."

Discreetly I beckon to the mamasan and whisper to her in Thai while the CIA studies the show. Even in Pat Pong not every girl zigzags, and I want Elizabeth Hatch on my side. The mamasan suggests a figure, though, that few girls would say no to. I tell the CIA, who nods. When the girl finishes her act, I watch the mamasan speak to her and catch the bright flash of curiosity that she casts at Elizabeth, the seductive smile. Elizabeth smiles back recklessly. As soon as she has dressed, the girl comes over to us, sits next to Elizabeth, and rests her head on the CIA's shoulder.

I say: "Shall I go now?"

In a lust-thick tone: "Just ask her, if you wouldn't mind, if there's anything she doesn't do?"

A brief discussion between me and the girl in Thai. "No, there's nothing she doesn't do. Don't hurt her."

She snaps her head around to face me. "Did you say that because I'm American, or because I'm female, or because I'm gay?"

"I always say the same thing to men," I reply with a smile.

The three of us leave together. I find Elizabeth a taxi and watch her disappear into the back with her trophy. They are moving away when all of a sudden she makes the driver stop, and she rolls down her window in back. Beckoning to me, then holding my arm when I'm close enough: "I appreciate this. I confess I'm not proud of what I'm doing." A pause. "I need air."

I smile: "I understand."

As she rolls up the window: "This is not what I generally do."

The girl beside her, now dressed in a low-cut black silk blouse and short white skirt that reveals her long brown legs, searches my eyes: *Problem?* I shake my head. No problem, just another gasping, life-starved *farang*. The taxi moves off.

It's one-fifteen a.m., which is to say forty-five minutes before the curfew. The street is alive with bodies already half conjoined on their way to the hotels all around. There are a few Western women with local girls, but the vast majority of the trade is heterosexual. Pat Pong is only a couple minutes' walk from the gay bars on the other side of Surawong, however. In the Grand Finale Club the format is much the same as in Pat Pong, except that the people on stage are all men. Most of them, in underpants, are late teens, early twenties, but quite a few are older, harder, tougher. And tattoos are everywhere.

I walk across the street to a gothic black door encrusted with nails that forms the almost-discreet entrance to the No Name Bar, a resort so sought after and so exclusive it never needs to advertise. You don't get to simply walk in without introduction, either. A child of the street knows the formula, though, and the burly, tattooed doorman lets me through.

Sure enough, the seats that surround the stage support a fair proportion of female backsides, most of which are Japanese, although quite a few are Thai working women on girls' nights out. The rest of the customers are gay, white, and male. The men on the stage are all naked and hand-picked either for their youth and beauty; for their testosteronic postures, the dimensions of their cocks; or for the quality of their decorations.

It happens that I'm just in time for the last act. The house lights dim, "Nights in White Satin" plays over the sound system, and a naked figure in black executioner's mask strides onto the stage; everyone, especially the Japanese women, gasps at the quality of the tats, which shine brilliantly under the spotlight. A naked boy and girl arrive to kneel and work his member. Soon, as the haunting sound track reaches its crescendo, the Battle of Midway arises magically from out of flaccidity. I have no idea if he has seen me or not, but even if he has, we both know it will make no difference.

I leave the club within ten minutes of entering. Back on Pat Pong the street is now so crammed with refugees from the curfew, it is hard to walk. I pause in the entrance to one of the bars to pull out my cell phone and press an autodial number. "If I give you my heart, will you give me yours?" I ask.

"Not if you're going to die."

"We have to stop him. You do know that."

A long pause. "This isn't easy. What do you want to do?"

"Live with you. Sleep with you."

Doubtfully: "Will that do it?"

My heart in my mouth: "It's worth a try, don't you think?"

A groan, then she closes the phone.

CHAPTER 39

I believe it is intrinsic to your cockeyed morality, *farang*, that when a man and woman engaged in law enforcement are forced to pretend, for strategic reasons (say, a decoy-stakeout situation), to be lovers, they must be scrupulous in preventing their false embraces from developing into full-blown copulation—correct?

Well, fuck that. Chanya and I, in our tiny love nest on Soi 39, which is the best I can afford in this expensive part of town, go at it like rabbits. Not only is she beautiful, she is also generous. Who am I *not* to love her? Her extraordinary beauty might not be of her making, but that tactile friendliness, that gentle concern that expresses itself in soft touches, sweet caresses, premeditated kindness—that is all from her soul, and I would have needed to be stone. Nevertheless, it is part of the job to parade our passion up and down the *soi*, especially in the evening when the Japanese clubs are open and the mamasans stand on duty outside, checking the street. During the day our duties are more practical.

It is a traditional little apartment, which is to

say ablutions are performed courtesy of a great tub of water out in the yard. There is a double gas cooking ring also in the backyard—oh yes, and a single rickety cupboard. There is no bed, so I bought a couple of futons that we keep side by side. I love her best in the mornings when, still sleepy, she rolls over onto her side to admit me from behind. Or do I love her best when she is horny late at night? Or is it when she's washing out in the yard, using her sarong to conceal her body from the neighbors? Don't ask me. Love is a form of insanity that pervades every fiber. It is also much increased by the knowledge that one stands a good chance of dying within the week. We keep our mobiles charged, and I check the Net every day at the local Internet café. Day after day, night after night, there is still no word, no attack. Perhaps we are growing complacent. When I remember I'm a cop, I try to elicit relevant information. Generally, she's happy to oblige but with heavy editing. Her story of the second half of her relationship with Mitch Turner is like the story of Othello without a single mention of Iago.

Chanya had returned to Thailand when the world was mesmerized by two office towers collapsing over and over on its television screens. She owned over one hundred thousand dollars and had no intention of selling her body ever again. She was twenty-nine and a little old for the Game in any event. She built a new house for her parents, set them up with twenty buffalo, which they used for breeding—a definite improvement on the hard labor of rice growing—sent her two young brothers to the best schools money could buy in Thailand, and already had proudly put her brilliant younger sister through a biology course at Chulalongkorn University. When all bills were paid, she did not have very much left, but then she didn't need much. Sometime toward the end of her Washington sojourn, beset by homesickness and self-doubt, she had determined to redress the karmic imbalance caused by her unseemly trade by dedicating her life to the Buddha. She was to be a *maichee*—a Buddhist nun. She was the queen of her village, the idol of her parents, almost a goddess figure to anyone who knew anything about rural Thailand.

Chanya did her best to make up for the lost years by spending as much time as possible with her parents, especially her father, a devout Buddhist with whom she had always been close. "To want nothing is ecstasy," he told Chanya. She knew that for him the *farang* drugs that would give him another decade on earth were a mixed blessing; they brought more obligation than joy. He really did not understand the purpose of extending his life artificially; he took the drugs out of politeness, to make her happy. She bought a Honda motorbike and took him to the *wat* most mornings for chanting, filled with envy for his innocence and vowing somehow to retrieve her own.

When she did not go to the *wat*, she woke before

dawn to watch her cousin, whom she had known almost since birth. Jiap was the same age as Chanya and no less beautiful, but she had never been tempted by money or ambition. She lived in the timeless zone of subsistence agriculture; Chanya watched the twenty-nine-year-old mother of three take the buffalo over the paddy fields in the dawn mist singing softly to the animals in the Isaan dialect, exactly as she had when they both were children and with the same weightless joy. The distance was no longer geographic; Chanya was separated from Jiap not by time or miles but by an invisible glass screen. In America, Chanya had generally felt light and free in comparison to the people she met; here she felt heavy, decadent, lost.

Gloom, though, could not squat long on her shoulders, and during the rest of the day quite different forces seemed to invade her mind. In particular there was the little problem that no one in the compound had dared mention, so it had taken a delegation from a neighboring compound to come and explain it to her one afternoon. Well, not a problem exactly, something really rather positive. The delegates, clearly, were adherents to the more worldly side of the Thai mind.

Quietly and with an infuriating reluctance to come to the point, they explained to Chanya just how brilliant her sister really was. Consistently top of her class every time, and with that extra little thing that was more than just brilliance, it was Buddha-inspiration definitely. Sure, with a little help here and there, a little sponsorship, she could get through Thai medical school, no problem. But let's face it . . .

Tired of watching them beat around the bush, Chanya finished the sentence: *Thai* medical school? The country's best doctors all spoke English fluently because they had been educated in the United States or the United Kingdom. It would take money, a quite exorbitant amount, but look what it would do for the country, to have a Thai woman from a dirt-poor background who understood the medical needs of the poor, boasting the very best medical education in the world. It would help the status of women, too.

Chanya understood very well what all the more worldly villagers were thinking, for she still thought that way herself from time to time: she had a couple more good years in her when she could make the kind of money most Thais could only dream of. After that there really were not going to be any more opportunities. Not for an uneducated girl from Surin—especially not for an ex-whore.

Chanya did her sums. She didn't want to leave Thailand again, but she reckoned that with what she had saved and maybe another year or so on the Game in Bangkok, she would have enough. What difference would one more year make in the scheme of things, especially if she made merit by turning her sister into a first-class doctor? She convinced herself the Buddha would approve and believed she could prove it mathematically. She used a calculator, and the arithmetic went roughly as follows: an average of three men per week for ten years equals 1,560, at a rate of two screws per john (one at night, one the next morning to put him in tipping mood) equals 3,120 units of negative karma. To achieve neutral karma her sister would have to effect an equal number of medium-to-heavy healings, which Chanya guessed would easily be achieved in a year or so. In other words, in return for her sponsoring her sister, the Buddha would liberate her from the karmic consequences of her trade within about a year of her sister's qualifying.

She was going to take her time, though. America had exhausted her more than she'd realized. She wanted to relax, Thai-style.

She'd left America in such a rush, thanks to Mitch's warning, that he had not thought to ask for her home address. Nor did he have her telephone number, because her American mobile did not work outside the United States. Had she wished, she could have closed the door on Mitch forever. Even with his access to CIA resources, it was unlikely he would have found her in Thailand. And that was exactly what she intended: to break off with him and his frightening (and delicious) madness forever.

There is a change of pace, though, in shifting from West to East that can be disorienting. The afternoons in her village were long and hot, and it never occurred to anyone to do anything except sleep, play hi-lo, and drink moonshine. (It was not for nothing they called it Sleeping Elephant Hamlet.) Even her cousin Jiap liked to gamble for pennies and drink cold beer. In her drive to accumulate wealth, Chanya had acquired just a little of the religion of purposefulness *(every night you make a short list*—the sober Mitch used to preach—*of all the things you need to do tomorrow. Review it at the end of the day. How much further have you gotten in achieving your goal?)*, which immediately translates into restlessness when moved to another country. If only she had waited a couple of months, the restlessness would have faded quickly, and she would have readjusted to the primal rhythms of her beloved home. But the village itself, no more than ten minutes away by motorbike, did boast an Internet café.

It was a shop house of the Chinese type owned by an old woman who, in addition to horoscopes, love potions, and astrologically based business advice, took in washing to make ends meet, and somehow along the way she had acquired a few desktop computers linked to the Net. Chanya knew that on any number of engines (Yahoo!, Hotmail, MSN), it was possible to open an account free of charge. No way Mitch could ascertain her whereabouts from those.

She didn't admit it to herself at the time, but in retrospect she realized that Mitch, with all his problems, was the nearest thing to a real lover she had ever had. (Thanee was wonderful, of course, but she was *mia noi* with him, not goddess.)

She didn't know how much she loved Mitch Turner, but that passion of his, she now saw, was immensely addictive. She did feel as if something vital had been brutally cut off from her life. There was a constant nagging at her heart—a new and quite bizarre sensation in her case.

Her first message to his Internet address at work was a masterpiece of coy:

Hi, how are you?

He replied within minutes on a private account:

Chanya? Oh my God, where have you been? Where have you been? I've been going totally insane! I've prayed every day since you left, I go to church every morning and evening now, I sit in the back of the pews, and when I'm not praying I'm crying. Chanya, I just can't make it without you. I know I'm fucked up, honey, I've got religion the wrong way, I'm totally out of touch with everything, I'm a hypocrite in my work, the whole fucking system here is a mess, I know all that, but for me the only way out is you. These last weeks I've known just one thing: only you can save me. I've just got to be with you. I'll do anything you want. You can do anything you want. You can go on whoring if that's what you need to do. We'll live in Thailand. Where are you? Look,

I know I can get a posting over there some-where. This whole Trade Center thing has got the Company totally wrong-footed. There are guys driving desks who will follow any hint, especially from someone who knows Asia. All I have to do is say I'm willing to hang out on the Thai border somewhere where there are Muslims, gather intelli-gence, check which way the beards are going . . . I can be there in maybe a month at most, probably sooner. Everyone wants to gain 9/11 points, sending someone like me to a foreign posting in Muslimland looks good on their books. Give me a telephone number, sweetheart. Please.

Couldn't we just chat on the Net?

You have to give me your number. I talked to my boss yesterday, told him I was ready to go over there, and he practically went down on his knees to thank me. Now in return you've got to send me at least your telephone number. Please, Chanya, I'm dying over here. PS: I watched The Simpsons for you last night. Homer became the official mascot for the Springfield Isotopes baseball team—it was a good episode.

Just as at the very beginning of their relationship, she found herself drawn in by some mysterious force. Perhaps that legendary *energy* that Americans were supposed to have? Or maybe just plain old female narcissism—you couldn't help but feel flattered when a man wanted you so bad he was prepared to give up Washington and live in a third-world dump just to be in the same country. She sent him her Thai mobile number. After that it was ring, ring, ring. To judge by the timing of the calls, he was a true insomniac and took the precaution of having a glass of wine before he called her, so she was protected from that heavy, preachy, serious side. Drunk, even over the phone, he cracked her up. All of a sudden those long, hot, sleepy, boring afternoons were punctuated by her straight-from-the-gut laughter.

A few weeks later he was calling her from a town she'd vaguely heard of, right at the other end of Thailand, on the Malaysian border, a place called Songai Kolok. She'd never been there herself but knew it to be a brothel town catering to Muslim men who came over in droves from puritanical Malaysia. In the flesh industry the women tended to be looked down on by the Bangkok elite.

She closed her mobile after that first call from Songai Kolok in a strange state of mind. So far it had been one long telephonic giggle, a hilarious injection of American wit, passion, energy, and optimism with not a single flash of possessiveness, intrusiveness, hypocrisy, preaching, or intolerance. She was getting the United States strictly as advertised, but she doubted he would be able to keep it up face to face. Despite his pleas she took more than a month to make that first visit down south. She steadily refused to give him her address in Thailand. He still did not know her family name.

He met her at the bus station in Songai Kolok, and she saw immediately something was wrong. It was early morning (she traveled by night), and he had not had a drink. That brooding, boiling, resentful, fragmented side was working his jaw as he took her bag, but there was more than that. He had lost weight and looked ill. Songai Kolok was not doing him any good at all. From his conversation in the cab on the way back to his apartment, he let slip how much he hated it. Quite simply, he was suffering from severe culture shock. The only other Asian country he'd visited (the only country he'd visited outside of the United States, period) was Japan, which had been a kind of reverse culture shock: in the minutiae of daily life the Japs were streets ahead of the United States, they had managed that almost-impossible thing of combining an ancient culture with hypermodern high-tech gizmos. In Japan everything was better than in America, the food, the hygiene, the nightlife, the women, the tattoos—especially the tattoos. By contrast Songai Kolok was, well, a third-world toilet.

He pointed out the window of his apartment at the police station with the hundreds of whore shacks leaning against the perimeter wall. "See that?

I watch them every night." Staring aggressively into her face: *"I watch them every night."*

So what? Perhaps he was not sure himself, but it chilled her heart when he showed her his little telescope. "They're always grinning and smiling. It's so . . . hell, I don't know."

"What is it, Mitch? What's the problem?"

A shake of the head. "How can they do it? Why aren't they in hell? How can they just do it, like they're taking a shower or something, and afterward it's all over, like nothing happened at all? Like they're good friends doing each other a favor, money for her, blow job and fuck for him? It's like, like . . . I don't know."

On her way from Surin she had changed buses at Bangkok, where she slipped into a downtown supermarket especially for him. She took out a bottle of Californian red, one of his favorites. He scowled at it but gave her a corkscrew to open it. She found a couple of glasses in his kitchen, poured him a very generous slug, and watched him drink. She waited to see if the magic still worked. At first it seemed not to, he continued to curse the filthy animalistic young people who congregated around the shacks every night, but little by little his mood altered. A light—slightly insane but preferable to the depression—came into his eyes. All of a sudden he was grinning.

Kneeling in front of her where she sat on his sofa: "Goddamned hypocrite, aren't I?"

"Yes."

"I'm getting on my high horse, and what do I really want right now more than anything in the world?"

"To screw the ass of a Thai whore."

A shocked look, then laughter. "My god, Chanya, what is wrong with me? What is it that I just can't deal with?"

She did not say: *reality*. To tell the truth, she was feeling pretty horny herself. It had been nearly five months since she'd had sex with anyone, and she'd been remembering his extraordinary stamina, when drunk. She allowed him to undress her.

After his usual command performance, he burst into sobs. "I'm so fucked up, honey. I'm sorry. Maybe this is a mistake. I don't want to see myself torture you all over again. Maybe I'm just a totally impossible, fucked-up freak?"

She buried a hand in his hair and did not reply.

She stayed with him three nights on that first visit and began to understand what had happened to him. His mind went through the same cycle as in Washington, with a vital difference. In D.C. his work had had the effect of focusing his talents, giving him something to chew on hour after hour; true, he left work and prepared for his change of personality in a grimish sort of state, but still with the feeling of having *gotten somewhere,* of having *achieved* something, of having made *progress.* In Washington, in other words, he had *purpose,* and to an American there is no higher god. Down in

376

Songai Kolok he had no purpose, his excuse to his boss for being here was false, as was obvious after the first day. With his quick mind, he saw that this brothel town was pretty much impervious to Muslim fanaticism for the very good reason that it was dominated by Muslim decadents who knew how to deal with troublesome beards. So night after night he watched the shacks. This had become his purpose. It was so *blatant.* The cops came in full uniform from time to time to talk to the girls, have a chat and a laugh, and drink a beer or two, and the johns came and talked to the girls *and* the cops, and everyone was kind of *partying.* There didn't seem to be any guilt at all. The Muslim boys were strangely respectful and polite to the girls, and as for the girls—well, you would never know they lived on the bottom rung of a feudal society; they didn't seem to carry any kind of inferiority complex at all. Actually, they seemed a lot happier than the average corporate drone. Come to think of it, they seemed a lot happier than anyone he knew, in the States or in Japan. Their gaiety seemed not in the least forced or brittle.

To a lesser spirit this would not have been so earth-shattering, but Mitch, to give him his due, saw the significance. These boys were Islamic, they were the skullcap-and-mustache equivalent of devout Christians, yet they sinned cheerfully, not appearing to notice the effect they were having on their immortal souls. *What was going on here?*

Chanya, veteran of that eternal battleground called the Western mind, supplied the answer. "None of them important, Mitch."

He blinked at her. Goddamn it, it was true. It didn't occur to any of them, not even to those young gallants, that they possessed the least importance in the scheme of things. But of course, that was where they were wrong, that was the mistake primitive people made because they had not yet received the great gift of ego.

A change of expression: Of course, in time all will change, even Songai Kolok would start to look and act like a first-world town once enlightenment had been brought to a permanently ungrateful world, and all the filth would be swept . . . under the carpet. In the meantime, though, the whole sick, immoral thing seemed to be *growing*. Through his telescope he'd seen five new huts appear since he'd been there. This was a *boomtown*, for God's sake. Booming on *sex. Muslim sex*. And no one was doing a goddamn thing about it.

Chanya had been watching the anguish pass and repass across his features. Now she said something that must surely have been the distillation of everything she intuited of him, of the West, of white men: "If you didn't torment yourself, there wouldn't be any difference, would there?"

It was quite literally too much for him to take, the idea that there was no difference at all between him and those horny young Muslim men, nor the whores nor the cops either come to that, apart from his needless self-torment. The West was mostly a structure of smoke and mirrors, after all; but it was exactly those with the biggest stake in it—men like Mitch—who found that rather obvious truth so difficult to swallow. He retreated into vanity, checked his body in the mirror, and muttered about that tattoo he was planning.

So she would open a bottle of wine, hand him a glass, and wait until that crucial thing in him started to loosen and he was able to forget purpose and laugh at himself. Purpose, though, was so ingrained, only alcohol could free him from it. At least, alcohol was the only cure she'd found so far. The problem: it seemed to make his grim even grimmer, once the effect wore off. And one other thing. This was the first time Mitch I and Mitch II had inhabited his body simultaneously, batting his mind from one end of the internal tennis court to the other and back again. She had no way of knowing that this was indeed a significant progression in the stages of psychosis. In her Thai way, she could not help seeing the funny side. With the best of intentions she seemed to have rather dismantled this big, muscular, brilliant, and incredibly important man. But how could she possibly have guessed how fragile he was?

Her visit did him good, though—there was no doubt about that. Even sober at the bus station wishing her goodbye, there was a healthier glow to his skin and a saner light in his eye. But she wasn't sure when she would be back. She refused to make any promises, and for once he was man enough to accept that. This discipline he was able to sustain for about as long as it took for her to reach home. In her handbag her mobile started ringing as she was getting off the bus.

So it went. Her worst fears were coming true. He called every day. If she didn't answer the phone, she felt pangs of guilt and fear for what might be happening to his mind. (After all, she was the reason he was in that sleazy town in the first place.) When she answered, he would seduce her with his humor, then just when she was molten, his mood would turn ugly, he would demand that she come see him, or give him her address so he could visit her.

Chanya, veteran of a thousand men, had so little experience with love tangles, she felt the need for ancient wisdom. The old crone in the Internet café seemed able to read her mind without the need for much explanation. Chanya told her it was not a love potion she needed, maybe something to cool him down. He was a *farang*, she admitted, with that excitable *farang* psychology that just could not accept life as it came. Why was he like that? He obviously wanted to turn her into an American, colonize her, in other words, as if she were some backward country that needed development. It drove him crazy that she resisted his attempts at psychic invasion. Worse, there was no hiding the fact that she owned a better mind than his. Of course, she had hardly had any education, but she could read his oversimplified moods as if he were a picture book, while at the same time he seemed to understand nothing about her. To tell the truth, he wasn't interested in who she was at all. This was understandable—he didn't want to focus on the way she made her living. But that was also ridiculous. If her work was such a problem for him, why had he come halfway around the world to be with her? This was him all over, a thoroughly divided mind: fatally attracted to the thing he loathed, or thought he loathed, driven to transform her into the thing he thought he wanted but actually hated. The minute he turned her into an American, of course, he would be bored and disgusted. He was a Christian, she added.

The crone knew nothing about Christians, but she knew a thing or two about crazy men, *farang* or otherwise. For her generation living in that part of Thailand next to the Cambodian border, there was a sure cure, a universal cure, that *farang* in their ignorance had driven underground. In her day if you caught the flu, suffered depression, needed an anesthetic, or simply wanted to improve your home-made soup, nature provided all you required in the form of the poppy. Try a little opium, she advised. Slip it into his wine or his food. Once he'd started to appreciate it, teach him how to smoke it. No one ever hurt anyone while they were on opium, and there was no hangover, no ugly mood change such as that caused by alcohol. The crone had once been married to a violent alcoholic and held all

381

fermented liquor to be an abomination that ought not to be legal. In her shop all alcohol was banned, even beer. She sold Chanya a few grams of opium and a pipe. She showed Chanya how to prepare the pipe, and also how to prepare the opium if she wanted to slip it into his wine. The next time Mitch called, she agreed to go see him again in a week.

Throughout the whole of the interminable bus journey down south, her stomach was in knots, and she resented him for it. If this was love, then maybe she'd had enough of it already. She was dreading his mood when he met her at the bus station, for once again she would arrive early in the morning.

Hard to say if it was an improvement or not, this unshaven man who met her bleary-eyed and exhausted. She was horrified at the deterioration that had taken place within so short a time, but at least he did not start nagging her. On the contrary, he seemed apologetic, quite unnaturally so.

He admitted he'd got hold of a couple of *yaa baa* pills the night before. After an hour, he'd been so terrified of the effect the meth was having on him (violent paranoid fantasies, a strong temptation to jump out the window), he bought a bottle of cheap Thai whiskey and drank it all. Probably the whiskey had saved him because it had made him vomit. Meth and alcohol don't mix, she told him. He could easily have killed himself. A shrug of indifference and a slightly insane grin. Incredibly for an American, he had not brushed his teeth that morning. They were dirty, and his breath smelled.

"So what? I feel like a dead man anyway. You're destroying me. I don't know how you do it, or why you do it. D'you know why you're doing this to me, Chanya? Is it because you hate Americans? Are you in league with our enemies?"

A hand to her mouth. "Mitch!" Then: "I'm leaving."

"No, no, please honey, I didn't mean anything, just a joke, you know, pretending to be paranoid, an American joke, you wouldn't understand. Stay, please stay. If you go, I'll kill myself, I swear it."

He was on his knees, holding her legs tightly as if saving himself from disaster. She thought of the opium in her handbag. "Have a glass of wine, Mitch. Calm down. This is crazy. You think I came all this way to be with a crazy man?"

She watched him drink the wine mixed with opium, wondering if perhaps she *was* destroying him. After all, wasn't she the one who'd taught him to drink? And now she was adding opium. Well, it might be a short-term expedient, but the atmosphere in the small flat was so claustrophobic, the madness in his eyes so frightening, that anything would be an improvement. She was administering emergency medical aid, she told herself. And maybe saving her own skin. This *farang* might be wasted, but that was an awesomely powerful body still.

CHAPTER 40

C ome on, *farang,* admit it—you've always wanted to try a little O, haven't you? Only the once of course, just to see, no? Naturally not with close family around, probably not even with any of your peer group who might snitch on you to the boss just when you were being considered for promotion, but if you got the chance to experiment (you know) on some private little vacation that you and your partner agreed you could take on your own to find yourself and your meaning during your midlife crisis (or your post-teen crisis, or your thirtysomething crisis), perhaps in some exotic foreign country somewhere in Southeast Asia? *Opium*—the word alone seduces, doesn't it? It's so alluring, so literary, so special, so rare these days.

They do O tours up north near the Laotian and Burmese borders, although they don't call them that, of course. *Adventure* is the word. You get the elephant trek through the jungle, the bamboo raft on the river, all the ganja you can smoke—and a couple of very special nights in one of those flimsy bamboo shacks you see so much of in Vietnam movies, sharing a pipe or ten with those colorful mountain tribesmen and women (whose children, for reasons lost to history, know all the words to the song "Frère Jacques" and are liable to belt them out at the slightest provocation). And why not? It's not as addictive as TV, than which there is no greater mental pollutant. For centuries the white man was a passionate trafficker, even fighting righteous wars to uphold his sacred duty to alleviate the burden of existence for Asia's teeming billions with a drug already deemed dangerous to white men. (Ring a bell, Philip Morris?) Nowadays there's a lot more profit in prescription tranquilizers and home entertainment . . . think about it.

There was a touch of Thai coolness (perhaps repugnant to you, *farang,* but somewhat charming to me) in the way Chanya watched for his reaction to the opium. The alcohol reached his brain first, with the usual effect. His mood changed, he joked with her and commenced to undress her. They took the ritual shower together (he called it *whore hygiene*), and her body worked the usual magic. There was no doubt about it, at these moments he literally worshiped her. She could not cynically characterize it as simple lust—there was such reverence in his love-whispers, such gratitude at the relief their coupling would bring to his feverish mind, such genuine awe at her beauty, especially when she smiled. What woman would not be impressed? This was heady stuff, better than the movies and apparently authentic.

Just when he slid his muscular thigh over her body in preparation for mounting her, he gave a long, slow incredulous grunt of satisfaction, like a man who has finally broken the curse of a lifetime. His right leg lay heavy across her own, and she was able to experience the progressive relaxation of the muscles. One by one they opened like flowers, giving up their insane energy, that mad grasping that the Buddha identified as the source of all karma and therefore all suffering. She was so surprised and impressed (the old crone really knew a thing or two after all) that all she wanted to do herself was to lie there, as if she also had taken opium. It was such a relief to experience this great masculine tornado finally let go, the catharsis was hers as well as his. They lay like that for fully ten minutes with him staring at the whorls in her right ear and her listening to the relaxed, deep breathing of a mind that had temporarily healed its terrible wounds. Peace rearranged his tormented features.

It was difficult to overestimate the effect this moment had on her: all of a sudden the expression on his face was normal, human. For more than a year she had assumed that this strange giant was a being—a *farang*—constituted differently from anyone she had ever known. Now she was witnessing a transformation in which he returned to the human family, with the inevitable implication that everything that went before was a form of insanity, a *farang* delusion leading nowhere, walking evidence of a whole society's failure to grow up. She was in shock. Finally she managed gently to push his leg off and lay him on his back. He held her for a moment, staring unseeing into her eyes.

"Marge," he whispered.

"Yes, Homer," she replied, doing her best to imitate the cartoon character despite her Thai accent.

The teeniest little chuckle as he spun off into some intriguing puzzle where she could not follow. She put a pillow under his head and wrapped a towel around herself and left him there. Eight hours later he came around feeling delightfully refreshed and in the most serene of moods.

"Opium," she told him. "I put opium in your wine."

The news didn't puncture his serenity at all. Just as the crone had predicted, he asked her for more.

CHAPTER 41

How like a *farang* to find a sweet spot in life and then ruin it by excess! In the golden days of opium, a gentleman smoker would restrict himself to a couple of pipes a night and might live to be a hundred, contentedly carrying out his daily chores with the confidence that an exotic vacation from the mundane awaited him on his divan in the evening. (Buddha knows where you get the idea that the unvarnished monotony of the inventory-obsessed mind is normal and *healthy, farang.*) No one thought the poppy was the answer to life's problems; everyone understood it as merely a break in the interminable workings of the mind; nobody expected to stay high all day.

Chanya made several visits to Mitch after his opium debut. The drug almost replaced her as his main focus of attention, and he always wanted more. He became expert in the use of the pipe, and she grew accustomed to his smeared eyes and stares into the middle distance. The upside was his great gentleness and gratitude. From the depths of serenity he was a perfect lover and husband, although their sex life did reduce in intensity. That also was probably no bad thing. She liked the long, contented silences, during which the *farang* obsession for filling space with noise was replaced with—glorious emptiness.

On each visit she brought more opium, but with a sinking heart. The crone was becoming alarmed at the amount the *farang* was consuming. She didn't see herself as a dealer at all—she simply gave people who needed it the traditional herbal cure that was part of her culture. It went with her role as village crone. Finally she warned Chanya she wasn't going to sell her any more. The last thing she needed was some *farang* drug enforcement agency on her back, or the local cops demanding a cut. Chanya determined to tell Mitch he would have to quit, because she couldn't get him any more of the drug. For once, though, fate seemed to intervene in her favor.

On her next visit Mitch told her a strange story that, in retrospect, she realized had a profound effect on him, although how much was truth and how much fantasy was impossible to say; he at least seemed to believe it.

One evening about a week before, on returning to his apartment from one of his interminable roams around the small town, which he now knew like the back of his hand, he slid his key into his door only to find it open. The truth was, he had grown somewhat absentminded with the various drugs he was abusing and could not be sure that he'd locked it in the first place. As he walked in, however, two pairs of hands pulled him into the front room and silently closed the door behind him.

The scene before him so exactly resembled his worst nightmare that for a moment he was quite paralyzed with fear. The two young men who were holding his arms looked like burly Malays in skullcaps. Seated on the floor was an imam of some kind with a long gray beard, Muslim robes, and a highly decorated cap. Seated around him were about fifteen men, most of them middle-aged, all in skullcaps, who clearly were disciples of the holy imam. The two young men forced him to sit on the floor, facing the imam.

After the first wave of quite devastating paranoia, which made it hard for him to breathe, his training returned to the extent that he panned the group to check for weapons. He saw none, and indeed even the two young guards were unarmed. Mitch's muscles were so developed from decades of pumping iron, he reckoned that he could probably overpower the young men and make a run for it. Evidently this thought had not escaped the minds of the imam and his group, who were making gestures with the palms of their hands that seemed to be requesting him to stay seated. He made a quick assessment. If this group intended to kill him, they could do so whenever they chose. If he escaped from this room, they could easily assassinate him before he reached the airport in

Hat Yai—before he could leave Muslim Thailand, in other words. His nerves were badly damaged from opium and speed, but he controlled himself enough to stay seated. He even tried to prepare himself for death. It was deeply embedded among his most sacred promises to himself that he would at least die like a brave American, even if his life had been less than perfect. *You can at least do that,* he told himself above the violent thumping of his heart.

His self-esteem was not much improved, though, by the imam, who seemed to intuit the depth of Mitch's terror and smiled somewhat patronizingly, as if to a frightened child. The other middle-aged men, at least some of whom Mitch recognized as respectable and influential citizens of Songai Kolok, many of them successful hoteliers, were also making calming gestures with their hands. When it was clear that Mitch was not going to make a run for the door, one of the young Malay guards respectfully seated himself next to the imam.

"Please forgive us, Mr. Turner," the imam began. "I'm afraid that if we had approached you in any other way, certain interests would have taken notice and your life would have been in danger, not to mention our own. Mr. Turner, we are here to help you stay alive. We will do you no harm ourselves, but our warning to you is not without self-interest, as you will see." A cough and a strange gesture that would burn into Mitch

Turner's memory: the imam had a habit of moving his hand in a curving, horizontal motion as if he were caressing a pet cat. "Mr. Turner, we know you work for the CIA and that you are here to spy on Muslims, especially fanatics from Indonesia and Malayasia who might be part of Al Qaeda or some other terrorist organization. Believe me, Mr. Turner, we are not at all out of sympathy with the cause, only with the manner of your country's serving it." A placatory raising of the hand. "But no matter, we are not here to convert you, only to try to help you. Mr. Turner, do you really think your presence has gone unnoticed throughout the Muslim world in Southeast Asia? Of course, no one believes your cover story about working for a telecommunications company, and of course your identity, even your photograph, has been broadcast throughout the Muslim networks. How many young fanatics do you think would be only too happy to dispatch you in a suicide bombing? We have been approached by three separate Indonesian groups, two groups based in Malayasia and a couple of young Thai Muslims who are enraged by your provocative presence here. You are an intelligent man, Mr. Turner, even a brilliant one, so I do not need to tell you about the advantages your ruling elite would derive from a permanent war with Islam. Oil and arms, Mr. Turner. America is so much easier to govern and exploit when it is at war, is that not so? Indeed, the world is so much easier to exploit when it is at war." Another pause. "Allow me to quote a very smart American: *America is a giant but a deformed one.* Yes, Mr. Turner, you are not the only ones who can eavesdrop on the electronic world—most of your components are fabricated over the border in Malaysia, don't forget."

A long pause. Mitch Turner was trying to come to terms: what the hell was going on here? That quote was from an e-mail he'd sent to a close friend in the United States.

The imam continued. "We do not want war, Mr. Turner. We are Thai citizens and happy to be so. However, we are also Muslims, and perhaps I do not need to tell you how ruthless Thai Buddhists can be when they feel the integrity of the kingdom under threat. If you are murdered down here in the south, Mr. Turner, Washington's screams will be heard worldwide. Enormous pressure will be brought to bear on the Thai government, which already has contingency plans to intern Muslims in camps if the security situation worsens. That of course will be the beginning of the end, not only for us but for peace in Southeast Asia. But I don't think your government minds much about that." A short pause. "We want you out of Songai Kolok, Mr. Turner. If you will not go to save your own skin, then do it for our sake. I believe you are a Christian, is that not so? Perhaps you know how deeply Islam reveres Christ? For Christ's sake, then, go away." Looking deeply into Mitch Turner's eyes: "Pursue your death wish in some other land, Mr. Turner. That way perhaps you will be the only victim, rather than half the world."

And with that the imam rose and crossed the floor with great dignity, leading the others behind him. He paused at the door: "Mr. Turner, there are so many problems with Western society, but there may be one above all others that will destroy civilization. I speak of your inability to conceive that you might be wrong."

Now Mitch Turner was alone. Down below in the huts around the police station the night was in full swing. Mitch Turner was shaking with shock. Pacing up and down his flat with his head reeling, it took him more than five minutes to notice a package on his coffee table done up in ornate green and gold wrapping and topped off with a gold ribbon. In the circumstances a booby trap was unlikely, but his nerves were in such bad shape, he fumbled time after time while opening it. Inside: a ball of dense black viscous opium, far bigger than anything Chanya had ever brought him.

He knew I have a death wish, he saw it, Mitch Turner muttered as he prepared his pipe.

CHAPTER 42

Now Chanya couldn't believe what a bad turn everything was taking. Mitch Turner was an opium addict, and it was all her fault.

A Thai shrug. Karma was karma. Perhaps she should not have introduced him to the drug, but the kind of obsessional behavior that turned it into a dangerous addiction came from his own background—she could hardly hold herself responsible for that. She had acted with the best of intentions, but as the Buddhists said, the only real favor you can ever do for another being is to help him or her on the way to nirvana. Everything else is mere indulgence. She felt it was about time she ended her own indulgence. In any event, she had now made the decision to come work for us.

With the simplicity of a Thai in a fix, she changed the sim card in her mobile telephone and stopped replying to his e-mails. With the determination of an American in the grip of an obsession, he found her after a few months at the Old Man's Club.

★   ★   ★

Chanya had nothing against my mother's bar, but it was a drag, frankly, to return to that sordid mind-set just when you thought you'd escaped. She had nothing against the johns either—in the whole of her long career, she had come across no more than five or six who'd given her trouble, and she knew how to deal with that. More than anything it was the indignity. Being twenty-nine simply was not the same as being nineteen. You couldn't laugh it off as some game you were playing on the way to growing up. Whenever she could, she avoided fellatio. Nothing to do but to put a brave face on it all, though. A sad whore is a bankrupt whore. The johns come to be cheered up; generally they had problems of their own— why else would they be hiring flesh? It was a sad and fallen world, under the surface, just like the Buddha said: there is suffering. She could hardly believe it when she saw him sitting there in the Old Man's Club that night.

She had already been with one customer, and it was her right to go home if she wished, but she was working at full power. She was taking it easy at that moment, though, and had just emerged from one of the upstairs rooms where she had been resting for half an hour, by which time the brooding *farang* was sitting in his corner, ignored by the rest of the girls. She caught my eye when she reached the bottom of the stairs and made it look as if she were following a hint from me to go and sit with him. She exercised all her powers of self-control, not because it mattered particularly that this customer was her lover, but because like all Thais she loathes any kind of public scene. She was thankful that Mitch understood enough about Asia to respect this. Indeed, she was impressed with his appearance. He seemed much healthier and mentally more together than when she'd last seen him.

His approach to her that night was quite new. He no longer relied on wacky humor to seduce her, but he obviously intended to impress her with his sobriety. Apparently he was able to drink a couple of beers without losing control. He was doing Cool with considerable success. He admitted to being lonely and to missing her badly, but strictly within the parameters of the sane. He wanted to try again, to show her that he was not nuts, that the thing could work. There was enormous charm in the humble way he told her how good she looked, how deeply he was in love with her, and offered to pay her bar fine.

He had rented a room in a reasonably clean hotel just a short walk from the bar. They held hands as they left, and on the way to his hotel she asked how he was managing to cope with the culture shock, the boredom, the lack of purpose down there in Songai Kolok, where frankly even she would feel lonesome.

"Stop," I tell her. "I can't stand any more of your lies."

CHAPTER 43

W hat lies?"
She is startled. Her narrative seemed to be going so well. Perhaps she had started to believe it herself.

"Lies of omission. The tattoo, darling. You have to tell me about that."

She takes a deep breath. "I do?" Checking my face with an ancient question in mind: *Can he take it?* "Okay."

Hard to say what happened first—Mitch's interest in Islam, or his decision to finally go ahead with a large tattoo. Somehow they seemed a product of the same desperate impulse. Even then his conversation had begun to lack coherence. Putting it all together as best she can, it seems that the CIA spy befriended the very imam who had come to see him that night to warn him of the threat to his life by radical fanatics. Chanya's memory of his conversation at this time is vivid but partial, like the intense but inexplicable images of an opium dream, which it may well be, for at this stage Mitch hardly left his room without smoking at least one pipe.

The imam lives out of town in a modest wooden house on stilts in the middle of a lush green hollow, of the sort his Arab brethren associate with paradise. An artesian well with the long crossbeam of former times joins land and sky. There are no electric or telephone cables here; this is an oasis undefiled by utility. Nestled still more deeply into the hollow and no more than five minutes' walk from the cleric's home: a mosque so cute, it might have been invented by a cartoonist. The dome's compass is no greater than that of a large house; the minaret is less intimidating than a radio antenna. On his first visit Mitch found himself at the center of a small gang of bodyguards, one of whom spoke to a servant woman, who reported that the revered cleric was in prayer but would see him in due course. He sat cross-legged on a rush mat, drank sweet peppermint tea, and exchanged small talk with the bodyguards who, apparently convinced by intuition that he was harmless, did not search him. Then quite different men began to arrive. They were bearded, wore the long robes and skullcaps of Muslim clerics, and took no notice of him at all.

Now five quite elderly men with graying beards arrived with the dignified bearing of magi, each one more straight-backed than the last, each smoothly descending to the floor and crossing his legs under his long robes with the fluidity of the enlightened, each composing himself with a sigh and a closing of the eyes. They communicated with brief unintelligible murmurs and paid him no attention. Finally the host arrived. He owned all the bells and whistles of an aesthete, including the gaunt features, the long gray beard, the straight back, the prayerful manner—but there was an extra energy in his gestures, a gleam in his coal-black eyes. A young man translated the imam's words for Mitch:

"We were speaking, were we not, of the great Abu'l Walid Muhammad ibn Rushd?" With a smooth flourish the imam adjusted his robe. His voice was hardly more than a power-laden whisper. "Shall we continue our study?"

"God willing," murmured the others.

Mitch realized he had stumbled upon a seminar of the learned in which the words of an ancient cleric were being examined and discussed. Mitch was enthralled. Nevertheless, he decided to wait outside the house until the seminar was over. With whatever grace he could muster, he stood up, bowed, and *waied,* and left the room. He feared his footsteps on the wooden stairs that descended to the path that led to the well were the loudest noise in this tranquil valley.

He waited by the well. It was nearly dusk; therefore the imam would go to the mosque to pray before he would have time for Mitch. He watched while they all trooped out of his house, crossed the short path to the mosque, and disappeared inside, exactly as the muezzin's song seemed to rise from the grass up to heaven. The sun set, the moon rose:

an impossibly large and shiny crescent hung haphazardly above a palm. It did not surprise him that the imam possessed the magical power to creep up silently from behind. At the sound of a cough, Mitch turned and there he was, leaning against the opposite side of the well.

The imam spoke softly in formal, accented English unconstrained by context:

"There will be peace on earth when Hollywood makes movies in which the heroes are non-Americans. According to someone called Ibn Qutaiba a certain rose bush used to be cultivated in the gardens of Hindustan, the petals of which were bright crimson and bore the text in Arab characters of the famous line from the Koran: *There is no god but God, Muhammad is the prophet of God.*"

"I see," said Mitch in the slow drawl of a man under a spell.

"That's it? That was his Islam?" I ask Chanya as we lie naked side by side in our poor shack, listening to the sounds of the night.

"That's all I remember. He was pretty in-coherent at this point."

"And the tattoo?"

The *horimono* was a different matter, one requiring some fairly concrete decisions. Chanya sees it as the male equivalent of a breast implant: the revolutionary modification that would surely change

401

one's destiny. All she knows of the origin of the tattooist is that he emerged from Mitch Turner's Japanese connections. Turner, as a nonofficial cover operator in Tokyo, built up a wide network of contacts with whom he kept in touch. As frequently happens in the spy business, not a few of these contacts were associated with the underworld, which was to say the *yakuza* mobs. From time to time the e-mail gossip still echoes with memories of the hilarious exile of a manic tattooist who got drunk one night with a *yakuza* godfather and tattooed the mobster on the forehead with a picture of Mount Fuji. It was thought the tattooist was in hiding in Bangkok. He was, the legend confirms, a master of his craft, a genius within the glorious tradition of the woodblock artists of yesteryear, but hard up and hungry for work and more than a little crazy. Using techniques known to all spies, Mitch located him without difficulty.

The Japanese tattooist came to stay for a week in Mitch's spare bedroom in Songai Kolok. He and Chanya disliked each other on sight. The segment of pinkie missing from his left hand disgusted her. When he stripped to his shorts in order to work, she realized she was sharing an apartment with a monster.

He did not speak to her at all at first, which she took to be the height of rudeness and an expression of contempt for her profession. Later she realized he was pathologically shy because of his stutter. He and Mitch huddled together over a thick wad of drawings the tattooist had made for the American spy's consideration, speaking in rapid Japanese. Mitch's instructions were quite specific, apparently. The *horimono* was to be a single gigantic work covering the whole of his back, from shoulders to hips. Ishy's right hand worked so fast it was a blur; he was able to produce elegant sketches at lightning speed. Chanya had never seen a man infected with the passion of art before. She was not offended that the Japanese cast not a single lecherous glance at her body. Even though she had decided to hate him, she respected his fanatical concentration. She watched, mesmerized, the first time he opened a long black lacquer box roughly the dimensions of something you might carry a flute in. She wondered if this man ever treated a woman's body with the reverence he showed for his *tebori*, those twelve-inch-long polished bamboo tattooing needles.

After the paper sketches came the painstaking computer work. Ishy brought a digital camera and a Sony Micro Vault. His software enabled him to impose a grid on the snapshot of Mitch Turner's back, which in turn enabled him to plan each pinprick with precision. There followed the painstaking transfer of the grid to the American's back, then broad outlines of the work using a Western tattoo gun. Finally ready, Ishy mixed his ink in another machine, which juddered quaintly. The apartment was filled with the indescribable odor of *sumi* ink, which she decided was neither pleasant nor unpleasant but exclusively Japanese. Stoically, Mitch endured the first deep penetration of his skin as he lay on the bed with Ishy sitting above him, using the full weight of his body behind the *tebori*, which the tattooist worked as if it were a long chisel.

Now a problem arose. Sober, Mitch had difficulty keeping still for hours on end. He could take the pain but not the boredom. Ishy grew irritated. He would not have his masterpiece ruined by American impatience. An obvious solution offered itself. Mitch would smoke a few pipes of opium before each session, which would keep him happily comatose for nearly eight hours. The tattooist was delighted. His concentration was such that he could easily work almost nonstop for the full eight hours. What he thought would be a two-week job could be accomplished in one, so long as Mitch remained stoned.

Chanya was not allowed into the bedroom, now an artist's studio, while Ishy worked. It was her duty to keep one bottle of sake warm at all times, that being the only sustenance the artist would tolerate while on duty. Finally she was amused at the way the tattooist emerged from the bedroom every couple of hours, went to the sake bottle, and returned to the bedroom without so much as acknowledging her existence. She had begun to understand that this was not bad manners so much as the behavior of a wild thing, a denizen of the electronic jungle that had never been socialized.

To test her theory one day, she stood topless in the kitchen while the artist emerged from the bedroom, gulped some sake, and returned to his work, pausing only to remark at the door that her nakedness would benefit from a *horimono*—perhaps a blue dolphin over her left breast?

"Dolphins are old," sneered Chanya when he reappeared. He grunted, but the next time he emerged from the bedroom, he brought a sketch of the most beautiful dolphin she had ever seen. The proportions were entirely consistent with her charms. Now, in between the long sessions with Mitch, Ishy worked on her bosom while she sat in a chair. She was astonished at the gentleness of his touch, embarrassed by the swelling of her nipples, enthralled by this guided missile of ruthless concentration. She had not realized how erotic male passion could be when raised above the level of sex. Or how elusive. She found herself exaggerating the pain a little. He ordered her to cup a hand underneath her left breast to keep it firm: "You're not hurting that much. Tits are not so sensitive except near the nipple. It's mostly just fatty tissue."

By the end of the week Mitch's tattoo was finished, and she and Ishy had become lovers. What can one say? The sexual preferences of prostitutes can be eccentric, I of all people should know that. She was ashamed of herself, ashamed to betray Mitch in this way, but what could she do? Mitch was a prisoner of a million rules and regulations, most of them contradictory; Ishy was a wild thing who knew no rules, not even of conversation. In terms of raw sex appeal there was no contest. And then there was the *donburi,* that outrageous and indelible challenge to the universe. The abused and desecrated skin that had appalled her at the beginning of the week was exercising a mesmeric appeal by the end. As a lover he was extraordinarily feline; the flashes of intense color when he paid silent homage to her body burned into her mind long after he had left her. Every night she dreamed of gigantic, vividly colored *nagas*: snake gods who possess an almost un-endurable sensuality. Every day when they coupled again, she thought of the American lying in a trance in the other bedroom, exactly as if she and Ishy were protagonists in his erotic opium dreams.

For the first time the balance of passion lay in her heart. When Ishy returned to Bangkok, she ached for him. She convinced herself that he needed her, that she alone with her street wisdom and undefeatable toughness could save this lost man-child who stumbled through life under the burden of a gigantic talent. But he did not reply to her text messages or her e-mails. This was a first. It had never occurred to her that when she finally fell for a man in this way, he might not respond. She went through the hackneyed stages of volcanic yearning, fury, a quaking in her guts, a sense of loss of power, and a conviction that his lack of response was connected to the onset of her third decade and/or her unsavory profession.

Her final attempt to contact her beloved consisted of a telephonic text message of the kind he favored: *Y the F don't U kal?* There was no electronic response, but a few days later an envelope arrived with a single sheet of paper. In the most elegant tradition of Thai calligraphy, a single sentence:

Because I am not worthy of you.

In addition to the single sheet of paper, Ishy included the last segment of his remaining pinkie. The sly reference to a certain Dutch impressionist was entirely lost on her, but not the message. Now she was ashamed for a different reason: she found her passion quite bourgeois compared to his. This great artist would sacrifice his hands for her. All she had done was yearn and groan. Thumbing the message feverishly into her mobile, she freed her heart from all restraints and resorted to the vocabulary of Oriental extravagance: *I would give both my I's to see U again.*

Ishy*: U don't No what U ask.*

Chanya*: I don't kare. I want U.*

With apparent reluctance Ishy agreed to see her in Bangkok, not in his home—which remained mysteriously anonymous—but in a bar on Sukhumvit. Finding his attitude incomprehensible and therefore all the more alluring, she arrived early, drank three tequilas to steady her nerves, and had no idea what to do about the great quaking in her stomach when the bashful genius walked awkwardly into the bar, ordered sake, and sat next to her. What could possibly be the matter? His eyes were on fire with desire for her, but he refused to take her to his apartment. He tried to explain, but his stutter was worse than ever and quite incomprehensible. Only after he had consumed three bottles of sake could she begin to understand what he was saying, but by then they were both too horny for words.

"I know a short-time hotel around the corner," she confided.

"I don't have any money."

Eagerly: "Don't worry, I'll pay."

In the heavily mirrored room, which was encumbered by the obscenity of a gynecological chair to serve those perversions that require it, she laid him on the bed and covered him and his outrageous tattoos with her flawless body, made him her own in the way so many men had done to her—or tried to. Now for the first time in her life she understood men and their need to possess in a total way through the act of sex. (She finally understood Mitch.)

She could not recall for how long they made love—it seemed to go on all afternoon. From time to time she sent out for warm sake for him, cold beer for her. It seemed they were satisfying a hunger accumulated over lifetimes. When their passion finally began to ebb, they switched on the TV monitor, which automatically played a hard porn video. Finally sated, with him drunk enough to lose his stutter, he talked as they lay on their backs, staring at their bodies in the ceiling mirror. What she saw there was a woman lying naked next to an extraterrestrial. She could not say why she found comfort in this juxtaposition, except that he seemed the male expression of herself at that moment; after all, for her as for him, there was no society of human beings worth belonging to, merely a torn cobweb of hypocrisy best avoided.

Ishy explained: Only through his work could he escape for a moment from his appalling sense of inadequacy, which stemmed from that lifelong problem with people. But what happened when there was no work, as was often the case? If he did not work for more than a day, he began to suffer mental torture of the most excruciating kind, a sense of suffocation—worse, of annihilation. His very existence was thoughtlessly eclipsed by people happily chatting together, by the merest glimpse of that effortless camaraderie to which Thais—especially our women—are particularly prone. Two old ladies nattering could send him into a jealous rage. (He was capable of envy provoked by the mutual grooming of cats.) His sense of isolation was of a degree no human should have to endure. He experienced the insane need to tattoo everyone around him, that they might carry proof of his existence all the way to the grave. After more than two days without work his mind filled with violent fantasies. On the inside of his skull, just above the eyes, cartoons of extreme sadism, murder, and death played out. There was only one activity that in its intensity could replace the solace of creativity.

"What's that?" Chanya asked, fearing the answer.

"Gambling."

"Gambling?" She almost giggled. She had suspected something far worse.

But as Ishy explained it, she realized this was not a vice to be taken lightly. The reason he spoke Thai so well, at least when drunk, was that he spent most of his time and all of his money at boxing contests, cockfights, horse races, and even cockroach races in cardboard cities under bridges among the city's derelicts. To finance his vice, he borrowed from loan sharks, who were invariably of Chiu Chow origin, specifically the Swatow area south of Shanghai, which has been home to the Pacific Rim's greatest financiers and thugs for a thousand years. His life hung permanently by a thread as he struggled to pay off one bloodthirsty gangster by borrowing from another. At the present moment he owed not less than a million U.S. dollars, most of it due to some Japanese financiers who saved him from mutilation at the hands of the Chiu Chow only by securing his agreement to a particularly onerous contract.

"So what does the contract say?"

"Don't ask," he replied. "Just don't ask."

Even in the grip of her passion, she saw the point. Everyone in Thailand knew about the Chiu Chow loan sharks, and she doubted the Japanese were much more humane. If they discovered a love in his life, she would become leverage; they would do to her whatever they thought necessary to squeeze more money out of Ishy. In his mad attempt to save his mind, he had mortgaged his life.

"Not only my life," Ishy replied with an ironic twist of his lips.

Desperate, Chanya found herself arguing exactly like a man: "But we could still do this from time to time, meet somewhere safe, go to a hotel, be together for a few hours?"

Ishy shook his head. The people on his tail were ruthless and extremely good at what they did. He could not risk it. He simply could not bear to think of what they would do to her. The steps he took to cover his trail today had been elaborate to the point of baroque, but still he could not afford to feel secure. This was their last moment together. He was resolute, unshakable. He would go to the grave with the comfort that at least he'd managed to protect her.

Chanya is looking at me with the shrewd eyes of a woman who has experienced every shade of male jealousy. I lick my lips and swallow to cure the dryness in my throat. "It's okay," I croak. "I'm okay."

"What d'you think? What's going on in your heart right now?"

"Actually, I'm thinking about Mitch Turner."

CHAPTER 44

I'm surprised at how often I *do* think of him (whoever he was). There was no real malice in him, he never once used those formidable muscles in anger, and even his savage words in moments of fury with the woman he loved were mostly an expression of bewilderment: how did he fall for a girl like that anyway? But I think of him mostly because he wants me to. Last night I saw him as a Superman figure, trapped in a cube of deadly kryptonite, unable to use his strength, for he dared not touch the walls. But that, it turned out, was no more than a reflection of my own prejudice. A second later he was a humble fellow in T-shirt and jeans, smiling gently at my folly. *Your back!* I exclaimed. He pulled up his shirt and turned: a rectangle in the form of a picture frame, within which foreign words were written in a code I could never decipher. He shrugged: it didn't matter to him anymore, he was merely trying to help me with the case.

I'm on the back of a motorbike again, playing Pisit's talk show through my earphones while we weave in and out of the static commuter traffic. (Cars, buses, and trucks are the only objects not subject to the law of constant movement in this Buddhist city.) Chanya was fast asleep in our love den when I left her in response to Vikorn's call: another T808. The old man finally seemed to be worried about something.

Well, Pisit is having a field day with the story of the abbot in Nonthaburi who had more than a hundred million baht in his bank account when he was gunned down last week. He quotes from *The Nation*'s short bio of the deceased monk: *Thanks to his cleverness and knowledge of magic he quickly rose in the Sangha and was appointed abbot when he was thirty-seven years old.*

Pisit, to Sangha spokesman: Is it common for ambitious monks to use magic as a promotion aid?

Spokesperson: Unfortunately, meditation brings many powers that are vulnerable to abuse.

Pisit: You mean like purple rain? Or hundreds of millions of baht?

Spokesperson: Buddhism has been fighting sorcery for two thousand five hundred years. Generally, we have an excellent success rate, but a few miscreants still slip through.

Pisit: The magic in this case seems to have worked through the mundane medium of drugs and sex. The rumor has it that the abbot was murdered because he double-crossed a certain army general.

413

Spokesman: Sorcery carries a heavy karmic price.

Pisit: Almost every Thai man learns to meditate in his early twenties. How much sorcery do you think we generate in this kingdom? I mean, how many of our most prominent figures in business and politics have got where they are today using dark powers?

Spokesman: We don't have any statistics.

Pisit: But if you were to hazard a guess?

Spokesman: All of them.

The destination this merry morning is a magnificent mansion off Soi 22, Sukhumvit. Vikorn sits in the kitchen flirting with an attractive Thai woman in her mid-twenties while a corpse waits in the living room. Blood has flooded the capillaries in my Colonel's face, which has acquired an obscene beam. He introduces his companion as Nok, and I can tell by the shape her mouth makes when she speaks to me that they have already fixed an assignation.

"You better tell him yourself," Vikorn says. With a quite disgusting grin at her: "I don't want to put words in your mouth."

"I'm the maid here," Nok says, standing up and leading me out of the kitchen. "When I arrived this morning, I found him like that. Naturally I called the police, and Colonel Vikorn himself arrived."

The middle-aged Japanese male is naked on the polished pine floor in a crimson lake that has

414

spread in a slow flood over sealed wood. Vikorn wanders in while I'm conducting a perfunctory examination of the corpse. The last segment of pinkie is missing from his left hand, a very old wound. I catch Vikorn's eye when I turn him over.

Vikorn shakes his head. "You'll have to stop this. Do whatever you need to do. Don't arrest him— shoot him while he's trying to escape. This has to stop." A shrug. "At least this victim is not American so we don't have to call the CIA."

"You're not going to tell them?"

"I've run out of hairs."

I turn to Nok: "Please tell me what you know."

"I came to work here a year ago," Nok explains. "I was recruited by his wife, a Japanese woman with a personality problem. I mean, she never stopped complaining. She was obsessive about the house." A wave of the hand: "This is all her."

I take a moment to look around. The place could not be more Japanese: sliding screens of translucent paper, a small nonsymmetrical pool in the middle of the room (in which a severed penis floats) surrounded by pebbles, *bonsai* in beige glazed pots, and carefully wrinkled natural-colored paper on the walls.

"I had to learn the Japanese names for every-thing. It took me ages with her bitching at me all the time—the place had to be spotless. Then, just when she had everything perfect, she dumped him and fled back to Japan, said she couldn't stand Thailand, that we were all primitive, dirty, and revolting. Nips are worse racists than we are."

"When did she go?"

"About two months ago. It didn't seem to bother him very much. He had whores back here from time to time."

"Did you sleep with him?"

Firmly: "No. He asked me to a couple of times, but I said I wasn't like that."

"If he'd offered something respectable, like the position of *mia noi*?"

"Well, he didn't. He just wanted a cheap screw, and he wasn't going to pay any more than he paid for his other women, so I said no."

"You never saw him naked?"

"No."

"Never saw his back without a shirt?"

"No."

"Any enemies that you know of?"

Vikorn stands frowning over the cadaver. "Forget it," he says to me. "This guy was the CEO of the Thai-Nippon Reforestation and Beautification of Isaan Corporation."

I was bending over the body; now I straighten to stare at him. He shrugs. "Don't ask me, I haven't the faintest idea."

"Zinna's going to think you're behind this."

"I know. It's one of those dreadful coincidences." He does not seem overly worried about Zinna. "I don't know what the connection is, really I don't.

This has nothing at all to do with me. What does it matter *why* when we know *who*?"

I exchange a nod with Vikorn.

"The forensic team will be here in a minute. I've got some urgent business on the other side of town," I explain to the maid as I make for the door. Out on the street I take a motorbike taxi back to Chanya. On the way I finally hear my mobile bleep with a text message:

They've taken her. They want her tattoo.

CHAPTER 45

O ur love nest echoes with ghosts of love's murmurs. I'm too devastated to move. Rooted to the spot, I experience an expanding vacuum in my chest that makes it difficult to breathe. Images of her likely mutilation flash across my brain. I loved her long before I knew her face or name. I am consciousness trapped in a pipe. Is there any need to explain? I never wanted anything before she illuminated my life. Now I cannot return to that pre-Chanya drabness, that routine of shadows. (Even the Buddha doesn't glow like her.) I fear nothing except her loss. I hardly have the will to look at the new text message on my cell phone: *Come alone, bring a million USD in nonsequential notes. Help me save her.* The message ends with an address on the other side of town, just off Kaosan Road. I call Vikorn. A million U.S. is an oddly modest sum in the circumstances—he'll send someone over with it immediately. "D'you want a team? We could just blow up the building."

"Kill her, too?"

Vikorn grunts. "Have it your way. If you lose the fight, I'm going in with a hit squad, and she'll have to take her chances. Fucking Chiu Chow."

The money, thrown carelessly into a plastic bag, arrives in the company of a young constable who, from the look on his face, has been suitably terrorized by Vikorn.

But the roads are blocked with the usual traffic jam, which stretches all the way down Sukhumvit, shutting out even the side *sois* where traffic cannot enter the main stream. Serenity eludes me. I cannot meditate. I'm another helpless creature, just like all the other creatures, from ants to Einsteins, lashed by karma. By the time we arrive on the other side of town, my nerves are jumping, my eyes darting, the hand holding the money is shaking violently. My brain is full of un-Buddhist images of what I will do to them if they've started to work on her. At the same time, like any amateur I'm attempting to bribe the Buddha. I'm up to three hogs' heads and a thousand eggs by the time we turn into Kaosan Road. As far as I can recall, even birth was less stressful.

Well, there's nothing like the Buddha when it comes to anticlimax. The house is an old teak structure on stilts in the ancient Thai style. There are still a few left in the Kaosan area, mostly turned into guesthouses for nostalgia-hungry *farang*. This one has not been well maintained; it looks almost derelict with luscious weeds and other stubborn growths crowding out what must once have been a tropical garden. On the wall next to the front gate is a forlorn sign in Thai, English, and Japanese:

419

TATTOOS. All the windows are shuttered. Parked in the road outside: a large metallic gray BMW with a driver waiting. At my knock the door immediately opens, a well-dressed Chinese man in his early thirties surveys me for a moment and allows his eyes to rest on the plastic bag, then bows slightly as he lets me in. He closes the door carefully behind him and points to the internal door, which leads to the great room that occupies the whole of the first floor.

For light we are dependent on knife-shaped shafts that penetrate the teak shutters and carve out brilliant elongated forms on the floor and furniture. Some of the light pierces the gloom of the walls, which I now see, with the expansion of my pupils, is chockablock with paintings, geometric designs, and grotesquely enlarged photographs of tattooed bodies both male and female, most of them naked save for the ink. The walls are so extraordinary, they quite eclipse the humans who sit below them. I think Gauguin's hut on Tahiti was like this. Here in this big old space the tattooist has let his imagination run riot. And what an imagination! Influences from the great Hokusai to Hieronymus Bosch to Warhol to Van Gogh to Picasso to graffiti on the Tokyo subway: Ishy's art is as eclectic as a magpie, but somehow, in the great heaping of color and shape, he has managed an appalling coherence. The walls are an extension of his own tattoos: extraordinary, intense, compelling, and ultimately incomprehensible, the product of a wild genius compelled at risk of madness to say: *I am.*

When my eyes drop to the sunken table, I wonder if I have not misunderstood the situation and clumsily stumbled onto a business meeting. Each of the seven Chinese is dressed in a business suit and tie, save for one man in his forties who is perhaps the chief negotiator and sports an open-necked shirt under his cashmere jacket. The floor has been dropped to accommodate legs and feet under the table in the old style, but from the other side of the room it looks like a congregation of dwarfs sitting on the floor around a long teak dining table below walls decorated by a mad god. A long shaft of light illuminates Ishy, who sits at the head in a splendid white linen open-neck shirt that reveals a wedge of his tattoos, with the inevitable bottle of sake in front of him. Chanya, in a silk shawl the color of old gold, sits next to him in near darkness. When I approach, she explains in a grumble: "They gave me an anesthetic. I can't feel my tits." To emphasize the point, she massages them with both hands. Without a word I walk to the head of the table with the plastic bag, which I dump in front of Ishy. Everyone stares at the bag, but no one grabs the money. What have I interrupted here? Finally Ishy clears his throat. I think he must have been drinking heavily, for there is no stutter.

"Unfortunately, it's no longer as simple as that."

"A pardonable misunderstanding, no one's fault," the Chinese in the open-necked shirt mutters, flashing me a ghostly smile. "But it will have to be cleared up one way or another."

Ishy engages my eyes. "It seems the million is in respect of Chanya's tattoo only. They were going to cut it out and cure it. Imagine, a million for just that little dolphin. I could have been rich if I'd had more time."

"So what's the problem?"

"They were assuming they could just take the other tattoos to sell on the black market. There's quite a demand for my work now, mostly in Japan among the *yakuza,* who use them as status symbols—the way Japanese businessmen used to keep Van Goghs in safes and only take them out at bragging time. It's quite depressing for an artist who wants exposure. After all, Van Gogh's financial problems are over."

"Where are the other tattoos?"

"Upstairs. The most recent are still being cured. Did you know the process is identical to that for pigskin?"

"How long has this—ah—trade been going on?"

"It's a long story. You could say Mitch Turner was the first. I never intended it to get out of hand like this. I didn't really intend to kill anybody except him." He gives a matter-of-fact flick of the hand in Chanya's direction. "I couldn't have her, but I couldn't stand any other man to have her either. You would have been next. But if one is going to kill, why miss the opportunity to make a profit? I've coveted that creamy white flesh of yours since the night we met, especially on your back."

I had already guessed all this, of course. Standing quite still about six feet from the table, speaking like a man calling across a valley, my voice echoing in the cavernous room, I say: "So why can't they take the other tattoos, cured and uncured?"

Ishy shakes his head at my obtuseness. "Because I've mortgaged them to the Japs already. The *yakuza* loan sharks. They're sending a team with a lawyer. Should be here any minute. With the Italian." At my baffled glance: "My dear fellow, you didn't expect a war, did you, in this day and age? I called the Japs with the full agreement of Mr. Chu."

"That is correct," confirms the Chinese in the open-necked shirt, speaking in a monotone. "We're all part of the global business community. It would be unfortunate if this little contractual matter were to come between us when we have so much trade with our Japanese colleagues. It would be unthinkable for us simply to take the works away, now that we are aware of a possibly prior and more lawful claim. I'm afraid Mr. Ishy is too much of an artist to trouble himself with legal niceties. He has mortgaged everything at least twice." A pained smile. "That is the problem."

Ishy opens his hands helplessly and makes a guilty face. With sudden eagerness: "D'you want to see them?"

He leads us up the stairs to a narrow corridor with two doors. The first opens onto a bedroom, the walls of which are covered with tattoo designs of the most intimate—and pornographic—variety.

He points to a pale skin curing on a single wooden plank."I figured if I was going to kill people for their hides, I might as well combine it with some form of community service. He was a *yakuza* thug, basically, very senior though, CEO of that phony corporation that is forcing peasants off their lands in Isaan so they can grow fucking chopsticks. He was the one who ordered the killing of that journalist who was a friend of mine—that butterfly tattoo was one of my best. Actually, this godfather was one of my first customers over here. Of course, he wanted a damned samurai on his back—my people really have a problem with mythology. Samurai were mostly drunken homosexuals with a psychotic streak, but don't say that out loud in Japan. I had to be subtle. Fortunately, he was too stupid to understand the message in his own skin. Not bad, is it?"

The tattoo on the hide on the board is, as a matter of fact, a triumph of subtle satire. To a cursory glance, the samurai in magnificent armor and helmet on the back of a great black stallion, wielding his voluptuous bow, is the very image of the perfect warrior. Look a little closer, however; with just a few deft strokes, Ishy has made his point: drunk and gay, there's no doubt about it, a bombastic narcissist all dressed up with nowhere to go.

"May I ask why you had to sever their cocks?"

Ishy frowns and scratches his head, then jerks a thumb at Chanya. "Her karma. I did it to Mitch Turner in a jealous rage, but after that I realized any man could have her. Any jerk in the street.

He only had to pay, right?" Chanya winces and looks at the floor. "I would have castrated the whole city for her. That's love."

"But the men you castrated were already dead."

"I said love, not logic. Love is a language of symbols—you should know that."

"Why did you have to kill people you'd already tattooed? Why not kill anyone on the street, then tattoo them later?"

He shakes his head gravely. "A recipe for mediocrity. For a start, the ink needs to penetrate far below the surface before you get that quality of color and shade. Secondly, you've failed to understand the market. I'm not just selling tattoos, I'm selling murder at the same time. People want that *frisson,* the cachet of owning the decorated skin of a murdered man, the very skin he wore in life, before he was cut down like a tree for the purpose of art. It's the civilized equivalent of collecting shrunken heads." A swig from the sake bottle he brought with him: "I'm also selling notoriety, of course. When this gets out, the prices of my work will increase a hundredfold." Thoughtfully: "What is murder but suicide by an extrovert? We are all part of the human family after all, and only murderers experience the unbearable passion of true love."

The man in the open-necked shirt nods in agreement.

The room next door contains only two wall hangings, both covered in silk cloth. Ishy uncovers the first. "A sad case, that young CIA spy. It was what he wanted—he was quite pleased with it. I guess it was all he expected from life, but he ended up with a Thai whore instead." The tattoo is deeply sad for anyone who knew Stephen Bright: a young woman, a Caucasian with long blond hair, cradling an infant in the tradition of Madonna and child. The sheer simplicity of the lines (perhaps Ishy was making a point, for it is a touch *too* simple) makes it all the more poignant.

"It's brilliant," I find myself saying with a gulp.

"But it's not as good as this," Ishy declares as he pulls the cover off the second, larger work. Chanya gasps at the sight of a familiar image in an unfamiliar situation. I also gasp, as does the man in the open-necked shirt. Even his thugs are impressed. "Mitch Turner," Ishy explains. "It was his idea, something he got from a book or an opium dream, or some spell he was under. Of course, I insisted on my own interpretation."

But for once Ishy has maintained a fierce discipline, which is a big part of the magic. An amazingly dense and virile green vine fills the whole of the tattoo with such vividness, it seems to grow up the wall on which it hangs. The rose blossoms themselves are downplayed, hardly more than crimson afterthoughts, highlighting the leaves, each of which, even the tiniest, bears the legend in blood: *There is no god but God, Muhammad is the prophet of God.*

Chanya bursts into hysterical sobs as we hear a polite knock on the front door.

CHAPTER 46

We have all returned to the great downstairs room. Hours have passed. The man in the open-necked shirt speaks fluent Japanese, and the negotiations have been continuing in that language with the newcomers, a somewhat muscular band of Japanese men in black business suits, all of whom have at least one pinkie missing. They are lined up against one wall, while the Chiu Chow thugs are lined up against another, each warrior perpetually marking his opposite number, while Chanya and I sit on cushions on the floor. Ishy, the chief Japanese negotiator, and the man in the open-necked shirt sit drinking sake at the long table. Quite drunk now, Ishy has undone most of his shirt, perhaps intentionally displaying his hero Admiral Yamamoto, who stares sternly out between the linen folds. The Italian, a slim, gaunt fellow with a mass of curly dark hair, wears a black short-sleeve shirt and a pair of jeans, slippers without socks. He squats in a corner of the room with his back against the wall. Ishy has explained, not without some disdain, that he is an art restorer, flown in from Rome. The

Japanese, it seems, are taking no chances. (*He can peel a micron of paint off a five-hundred-year-old masterpiece,* Ishy reported.) It seems that at least one of the Japanese thugs is also a surgeon. In the circumstances, Ishy's good humor is inexplicable. He grows more cheerful by the minute. Finally there is a pause in the intense discussions.

"They've decided the main point," Ishy calls out to me. "It's only details they're discussing now. Copyright, merchandising, that kind of thing."

Simultaneously Chanya, who has understood more than I have been able to, from some Japanese she picked up in the course of trade, has collapsed in another great torrent of sobs, taking frequent moments to stare disbelievingly at Ishy, her eyes great saucers of horror and disbelief. When both the Italian and the Japanese surgeon make toward us, she clasps her breasts possessively.

But they pass by us just as Ishy removes his shirt, then the rest of his clothes.

"The *yakuza* are very humane," he explains while the surgeon takes a syringe out of his pocket and a small vial out of another. He pulls the hygienic paper off the syringe, pulls the protective cap off the needle, and plunges the needle into the vial. "They said I could die first. I said no, I want to preside over the removal of my masterpiece. One wrong move by that wop, and I'll curse him for eternity." Shaking his head at Chanya: "Don't worry, love—it'll pay for everything. There's nothing more to worry about. This way you get to keep your tits." He pauses while one of his country-men ties a white scarf with black Japanese char-acters around his head in the tradition of kamikaze, then watches while the surgeon injects him in the arm: "It's one of those new brain drugs. I'll be able to follow everything painlessly, like a great fog of consciousness looking down on my exfoliation. I see this as a personal triumph—like the snake I am, I'm shedding my skin, my ego, and my life in praise of Buddha and for the love of man. After all I've been through, I think that's heroic. You may not want to witness this, though. You're free to go. I told them you won't tell anyone."

I tell Chanya to get the hell out while she still can, even though these men seem to pose no threat to her and indeed have more or less ignored her since they cut their deal. Am I protecting her, or is there some other motive? Perhaps I'm ashamed of my morbid curiosity. Perhaps I don't want her to see how fascinated I am by what will happen next. (Maybe I don't want to see how fascinated *she* might be.) I take her to the door, kiss her, and push her away. By the time I have returned, the drug is already taking effect—Ishy is losing control of his legs. The surgeon barks orders in Japanese, and five men immediately surround the artist and lower him gently onto the long table. Already he has lost all control over his body, there is no connection between his mind and his nerves, but light remains in those unblinking eyes. I would love to know what he's thinking.

Under the direction of the Italian, the surgeon makes some deft strokes with a scalpel from armpits to hips and along the length of the underarms. He makes light circular incisions at the ankles and wrists and along the length of the penis. With quite astonishing speed, assisted by the Italian and one other man, they unpeel him. As with any master-piece, the Italian carefully rolls up the hide to take it upstairs for curing. All the others follow, leaving me alone in the cavernous room with his brilliantly colored work glowing from the walls, while Ishy, finally naked, presides inscrutably over his own slow dying.

PART 7

PLAN C

CHAPTER 47

W ell, we've received the final official lab results," Elizabeth Hatch says in that level, hypercontrolled way of hers. Nevertheless, she casts a slightly sheepish glance at me. (I have my spies: I heard on the grapevine she went on another tour last night and ended up with the same girl. This could be love—I have a feeling she'll be back.) "It seems the DNA is identical in the Stephen Bright and the Mitch Turner case. The only problem: the DNA, according to our database, belongs to the terrorist Achmad Yona, who was killed in the bomb blast in Samalanga in Indonesia a few weeks before Bright."

"So he killed Mitch Turner, died in the bomb blast, came back to kill Stephen," Hudson says.

I'm not totally convinced of an ironic intention. The conversation, in the CIA's suite at the Sheraton, possesses the surreal quality of a rehearsal. These two officers will be filing their own individual reports, of course; this is a practice session.

"So you narrow down the possibilities. One, Achmad Yona had nothing to do with any of the slayings. He distributed hair from his beard and two of his fingers to colleagues in order to create a red herring and/or to enhance his reputation. Two, Yona did both killings and the DNA evidence found at the Indonesian bomb blast was a plant."

"The way to handle it," Hudson declares, straightening his back (he has miraculously mutated into Paper Warrior First Class), "is to play down the Indonesia thing. So they found DNA belonging to him in that bomb blast—so what? They burned all the other remains before we could get to them, so we don't know for sure what they actually found, if anything. We can't rely on the Indonesians to play totally straight with us. They're Muslim, after all—under the skin they're not totally unsympathetic to the radical cause."

"That's it," agrees Elizabeth. "We finesse the Indonesia thing into a footnote."

"That's the way to play it," from Hudson.

The two suddenly remember my presence. "Oh, we brought you over here because we wanted to make sure we're all singing from the same hymnbook." Elizabeth smiles. "Anything we've said so far inconsistent with your understanding of what went on?"

Tired of lying for Vikorn and suddenly haunted by an image of Mustafa and his father, I experience a reckless, liberating, and profoundly Buddhist compulsion to tell the truth. "Actually, Mitch Turner and Stephen Bright were killed by a mad Japanese, a tattooist with a terrible personality problem who confessed before he died. The killings had nothing to do with Al Qaeda."

I am more than a little curious at the effect this bombshell will have on these two professionals. Which only goes to show I'm not so smart; I should have remembered that *farang* inhabit a parallel universe. The two suffer from a moment of collective deafness. Or are they embarrassed? Third-world cops do come out with the most ridiculous crap after all.

"Well, that's great," says Elizabeth after a long moment when no one looks me in the eye. "We can report that local law enforcement agrees with our initial report." She gives me one of her superior-librarian looks as I make for the exit. "I know his Colonel sees it our way, too."

When I glance back from the door, Hudson mouths an apologetic explanation: "GS Eleven."

The Sheraton is only a short walk from our primitive love nest. We should probably have moved out by now, Chanya and I, but we've both got used to being what we really are: a couple of third-world peasants grabbing a sweet moment, favoring quality of life above standard of living. We're both particularly fond of the big water trough in the backyard, where we wash each other down like elephants. She has to cook in the yard, too, and I've become fond of watching her pounding chiles with the mortar and pestle wearing nothing but a sarong. A couple of beers, the odd spliff, the sounds of the street at night while we cuddle up under the fan—what more could a sane man want?

Well, there is just one gigantic loose end that troubles me. I wait for the moment—we've just made love, and Chanya, who has morphed into traditional Thai wife, goes to bring the beer from the cooler. I clear my throat. She glances at me. I'm tilting my head in the cutest possible imitation of a question mark. She's way too smart not to get the point. She puts the bottle down next to my arm, goes to rummage in one of her bags that she dumped in a corner of the room, and returns with a late-model IBM ThinkPad. My eyes turn to saucers while she expertly switches it on, connects the modem to our landline, and types in a code.

In a sweet tone: "What is your question, exactly?"

I stare at the screen while Windows XP Edition radiates its deep blue glow and those stupid Windows icons spread like a virus. "Vikorn. Why exactly was he so keen to protect you after Mitch's death? I've never seen him like that before. He even flew to Indonesia. Did you sleep with him?"

She scowls. "Of course not. He was just terrified that if the CIA interrogated me, I'd spill the beans and Zinna would have him run out of town."

"How did you get this?" I tap the IBM.

"Mitch checked it into a safe box in the hotel he was staying at when Ishy killed him. I took the key when I left the room because I knew he would have some opium in the safe box. I took the ThinkPad at the same time."

"You better tell me what really happened, just in case there's something I need to finesse with the CIA."

"Sure," she says as she works the keys. Now we're out of Windows, into a dire warning of how the U.S. government will systematically hunt down and wreck the lives of anyone and everyone entering this supersecret database without authority.

"It goes like this," Chanya says.

The scene is Mitch's apartment in Songai Kolok in the early days, quite some time before Ishy arrived to complicate their lives, the time of day about three in the afternoon. After watching Mitch slip into opium heaven—much to her relief, since he had been particularly tense on this visit—Chanya had pottered contentedly around. No doubt about it, there was something rather special about their relationship, particularly when the White Tornado was deeply opiated. He was stark naked on the bed, and she liked to have his amazing body in the best perspective. Once, wickedly, she placed a cotton towel over his head and imagined what his face would have been like if it had mirrored the beauty of his body. She found a tiny American flag in one of his drawers and stuck it in his hand, spending some time on getting the fist to clench. Out of curiosity she tried working his penis; the erectile tissue was off chasing dragons.

Growing bored after a while, though, and allowing that she wouldn't have minded if he'd said a word or two, or even simply moved a finger, she wandered into the room he used as an office. He had been particularly voracious for his opium that day when she had arrived, and smoked a pipe as soon as she had handed him the black viscous package. In his haste he had forgotten to turn off his laptop, the screen of which was now swimming with a particularly banal screen saver. A mere jog of the mouse, though, took her directly into the much-vaunted secret world, for he had forgotten to turn off his Internet connection, too.

Which turned out to be as boring as the screen saver. An apparently mindless chatter of international gossip came through on the incessant e-mail: American woman almost raped in Durbar Square in Kathmandu; gang of teenage American cannabis traffickers caught in Singapore; China cracking down on American businessman because he was making too much profit, now accused of being a spy (actually he *was* spying, the e-mail confided), State Department outrage recommended. Tip-off for the DEA: big shipment of heroin believed to be moving out of the Golden Triangle, down to Udon Thani. Obviously headed for Bangkok.

Interested now, she traced the sequence of messages back through time. Relay teams of CIA, FBI, DEA, Thai customs, and Thai drug enforcement police were chuckling while they secretly followed the shipment from northern Laos, across the border into Thailand; like a snowball it collected more perps the more it rolled. The plan was to wait until it reached Bangkok, so the kingpin would be revealed. As she watched, they lost the shipment, however. Somehow on the outskirts of Krung Thep the van, surreptitiously followed by a great motorcade (of Japanese four-by-fours, so beloved of foreign government agencies), disappeared. Sighs, groans, and moans over the instant messaging. The Americans suspected the Thais of pulling a fast one. So did most of the Thais, who salivated at the probable size of the bribe someone had extorted.

"We think it's General Zinna again," one of the real-time dialogues revealed.

"Really?"
"Yeah really."
"You really think it was him?"
"Yeah, that's what I think, that it was him, yeah."
"Well, you don't know it was him?"
"No, I don't."
"It could have been someone else."
"Yes, it could. But it wasn't."
"How do you know that?"
"I don't know that. I just know it."
"Like a hunch or something?"
"Like a hunch, but not really a hunch. A kind of—"
"What?"
"A kind of faux hunch."
"What's a faux hunch?"

"Like a hunch but it's not? I get them from time to time."

"I've never heard of a faux hunch before. I have a conceptual problem with that."

"I understand that."

"But cutting to the chase, you've got one now?"

"Yeah. Right now. That it was him, yes."

"Zinna?"

"Yeah. Zinna."

"I'm bored out of my friggin' mind. You?"

"If I wasn't, like, catatonic with boredom I wouldn't be talking to you like this. You're my last link with humanity. It's like, I'm that spaceship captain in that David Bowie song from way back? Thousands of years ago they launched me into cyberspace, and this is all I've known—if it wasn't for this dim, tenuous link with you, I'd be like a cipher by now—a shade. I guess that's all I am. I'm like those Japanese kids who can only communicate via computers."

"You need to get laid."

"Or smoke some dope."

"Yeah. That's kind of funny."

Chanya saw an intermittent cure for boredom in the future: there was something homely and warm about this faceless American conversation—it reminded her of those people in the States who had been good to her. It so happened that Mitch was slowly coming out of his trance, although still a long way from sobriety. He glanced up at her as she entered the bedroom, but his eyes immediately switched back to the ceiling. "Marge, I saw it, Marge."

Chanya, doing her very best Marge Simpson impersonation: "Saw what, Homer?"

Ecstatically: "I saw the beginning of the world, Marge."

"Really?"

"Yeah." Crestfallen: "Then I saw the end of it."

"Did the Company send messages again?"

"Yeah. That's how I saw the beginning and the end of the world, Marge. The Company knows everything."

"Homer, honey, remind me again of the secret code for accessing encrypted messages from the Company over the Net."

"AQ82860136574X-Halifax nineteen [lowercase] Oklahoma twenty-2 BLUE WHALE [all uppercase] Amerika stop 783."

CHAPTER 48

After Chanya left him that day, she thought about the heroin shipment that had disappeared, and Zinna. In no time at all, she fashioned a plan. She bought a large calculator that coped with more than twenty digits on the screen, but it didn't come close to telling her how dramatically her karma was about to be improved.

> Not enough zeros in the world. Chanya going to the stars this time.

She could hardly believe the brilliance of her idea, or the great waves of relief that were rolling over her. She felt cleansed already, and during the journey she experienced repeated pleasurable shudders, the very shudders that the books associate with the first true experience of *samadhi*—your mind just cannot comprehend the relief: at first it has enormous difficulty admitting that life, finally, is an ecstatic experience, contrary to all news reports so far received.

She covered her mouth to stifle laughs of joy, kept grinning inappropriately, and sometimes could not resist a sob. This was salvation, big-time. This was exactly what the Buddha taught: you acted with total selflessness, even putting your life on the line, certain that you were following the Path exactly as it presented itself to you in the context of your karma, grabbing at opportunities to liberate all living beings from the chains of existence. She understood that famous Buddha anecdote as if it were happening to her right now: wild strawberries had never tasted so good. She offered a vow that even though she was not yet a nun, she would continue, lifetime after lifetime, to the very end of time, to return to help and heal. Especially to heal. Like Joan of Arc she was a girl suddenly certain of her link with Up There. The only problem: finding the right *jao por* to whom to sell her plan.

As often happens, though, with grandiose plots to dramatically improve one's karma, the idea soon began to diminish in her mind. She wondered if she had not spent too much time alone with that madman Mitch: how could an insignificant girl, a whore, hope to pull off something like that?

Her devastation at the manner of his death, though, caused a seismic shift in her state of mind. She and Mitch had already been naked, about to make love, when Ishy burst in with that huge military knife, his face distorted with an insane jealousy. It happened so quickly. She was still lying next to the American when Ishy jumped him, plunged the knife into his guts, tore upward with the blade, then made her watch while he severed the penis, held it in her face, then chucked it on the bedside table. Ishy the artist had been totally eclipsed by Ishy the monster. There was even a righteousness in the tattooist's rage: a face bursting with self-justification as he held up the severed member. Here was a tortured mind that had given up the last shred of resistance to its demon. Here indeed was the demon in purest form. Her face expressed total revulsion: she was not afraid to die. Clearly Ishy had misunderstood. For her, this could never be an expression of love. Further enraged, he grabbed the telephone and stretched the cable until it was close enough for her to use. *Go on then, call the cops,* his expression said.

But she turned her face away. She dared not; her humiliation was complete. She would have let Ishy kill her without complaint, but the thought of spending the rest of her life in a Thai jail was more than she could face. (She was a whore and Ishy's former lover, of course the cops would charge her too.)

With an expression of contempt, Ishy turned the American over and began expertly to remove his tattoo using the knife. Next to her on the bed, Mitch gave his last groans: she watched the light fade from his eyes, which fixed on her in eternal sadness.

Ishy's face was a hideous caricature, like something from Japanese demonology, as he carefully rolled up the tattoo with both hands and placed it in a plastic bag that he dumped on the table. He picked up the knife again, held up her left breast for inspection, and traced the outline of the dolphin with the tip of the blade—then abruptly chucked the knife on the bed and left.

Shock set in, spasms invaded her body. She forced herself from the bed, staggered around the room like a drunk until she found Mitch's pipe and smoked some of the opium before she could control herself sufficiently to leave. Tripping a little on the drug (entering the smoker's world of symbols), she picked up the rose she had discarded on entering the room, put it in a plastic beaker that she filled with water from the bathroom, and placed the beaker at the opposite end of the bedside table to that where the penis lay. Somehow these two icons now balanced each other.

She had nowhere to go but our bar. On her way out, she caught sight of the key to the hotel safe box, where she expected Mitch had stashed more of the opium. She did not consider the IBM ThinkPad until she saw it there in the box the next day. She bribed the hotel receptionist to keep his mouth shut.

When the opium dream began to melt, a great black cloud of guilt gathered in its place; the terror of the kind of karma that her involvement in this hideous crime might involve (there was no doubt, surely, that this murder sprang directly from her lust for Ishy?) produced in her soul a colossal struggle that seemed to take place in the region of her guts. Little by little she began to resume sovereignty of her mind.

She adopted a mask of nonchalance, but her inner life was quite otherwise: faced with hell, she found the strength for one desperate attempt to make amends and was prepared to risk anything. She revived her plan and went to Vikorn with it. The intensity of her advocacy, together with the political benefits from Vikorn's point of view—and the chance finally to get one over on Zinna—for once overcame the old man's greed. Yes, he would forgo all profits if she would use the CIA's laptop in the way she suggested. He would personally arrange the hijack, once the coordinates of General Zinna's next shipment were known. His only stipulation: that he would retain naming rights to her grand project.

The thing turned out to be quite amazingly simple. She studied the e-mail chatter on the CIA encrypted line until Zinna's name came up, together with information about the size, direction, and likely destination of this new shipment. She called Vikorn, told him where the drug haul was presently located according to CIA information, and monitored the e-mail while Vikorn made his move. With a troop of plainclothes cops under Vikorn's personal direction, the sting went off like clockwork. As luck would have it, the haul consisted of a massive amount of newly processed heroin from finest-quality Burmese opium refined to professional-level purity in labs up in the Northwest in the no-man's-land where the Karen tribe have been warring with the Burmese for more than fifty years. (According to the beat on the street, Zinna no longer touched morphine.) Using his own network, Vikorn was able to sell the haul wholesale within days and use the dough for Chanya's project, which Vikorn now took over with enthusiasm. Naturally, there was no obvious scream of outrage from Zinna, and for the time being he could only remain in a state of muted eruption. Of course, once Chanya's plan was fully realized, there would be no doubt about who stole the dope or what he did with it. That suited Vikorn, who was in the mood for some in-your-face revenge.

"Look," Chanya says, pointing to the stream of instant messaging passing over the screen:

"The latest we have about that Zinna shipment is that it was hijacked by the cops."
"Yeah?"
"Yeah, the rumor is pointing at his arch-enemy, Colonel Vikorn."
"You're kidding me?"
"Nope, there's quite a lot of anecdotal evidence."
"Like what?"
"Like they are breaking ground on a big site just outside Surin, for a massive general hospital."
"I don't get it."
"It's gonna be called the Colonel Vikorn Memorial Hospital."
"Right. Now I get it."

I stare at Chanya. "A hospital?"

She takes out a large calculator and shows me how quickly her negative karma will be eclipsed by the number of lifesaving operations the hospital will perform. In less than a month after the hospital is fully operational, she'll be free of all defilements.

My jaw has dropped. "You were the one with Plan C, not Manny?"

"Who?"

"Lieutenant Manhatsirikit?" She looks at me blankly. "Did Vikorn give you the hundred-thousand-dollars' reward that he was promising to anyone who successfully needled Zinna?" This is not a disinterested question; for more than a week now we have not used contraception.

"I gave it away to a charity that helps rehabilitate prostitutes. I want clean karma. I don't want any dirty money."

So she's even a better Buddhist than me? Well, at least I can see the funny side.

"What are you laughing at?" She hits me, a good strong punch in the arm. "You think I'm just some dumb half-literate superstitious whore, don't you?"

I'm laughing too hard to reply.

CHAPTER 49

We're packing the eggs and other offerings into the back of the taxi, Chanya and I. While flattered that I considered her worth five hogs' heads (that was my final bid), she didn't appreciate the cooking, which, what with one thing and another, took us all night. (Ever tackled the logistics of boiling a thousand eggs over two gas rings? You're lucky if your saucepan holds more than a couple dozen—think about it.)

Sharing the backseat with the fifth head, which would not fit into the trunk, we tell the driver to take us to Wat Sathon. It's a power *wat* about forty miles outside Bangkok frequented only by Thais (a no-frills magic factory renowned for its capacity to fructify the barren, resurrect the impotent, heal the broken, and provide winning lottery numbers to true believers—not to mention the excellence of the cooked food stalls that surround it). The driver plays some upbeat Thai country pop on his music system.

When we arrive, we haul the eggs and heads, marigolds, lotus garlands, fruit, and vegetables into the temple, which is crowded with satisfied customers like us anxious to pay their dues. (I would guess at roughly a hundred and fifty hogs' heads all told, and the boiled eggs numbered in the tens of thousands.) We lay them out to be scrutinized by the Standing, Walking, and Sitting Buddhas who populate the raised platform. Chanya and I light incense, hold the bunches to our foreheads in deep *wais,* and give thanks to be still alive and in love (you must value every minute), then break open the packs of gold leaf. You need to be nimble. Lesser practitioners end up with the frail leaf disintegrating all over fingers and faces, but Chanya and I manage to stick it on target every time. She favors the great fat Laughing Buddha, while I myself have a weakness for the Walking Buddha With Left Hand Raised (meaning: *Don't be afraid*). Little by little, though, we work our way through all of them, plastering their heads and limbs with the gold as we go, making sure no one is left out. We return to the floor to kneel, *wai,* and pray. (I think she prays for a daughter; I pray she won't leave me—how pathetic!) Now it's time for the cooked food stalls and fried mussels in chiles (they really make the best here), *miang kham* on a lettuce leaf with coconut shreds, *laap pet* (spicy duck salad), and a few beers.

In the cab on the way back, in a jam on the outskirts of Krung Thep, I ask the driver to tune in to Rod Tit FM. Pisit is interviewing a famous abbot from one of our forest monasteries.

Pisit to abbot: The more I think about Thailand, the more it drives me insane—I mean, totally crazy, insane, mad.

Abbot: Because of our overwhelming problems?

Pisit: Yes, our overwhelming problems, exactly.

Abbot: Which problems are you most overwhelmed by?

Pisit: All of them.

Abbot: Excuse me, but are you really expressing yourself accurately? Is it not more precise to say that it is not the problems that are overwhelming—after all, they are just problems out there somewhere—but the difficulty in solving those problems?

Pisit, resignedly: If you like. Yes, the difficulty in solving them.

Abbot (with satisfaction): Ah, then Buddhism can indeed help you. At first I thought it could not, but now I am pleased to say that it can.

Pisit: Yes?

Abbot: Well, it's very simple. It is not the country's problems that overwhelm you but your egotistic belief that you can be instrumental in solving them.

A scream from Pisit, then silence.

Kalpa, farang (if you are still wondering): Imagine a mountain consisting of a solid cube of rock, one league in length, in breadth, and in height. If with a piece of cloth one were to rub it once at the end of every hundred years, the time that it would take to wear away such a mountain would not be so long as the duration of a kalpa.

Pichai: Last night he finally admitted the whole case had been a ploy on the part of the Unnameable to enable him to reincarnate in Chanya's womb using my seed. *She's the best stock on the planet,* he explained. *Is there nothing from me you want?* I asked, but he disappeared with a pop.

Breaking News: Superman is due to arrive in two days. (I have knots in my stomach from time to time, and Nong has resumed her diet; we've bought an extra half-kilo of grass and a little opium, just in case he's still in Vietnam mode. Nong says that with *farang* on R&R, you never know.)

Lek is still popping the estrogen and giving me a daily bulletin *re* his breast size (still modest and disguisable at the time of writing). He can't decide whether or not to have the full operation, though: maybe half and half isn't so bad?

Consciousness trapped in a pipe: the human condition, the pipe being the body.

Nirvana: We look out on the world and see only a dust-laden collection of homemade symbols. Those that fit our prejudice of the moment we keep, the rest we dump. We are distracted from distraction by distraction. Nothing is happening. Nothing has happened. Nothing will happen. Emptiness is the ultimate challenge; identity is for suckers. Says the Buddha: *All meaning is realized, the universe is nirvanic.*

Be generous and grateful (and honest when you are not), humanity lives at the busiest crossroads in the seven thousand universes, I am yours in dharma, Sonchai Jitpleecheep (there is no ending and therefore no period)

AUTHOR'S NOTE

Bangkok is one of the world's great cities, all of which have red-light districts that find their way into the pages of novels from time to time. The sex industry in Thailand is smaller per capita than in many other countries. That it is more famous is probably because the Thais are less coy about it than many other people. Most visitors to the kingdom enjoy wonderful vacations without coming across any evidence of sleaze at all. Indeed, the vast majority of Thais follow a somewhat strict Buddhist code of conduct.

On a related topic, I am bound to say that I have not myself come across police corruption in Thailand in any form, although the local media reports malfeasance on almost a daily basis.

John Burdett is a nonpracticing lawyer who worked in Hong Kong for a British firm until he found his true vocation as a writer. Since then, he has lived in France and Spain and is now back in Hong Kong. He is the author of *Bangkok 8*, *A Personal History of Thirst*, and *The Last Six Million Seconds*.